English Weather

Born in 1947, Neil Ferguson spent several early years in a Church Army children's home. Later he attended Holland Park Comprehensive School. He lives in London where he is responsible for Refugee Education at an FE College. *English Weather* is his third novel.

Bars of America
Putting Out
Double Helix Fall

NEIL FERGUSON

English Weather

INDIGO

For Joan Haworth (1922–1993)

First published in Great Britain 1996
by Victor Gollancz

This Indigo edition published 1997
Indigo is an imprint of the Cassell Group
Wellington House, 125 Strand, London WC2R 0BB

© Neil Ferguson 1996

The right of Neil Ferguson to be identified as author of
this work has been asserted by him in accordance with
the Copyright, Designs and Patents Act, 1988.

A catalogue record for this book is
available from the British Library.

ISBN 0 575 40061 7

Printed and bound in Great Britain by
Guernsey Press Co. Ltd, Guernsey, Channel Isles

97 98 99 10 9 8 7 6 5 4 3 2 1

1

PETROS TECKLEMARION

The day was grey and cloudy, as it sometimes is in my country at the end of summer, just before the rainy period. My mother had gone with my older sister Rigbe to visit my auntie, who was going to have her baby soon. My father was inside our house, sleeping, and my little brother Samuel was asleep in his arms. I was outside our house, playing with my little sister Neguste on the piece of land next to the house that belonged to my father. From the east, where the sea is, there came a sudden loud roaring like thunderclaps. At first I thought it was the sound of a storm breaking I could hear. Finally the rains had arrived. I looked up into the sky to see where the thunder was coming from just at the moment fast bomber jets dived out of the clouds and fired rockets on to the city, on to houses and shops and mosques and churches, wherever they wanted to. There were some big explosions by the North Gate.

As I stood watching the planes – I did not think to lie down – one plane flew low over our quarter and fired a rocket on to our house and the house of Mister Adam, our next-door neighbour. There was a terrible explosion, and that was when my father and my brother Samuel were killed. I was thrown into the air by the blast and Neguste lost one eye. Neguste's blood was all over me. At first I was afraid that her blood was mine, but it was God's will that I was spared that day.

This was a very bad time for my country. The Government soldiers had started to bomb and shell towns and shoot anyone who supported the Liberation Front – and everyone in my country supported the Liberation Front. If the Front soldiers shot a single Government officer the Government Army destroyed a whole village, burnt their fields, shot their animals, dishonoured their women. They showed no mercy to anyone, priests or mullahs or children. Their soldiers were thieves and murderers but they were not good fighters because they were a long way from their homes and they were hungry and frightened. Most Government soldiers were farmers who had not been to school and could not read or write.

Recently our fighters had started to win battles and to push the Government Army back so that they were afraid to leave their barracks or the capital and one or two other big towns. My family and our neighbours were happy because the EPLF freedom fighters were winning the War. In our town, which is called Nacfa, we had no Government soldiers any more and the People's Liberation Front were in control. We could walk in the streets without fear of being beaten or shot. The women went in public with their faces uncovered, smiling again. The hospital and schools were open again. The Tivoli cinema began to show Indian films again. We played football on the football field. Young people took the chance to get married in a church or a mosque and there was dancing and plenty of *zigne* to eat. The markets were busy again and there were fresh eggs and vegetables to buy. The nomad tribes had returned to the hills with their sheep because the hills were safe now. The Front soldiers guarded the farmers when they brought

10

in the sorghum and maize and barley from the fields near the town.

In the city every person, Christian and Muslim, supported the Front and hated the Government soldiers, who were all communists. Then – just as soon as we thought the EPLF was going to cut the Ethiopians off from Ethiopia and make them leave Asmara and Massawa and we would be free of them for ever – we started to lose battles. The Russians and Cubans, who had been our friends before, began to help the Government soldiers with tanks and field guns and bombers and fighters so that the EPLF were forced to retreat. We were all afraid that our soldiers would have to leave Nacfa and go back into the mountains and that the Government Army would return. This was when the jet planes attacked my father's house with rockets.

As soon as she heard the bombs falling in our neighbourhood, my mother ran back home with my sister Rigbe as quickly as she could from my auntie's house. When she arrived and she saw the terrible ruin of our house, she began to pull away the bricks and cement with her own bare hands until they were bleeding, but she could not find my father. Then Mister Adam and some men came to help her and they found him in his bed – and little Samuel, who was in his arms. An ambulance came and took Neguste to hospital. I cried and my mother and Rigbe cried. My mother could not speak for a long time after that because in one day she had lost nearly everything she had – our beautiful house, her husband, one son and all our money. Now we had nothing.

The family of my father took us in. We lived in the house of my uncle Zilas for four months but it was not good there. We were not happy. In my country poor family members and their children are nearly the same as servants. They must wash and cook and serve at table and look after the family to show thanks. My uncle wanted to sleep in my mother's bed. She was too proud to lower her eyes in front of her husband's brother. Because my mother was not a servant and she did not want him to sleep in her bed, she took me and my sisters Rigbe and Neguste from Nacfa into Sudan to find a better life.

To get to Sudan we had to walk across the Barka region of Eritrea which is like a desert. It was very dangerous, even though we had guides and we rode on camels. We travelled at night because it was very hot. We had dressed ourselves as villagers dressed and all we carried was what villagers usually carried, a blanket and some *koronsha*, dry bread, because the guides were frightened that Ethiopian soldiers would catch us and, if they thought we were trying to escape, kill us. I had never been on a camel before and it made me feel sick.

It took my family one whole week to cross the Barka region. At night we were bitten by mosquitoes and I kept my hand on my dagger because I was afraid of the wolves which the Barka region is famous for. After ten days we reached Kasala in west Sudan. It was very hot there and too crowded. We were hungry and thirsty and we were without money to buy food. Eritreans already in Kasala looked after us until we could go to the EPLF refugee camp.

I was very sad to leave my home town, which is like paradise, with beautiful houses and palm trees and rich land in the valleys between the mountains, good for grazing cattle. There were many Muslims and Christians in Nacfa. Some of our neighbours, like Mister Adam, were Muslim, some were Christian. My mother would go to Muslim shops and Muslims would go to Christian shops. Some Muslims are good, some Muslims are bad, just like Christians. The Addis government, the Dergue, was communist and the Ethiopians wanted our sea ports and the things which the Italians had left: factories, businesses, roads and railways and many beautiful buildings. They hated all the people of Eritrea and bombed the churches and mosques. In the EPLF Army, Muslims and Christians fought side by side for Eritrean liberation from Ethiopian rule. Our slogan was 'Freedom, justice and equality for the Eritrean people'.

But Muslims who left Eritrea had the chance of going to Saudi Arabia, of working in Riyadh and making some money. Most of the money that was sent to the EPLF came from Eritrean refugees working abroad in foreign countries. For Christians it was more difficult. They had to stay in the south of Sudan where there was no work and not enough food. North Sudan is Muslim and the people there do not like Christians. We stayed six months in Kasala.

I went to an EPLF school in Sudan. The teachers there were very good and I ate *zigne* and *injeera* every day. I learnt many important lessons. I learnt that all people are the same. Christians, Muslims, Palestinians, Jews, Americans, are all the same. Women and men are the same. In the EPLF camp Eritrean women carried Russian guns alongside the men. There were doctors and teachers and soldiers who talked to us at political meetings.

In the EPLF school I learnt how to write in Tigrinya for the first time. Before then I had only learnt Amharic, which is not my language. I had my first lessons in English and our teacher was Hewet, an Asmara woman who had lived a long time in Canada. She was a very beautiful woman who spoke English like an American. I liked her too much. I was only seventeen years old and I wanted to be near her all the time, but she had already promised to marry a famous EPLF soldier. I learnt how to hold a gun, how to live as a guest in another people's country, how to smoke cigarettes and to speak a little English. In camp there were not too many bad people, but in the south of Sudan there was not enough food and some Eritreans made trouble and angered the Sudanese people.

Because Neguste's eye was still bad – and because my mother is a very clever woman – a Sudanese man in the Red Crescent drove us from the camp in a lorry to Khartoum. After six weeks in Khartoum, staying with some friends of my father, we took an Air Egypt plane to Riyadh and then to London. In London we waited a long time in the airport until a white man with a red beard, an Irishman from the BCAR, came and took us on a train to the Splendid Hotel in Bayswater. We went down under the city. It was like a journey into hell, very noisy and dirty. We were very frightened. We had never seen so many white people before, and London was cold and wet. The weather in England was very bad and we were wearing clothes for Riyadh. We did not even have an umbrella.

The hotel was a bad place. The corridors were yellow and dirty. There were many small rooms where people with the faces of thieves lived, a few refugees and people who had not enough money. There were beetles in every room, and in the corridors a very bad smell from the toilets and the cooking. My mother and Rigbe always raised their scarves to their eyes when they left our rooms to go out into the street, something they did not do in our country.

But close to our hotel there was a very big, beautiful park. Neguste was eight years old now and every morning I took her to play in that park while Rigbe and my mother went to buy food from the market. Neguste liked to play in the children's playground because there were swings and slides and other children of her age. There were many trees, not like the trees in Nacfa – but they were very old and beautiful trees. That park did not look anything like my country but I always thought of Eritrea when I was there. While I pushed Neguste's swing I remembered Hewet, my teacher in EPLF school, who I would never see again.

On Sundays we went to the Greek church in Moscow Road. After church I went with Neguste to watch the old men race their model yachts across the pond. They were quiet, old Englishmen without women or children and when they were there, the pond looked like a beautiful ocean. I made Neguste her own sailing boat from pieces of wood I had found in the street and she pushed it out into the water, but it fell over on to its side. It was not a good boat. An old Englishman who was watching us spoke to Neguste. I could not understand what he said because I did not know English well then. The old Englishman noticed that Neguste could see with only one eye and he was very sorry for her.

The next time we met that old Englishman at the pond, he had with him a small sailing boat which he gave to Neguste as a present. It was like his own beautiful yacht, yellow with a mast and two blue sails. Neguste was so happy she ran to him and kissed his face. She is a warm-hearted, pretty girl. We – Neguste and I and the old Englishman – sailed the little boat all the way across the pond and then Neguste ran back to the hotel to show her boat to our mother. I liked English people after that. I thought they were very good people.

In the EPLF camp I learnt the history of my country. All boys and girls studied Eritrean history and the English language as well as their own language – Tigrinya, Tigre, Sahho, Danakil, Beja, Baza, Barya, Bilayn. I learnt that England had betrayed Eritrea to Haile Selassie when the United Nations gave our country to England to look after, when their war with the Italians was over. The British did not do what the United Nations wanted. They gave Eritrea back to the Ethiopians and from that came the war between us.

The British soldiers were very bad when they were in my country. First, they wanted to divide Eritrea, give the Muslim half to Sudan and the Christian half to Ethiopia. It was lucky for Eritrea that most of the Muslims do not live in the north and that most of the Christians do not live in the south. We live as neighbours all over Eritrea.

Second, they fomented trouble between the Muslims and the Christians, to make them hate each other and so make a war between us. When the British were looking after Eritrea for the United Nations, the land continued to be stolen from the Eritrean people and given to the Italians who were there, who they told us were Fascists. I learnt that the British were very bad racist imperialists, even worse than the Italians.

My teachers said: 'London did not want a plebiscite in Eritrea. London wanted to have its own colonies back. London wanted the Suez Canal.' I thought London must be a very bad place. I know now that there are poor and rich people in London, and good and bad, just like in Eritrea.

Every two weeks I went with Neguste on a 25 bus to Holborn, where Moorfields Eye Hospital is. We always sat in the front seat at the top of the bus and looked through the window at the people in the street because we had never seen such strange clothes and faces before. An Englishman in a bowler hat, a Sikh man with his turban, girls of Rigbe's age with green and pink hair wearing skirts high above their knees – all at the same bus stop! In London people dress how they like and do what they want. When they pass you in the street you are not supposed to look at them. If they see you look at them they become angry and ask you what you are looking at.

At Moorfields Eye Hospital an old eye doctor, Mister Trevelyan, looked into Neguste's eye with a torch and made her laugh. He told my mother that he did not know if he could do anything to help Neguste's eye but he would try. Neguste had a splinter from the bomb in her eye. He said he thought he could take out the splinter but he did not know if that would make her see from that eye. He operated on Neguste's eye and now she can see a little bit – light and dark things and coloured shapes.

My mother wanted to give Mister Trevelyan something valuable as a gift, of gold or silver, but in England you must not give presents or money to a doctor. Everything is the opposite in England to what people do in my country. My mother invited Mister Trevelyan and his wife to our hotel to eat *zigne* and *injeera* and drink beer, and they came and we all laughed and sang songs. My mother loved Mister Trevelyan and always sent him a card at Christmas.

Our two hotel rooms were not very splendid. The paint was dirty and the furniture was old and smelly. We did not receive very much money from social security and everything in London is very expensive. My mother bought our clothes in the second-hand market in Portobello Road. In England people buy and sell clothes and things which even in Eritrea we would throw into the dustbin. I took Neguste to school every morning and collected her at four o'clock while Rigbe and my mother went shopping and cooked. In the day I had English classes at college and my teacher was Colin, who was very good. I worked hard and after seven months Colin said I was nearly ready to do First Certificate.

In July the college closed. It was the summer holidays and I did not know what to do. I did not have to take Neguste to school or to meet her at four o'clock and I had nothing to do in the time in between. I walked all around north London, hungry and sad, thinking of Hewet in Sudan who was married to an EPLF fighter. Sometimes a black woman, an African or a West Indian woman, would look at me and see what my face said. She would give me something to eat, an apple, a piece of bread or some money. There are many different people in London, people from all over the world, but the only people you know for sure you can trust are old black women – it doesn't matter where in Africa they come from.

In London, when you speak to a person for the first time you never know if they speak English like an Englishman, as badly as you do or not a single word. Boys from Jamaica spoke English like cockneys and their mothers spoke a Jamaican kind of English I could not always understand. I knew one or two black boys of my age and Colin, my teacher at college, said I was speaking English with a London accent. He said this was

17

good. My mother, however, wanted me to speak only correct English. I told this to Colin and he laughed. He said when I was with my friends I should speak like my friends and when I was with people who spoke correct English I should speak correct English. That was what *he* did. Colin was a wise and clever man.

Once I was walking in the subway under a big fast road in a part of north London I had never been to before. I was just walking. I did not know where I was going. Two white boys came towards me and started to punch and kick me. I was surprised because I did not know them and they wanted to kill me. I ran away fast and they chased me but they could not run as fast as I could. I told my friends, the black Jamaican boys I knew, what the white boys had done to me and they all nodded and said I must be careful. London was a bad place for black people. They wanted to give me a knife to carry and they all had one in their hands for me to choose. I said no, I did not want to carry a knife. But I was more careful when I went into subways after that.

In my country the people fought the enemy, soldiers from another nation. In England people fight each other, one class against another class. In Eritrea the EPLF gave political education to each class, to the small landowners and the big landowners, the farmers and the nomads, men, women, Muslims and Christians. In Eritrea we started to have a civil war between the ELF and the EPLF, which was what the English had always wanted, but the people stopped that and all classes made a common cause with each other against the Ethiopians. The war in England – like everything in England – was the opposite to the way it is in my country.

The black boys I knew – Joseph and Dexter and Harman – asked me about Africa and Ethiopia. They knew that I could speak Amharic and could write the Amharic language. They all wished they could do that. Some Jamaican people believe that

Haile Selassie is king of all the black people in the world. I told them Haile Selassie was a wicked old man who had sent his soldiers into my country and now he was dead. They shook their heads and said no, he was the Lion of Judah, the descendant of King Solomon. If the Jamaican boys wanted to think Haile Selassie was the Lion of Judah, descendant of King Solomon, I did not want to argue with them. One thing I know is that it is never good to argue with people who have a different religion to you.

These boys were not good boys, I knew that, but they were my friends. They knew a lot of black people and they took me to their houses. Their mothers looked after me and gave me food to eat. I like Jamaican food very much. Just the smell of English food makes me feel sick. My friends gave me cigarettes and it was with them I first smoked ganja, but I did not like to smoke it very much. Ganja made me dizzy. I smoked with my friends because they said I was their brother and now that Samuel was dead I had no other brothers. Sometimes older Jamaican men gave Joseph and Dexter and Harman money to take things across London for them and I went with them on the Underground.

At weekends they would let us come to their party where there was always loud reggae music and plenty of Red Stripe beer to drink. They were good parties and we always got a little drunk. I liked Jamaican reggae music and being with black people.

There were never white men at these parties, although there were always a few white girls. Jamaican men like English girls and English girls like Jamaican men. Even my friends knew some white girls, girls they had gone to school with, and these girls would come with us sometimes. They would do anything my friends asked them to do. For example, they would go into shops and take things for them. My friends would break into a beautiful house and in the bed of the owner of the house they would do jig-jig with their girls. I myself first did jig-jig with a girl in the bed of a house we had broken into. I did jig-jig with Samantha, a white girl with blonde hair, and afterwards I gave her some ganja.

I never took things from the houses of the people my friends broke into because I am not a thief. I went with them and helped them but I never took anything. Except for money, the things my friends took – cameras, jewellery, radios – they sold to the older Jamaicans or gave to them for ganja. The money they always kept for themselves. I went with them because I wanted to see inside the houses of rich people. In the Bayswater area there are plenty of big old houses where rich people live, one family inside a whole house. In those houses there was beautiful old furniture and expensive decorations.

My friends taught me how to break into a house and a few times, if I had nothing to do, I went by myself into a house just to look inside it. First I rang the back doorbell and if nobody answered the door, I climbed in through a window and walked all over the house without making a noise on the thick carpets. I sat in the leather armchairs and turned on the television. Those houses were like palaces and the bathrooms were good enough for a Saudi princess. I looked into the cupboards and felt the expensive dresses and shirts and shoes.

In the fridges there were bottles of champagne and food I had never even seen before. I wanted to take some of the food for my mother and Rigbe and Neguste because I knew they were in the hotel, cooking rice in the kitchen everyone used so that the windows misted up and the air smelled of cooking. It was hard for me because I was hungry and I knew I was the only man in my family now, but I did not want to take a single crumb, not even a tin of Coca-Cola. I used the toilet if I had to and once I had a hot bath, careful to leave no signs that I had been there, but I never stole things. My father taught me that stealing was very bad and that was the reason our people were fighting the Ethiopians, because they were stealing Eritrean land and property. My mother told me that my father was in heaven watching me all the time and if I did a thing which he had taught me was not good, he would be sad and perhaps stop watching me. Then I would be alone.

My family stayed a long time in the Splendid Hotel. Rigbe went to Westminster College every day and – because she is very clever – she passed her exam in English. Neguste went to school for children her age and she was very happy there and talked about her little friends all the time. Even my mother, who had never gone to school in our country, went to adult college in the afternoon where she learned to speak some words of English and to write the alphabet. I was supposed to go to college when it opened again in September and I did go some-times, but often I did not go because I had a new teacher, a New Zealand lady who was not so good as Colin. Colin had moved away to another part of London to live and work.

My family thought I was going to college every day. Instead of going to college I went with Dexter and Joseph and Harman to sit in their houses and watch television or walk the streets and do stupid things. We broke into houses because we could not think of anything else to do. We ate fried chicken and chips in the street and drank beer and smoked ganja and, if the white girls they knew wanted to, we would go under the motorway and do jig-jig into their mouths. English girls are not modest like Eritrean girls are.

In December it was very cold in London and English people were getting ready for Christmas. It was already dark at four o'clock in the afternoon and often it rained and the best thing to do was to stay indoors. The weather was terrible. You needed money if you wanted to go out. Once Joseph and Harman and I broke into a big house in Campden Hill because we were cold and we wanted to be inside and be warm. We did the usual things to find out if the owner was at home – looked at the name on the door and then got the telephone number from the operator and phoned up the house. There was no answer, and so we went over the wall and climbed in through a window that was open in the back of the house. It was easy. The house was decorated with silk wallpaper and the curtains had golden ropes to pull them open. I sat down on a velvet sofa and turned on the television with the remote control while Joseph and Harman went into all the rooms in the house, looking for money or valuable things to take.

While I was watching the television – it was a horse race – I looked up and saw an old white man standing in the doorway. He was wearing a dressing gown and he held a long hunting gun in his hand, pointing it at my face. I didn't say anything. I was too frightened to move. I turned off the television with the remote control.

The old man said: 'Don't move. I have called the police. They are on their way.'

The old white man was shaking, but I don't think he was as afraid as I was. I thought his finger was going to pull the trigger of his gun because his hand was shaking so much.

While he was standing in the doorway, pointing his gun at my head, through the door behind him I saw Joseph moving quietly down the stairs. I could not see Harman. Suddenly Harman shouted out something and the old man turned round quickly but the end of his gun knocked against the side of the door. Joseph jumped towards the old man and hit him in the chest so that he dropped the gun and fell down. I did not know how much he was hurt and we did not stop to look. We were all running to the back of the house, to the window where we had come in. When we got there we could see a policeman standing outside in the garden. We ran back through the house and opened the front door. Outside there were many policemen who grabbed us and put handcuffs on us and started to slap us.

I only found out then that Joseph had stuck his knife into

the chest of the old white man and that the old white man was already dead. I was sorry to know that and I started to cry.

That was the beginning of a lot of trouble for me.

In the police station the police asked me many questions and I answered all of them truthfully. I told them I was watching the television in the house we had broken into and when I looked round an old white man in a dressing gown was in the room pointing a gun at me. Joseph came down the stairs and Harman called out and the old man turned around and the end of his gun hit the side of the door. It was then that Joseph had hit him in the chest. I did not know until afterwards that Joseph had put his knife into him. I told the police I had not killed the old man and they became angry and slapped me until I cried. The old man, they said, was a hero, a famous fighter pilot who had shot down many planes during the War. They said everyone in England was very angry at what we had done. Then they sent me back to my cell. I cried when I was alone. The walls of my cell were made of white glass bricks and the only window was high up above my head. Every night, after the traffic had stopped, a bird sang in the tree outside my cell window.

Every day the police asked me again the same questions a hundred times and every time I gave the same answers. They got very angry with me and they beat me. After a week the Law Centre sent a lawyer to see me and I told him the same thing I told the police. The Law Centre lawyer said he believed me. Then my mother and Rigbe visited me and I told them everything I had done. They cried and held my hand across the table and I cried too. It was good to speak Tigrinya. I make mistakes when I speak English to English people, but I cannot tell a lie by mistake in my own language.

The trial was at the Old Bailey. The judge was an old English-man who wore a red coat and some false hair on top of his own hair. A woman from the court showed me a knife and the judge wanted me to say that it was my knife. I said no, I did not like to carry a knife. Another man, who was the Queen's barrister, said: if there were three boys and three knives and two of the knives were found in the pockets of two of the boys, who did I think the jury should believe the third knife belonged to? It was like a riddle. I thought he was going to tell me the answer but he did not.

Then Joseph and Harman were asked questions by the Queen's barrister and they both said that they had come down the stairs and found me standing over the old Englishman and my knife was in him and so they had run away. My barrister told the jury what I had said and they all listened carefully. All the jury were white people, seven men and five women, and they looked like very honest people to me. I told them that I was not a thief and I had never stolen anything in my life and I only went with Joseph and Harman because I wanted to see inside the houses of rich people. I sometimes touched their clothes and things but I never took any of them. The judge asked me if I expected the jury to believe me. I told him yes I did because I always spoke the truth.

The Queen's barrister asked me if I smoked cannabis. I said I did sometimes. When I was with my Jamaican friends.

When the questions finished the judge spoke for a long time. He told the jury that I was an Ethiopian and that Ethiopians are Africans, who are people who do not know the difference between a true thing and a lie. He said Africans are the best liars in the world. The jury listened to the judge and then went away to talk about the evidence they had heard. They came back into the court and said I was guilty of murdering the old Englishman. The judge thanked the jury. Then to me he said I, Petros Tecklemarion, was a very wicked boy and I must go to prison for ten years. I was very frightened and I started to cry, and my mother and Rigbe cried. The jury said Joseph and

Harman were not guilty of murder but guilty of burglary and, because they were under eighteen years old, they were only sent to a detention centre for two years. Harman and Joseph looked very happy when the judge said this. Their families and friends in the courtroom laughed and cheered. My two brothers who believed Haile Selassie was the Lion of Judah, descendant of King Solomon, were in the detention centre for one year and two months.

During the trial I was in a prison in London, in Brixton where there were many black prisoners. It was a bad place but I was allowed to wear my own clothes and I could see my mother and Rigbe once every week. I missed Neguste so much. I wanted to see her but I did not want her to see me in prison. After the trial I was sent to Leeds Prison, which is far from London, too far for my mother and Rigbe to come many times. Nearly all the prisoners in Leeds were white men. There were a few Jamaicans but no Africans. Everyone in Leeds called me Sambo, the other white prisoners and the prison officers. That was my name.

It was a terrible place. The job they gave me was to empty out all the buckets in the morning, which is called slopping out. I did not know then that every prisoner must slop out his own bucket every morning. In Leeds they told me it was my job to do it. Prisoners bumped me when I carried the buckets so that the urine spilled on to my shoes and the prison officers watched and laughed. I told a Jamaican prisoner about this and he wrote a letter to the Governor. After that I did not have to slop out other men's buckets any more.

My life was hard when I was first in Leeds and I was unhappy. There were all kinds of thieves, murderers, men who did jig-jig with children, young men and old men, all mixed up together. In my cell there were two ugly white men who did not keep themselves clean. They farted loudly whenever they wanted to, when they were lying on their beds or eating or whatever they were doing. Then they smelt their fart and laughed. If I farted, even if I farted without making a noise or I did not mean to fart, they beat me. Those men liked their own smell but my smell always made them angry.

All the white prisoners spat at me and bumped me. They did not talk to me and I did not want to talk to anyone, black or white. I think many prisoners did not know I could understand their language. Inside my head I talked to my mother and Rigbe and Neguste, and in my heart I listened to the voice of my father and Samuel. Often I prayed to God. I wanted to sleep all the time because when I was asleep I sometimes dreamed I was in my country. I dreamed I was in Nacfa with my family, eating my mother's *zigne* in my father's house. I was playing football with my schoolfriends or watching Hindi films with them in the Tivoli cinema. Sometimes I dreamt of Hewet and woke up with my own jig-jig juice inside my bed. I always dreamt in my own language. Samuel and my father were still asleep in my father's bed and I was with Neguste in our garden and my mother and Rigbe were at my auntie's house helping her to have her baby. When I woke up from my dream and saw where I was I cried and the other men in my cell shouted at me and, if I did not stop, kicked me. In Leeds Prison I learnt to cry as silently as I learnt to fart.

After my trial, when I was in the police van that took me from my first prison to another prison, I saw a newspaper which had printed what had happened in my trial and what the old judge had said about me. I knew then that everyone in England, even people who did not know me, believed I was a thief and I had put a knife into the old English fighter pilot in his own house. The prison staff and the other prisoners believed that I had killed the old man. Eritreans in England who could read English thought so and hated me because I had brought shame on to our people.

Everyone except my mother and Rigbe and Neguste hated

me. Only my father, who spoke to me in my heart, said that I was not a thief nor a murderer, that I was a good boy and that he still loved me and promised always to love me.

My job in Leeds Prison was in the yard outside the kitchen. I was not allowed to touch the food when it came in or do the cooking, or even wash the knives and forks or the dishes. My job was to empty the dirty bags of rubbish into the metal container. Every two days a council lorry came into the yard and collected the containers and took them away. Prison officers watched us all the time I put the bags in the back of the lorry. The work was dirty. I did it because no other prisoner wanted to do it. But it was all right. While I was in the yard I was alone with myself and I preferred the smells of English food to the smell of the other prisoners. The council lorry drivers who came to take the prison rubbish away were free men who worked outside the prison, and I liked to be near them. I liked to hear the council men laugh and shout to each other. I could hear from their jokes and talk that they were free men.

I liked those working Englishmen. Sometimes they left me a bar of chocolate or some chewing gum, hiding it so that the prison officers who were watching could not see it. They called me Sambo too. That was the name everyone in Leeds called me.

I became very ill in Leeds Prison. I did not eat anything there because the food made me feel sick. I was never hungry. I wanted to die. Every night I prayed to God to take me to His bosom so that I could be with my father and Samuel. I became thin. The prison doctor gave me some tablets but I threw them away. Then one day I fainted in the yard and the Chief – they called him the Bully Beef or sometimes just the Bully – told me the Governor had decided to send me to another prison. I got my things together and I was taken by bus to Sellswood Prison in Lancashire.

Sellswood was an even worse place than Leeds because the

27

POs there beat prisoners when they wanted to, just as the Ethiopians bombed houses and mosques and schools. They hated us all, whoever we were. The prison was very crowded and most prisoners were three in a cell. I was lucky because I shared my cell with just one other prisoner, an Englishman who was not an animal and did not taste his own smells like a dog. This man had been to many countries and knew their languages. He spoke to me kindly and talked to me about many subjects. When I told this man my story he believed that I spoke the truth. My life got better after that. I started to eat again. Most white prisoners do not want to share a cell with a black man. The prison staff found a white prisoner who did not mind being with an African.

This prison was a very old building. The walls were damp so that you could put your finger into the mould on them. Because it was too crowded, prisoners and staff were angry all the time and there were often fights between prisoners who did not like each other. They scratched themselves because of the insects in their hair.

The food in Sellswood was worse than the food I used to put into the rubbish lorry in Leeds. Even the English prisoners did not want to eat it. There was always a terrible smell coming from the food. Sometimes men refused to eat and they made demonstrations about the food, but nothing happened except the prisoners who threw their food on the floor were put into the punishment cells and beaten. The demonstrations against the food only made the prison officers more angry. Then they would go into cells and beat prisoners they did not like, usually with their fists but sometimes with sticks. I saw men with their faces bleeding and bruised after they came back from the punishment cells. The way the POs treated prisoners was worse than a person in my country would treat an animal.

The prison officers hated us. I know that they were angry because they did not get enough pay but that was not our fault.

I felt sorry for them because I could see that they did not want to be in prison any more than we did. The prison staff were like Ethiopian soldiers. They did not like their work and they hated their bosses. They were very sad men. Many Ethiopian soldiers did not want to fight because they were farmers just like us.

The worst thing about prison is not that you are away from your family or the terrible work you must do or even the food, but the way the POs talk to you and punish you for the smallest thing. All prisoners hate screws – this is the name prisoners give to prison officers – but in Sellswood they wanted to kill them. Even though it was worse than Brixton or Leeds, I was glad I was there. I had made a friend, somebody I could talk to. His name was Gregory and he was the first white person to become my friend.

Gregory was not unhappy to be in prison. If he was unhappy he did not say he was. He read books and wrote letters and played his guitar and he spent time in the gym training. From the other prisoners he had respect because he knew all about boxing. He said that going to prison was the same as taking a long journey in a very slow train, like the train my father sometimes took me on from Nacfa to Asmara to visit his grand-mother who lived there. He said: after you enter the train compartment, you can do nothing to change anything until the door to the compartment opens again. If there is a cow on the line you cannot stop the train. Whatever is on the track is waiting for you. You can play cards or dominoes. You can read or you look out of the window, or you can become friends with the people in the compartment with you. Since you cannot stop the train you might as well make the most of it. He told me the story of a famous Greek philosopher who lived all his life in a barrel and boasted that he was the freest man in Greece.

Gregory understood Greek and soon he began to learn my language. Every day he made me tell him new Tigrinya words and he quickly learnt how to write the letters. He called me his teacher and often we spoke to each other in my language. He made the Governor order a Bible in Tigrinya to be sent from London. Gregory had an English Bible, which he read to me to help my English.

If I had a dream I always told it to Gregory in the morning. He asked me to tell it to him in every detail.

'I am going from my house to Dawit's house . . .'

'What is the name of the street?'

I had to think. I had lived in England so long I thought every street must have a name. But only the old people know the names of the streets in Nacfa, because they speak Italian. My friends and I did not like to use Italian words. The big roads we knew, the Via Dante and the Via Gabriele D'Annunzio. Gregory wanted to know where Dawit's house was, how near it was to Via Dante. I had to draw him a map and show him where my school was, where the Tivoli cinema was, where the football field was. And so on. After I had finished he knew Nacfa very well, nearly as well as I. He knew the names of the fruits in the market, the names of my family. My cousins and aunts and uncles, all my grandmother's names. He made me tell him where each tree was in my father's garden and what it looked like and what the fruit tasted like.

He lay on his bed in the dark and I lay on my bed.

'What do the petals look like?'

'Round and sharp at the end . . .'

'Spiky?'

From Gregory I learnt many new English words.

He travelled into my head. In the dark we went to Nacfa together and I showed him round our garden. I introduced him to my schoolfriends. We sometimes played football together.

'I'm running into midfield . . .'

'Hebte has the ball . . .'

'. . . He has to get past Silas, the right back . . .'

'Ibrahim goes for him . . .'

'. . . Hebte passed to you on the wing . . .'

'I cross . . .'

'. . . Which wing am I on?'

'The right wing, of course!'

When we played football in Nacfa in the dark in our head we always both scored lots of goals, but sometimes we ran into each other. With Gregory Harris I laughed again.

Gregory played his guitar and sang me all the songs he knew – and he knew many beautiful songs, songs of black American slaves and English songs – and he learnt the songs my mother sang to Neguste and Samuel. He made me explain how the women in Eritrea make *injeera*, our bread – which takes three days to make. He had not even seen *injeera* until my mother sent some *zigne* and *injeera* into the prison for our Christmas, which is seven days after English Christmas. Gregory converted to the Orthodox religion. I know he only did this because he wanted to hear the Greek language spoken. There were some Greek men from Cyprus in the prison and on Sundays, a Greek priest came in and held a service for them. I went to that because in Eritrea we have the same church rites, even though I did not understand Greek. Gregory asked the Governor if he could be at the service and the Governor said he could.

Gregory's name for me is Mikaree, which is not my name but the name my father always called me – and still calls me, when he is pleased with me. Mikaree means honey in my language.

Gregory had no family any more, but he loved a woman called Susan Thomas who visited him every month. He had to sell his house and Susan was looking after his property for him. Susan loved Gregory very much, and when he came out they were going to get married and have children. She wrote beautiful letters to him. Gregory gave me all her letters to read because I had no girl writing to me.

Gregory wrote letters for any prisoner in C-wing who asked

him to. A lot of prisoners could not read and write English very well and Gregory helped them to write to their lawyers and their family and girlfriends. He did this for free, although in prison nothing is ever for free. After six months in Sellswood nobody in C-wing called me Sambo any more. They called me Petros, which is my name.

Gregory wrote a lot of letters of complaint to the Governor and to the prison Visitors about the bad state of the recesses, which is what they call the toilets in prison, and about the food and the beatings which the prison officers gave prisoners. He wrote to the newspapers and to the Home Office. He said to me that if something was not done soon there was going to be some trouble in the prison. None of his letters was ever answered.

He helped me to write to my solicitor at the Law Centre who was in charge of my appeal case. My solicitor was appealing against my conviction because I was innocent of the crime of murder. My solicitor came to see me with a man who was my barrister, called a Queen's Counsel.

My friend Gregory was not like the other prisoners. He was not a criminal. He believed me when I told him that I had not killed the old Englishman because the same had happened to him. He also had been accused of a crime which another person had committed. He also had been betrayed by a friend. Gregory told me his story and I believed it was true.

On the day the trouble started we were all in the dining hall. It happened during lunchtime on a Sunday. Lunchtime in Sellswood was called a period of free association, which is when prisoners are given permission to move about and talk to each other, watched by the POs. First, there was a bit of shouting from some prisoners sitting at a table behind us. We all looked round because in a prison, anything that happens that does not happen every day is exciting. Two prisoners were fighting and swearing at each other. The men wanted to hit each other and were held back by their friends. All the men in C-wing began cheering.

In Sellswood we ate our meals in a large hall. We queued and collected our tray of food from a hole in the kitchen wall. To me the smell of the food was even worse than the look of it. I still did not like to put the food in my mouth but I learnt how to swap things I did not like for food I could eat. I ate the soup and the bread and the cake puddings. English bread comes in exactly the same sized slices and it is always white like boiled cotton. The bread is not disgusting because it has no taste at all, although I did not like the grease they always put on one side of it. I ate a lot of English bread. Sometimes in summer we had tomatoes and salad and in winter, small bitter English apples. The prison officers watched us eat from the sides of the hall. When a prisoner wanted more food, he had to ask for permission to go up to the serving hole. Some men ate a lot of food. If I looked at them eating my stomach started to turn inside out and I had to look away in case I was sick into my soup.

When the fighting started the men at our table stood up to see what was happening. The POs shouted 'Sit down!' and ran to the place where the men were hitting each other. The officers made a line between the fight and the rest of the prisoners. I had seen this happen before in Leeds but this time, plates of food and spoons and forks were thrown at the prison officers. It looked to me that the men were waiting for this fight to start.

Soon the prison officers were covered in food – custard and duff pudding – and all the prisoners were laughing. English people laugh when they see men with custard all over their faces and clothes. The prison officers moved towards the place where two of their men were trying to separate the prisoners who were fighting. I was standing on my chair like a lot of the prisoners, who were cheering like boys at a football match. I could see what was happening. Gregory, who was standing next to me, was not laughing because two prison officers were being beaten. One of the POs was lucky. He was pulled away by his comrades, but they could not save the other one.

Then trays began to be thrown and the prison officers were forced to go backwards towards the kitchen. I saw Gregory run into the crowd of men, but he could not get near to the prison officer they had because men were crowding round him to kick and punch him. At that moment they dragged the prison officer past our table and I saw who it was they had. It was Mister Crogan. I was not sure because the face of the man was red with his blood. He looked very scared.

We waited in the hall, the rest of us. About twenty prisoners had dragged Mister Crogan out of the hall to the area where we used to watch television. Then the prison officers began chasing the prisoners out of the hall. I watched them run but soon I had to run myself. A PO with a stick ran towards me and I did not know which way to go, towards the kitchen or out of the hall into the television area. I would have stood where I was and let the PO push and hit me, but in my heart the voice of my father told me I must go with the prisoners who had Mister Crogan.

At that moment more prison officers charged. They had sticks in their hands and they hit every prisoner in front of them, those who wanted to go back to their cells and those who wanted to fight. You could hear the noise of the sticks against the men's heads, and men were falling on the ground and then the prison officers kicked them in the face and between their legs. But most of the men they were hitting were the prisoners who were not fighting. They were not the rioters. Then the men who had Mister Crogan charged and joined in the fight. Some had weapons but most men used their fists or their heads. The prison officers were outnumbered – it was a Sunday and there are always less POs on duty on Sunday – and they were pushed back again towards the kitchens.

Gregory, who was with the men who had Mister Crogan, saw me and shouted 'Kida! Kida!' *Kida* means 'go away' in my language. But I did not go away. Men were throwing things at the POs and Gregory pulled me from the fighting.

There was terrible confusion everywhere. Men ran to and fro, shouting to each other. They carried things from the television room to make a barricade and then they ran back to find more things. Their faces showed that they were not animals. They were men who were angry, happy to be doing what they were doing. I stood and watched, an African in a crowd of running, frightened, white Englishmen. Some men I saw angry, some laughing, but they did not see me. I was invisible.

I felt nothing for what was happening in front of me because I was not one of the rioters. I had no fear for myself because I knew my father was watching over me – but still I was afraid. I stayed close to Gregory because I was afraid for him. I had a strong feeling of love for Gregory, and I did not want to leave his side. I wanted Gregory to be my brother. This was why my father had told me which way to run.

A few minutes later, fifty prison officers rushed into the hall from the kitchen. These men were wearing helmets and carried sticks. The prisoners who were still in the hall stood still or put their hands up. Most prisoners wanted to go back to their cells and did not like what was happening. The prison officers ran forward to the place where the rioting prisoners were, but there was now a barricade at the entrance to the dining hall and they could not get past it. The men had made a fire of the furniture and the smoke kept the prison officers from reaching where we were. As soon as the POs came near to the entrance to the television room some prisoners set a fire hose on to them and that stopped them from rescuing Mister Crogan.

I write only what happened, what I saw. I want to write

only the truth because I was there and my father, who is in heaven and is watching me, will know if I do not. If I write lies he will know and he will stop watching me.

By the afternoon the men were in control of the whole of C-wing, because no prison officers could enter from either end. Some men climbed up to the roof. Like all the officers, Mister Crogan had a key to the doors leading to the fire escape.

There were forty-three prisoners in the protest about the food and the beatings. I knew most of the men, who were all from C-wing. Only C-wing prisoners were in the dining hall when the fighting started, although afterwards we could hear men in the other wings shouting and banging on their cell doors to show that they were with us.

The leader of the C-wing men, who had organized the protest, was a prisoner called Loafer. He was giving the orders and men ran to do everything he said. He had made the plan. Loafer was a strong fighter and when the prison officers charged the second time, he was the man they wanted to take. He beat them off until the water from the fire hose stopped them from taking him. All the POs wore masks so that prisoners could not see who they were. A lot of prisoners had put handkerchiefs over their faces also because they did not want to be known and pointed out later. Loafer could have worn a mask if he wanted to but he did not want to. He could never hide the man he was.

While the prison officers and the men were fighting in the big corridor between the dining hall and the television area, I and a few other men were in the television area where Mister Crogan was tied to a chair. His uniform jacket was off and his white shirt was covered with his blood and torn so that you could see his fat belly. His bald head hung down on to his chest. As soon as I saw him my father spoke to me. He was very angry. He reminded me that Mister Crogan was a man. According to our religion I must not watch another man suffer pain and do nothing because if I did nothing I was the same as those who caused his pain. My father told me that I must give Mister Crogan some water and so I did. I ran to obey my father. I found a cup and I gave Mister Crogan a drink of water. The other men around him did not try to stop me. They knew that what I did was right, but they were too afraid to do it in front of each other. It was nearly dark – the Governor had cut off our electricity – and perhaps they did not see me.

It was when the fighting had stopped, after the prison officers had gone away from the dining hall, waiting for more men to join them, that the prisoners held a meeting to decide what to do next. A few men said that we had protested enough and now we should surrender. Most of the men wanted to go on. They wanted to make a protest about the terrible food, the crowding of prisoners three in a cell, as well as the beatings, because people outside the prison did not know about these things. If they did, they would make the politicians stop them. The prisoners wanted to tell the newspapers and the television. We all knew that the more we resisted the worse it would be for us afterwards, but as long as we had Mister Crogan prisoner we had something to make the POs stop fighting us.

Gregory spoke then. He talked in their language, their cockney way of talking. He told them that there was a telephone in the room next to the television annexe and that he had used it to tell the local newspapers our story, to explain that what we were doing was not a riot, it was a protest. The men were very pleased to hear him say this and Gregory was cheered for doing it. Gregory told the men they must make a list of their complaints and he would write them all down and if the newspapers printed it we would let Mister Crogan go and surrender. The men all agreed to his plan because they knew that only the newspapers could stop the POs from beating us. Even the big man called Loafer saw that it was a good idea. Gregory said we must look after Mister Crogan well because that – fair treatment – was our chief complaint. We wanted to be looked after as human beings, and it was bad of us to look after our prisoner worse than we wanted the prison staff to look after us. There was a big argument about that. In the end everyone agreed that there must be no more hitting Prison Officer Crogan.

Gregory was a brave man. He did not care about his own safety. He went to the barricade and stood without a mask on his face in front of the POs and asked them for a medical box to look after Mister Crogan. He said Mister Crogan was all right. He gave his word that their colleague would not be hurt or spat on any more. After a few moments, one of the POs gave Gregory a medical box and Gregory gave it to me and asked me if I minded looking after Mister Crogan. I did not mind. I bathed Mister Crogan's face, which was covered with blood and men's spit, and I put antiseptic cream on to his cuts. I found his jacket and I helped him to put it back on.

Mister Crogan looked at me and said, 'Thanks, lad.'

I gave Mister Crogan some more water to drink and a cigarette to smoke. None of the men wanted to touch Mister Crogan, either to put the cigarette into his mouth or to light it for him, but they did not mind if I did this because I was only an African.

Nothing happened for a long time. We listened for something about our demonstration on a radio. It was on the news because we had a prison officer as a hostage, but nothing was said about our complaints.

For the night Mister Crogan was put inside a cell. His hands were untied so that he could lie down on the bed and he had a bucket to use, just as we did.

All night the POs waited and we watched them waiting. Every hour they made a noise to keep us from sleeping. We found out that the telephone had been cut so we could not talk to people outside any more. C-wing was quiet. I fell asleep. The other men were tense from waiting but nothing happened. While I was falling asleep a voice sang out over C-wing. It was a very quiet, sad song which I had often heard Gregory sing before. A prison is a very good space for singing in, like a church, and his voice was beautiful.

Roses are blooming in Picardy . . .

The prisoners who were awake and the POs and Mister Crogan, listened. Everyone could hear it.

In the morning we found that Mister Crogan had been beaten in the night. We looked at each other. No one knew which one of us had done such a terrible thing. Mister Crogan was lying on the floor of his cell with his blood all over him. I went to him and put my hand on his heart. He was not dead and he was conscious. I thought he must have some broken bones. Because of that, prisoners started shouting at each other and some wanted to give up then, because they said Mister Crogan needed to go to hospital as soon as possible. There was a big argument among all the prisoners and I listened to them, but no one asked me what I thought and so I said nothing. Gregory was very angry because he had given his word to the Governor that nothing bad would happen to Mister Crogan. He said if we acted worse than animals we must not complain if we were treated as animals. Already some men were thinking about the beating they were going to get after they gave themselves up.

It was agreed that all those men who wanted to should be allowed to give themselves up and let Mister Crogan be taken to hospital, but those men who wanted to go on with the protest should go up to the roof where they could not be attacked. Before the men parted they promised not to blame each other and they shook hands and hugged each other. They were all afraid, but nobody wanted to show it. Only Gregory shook my hand and hugged me.

'Soon it will be all over, Mikaree,' he said.

He was right. Soon it was all over.

Gregory spoke to the chief prison officer and told him that most of us wanted to surrender. The chief prison officer promised we would not be beaten. He said we must send Prison Officer Crogan out first and then come out into the dining hall, with nothing in our hands, one at a time. Those of us who wanted to did what he asked, but as soon as they saw Mister Crogan, who had to be carried on a board, the POs started to punch and kick the men who carried him. The men who were waiting to surrender became very angry when they saw the POs do this, because the beatings were the reason why they had made their protest, and so they started shouting and throwing things again. Then the prison officers charged. The men charged too, and there was another big fight in the dining hall but this time the POs were better armed and there were too many of them. They were ready for us. They beat and hit men to the ground and dragged them away by their hair. The man could not do anything except fight with their hands even though they had lost the will to fight. I myself was punched and kicked in the head and because of that I cannot hear anything in my left ear now.

I saw two of the POs hit Gregory even though he did not fight back or try to resist. Gregory knew how to box but he had his hands up and they hit him on his head again and again with their wooden sticks. He fell on to the ground and then they kicked him in the face with their black boots. They smashed their sticks into his head. I waited for them to stop hitting him but they did not stop. They could not stop. They hated Gregory because he had given his word that nothing would happen to Mister Crogan. They wanted to kill him.

There were many prisoners badly hurt in that fight. Some

men had bones broken. Nearly all the wounds were done to the head and the face. I was lucky. I was not very badly hit, but I saw some terrible things done that morning.

After the Disturbance, as the protest was called, all the prisoners were beaten and soon transferred to other prisons. I was not badly beaten. Mister Crogan was taken to hospital where he stayed unconscious for a long time and they thought he was going to die, but it was God's will that he did not die. Gregory was looked after in the same intensive care unit of the same hospital. I prayed for Mister Crogan, but I prayed more for Gregory. I was very sad when a PO told me that my friend had died. I cried. I loved Gregory more than any person in England. In my heart my father and Samuel cried too, because they had loved him as much as I did.

My mother and my sisters, Rigbe and Neguste, were at Gregory's funeral. They were invited by Susan Thomas, the English girl Gregory was going to marry and wanted to have his children with when he came out. There was an English church priest and his wife who had known Gregory when he was a boy and had always been his friend. There was a Greek Cypriot girl called Rita who had been to school with Gregory. She told Rigbe that she had always loved him then, but he had not looked at her. He had liked her best friend more.

Many times afterwards I was asked what had happened in the dining hall – where I had been, who I had spoken to. There was an inquest into Gregory's death and a trial of the prisoners who had been in the Disturbance and, later, a report to the Government. I told the policemen and the coroner everything I had seen. I told a judge the Government had asked to make the report all about the Disturbance. The judge asked me if the men had charged out of the television room and attacked the prison officers. I said no, that was not what happened. The POs had charged first, and two of them had kicked Gregory even after he had stopped moving. His secretary wrote down

41

everything I said, and she read it back to me afterwards and I signed my statement.

But no prison officers got into trouble because of the beatings they had given to the prisoners, because nobody except the prisoners said they had been beaten. No prison officer wanted to say who had killed Gregory. One PO said Gregory had fallen down the iron staircase into C-wing. Mister Crogan, who was out of hospital by now, told the judge that it was a black man who had looked after him. He pointed me out because I was the only black man in C-wing. He said he had not seen me in any of the fighting. A solicitor told the judge that I could not hear in my left ear any more because of my beating. The judge said I was with the rioters but, because I was an African, I probably did not understand what was happening. One prison officer told the judge he had seen me throw a chair, but the jury all agreed that I did not do what he accused me of.

Because of Mister Crogan I did not lose any remission in my sentence. Most of the men had extra years added to the time they already had to spend in prison. Loafer was given five years extra time because Mister Crogan had pointed him out as the man who had beaten him. I was lucky because I had listened to my father and done only what he had told me to do.

Soon after that trial I was in court again. My appeal case was held at the Old Bailey. In Sellswood Prison Gregory had written many letters to my solicitor but it was only later, after I came out of prison, that my mother told me it was Mister Trevelyan, the eye doctor at Moorfields Hospital, who had paid for my Queen's Counsel with his own money. The second trial was very short because my Counsel was good. He said that I could not be accused of murder only on the evidence of other persons who had also been accused with me. This was against the law of England, which has the best law in the world. The three judges in charge of the case said he was right. They said I was innocent. After three years in prison I was free to go home.

After the judges gave their decision, I walked out of the court into the sunlight. I was free to go home.

We had a big party in the flat the council had given to my mother. There were many Eritreans there, Mister Trevelyan and Mrs Trevelyan and English people I did not know then. We had beer and *injeera* and *zigne* and we danced all night to Eritrean and disco music. I met Miss Susan for the first time that night. I was very happy.

My mother and Rigbe became very friendly with Miss Susan. She is a very beautiful and kind woman and I have become friendly with her too. I asked her if she had something belonging to my friend Gregory that I could have to keep and she gave me his lucky silver shilling that he always had with him, she said, except when he went into prison, when he had given it to her to look after. She said he had once told her it was all he had that was his. If he had had his lucky shilling with him in prison, perhaps he would not have been so unlucky. She also gave me one of Gregory's guitars. I am learning to play African music on it with my one good ear.

I do not live with my mother and Rigbe and Neguste any more. I live in Brixton, which is on the other side of the River, in my own room. I decided it was time to make my own life. I study maths and English and electronic engineering at Brixton College. My room is very near to my first prison where I lived for eight months. Sometimes I see the blue police vans carrying prisoners and my heart hurts for the men inside. I always wear my friend's lucky shilling round my neck on a silver chain.

My old teacher, Colin, lives in Clapham and I see him and his friends sometimes. Nearly all Colin's friends are men because Colin is gay. In my religion it is forbidden for men to love each other in that way, but Colin and his friends are very kind to me. I see my family and people from my own country when I want to see them, but after I came out of prison I did not want to be with them all the time. I was different. In prison I had seen too many things that I did not want to talk about to Rigbe or Neguste. I have a beautiful girlfriend from Asmara who is studying English at my college. I love her very much and we are going to be married soon. Although there are many black people in Brixton I do not have any Jamaican friends, because I do not want to go back to prison again. Colin said my English is very good now and next year I will study electronic engineering at a polytechnic.

I was very sad after I came out of prison. I wanted to cry all the time but I could not. It was Colin who told me that I must write down my story. He said my sadness might go away if I wrote down why I wanted to cry, without making any mistakes. I wrote this for Colin, who helped me with my grammar and spelling.

I came to England to escape the war in my country, but I have seen many more terrible things happen in England than I ever saw in Africa. My childhood ended when I left Nacfa and I will never return there again.

I still talk to my father sometimes and he sometimes talks to me, but more often now I talk to myself while my father and Samuel listen in silence.

ALAN LOMAX

I have always chosen the cities I lived in on aesthetic grounds. Venice. Isfahan. Bath. San Francisco. To me there seemed no point living anywhere second-rate. No one in their right mind would willingly spend their days in Walthamstow – as I did until I was seventeen – unless they had to. But people do. People live and die in places like Dallas and Fort Worth out of choice. From the window of my room in Ca' Foscari on the Accademia I was able to look out on to the lovely dome of Bernini's Santa Maria della Salute whenever I felt like it. To be able to walk in the shadow of Renaissance architecture between a business meeting and shopping for bread and coffee was, I decided, a small triumph over fate. My fate was to live in Walthamstow, Chingford if I was lucky. Whenever I am surprised by a view of the Golden Gate Bridge or the Trans-America Pyramid, even today, I am reminded of my good fortune. I am – I inwardly crow – still ahead of the game. As long as I am free to roam one of the world's most beautiful cities, the bastards haven't ground me down.

Most cities, even most beautiful cities, have their drawbacks.

Bath is situated in a bend in a river valley and during the winter the damp creeps into your bones. I have never understood how the place earned its reputation as a spa for arthritis and rheumatism sufferers. Venice is a suburb of the gas-refining plant at Mestre and the air is noxious. Isfahan, ancient Saffavid capital of Persia, whose delphinium-blue domes tower over a graceful honey-coloured city, has – or did have when I was there – primitive standards of sewage disposal and cholera is periodically pandemic. It's probably better now. But San Francisco has no drawbacks. It has everything anybody could want from a city – and more. Even the Bay fogs the inhabitants complain of to deter visitors lend a subtle mood to the city which, notwithstanding their complaints, the inhabitants secretly enjoy. A US city Europeans feel at home in, it has to be the dernier cri in modern urban living.

In whichever part of San Francisco I find myself – in the Western Additon where I have my premises, in Golden Gate Park, in the hills, in Specs's Bar in North Beach drinking up Martinis that Specs himself has just mixed for me – I feel lucky. I am blessed. One of the Chosen Few. Only a handful of people have this much luck.

Only a handful of cities at any one time possesses that elusive Paris Factor, the quality that makes a city *the* place to be at a particular moment in history. Isfahan had it around 1570, and Venice on and off for nine hundred years – but not, alas, in the late 1960s, when I was living there. Bath was chic for less than eighty years, if that. San Francisco, everyone here is agreed, has PF in spades.

In Walthamstow only about half a dozen people are of any consequence. Here, practically everyone is interesting. The gold-rush hedonism of San Francisco gives you permission to put yourself at the centre of the universe. I can't see myself embarking upon so self-regarding a narrative as this in any other city in the world, certainly not one in England. I would never have presumed to take myself so seriously. Only because Greta, my therapist, nags me to *open up on myself* have I agreed to do this. She has put the same question to me on so many occasions that I have decided to try and answer it. If I can do so to her satisfaction, she says, I can stop seeing her. She has convinced me it will be to my financial advantage if I do. If I don't, I have to continue paying her twenty-five bucks a session, increasing with inflation, for the rest of my life.

The question she puts to me takes several forms. At its most simple it is: *What am I doing here?* (As far as Greta is concerned, 'here' can mean anything from here on the West Coast to here on the planet Earth in the late twentieth century.) Another way she poses the same question is: *Where did I come from?* – encompassing everything from my journey from Walthamstow General Hospital in 1947 to my counsellor's two-storey house in Potrero in 1984. *Why did I leave England? What do I expect to find in America? Who am I?* They are all the same question, Greta tells me. When I know the answer to the question I will *know myself* and can dispense with her services.

She has agreed to let me write what I want. Writing is a legitimate means of what she calls *opening up on myself*. She probably expects me to write about what my lousy childhood was like, and my parents, and all that David Copperfield kind of crap. Fortunately I didn't have a lousy childhood. My mum and dad were ordinary working-class Londoners who voted Labour, supported Spurs, went to the Holborn Empire to see Max Miller and were rehoused in the suburbs after the War.

My name is Alan Lomax. Practically everyone here calls me Al. I have a two-storey apartment on Jackson and Fillmore, which is in Pacific Heights, and I have a business address on O'Farrell. I came here in 1974 and, unlike most of my fellow compatriates, I work here legally. I have a green card and I pay federal and city taxes. I left Bath because in winter the damp creeps into your bones and it was also too small-town for the kind of intercontinental business I conduct. Forty per cent of my customers in England were from the US anyway. It was inevitable, if my business was to expand, that I should cross the Pond. Like everyone else, I'm here to make money. You would think that was enough to satisfy anybody.

You don't know my therapist.

I went to live in Bath in the autumn of 1971, when it was still part of Somerset. Until then, ever since I finished my university course, I had been living abroad. I was ready for a spell in Blighty. Living in foreign parts is fine if you have an independent income or an understanding bank manager at home. If you haven't, you're just a sadhu or a footloose fucking hippy. I met enough of the latter in the East to know.

To be honest, when I first went to Turkey and Iran and Pakistan I wasn't so different to them, at least to look at. I wore a kaftan and a sarong in India and in Iran *shalwar* and *giveh*, Persian zouave trousers and gondolier shoes. I was just as hip and full of shit. In my case, though, I never believed in the shit. I didn't give a toss about the Bomb or L. B. J. or what happened in South-East Asia. But I repeated the mantras, which were easy enough to learn. I read the right books – Kerouac, Tolkien, Huxley, R. D. Laing, Jung. I could sit around the Amir Kabir Hotel in Tehran and smoke bhang and shoot the breeze with the best of them. All you had to do was turn a humdrum idea on its head – 'All property is theft' – and they thought you were fucking far out.

On my way home from my first trip East I picked up two fine old silk Isfahan prayer mats. Mihrabs. I bought them because I liked them, for no other reason. I got them cheap because it made no difference to me if I owned them or I didn't, which gives you the edge in any bargaining situation. I knew nothing about bargaining then – or knot counts or dye tones or pile. If I didn't pay import duty on them, it was because I didn't even know that import duty was payable on carpets then. I hadn't a clue. On my return to England I hawked them around a few carpet houses in London, eventually accepting an offer from Rackham's in the Strand of four hundred pounds apiece.

Although I made a handsome profit I soon realized I had been robbed. I had no idea how to sell a rug then, but it opened my eyes to the money to be made in the carpet retail business. Every place I took the mihrabs I was asked the same question: could I get hold of any more like them? Well, of course I could. I returned to Iran and Baluchistan immediately and bought some Kirmans and Kashans and some old Baluchis. Baluchis then were unappreciated. They were considered too crude and prices were low. Not that I knew that. I didn't know anything about carpets. I simply bought what I liked. I had a good eye, and I was lucky. I still am.

From that point on I was in business. I stayed in better hotels, ate in good restaurants and slept with Iranian girls. I still rubbed along with the hippy guys and their chicks when I ran into them, had a smoke and talked shit with them. I would happily travel down to Hyderabad or up to Bukhara in their company. I always got on with them. But in addition to my *shalwar* and *giveh*, I had a shirt and tie in my travelling bag. I was a businessman – the most respected group in Iranian society. I had a razor and a fountain pen. As well as passing the time of day with the dharma bums, I needed to deal with bank staff and bribe government export officials.

I knew a lot of hippies who, on a smaller scale, were doing much the same as me: buying saris in Madras to sell in Colombo, spices in Kandy to sell in Rajasthan, turquoise in Kabul to sell in Istanbul. Primitive mercantilism, apparently, was not at odds with their philosophy of self-sufficiency and the quest for satori – but big or even medium-sized business was. This is just one example of the shit those hippy guys talked.

The fact is, they didn't have a philosophy. They had some

half-baked ideas and a handful of borrowed nostrums. They affected to despise money and politics and power, as well as academic pursuits and anyone who was interested in those things. I have to admit it was a good playground strategy – to refuse to recognize the objectives of the ruling clique. I had a lot of sympathy for it myself. Those old cold war warriors were wankers.

When it came to sex, hippies were right on. They put fornication right at the top of the agenda, where it belongs. Even then, if I were a feminist historian – God fucking forbid! – I would probably say that it was the pill did that. There would have been no Woodstock, no Isle of Wight, without that little daily dose of oestrogen into the obliging lady's hormone system.

The hippy movement was the result of social change, not the cause of any. I don't know if anyone has said so before, but it wasn't the hippies that put an end to the war in Vietnam; it was the war in Vietnam put an end to the hippies. Once those freaky, far-out guys and their sexy chicks occupied themselves with the Big Political Issues of the Day and took on the police in Washington and Chicago and Grosvenor Square, their days were numbered. They became just like any other silly interest group with an axe to grind. They lost their virginity and with it their moral authority – which up to that point had been considerable. The movement was finished. Its adherents put on Hudson Bay plaid shirts and Levis and sensible boots and got into *The Whole Earth* catalogue. They built up right-on businesses – opened wholefood shops, carpentry workshops, imported carpets – or drifted into straight jobs, teaching or selling insurance. The unlucky ones became armchair Buddhas in provincial nuthouses.

It's thirteen years since the period I'm writing about. I don't know where any of the people in my narrative are now, and I don't want to. They have disappeared out of my life. For me, the past is literally another country. Margaret Thatcher has been in power in Britain for five years. The hippy dream is ancient history and I can safely come out of the closet. My time has come! Richard Branson is no different to me, just a lot more successful. Like me he still has a beard, wears his jeans during office hours, for old times' sake. He probably still smokes dope, for all I know. But he and Maggie see eye to eye. Having navigated themselves to the same position in the political ether, after setting out from opposite points on the compass, they validate each other.

I feel pretty pleased with myself that I got it just about right. I had all the sex and drugs and fun there was to be had in the late sixties and the early seventies, but I was never stupid enough to believe that deep breathing and chanting *Ommm* would make Alan Lomax a happier person, never mind Allen Ginsberg. What did that was *money*. Freedom, paradoxically, is not free. It's not even cheap. I made an effortless transition from freewheeling, dope-smoking member of the love generation to freewheeling, Armani-dressed businessman. I know several other people who pulled the same stroke.

It wasn't as hard as you might suppose. Essentially there is no contradiction between the primitive capitalism of my hippy days and the big-bucks capitalism I am into today. They work from the same premise: buy cheap, sell dear – and caveat emptor. They both rest on a Hobbesian view of the world: it is human nature to put your own interests first. Ideas are unimportant. If you make yourself wealthier, the world will be a better place.

I rented a spacious, high-ceilinged flat in Rivers Street, which runs between Royal Crescent and the Circus – as Jane Austen had done a hundred and fifty years before me. If you have an eye for classicism and symmetry – as, I suppose, after gazing at thousands of carpets, I must have – you could do worse than choose a harmoniously planned Georgian town to live in. Versailles is a palace for a single monarch to reside in, Lansdown

Crescent a palace for seventy-odd families. Bath is an arriviste middle-class Jerusalem – no less than I deserved, I thought. I took pleasure in walking along Rivers Street to the field below the ha-ha in front of Royal Crescent to throw a frisbee or join a handball game, stopping at the Crossed Keys afterwards for an early drink in the company of ordinary blokes and their wives who spoke West Country.

Today all the houses in Rivers Street – and, indeed, throughout Bath – have been dandified. The portland stone has been repointed and cleaned up to an eye-achingly yellow ochre. Repro ironwork has replaced the rickety original. But in the early seventies all the houses were blackened from centuries of coal-burning fires. They were interestingly different in their uniformity. Their crumbling elegance had charm and character. Now they are the collateral of company directors and accountants and their families, but back then they were multi-occupied by old dears, maiden aunts, forgotten Arnhem veterans, retired French polishers, council employees, students, even a few black people.

And, of course, what the townsfolk called hippies, amiable layabouts who lived the life of Riley on the dole.

Bath at that time was a Mafeking for old hippies, the redoubt they chose for their last stand. Already the more intelligent among them were beginning to get into things. Walcott Restoration, for example, was a thriving business, returning the interior decor of old Bath houses to its Georgian original. Not only was it organic and holistic and right on, it was a fucking gold mine. These new paladins of the whole world started taking up local issues. The city council had a plan to put a motorway through the city, with a tunnel coming out at the top of Walcott Street, to link the M4 with the M5. It was a nutty idea, but the local Tory councillors had their noses in the trough. They had heard from their Freemasonry pals in Newcastle upon Tyne and Birmingham of the large sums of money to be made out of big construction contracts. If today Bath Spa is not a glorious motorway service station, we have to thank the Walcott ex-hippies and the Labour Party members who mobilized the Old Dears and the Tory vote against the idea.

The word ecological was not on everyone's lips then, but a holistic view of the environment, a complex place we share with other creatures, is the only Big Idea to have survived that loony era.

I voted Conservative for the first time, for Ted Heath, in 1970, and I would probably have voted for Margaret Thatcher in 1979 if I had been in England then. I was not a Conservative out of conviction but from persuasion. I was – still am – Walthamstow boy made good, and I came to accept certain verities. I had never believed in an egalitarian distribution of the means of production, all that Clause 4 shit that exercised my dad and his mates. That does not mean I liked Tories more than other, more liberal-minded folk. Quite the reverse. My friends were teachers and public service employees, artists and working people who would have been dismayed to discover how I cast my vote. If you had pressed me I would have confessed a preference for the education, health and defence policies of the Labour Party. When it came to the economy, however, I was a Tory – albeit a Heathite one, someone Thatcher later would call a Wet. I hate to think what my dad would have called me.

Conviction Toryism is a condition, not an intellectual position. Having spent your formative years away from your mother and father and brothers and sisters and neighbours, in a closed male community that promulgates an ethos of self-reliance, there isn't much chance you won't turn into a fledgling little fascist cunt. Alienation is all you know about. The point of sending your child to such a school is not to sharpen his wits, but to cripple his soul. Public school does to the heart what silk bandages did to the feet of aristocratic Chinese girls. That is the mistake socialists always make: their answers to the problems of capitalism are intellectual. They don't understand, as Orwell did, because he went to Eton, that Middle England is not interested in culture or ideas. Margaret Thatcher wouldn't know a prayer mat from a door mat. She despises all forms of intellectual and artistic activity.

My antipathy towards my political allies put me in an ambiguous position. I loved England, but I detested the people whose cause I voted for and was rather attracted to their adversaries. In America politics is a lot more straightforward because both sides of the debate are in agreement about how wealth is created, and I may sympathize with the Democrats with a clear conscience. In the US, an English Tory Wet is called a liberal. Because there is no serious opposition to capitalism, everyone is humming the same tune, from the shoeshine boy to the person in the shoes he shines.

Where there is no ambiguity there is no room for doubt, not to mention irony. I find the political air freer here and I feel comfortable. There is a lot of claptrap talked about morality and religion in the US, especially in the Midwest, but it is just talk. That's all. America is the same old sleazy place Dickens lampooned in *Martin Chuzzlewit* for its venality and hypocrisy. In England, where it is infra dig to discuss matters of morality, notions of what a chap should or shouldn't do run deep – and are not openly discussed for that reason. It was the moral and political climate I forsook as much as the meteorological.

In Bath, all the serious drinking was done in Walcott – in the Bell or the Star, the Curfew or the King Billy. But it was the Hat and Feather you went to on a Saturday night. There are rare moments in a pub's life when it hums because it is the hub of the social life of a large circle of people. I have known many fine pubs and bars but I have never known one – not even in North Beach – that approached the Hat and Feather on a Saturday night during the period I'm talking about. The Hat was something else. A sublime, roaring, funny, libidinous drunken thrash from dusk until closing time, the jukebox belting out old Stones or Wilson Pickett numbers or the DJ playing Captain Beefheart or Frank Zappa requests. Dionysian is the only word for it. As far as the Bath townsfolk were concerned – and, to judge from the *Bath Chronicle*, they were very concerned – we were all hippies and layabouts. Certainly such characters were adequately represented, but the Hat tolerated a diverse client group. Besides the usual inadequates and rogues, there was the deliciously under-age Bath Convent School Girls' clique and the rough diamonds they collected as their male escorts. There was the Antique Dealers' clique – wide boys with beards and paunches, expansive and funny, who dominated the bar-football table. The Natural Theatre clique – an anarchic fringe company which put on plays and silly stunts to keep us amused. A number of individuals – I was one of these – moved from clique to clique, and no one minded if you went back to their place after closing time for a smoke or a roll in the hay, no strings attached. The pub reeked of cannabis and sex. Everyone was horny. If a fellow couldn't score in the Hat and Feather on a Saturday night, he wasn't trying.

But the clique I took a shine to and attempted to infiltrate was the one I called the No Hopers. The No Hopers were all exactly the same age – twenty-five or twenty-six – having attended the same university contemporaneously. They all had fancy degrees in useless subjects: fine art, Italian literature, European history, philosophy – and no idea what to do with their lives. Like me they were Bulge babies, children of Second World War soldiers for whom Beveridge had planned a cradle-to-grave welfare state. They had everything: looks, education, charm, a nice line in ironic repartee and a social conscience. All they lacked was ambition. They were completely without that necessary life skill. They had no desire to make money or to tell other people what to do.

This − I must confess − was what made them so attractive. They weren't competitive. Their state-school education had not encouraged them to strive for the summit at all costs. They couldn't give a toss. They lounged around each other's Georgian rooms, threw frisbees on the grass in front of Royal Crescent, painted a picture or two, read and talked about literature, played musical instruments, got drunk and stoned and laid each other every night of the week. They either had no-hoper jobs − working as hospital porters or behind a bar − or they lived off the dole. They were incorrigibly indolent.

I liked them all, Ed and Paul and Steve, and their girls − Liz, Carol, Sue, Daphne − were lovely. I got the impression they had all slept with each other at one time or another. They seemed to exchange partners by mutual consent and without acrimony, which made them a formidably tight-knit group. They were prepared to meet outsiders like me on equal terms, but there was no way I would ever be allowed to become a member of their clique. I didn't care about that. I had plenty of other fish to fry. What drew me towards them was their intelligence and wit and − I was appalled to discover − because I had fallen for one of their number.

Sue Thomas was a dark beauty. Dark in the German Romantic sense of the word rather than the Confucian. She had flowing jet hair and dark eyes and she was both comely and come-hither. Eustacia Vye. But she was also the intellectual equal of any man she was with. In the *I Ching* Confucius he say: *The wisdom of man is of Heaven, the wisdom of woman is of Earth.* After spending time in Sue Thomas's company you realized that Confucius, he not hang around with right girl. As much as her natural voluptuousness, it was her frank disregard for what anyone thought of her that attracted me.

One reason I liked Paul, by the way, was that it was he who said: the only place to throw the *I Ching* is out of the window.

Sue had trained as a historian but I never saw any evidence

that she practised her trade. I think she helped out part-time in some private Montessori nursery. She embroidered her dresses, painted the odd picture or two, wrote poems in a rather lazy way. She was like a lazy cat, the cat that walks by itself, completely without morals. As she never judged, so she never expected to be judged. She couldn't care less whether or not the dishes sat in the sink all day or what you thought of her if they did. She was more like a bloke in that respect. I was smitten with her. It was stupid of me, but there you are.

Jung has this theory that the beautiful female stranger whom you occasionally encounter in your dreams and want to have sex with but cannot for whatever reason is, in fact, a manifestation of your anima, your soul — a representation of your own mother. Perhaps this is crap — what Holden Caulfield called *phoney* crap. I don't know. But I have often had that dream myself and I know how painfully sweet it is to be in her company: to have and to have not. Sue Thomas was the only girl I ever met who aroused in me such a degree of desire and foreboding in equal measure.

I was a No Hoper myself when it came to Sue. I didn't get anywhere. *She* chose which men she wanted to go to bed with, not the other way about. Thoroughbreds, young boys, older men, lost souls, sugar daddies: she selected her sleeping partner as a punter runs his pencil down a string of runners before placing his bet; as I had been accustomed to choosing my women, as the fancy took me. Like all would-be great lovers — as opposed to the merely sexually promiscuous ones — she was discreet. A reputation for not advertising your liaisons is the sine qua non of the libertine.

It was months before I found out that she was seeing someone on a regular basis. He was a guitarist in one of the local bands that played in the Village Hall, a venue on the Burial Ground, between Walcott Road and the river. He seemed a likeable enough bloke, tall and bearded, good-looking. At least he didn't wear loons and batik T-shirts. I had heard him play once but I can't say how well he did. Like most people with a large record collection, I don't know anything about music. He did not frequent the Hat and Feather. I found out he didn't even live in Bath, which explained why I never saw them together. I resigned myself to a long haul.

It was then – while I was in mid-stride, when my business in Bath was beginning to take off, while I was having a whale of a time with my social life and ran around in a not-so-old Ford Cortina, after I had met a woman who stopped me in my tracks – it was then I made a small error in judgement. My therapist would have called it hubris, a result of a sense in my ability to defy my fate. The blunder was not in itself important but many consequences flowed out of it, not least of which is my current residency in the Sunshine State and the reason I am writing this down.

By now I had already established my buying and import routine. I travelled to Iran and bought each piece as it caught my eye. I occasionally bought in bazaars in the big towns, because there are sometimes bargains to be had there and a greater variety of rugs to see – and they are fun. Although I enjoyed haggling with rug dealers I preferred to go out to the villages and visit the small rural factories, and I often bought direct from families. I have always liked to cut out the middleman. It is not always practicable to buy direct from nomads, unless you are prepared to follow their flock on its journey from old pasture to new, but I preferred nomad work. The patterns are cruder and less regular, the knot count generally under three hundred a square inch, but I loved them. I still do.

A single family takes the wool from its own sheep, dyes it and cards it, designs and produces the entire carpet. Such a rug, made on a portable horizontal loom resting on the desert sand and then washed in a river and dried in the sun, is like a living creature. When you behold one you are in the presence of a thing of great purity. Not many people saw it that way when I started out and so nomad rugs and kilims were a bargain. Carpet connoisseurs and buyers – not always the same thing – preferred the fancy, detailed silk work from the old cities, Isfahan and Shiraz and Heriz. Not me. I bought what I liked and I liked the luscious bluey vegetable-dyed colours of Baluchi rugs – called *luckee* in Persian. And, for me, lucky was what they were.

London has been the centre of the oriental carpet market for two hundred years. There were a lot of carpet buyers, all of whom knew more than I did. The language of carpets is arcane. When I started out it was unusual for a London seller to go to Iran and haggle in the bazaars and make his own way to villages, leave the beaten track, as I liked to do. I built up a network of friends and village master knot-tiers, dealers who trusted me and learnt what I liked and how much I was prepared to pay. I flew to Tehran once or twice a year and visited my contacts: down to Shiraz for the Bakhtiari nomad rugs, up to Herat for the Baluchis – avoiding Meshad whenever possible.

Iranians are the most hospitable people in the world. The further away from Meshad they live the more hospitable they are. Fierce and gentle in equal measure, as their rugs are strong and delicate. The rug of the nomad is a tangible expression of the spiritual integrity of its makers. There is something human and fallible but movingly sincere in a Baluchi wool rug that I missed in the artfully manufactured silk Kashan with its intricate teardrop medallion design in fancy German chromatic dyes.

It was my good fortune that public taste changed over the years. As people wanted something organic and authentic, the prices of Baluchis slowly rose. I don't delude myself that I contributed towards this shift in public demand.

I chose my rugs and carpets personally and they were

packaged up for me in Tehran. A bill of lading was made out and the stock was bonded and flown to England where duty was paid and they arrived in Bath by special delivery. It was always a pleasure to open and inspect again the stock I had bought several months before. The carpets were rolled in batches of three or four and then crated. Customs officials in England inspected each batch but never troubled themselves to check each individual carpet, since the bonding in Iran gave all the information they needed in the form of lead seals and a description, both of which were clearly visible and tallied with the bill of lading. I knew that the batches were not tampered with because over a period I had several small articles sent inside them – sealed packages containing, say, a paperback book, which always arrived unopened.

Encouraged by the security of this route, I bought and sent myself a weight of the finest Afghan bhang – soft, freshly pressed cannabis resin from the valleys around Mazar-el-Sharif. I did this because I was fed up with paying over the odds to the black guys in Twerton or the hippy guys in Snow Hill for wretched stuff, when I knew I could supply myself with higher-quality cannabis at a fraction of the price. A single weight would keep me from hustling for years. It was plain old-fashioned home economics, as I saw it. It went against my instincts to pay good money for an inferior product, and logical for me to cut out the middleman and take the risk myself, especially since the risk was so small.

I first knew that I was in shit up to my armpits the morning I received a visit from two men in suits. I was alone in the shop. Silvia, my heavily pregnant personal assistant, was in the back making tea, having just taken delivery of a consignment of stock from the airport carrier. I was looking forward to opening the crate. I had forgotten that this particular consignment contained anything more than rugs, an indication of how little importance I attached to the situation. The two men browsed in the front of the shop for several minutes. I took them for passing trade until one of the men approached me and spoke.

'Alan Lomax?'

I instantaneously knew that they were police officers and that I was about to get clobbered.

'Yes?' I said.

'Your secretary has just taken delivery of an import package from Iran.'

'Yes,' I said.

'Are you aware of what this consignment contains?'

It was one of those are-you-still-beating-your-wife type of questions. You are fucked whichever answer you give.

'Yes,' I said.

'Do you mind if we are present when you open the crate?'

There was nothing I could do. Silvia brought us each a cup of tea and I sent her out on an errand. I opened the wooden crate, unlaced the batches, rolled out the carpets and, lo and behold, there was a weight of freshly pressed cannabis in my hand. They let me touch the sealed package but not the dope itself which, Inspector Carson later told me, would have to be examined for prints. I was bhanged to rights. The two policemen watched me scratch my head and look baffled while they sipped their Earl Grey, unmoved by my performance. English police can be cunts when they want to be. A weight of dope was a serious amount to be busted for, but it was a much more serious amount to be busted for importing.

The two men, I soon learnt, knew all about me and my business, which by then had a twenty-five-thousand-pound annual turnover. I could be given six months, a couple of years if they played their cards right, but even a conviction would ruin me, since it would prevent me from trading.

Carson politely asked me to stop play-acting. He urged me not to worry.

'If you want to keep out of the *Chronicle* we can probably come to an arrangement.'

He did not specify what form the arrangement would take.

I accompanied Carson and his DC to the police station in Manvers Street. I had dealt with enough corrupt policemen in my travels to think I knew what I was doing. I noticed that at no point was I booked in or spoken to in the presence of a uniformed officer. This was an encouraging sign. While I was being led down a labyrinth of corridors I calculated how much I would have to pay. In a quiet room Carson put it to me: either I would be charged for importing an illicit category-B drug or I would sign a statement admitting I had done so. I would have to agree to one or the other, but not necessarily both. If I wanted to call a lawyer I was free to do so, but if I did that the legal process would take its course and he would do his best to see me sent down for a stretch. If I agreed to sign a statement I could go home.

'What's stopping you from charging me after I've signed a statement?' I asked Carson.

'Nothing at all, Alan,' he said. 'I give you my word you won't be. That will have to do.'

They left me alone in the interview room with a cup of police canteen tea and my Rizlas and packet of Golden Virginia and an ashtray while I thought the proposal over. If the case went to court I would have no choice except to plead guilty since, *inter alia*, the bhang was covered with my prints. The case would be heard at the magistrates and I would probably get off, since it was a first offence, with six months. If I pleaded not guilty, the case would go straight to the Crown Court and I might end up doing a long sentence. It would be in my interests to cooperate with the police. That would go down in my favour. Since I would have to plead guilty anyway I chose to make a statement. Perhaps I should have called a lawyer, but my instinct was to cut out the middleman, which on this occasion was the British legal system. I preferred to make a deal with the police than to throw myself on the mercy of the court.

Carson kept his word. I dictated a short admission of guilt and signed it. He had it typed out and handed me my copy. Then he said I was free to go. I walked out of the police station and straight into the Saracen's Head, where I downed a brace of double brandies.

Often I didn't hear from Carson for months on end. He would telephone me and we would meet in a pub called the Retreat on Sion Hill behind High Common, now the golf course, with a fine view across the valley to the beautiful gas-holders on the far side of the Upper Bristol Road. He would buy me a pint of Bass from the wood and ask who was selling dope in the Hat and Feather. (Every tenth person, practically!) I gave him the names of the Snow Hill hippies who had burned me with their lousy Moroccan, because I knew he knew about them already. I kept back the names of the black guys in Twerton, who had always given me a straight deal. The information I let Carson have was useless, even I knew that. He didn't seem to mind. He never put any pressure on me.

He said: 'Alan. I don't expect you to grass up your mates. That wouldn't be in either of our interests. I'm not interested in who's giving quid deals to the Bath Convent schoolgirls for a blow job after the pub shuts. I just want to know about any new stuff that comes on to the market. Who's selling coke or acid or H?'

I had no idea who was selling acid or H, since neither of them was my own preferred recreational narcotic, and there was precious little coke around.

I mentioned that there had been some amyl nitrate in circulation, omitting to say that most of it originated from one of the No Hopers, Steve, who worked as a porter in the Royal United Hospital and had access, via the nurses he slept with,

65

to a connoisseur's supply of restricted drugs such as ether and tincture of morphine as well as amyl nitrate. Steve swore by Entonox, an oxygen and nitrous oxide mix, but that was only available in-house, on the maternity ward. Carson nodded but he wasn't interested. It was the big fish he was after.

The truth was, there were dozens of people dealing dope in Bath in 1972, but no one was into serious import and distribution. Those were all London-based operations. You either bought quarters of soft Moroccan black or brittle Lebanese gold. Dealing was seen as a legitimate, counter-culture means of making money without working. It was a living not so different from my own.

The arrangement I had come to with Inspector Carson hung over me for almost a year, into the summer of '73. Naturally, I didn't tell anyone about it and, as far as I know, nor did he. My life continued as before. I forgot about Carson from one month to the next. Silvia left to have her baby. Business boomed. Britain joined the Common Market. When the necessity arose for me to make a stock-buying trip to Iran, I mentioned to Carson that I had to leave the country. He shrugged and wished me bon voyage. He knew I had to come back. He had my statement in his file. I could bolt to the United States, but he probably had the means to put the FBI darbies on me if I did. If I wanted to go on living in England, selling carpets and fucking girls in the back of the Cortina, I would have to come back. Which, of course, is what I did do. A conviction for a narcotics charge could – still can – block your entrance to the US. That was always at the back of my mind.

It was during this period that Sue Thomas picked up that I had the hots for her. I may have said something to her. I honestly can't remember. She went out of her way to be friendly to me, but also to let me know that I was out of the running. I hardly ever saw her because most weekends she was with her bloke, Greg. I ran across her now and then in Paul's flat in Bennet

Street or Steve's in Chatham Row. The No Hopers were all very bitchy about each other and terrible gossips. Behind her back Sue was referred to as the Whore Goddess or simply La Belle – short for La Belle Dame Sans Merci.

One Saturday Sue appeared in my shop on Walcott Street with her beau on her arm. I don't think she was deliberately trying to make a point, but I got the message. I had never seen them in each other's company before and I had to admit they made a good-looking couple. At first I assumed it was a social call. Friends often dropped in for a cup of Earl Grey between three o'clock and five, to browse through the kilims while the pubs were shut. They never came to buy. I didn't mind. A cat may look at a Qum. My customers were from America or London, or were expensive Bristol interior decorators who made the trip to Bath with their clients because they knew they could pick up a Persian twenty, twenty-five per cent cheaper than they could at Rackham's in the Strand.

It was explained to me that Greg wanted to buy Sue a carpet. He wanted her to choose one herself. My heart sank. Such a generous impulse on his part showed a degree of commitment to her. He wanted her to select a carpet, but he also had ideas of his own about the sort of thing she should choose.

Greg asked to see everything, not just the run-of-the-mill stuff. From the way he browsed I could see he knew what he was looking at. You can tell when a person has looked at carpets before, not only by the way he fondles them between his fingers, but by which he pauses over and chooses to fondle. Greg liked carpets I liked, which should not have surprised me as much as it did. On a fine old Turkoman he pointed out to Sue the lovely *arbrush* – the accidental change in colour where the weaver either ran out of wool from one dye batch and had to finish with another, or where, over the years, the effects of light had affected the sections of the carpet differently. At one point he squatted on his haunches and gave a very good impersonation of a Herat carpet dealer, broken English and Pashto all jumbled up. That changed my opinion of the man at a stroke.

But they couldn't decide. Or rather he wouldn't let her. He tried to steer her in the direction of what was old, irregular and beautiful. He wasn't snobbish about looking at wool rugs. I was pleased to see that. If you want to use your rug, as opposed to hang it on the wall and look at it, wool is what you should go for. The more you walk on a wool rug, the more beautiful it becomes. I cordially despised the American matrons who came into the shop and went into ecstasies over some fancy silk Isfahan or Nain, which they bought without even turning over to examine the reverse.

Persian carpets have evolved out of the collective imagination of generations of Persians, of nomad tribes and villagers, of single families even. In the inhospitable desert they are a window into God's garden which they call *bahesht*. Paradise. Just talking about carpets brings out the old hippy in me.

Greg was taken by an old Baluchi prayer rug with a stylized tree of life design, the *luckee* colours, the deep reds and purples. I was very fond of the piece myself. I was amused at the way he kept placing it in front of her like an old bazaar dealer. Sue couldn't see it, and Greg didn't press his preference. He was happy for her to consider others. The man was so at home among my carpets it did not cross my mind that he might not be able to afford to buy one. The prices were clearly marked for the American matrons, who like to know where they stand, and I made it clear to him that these were just an upper price range. I expected him to haggle. I would give them a good price because they were my friends. I would have done the same for anyone I knew who was interested in buying a carpet – as any good Muslim would have done.

'Look, Sue,' he said eventually. 'It's crazy looking at carpets alongside so many others. It just confuses you. Why don't we ask Alan to bring out half a dozen you like most so that you can look at your carpet where it's going to be?'

He was right. I wasn't selling washing machines. Carpets are practically living things, and I like to know they are going to a good home. We settled on a selection – a dozen, in the end – which covered a wide price range. We were talking about five-by-three rugs of between five hundred pounds and upwards of a thousand – so I understood that money was no object. Greg gave me his address, which was a named house in a village in south Wiltshire, and a map to help me find it.

The next day, in the afternoon, I piled a dozen carpets into the back seat of the Cortina and, following the map, drove to Laxfield. One look at the house and I knew he wasn't wasting my time. It was one of those square, eighteenth-century red-brick houses, the kind of genteel rural residence I have always imagined the Bennet sisters lived in. Its symmetry appealed to me. Like most Conservative-minded people I'm a sucker for the rectilinear, the uncluttered, the classically formal. It appeals to our need for order. I was impressed. Sue's beat-up old Mini was in the drive, where a Stubbs horse and brougham more properly should have stood. Now wasn't the time to ask myself where the owner had got the bread to buy such a beautiful house. I didn't suppose Greg had paid for it from what he got playing guitar at the Village Hall in the Walcott burial ground. He was Gatsby without the bad taste.

They amused themselves with the rugs, placing one here, another there. They could not agree where the carpet should lie, never mind which one to buy. I approved of their indecision. Buying a carpet should not be hurried. Your final choice may be one you have to live with for the rest of your life. On rare occasions it can be love at first sight, it's true, although it will more likely be an affection that grows after a period of cohabitation under the same roof. The relationship can take years to develop.

Sue wanted an intimate carpet for her bedroom, one she could put her feet upon as she got in and out of bed. In my mind's eye I saw them sliding from under the sheets on to the carpet. I saw her thighs, her breasts and her lovely skin. It was not myself I saw lying beside her but some other bastard and I inwardly gnashed my teeth.

She chose a cheerful wool Yallameh rug with a clear running-dog border and recurring design of dark and light *guls*. Although it was new it was a good choice. Greg was disappointed she had not been as taken by the old Baluchi as he was – so he bought it for himself. We didn't haggle. I gave them a thirty-five per cent discount off the marked price and he wrote me a cheque for nine hundred pounds on the spot. I have rarely agreed a price for a carpet so quickly. Greg asked for two separate bills of sale, one for each of them – which I respected him for. Sue might be sleeping in his bed at the moment, but this time next year who could say where either of them would be? When she left him, the Yallameh would leave with her.

We completed the sale over the traditional cup of green *cha*. Greg filled a chillum with some Leb while Sue left us to prepare something to eat. We nattered about the East, places we had both visited, carpets and cannabis. The man had travelled. It was eerie how much we had in common. I told them if they wanted to change either piece, they were free to. We ate and then I collected up my carpets. While I did, Greg cut his piece of Leb in two and made me a present of the larger part. Sue kissed me and then I got into my car.

Dusk fell as I drove back to Bath along winding valley roads, feeling a little bit woozy and mildly paranoid from the effects of the pipe. My brain raced. I couldn't help liking Greg, and yet his aplomb unnerved me. I was accustomed to feeling a cut above the amiable losers and witty No Hopers that thronged the Hat and Feather. Greg was not just amiable and witty, he was successful, perhaps even more successful than me, and I had not met many men my age of whom I could say that. His familiarity with my own area of specialization demeaned me in my own eyes. It mortified me that his grasp of Persian was greater than mine, which was – still is – not bad. The bastard had everything I had and more. It didn't help, knowing that he had La Belle Dame Sans Merci in thrall. I was consumed with envy for a man I had just sold nine hundred pounds' worth of Persian carpets to.

I could see why Sue Thomas chose to stick with this one. It made sense. Without going as far as to accuse her of gold-digging, I was cynical enough to believe that any woman who got a man like Greg interested in her was not going to let him go in a hurry, not even a free spirit like Susan Thomas. I didn't blame her. She wouldn't have been the first woman to embrace with open legs the opportunity to make an eligible match. She had scored. This was Jane Austen country, let's face it.

No, I didn't hate Greg. I was just pissed off by his good fortune. He stood between me and the sun and consequently I was in his shadow. I had been basking in my own good fortune for so long by this time that I took my besting with very bad grace. I have always been a bad loser. I admit it. For that reason I make sure never to compete unless the odds are in favour of me winning.

Frankly, that was all there was to it. If I had met him in Iran or Afghanistan we would have hit it off together. It was not just the business over Sue. It went deeper than that. He daunted me and that affected my self-esteem, which is normally pretty high. He was like me, only a better version. A kind of improved dopplegänger.

'How did you enjoy the party at Summerfield last weekend? Quite a bash, I hear.'

It was an innocuous remark, such as anyone might make to the person he was having a drink with.

During my second-to-last interview with the head of the Bath drugs squad, he mentioned some details about my private life which put the wind up me. He mentioned them with the sole purpose of putting the wind up me.

Summerfield was a large Elizabethan country house near Marshfield that was collectively owned by some English aristo cranks and run on Gurdjieffian principles, whatever *they* were. It was the sort of enterprise you could easily imagine existing in the thirties. Members of the collective – tall, blond vegetarians with silent letters in their names – shared responsibility for household chores and the management of the animals and claimed to be self-sufficient in dairy produce. I can't say whether or not this was true. All I know is that once or twice a year they threw fabulous parties at which there was always plenty to drink, a band played and quantities of expensive proscribed drugs were consumed. A close blood relative of the Queen was an occasional visitor to the house, although I never actually saw her myself. I did drink a glass or two from the crate of Tanqueray gin I understood she had brought with her as part of her week-end luggage.

What Carson was telling me was that my presence at one of these thrashes deep in the Somerset countryside had been noted – presumably by another guest. He was letting me know that I wasn't his only source of information. He had others. He had a complete list of visitors to Summerfield in his file – including, no doubt, any with a blood connection to the monarch. He was saying: put that in your hashish pipe and smoke it.

On this occasion Carson was not the smooth bastard he usually made himself out to be. I detected a certain unease. I am quite good at picking up the vibe a person is putting out but is unwilling to put into words. You don't haggle for carpets in Persian bazaars without learning a lesson or two in human psychology. (I call it business acumen. My therapist calls it *being in syntony* with other people.) Carson wanted me to give him some names and addresses. He let me know that if I didn't come up with anything more noteworthy than the Twerton black guys, he would have no choice except to activate my own case. He almost apologized. I almost felt sorry for him. He practically begged me to deliver. He didn't care whose names I gave him so long as they were names he didn't have already. I had no information that was of any use to him, but as soon as I intuited the desperation of his mood the boot was on the other foot.

'I can probably give you something,' I said.

When I spoke those words I swear to God I had no idea what I was talking about. Buying and selling is not always based on reality but sometimes on dreams and emotions, hunch and guesswork. If the policeman wanted information from me as badly as that it meant I had something to bargain with, or he thought I did, which came to the same thing. Of course, he tried to persuade me to hand over my information there and then, but I would not do that. I could not. Not then. The idea had hardly formed in my brain. Nevertheless, the invisible worm had found out my bed.

I said: 'I'll meet you here tomorrow. You'll bring the original of my signed statement. If you are prepared to hand it over to me, I'll let you have something none of your other informants know about.'

He looked at me over his pint while he considered my proposition. We were two drowning men clutching at the same straw. Finally he nodded. It was a deal. All I had to do to get myself off the hook was produce a name for Carson within twenty-four hours. Some deal.

I didn't go into work the following morning. It had been a sleepless night, but I had not tossed and turned. I had lain in bed and calmly examined from every angle the course of action I was about to undertake. If I am to be honest, I have to admit that I had already arrived at a decision. It was simply a question

73

of convincing myself that it was one I could live with. As things turned out it was not, but I wasn't in possession then of information that only emerged later. You have to remember, I was haggling my way out of deep shit.

I was at the rendezvous before my adversary, seated with my pint on the narrow first-floor balcony. I seemed to be the only customer in the pub. I rolled myself a cigarette and waited. The view across the Avon valley was superb. The sun was on the gasholders in East Twerton. I have always been fond of gasholders, the only truly kinetic architecture.

The Retreat – so aptly named – was a pretty detached Georgian house on Sion Hill, not ideally sited to attract passing trade. An estate of new houses had recently joined it to the city, but originally it must have been at some distance from Bath. Unless you arrived on foot, you had to leave your car by the golf course and walk. The building was set back from a footpath behind a walled garden. You had the choice of either drinking in one of the two unlit front rooms or of taking your beer outside and climbing up to the Regency iron balcony, the kind which was sometimes appended as an afterthought to the façades of Georgian houses.

If the Hat and Feather was always packed, with wonderful young ectomorphs spilling out on to the pavement, the Retreat was never quite empty. It was a place for reflection and I would go there if I had accounts to look over. I loved the pub for the same sort of reasons I loved nomad kilims. It belonged to a particular place at a particular moment in time – and soon it would disappear for ever.

Carson arrived accompanied by his lieutenant, Detective Constable Cooke. I spied the two men approaching long before they saw me. I descended the staircase and was halfway down the garden path when they pushed open the wooden door off the footpath. I was not in the mood to argue the toss.

'What's he doing here?' I said.

I had no intention of putting myself in the position of being one against two. When a pair of buyers are dealing with a single seller they have a lot of advantages. You can't eyeball two people at the same time whereas they can you. I said I was leaving if he didn't send Cooke away. I wasn't bluffing either. I would have left. I'm sorry now I didn't.

Carson sent Cooke back to wait in the car and I immediately knew I had an edge. Trying not to spill his pint, Carson negotiated the spiral staircase up to the balcony. He sat down and admired the view across the valley and sipped the froth on his Worthington's.

'I'm sorry this is going to be the last time we meet like this, Alan,' he said. 'I do like the beer here.'

I believed him. For a policeman, Carson could be unnervingly human.

He placed the original of my signed statement on the table in front of me. I took from my pocket a foil-wrapped package which I placed on top of the statement. Carson picked it up, unwrapped the foil and sniffed the contents.

'Leb,' he said. 'And quite fresh, too.'

His face lit up as if he were a punter examining a quid deal in the Hat and Feather.

My pack of Golden Virginia was lying on the table and Carson took a Rizla and placed some tobacco into it. For a moment I thought he was going to pick some specks off the lump of Leb and roll himself a joint – but he didn't. He lit his cigarette and then pushed the tobacco across the table. The intimate gesture was in bad taste, I thought. I wouldn't have minded a cigarette, but I could not bring myself to smoke with the bastard. I just wanted to get it over with. I told him the name of the person from whom I had obtained the Leb and the address, which he jotted down in his pad. Both were new to him, I judged, otherwise he would not have done that. While he wrote I folded my statement and put it in my pocket. I walked down Lansdown Hill a free man. But not a particularly happy one.

I suppose I thought that Greg would get done for possession, that the piece of stuff he had in his tin would cost him a fine which he could easily afford. I hadn't foreseen that the consequences of what I had done would be so enormous and far-reaching and that, even though they were not the consequences I had anticipated, I would still have to live with them.

In the *Daily Mirror*, on the radio and TV, in the street, in the Hat and Feather, the news broke that there had been a big police operation, so big it even had a name: Operation Josephine.

According to the junk press a London dope-dealing ring had been smashed. As well as the big fish, the medium-sized fish had been netted – and even, we soon knew from direct report, some of the smaller fry. The Establishment hacks, of course, were cock-a-hoop, slavering with bile. Newspapers like the *Daily Mail*, which had supported Franco and Hitler and Mussolini, were outraged by a handful of harmless, mildly anarchistic *hashishim*.

It was a bad moment for us, because it disproved one of the cardinal truths members of the counter-culture clung to: we were brighter than they were, not only because we appreciated Captain Beefheart and wrote haiku, but because *we smoked dope and they didn't*! The police were without intellectual, moral or aesthetic discernment. We, on the other hand, had funnier gags and the sweeter lays. You can imagine how chagrined we were to learn that these tossers possessed the mental stamina to mount a coordinated operation that had successfully closed down a large London importer and an entire network of regional distributors.

It was a blow. Our *soi-disant* counter-culture of cool, dope-smoking rock 'n' rollers had been penetrated by rock 'n' rollers who smoked dope and were every bit as cool as we were. We had been infiltrated by people like us! Our worst nightmare –

best represented in Don Siegel's 1957 movie *The Invasion of the Bodysnatchers* – had come true. One of us was one of them! The Enemy wasn't at the gates, it was within.

OK, so we had not lain in the mud at Cambrai nor gone over the top at Tobruk with *The Waste Land* in our pockets. We had not done anything heroic for anyone. All we ever did was get wrecked and smashed and fuck each other's brains out to *Highway 61 Revisited*. In the Great Balance it isn't much. Nevertheless our understanding of and resistance to paranoia will go down in history as our contribution – our only contribution, perhaps – to world history.

After Cuba – about the time Roy Orbison LPs were first available on imports – we laughed and romped and behaved like fucking lunatics. We wore outrageous clothes and screwed like crazy – *in public*! We behaved like people for whom there was no tomorrow: not the first generation to do so, but the first for whom it had been literally true. Gary Powers was a spy as much as Kim Philby, only not such a successful one. We wished a plague on both their houses. All the same, walking down the high street of any English town twenty minutes after having dissolved a tab of lysergic acid diethylamide under the tongue, we understood what Philby must have gone through. He was one of us. Gary Powers was a cheap hitman in comparison. Munich, the Nazi–Soviet pact, the Cold War. To say we thought we understood betrayal and the fear of betrayal would be an understatement. We considered ourselves connoisseurs of the subject.

Sue Thomas was walking down Walcott Street just as I was locking up my shop – so it must have been about five-thirty in the afternoon, opening time – the day the news broke. She almost fell into my arms and burst into a flood of tears. I took her down to the Bell and bought her a large Jameson's. I learnt then, for the first time, that Greg had been arrested and that he was in Bath police nick. Initially I was disconcerted to be confronted with the consequences of my actions so soon. I can't say I was surprised, although she might have got the impression I was.

After she made the connection for me between his capture and Operation Josephine, I was aghast. It had never occurred to me that Greg was a big-time dealer – I could have kicked myself at my obtuseness – but as soon as she told me how many policemen had been involved in his bust and I reminded myself of the hitherto unexplained source of his wealth, it all fell into place. I was genuinely sorry. I had never intended to shop someone as guilty as all that.

I would be lying, however, if I said I did not immediately see the advantages of my situation. Amid the maelstrom my luck had held. I was at large, still ahead of the game. The weight hanging over me had been removed. I was a free agent again. The woman of my dreams was in my arms with her head on my shoulder – while her old man was behind bars. Things could have been worse.

I spent the rest of the evening trying to reassure Sue that her bloke's situation was not so bleak as it looked – a lie I wanted to believe almost as much as she did. We had that in common. I took her to the Assembly Inn for something to eat, and we finished up in the Star in Guinea Lane – a town version of the Retreat. At closing time I walked her back to her flat in Northampton Street and she invited me in. We had some more to drink. Her bedroom was a slattern's lair, a jungle of discarded petticoats and dresses, unwashed underwear, books and paints and *objets trouvés*, the bed unmade. Sue Thomas slept with me as an act of gratitude, out of the goodness of her heart. I didn't delude myself that there was any more to it than that. Still, it was a source of satisfaction to me to bed my rival's woman. It quenched something.

Through his solicitor, the details of the case against Greg emerged. The police had raided his Wiltshire house and taken away a load of illicit narcotics: a quantity of acid and a weight of cannabis. The acid connected him directly with the factory in a leafy suburb of south London. The solicitor was glum. He didn't hold out much hope.

It was only after I came back from India, after the trial at the Old Bailey seven months later, after I had seen a photograph, that I recognized among the Leb and the acid the weight of bhang I had bought and sent to myself from Tehran. Carson, having only found a relatively small amount of hash in Greg's house and realizing that it was not enough to put him away for long, had planted my unopened weight on him to raise his haul to one that would ensure a more substantial custodial sentence. Under normal circumstances such an amount would only have been worth a year or two, three at most, but with the acid and the conspiracy angle he was sent down for eight. The big fish were put on trial first and then, after they had been found guilty, those accused of lesser offences. It did not help Greg that his case was heard alongside ten others, each of whom was almost certainly guilty. The harshness of his sentence reflected the severity with which conspiracy is viewed in English law.

I assumed that the acid, like the cannabis, had been planted – which was Greg's defence – but I never found out for sure. He must have paid for his grand country house with coin of the realm.

Carson had been pulled into the magnetic current of the operation the big boys at the Met had set up. It was a question of prestige for him. He needed to produce something solid if he wanted to be a player. All he had were the quid-deal hippies on Snow Hill and the black boys over in Twerton. What he needed, what the Met and the Attorney-General wanted, was not dealers but the suppliers to the dealers. Greg fitted the bill. That or the Bill fitted him up for it.

Interestingly, while every known dope scene in Somerset was being busted and every two-bit hustler was being pulled in, the

Elizabethan house near Marshfield remained inviolate. No police sirens disturbed that tranquil haven. The cows at Summerfield continued to be milked, the carrots grown and cooked according to Gurdjieff's principles. One had to presume that the Queen's close blood relative provided the commune with more than crates of Tanqueray gin.

Shortly after Greg's arrest my business took me to Iran for several months. For obvious reasons I had no desire to be in England. From Iran, on a whim, I made my way to India and Sri Lanka. For several months I fooled around with an Australian girl, Gina, on the beach at Trincomalee – which Nelson called the finest natural harbour in the world. (Nelson had not had the opportunity of seeing San Francisco.) I often thought about Greg while I was away. He slipped in and out of my thoughts – as he does occasionally even now. By the time I returned to Bath – in the spring of 1974 – the affair was history.

I was glad to be back home. Nothing much ever changes in Bath, neither the composition of the council nor the weather. The Hat and Feather was still the place to go on a Saturday night. I was secretly pleased to learn that the Retreat had been sold by the brewery during my absence and was in the process of being converted into a private residence. It must have been a hole in the pocket as far as Bass Charrington were concerned. As much as I had been fond of the pub – ale sold from wooden casks in the front room of a domestic residence – I knew I would never go back. It was better that the place disappeared off the face of the earth and existed only in fond memory.

I did not know then that my ambivalent feelings for the Retreat were but an early symptom of my condition, one which would eventually force me to reject everything in England: the politics, the climate, the market it offered my business.

In the shop it was business as usual. In the city I sensed that my relationship with people had changed. I was no longer tuned into the same wavelength as the crowd who lounged around Walcott and played bar football in the Hat. By small degrees I was forced to acknowledge to myself that it wasn't them, it was me. I was the one out of kilter. The No Hopers made conversation with me, but they did not invite me back after the pub shut any more. Folk still helped me prop up the bar: the lovely Bath Convent School girls, the Antique Dealers and assorted rogues, the Bath Restoration crowd. There were no ugly incidents. I didn't get the impression that I was looked upon as a bad penny. It simply dawned on me one day that I didn't want to live there any more.

The next day I loaded my stock into the back of a box van, closed up the shop and drove to London. Over a couple of weekends I completed the move and I was soon trading from premises in Islington, N1. My ability to do that, to up and go, has always been one of my strengths, the reason I have stayed ahead of the game. The nature of my business allows me to take my trade where the whim suits me. Persian carpets are as good as international currency, better because their value does not depreciate with inflation. Inflation then was running at about eight, nine per cent.

I traded from N1 for almost two years. I didn't do badly, but there is a surfeit of oriental carpet expertise in London and consequently too much competition. The discriminating customer is spoilt for choice. The arguments in favour of moving my trading base to America were becoming overwhelming, not all of them strictly commercial. Perhaps if I had been able to look into the future and see how much Margaret Thatcher was going to alter British society, I might have stayed. Who could have foreseen that in 1974?

N1 is an elegant part of London, similar to Bath in some ways. But it isn't Bath – still less is it Venice or Isfahan – and it is frighteningly close to Walthamstow. It wasn't all that far from the site of the old Holborn Empire where my dad had taken my mum to see Max Miller. My fate was catching up with me.

Greg Harris died in prison in the summer of 1975. He was killed during a prison disturbance. His assassin, allegedly a prison officer, was never identified, and the Home Office coroner brought in an open verdict. That was all I knew – and I wouldn't have minded not knowing that. It was possible I might have caught the story at the foot of an inside page of *The Times*, or on the TV news – but I didn't. I missed it. I received intelligence of the event through the post, in the form of a cutting from a local newspaper. Someone wasn't taking any chances.

The cutting, which was already six months old, arrived in a manila envelope with a first-class stamp on it – and an SW9 postmark. I was baffled. I didn't know anyone in SW9. To judge from the irregular letter formation on the envelope, I was pretty sure that the person in possession of information about my connection with the deceased was a non-Roman-script writer. I have looked often enough at the writing of Muslim speakers of English to know. It gave me a fright to think that somebody out there, whose identity I didn't know, had the key to the cupboard I kept my skeleton in.

I didn't hang around to become better acquainted. The bulk of my stock, the run-of-the-mill pieces, I sold through connections in the trade. On the whole my colleagues gave me good prices, but they were still buying carpets for less than they would be selling them at. I took a further loss in paying US import tax on the stuff I took with me. A walk around the department stores and the specialist shops in and off Fifth Avenue soon reassured me. Prices were about fifteen per cent to a third higher than they would have been for equivalent pieces in Rackham's in the Strand, whose catalogue I knew off by heart. Buying direct from producers, as I did, I was laughing.

I gravitated towards San Francisco, a city whose elegance

and charm, domestic architecture and changeable climate – like Venice, Bath and Isfahan – cry out for the sumptuous feel of a fine carpet underfoot. I rented a shopfront on O'Farrell, put my stock in the window and opened a bank account. I have never looked back.

Every carpet, even the finest Kashan or Isfahan, possesses a single unobtrusive fault in its design. It might take you a long time to locate it, but you can bet your last dime a fault will be there. It is Allah's privilege to create the thing without imperfection, not man's, nor – especially in the case of carpets – woman's. The fault will be in the design, never in any of the stages of production. It will be some minuscule departure from an other-wise formally regular sequence – one leaf different in a thousand. Its very unobtrusiveness contributes to the carpet's splendour. There are rugs I have owned for years before the sly old weaver's deliberate error leapt up at me when I least expected it to.

The word for this in Farsi is *jofftee*. *Jofftee*, though, also carries the secondary meaning of copulation. (Two strands divided by a single strand is the etymology.) To Persians, in other words, a rug-maker's deliberate mistake and copulation are synony-mous. I have often wondered whether this is because they consider fucking to be God's own deliberate mistake in the design of the great carpet of His creation.

When I first bought carpets, I always examined every detail immediately and I was never satisfied until I had located the *jofftee*. Now when I buy a carpet, whether a splendid fine silk from Qum or a tough wool rug from the desert, I try not to look too closely for the fault. It will almost certainly reveal itself after an appropriate period of contemplation.

MARGERY UFFORD

Me and Thomas were both borned in Laxfield. Well, you knowed that, uv course you do, m'dear. But did you know we were borned athin a year on 'ch other? Well, we were. Jus' a year do part us. He be's old as the cent'ry and me younger be a year. That do make it easy to call to mind the year when summat did happen on. You want t'aks Thomas when were the King's abd'cation – or that airship as did blow itsel' up. He can tell you what partic'lar year 'twere.

I uv knowed Thomas all my days. Both on us were tiddlers at Laxfield School. We did fish for newts from dew-ponds and mooch berries athin Lacey Wood when we ud better uv been at school.

When I were fifteen, sixteen, I were's pretty as a March primrose. I had my share of a'mirers. All nice boys they were too. I could uv had me pick uv they boys. I were a handsome young thing . . .

(Laughs)

Well, I *were*! I can show you a photygraph, you don' believe me!

Of course I believe you!

I weren' a-courting Thomas then, mind. When they boys did first march off wearing the King's uniform I were tilting my cap at a Stourbridge boy – Arthur Marrick. Thomas were sent to France, but he weren' hurt – he were lucky there – and when 'twere all over he come home in one piece. Seven boys from Laxfield School weren' so lucky as he, poor devils. Arthur Marrick were one uv they seven as never seed Laxfield agin. And there were on'y twenny-two athin the school! The village were *all-to-hame*, as my old gra'mam ud say.

What did she mean by that?

Smashed to splithrins, good for nought.

(Sighs)

Who can say? I might uv married Arthur – or one uv they other boys – if things ud happen' a bit diff'n'.

(Pause)

If. There be a power uv summat in sich a bitty word.

(Pause)

You mean t'say . . . that box uv yourn ull catch ev'y word I do say? And ull play it back after – like a wireless?

'. . . *word I do say? And ull play it back after – like a wireless?*'

88

(Laughs)

Well, I never! I best be more partic'lar what I do say then, m'dear!

Where were we now?

1918.

'Twere bad ev'ywhere after the War finished, not jus' 'mong us county folk. All 'cross England 'twere bad. Athin the cities and the big houses. Ev'yone you knowed ud lost some'dy dear to they – a father, a brother, a son. There weren' many as come back brave. So when Thomas Ufford come home in one piece, well, I made sure 'twere me he were sticking up close to. Good-bodied men were's hard to come be's gold sovereigns after the War, where's young maids were common as daisies. Down be Bottom Combe we did caddle worse'n chil'un! I plucked he some wood-enemies and along on that he did give me his gage-ring. We were married at St Wulfred's next Lady Day – March 25, 1919. No honeymoon. 'Twere back to work come Munn'y morning in them days.

Be then I were 'ready at Holmwood, where I were maid for Missus Helen. Thomas, he ud learned hissel' how to drive motor cars in the Army – *and* how to repair they, too. In his heart he allus wished to start up his owned garage business, but nothing come out on it. He din' have the money to put down. He ud to go to Mister Dilke's farm over Burstock way. Stayed there ten year too, poor devil.

I had Charlie in 1920. April 27th. We din' waste no time!

(Laughs)

The Laceys weren' bothered. Then, a maid got hersel' with child, could 'spect to be let go, athout she had some'dy handy to take care on her babe for her. The Laceys din' let me go. They keeped me on a'cause on'y six week after Charlie were borned, Helen Lacey ud her owned boy and so I nursed the both uv they. One each side!

Charlie and Master Peter were same's two peas in a pod. I loved they both. Ev'yone did. I ud play creep-mouse with they till they did chuggle. I were charged to take care on they two babes and help Cook athin the kitchen best I could. Well so I did – and Cook did podge me up for it. Did suit all on us. Master Peter ud a friend to play with, and Missus Lacey din' have no cause to fret hersel' what mischuff her boy were up to. They boys did eat off uv the same trencher and sleep in the same cot. Weared 'ch others' clothes. I did treat they both equal – and so Missus Lacey did do too. The way they tiddlers did roll 'round the kitchen floor, you ud never knowed who uv they were the Lacey boy and who the ladysmaid's!

(Laughs)

It do make a person think, don' it?

Who were the Laceys?

The Laceys! Lor, that you should uv to aks sich a question! The Laceys ud lived in Laxfield hunnuds uv year. Walk yoursel' down to the churchyard and see for yoursel' how far back they do go. One uv they were a admirable as died in a famous sea battle. Don' aks me which one! There were oil paintings uv they in the house. (Don' I know, as uv dust they 'nough times!) Holmwood were built for the Laceys and be a dainty house. Well, you uv seed it for yoursel'. But *then*, in the twennies when I were nursing they two boys, one each side, there were a power uv folk familied athin it. Along uv the Laceys there were seven, eight servants, horses in the stables. A groom. Farm offices. Seven hunnud acre were with the house then.

Peter Lacey, when he weren' hard'y more'n seven, were packed off lick a parcel to Osborne, the Royal Navy school in Hampshire – and soon's he turned 'leven to Dartmouth College, where they learned he to stand with his shoulders straight and talk fast as a gen'leman. That were'n easy for Charlie – 'twere hard for both uv they – but they stayed thuck with 'ch other. Soon's he were back home from school for the summer hol'day, Master Peter teared his uniform off uv his back and were out with Charlie into they woods and farm fields, roaming and mooching squailing apples, ketching vowels, building trenches and fighting 'visible Germans . . .

(Pause)

Please don't stop!

I bisn't stopping, m'dear. I jus' be a-harking back to m'sel' how dear to me were they two boys!

Sorry!

Come 1931 John Lacey – Mister Jack we ud allus called he – took on Thomas as jobber and driver, which suited he. Thomas were never framed for farmwork. It wore he down. But give he a machine with an engine to be tentful uv and he were happy's a boy. So there we were, all together under one roof. They were good years. But didn' they go by fas'!

Thomas 'ud take they boys up into Lacey Wood to ketch coneys clean in a net, what Cook ud jug in cider for all on us, servants and family both. Eggs, bacon, cheese, butter we ud from the Lacey farm. We din' eat no worse'n kings nor queens! You 'ud on'y to read in the newspapers how other folk weren'

91

having it so easy. 'Twere worst athin the cities, I do know that. We were lucky.

But they were respec'ful county folk, the Laceys. Old Mister Jack and his son Oliver and Missus Lacey, they 'ud sich Christian ways. Allus very respec'ful on you, they were. Aksed if you ud mind so very much fetching a thing – 'stead uv telling you outright you must. They were consid'rate. You don' want to run off thinking 'twere so ev'ywhere, 'cos 'tweren'. Oh no! Servants I did talk to athin other houses – where I ud been with Missus Lacey – they ud tell you a diff'n' tale. I heared for m'sel' mistresses speak to they maids rough 'nough to make your small hairs curdle. We were diff'n'. We ud rolled around the same skillet. Ud growed up together and knowed 'ch other's family – same's Charlie and Master Peter knowed 'ch other as tiddlers – and so we were respec'ful uv 'ch other.

Mus' be hard for a young girl sich as yoursel' to unnerstan'. Be all changed now – and for the best, I ud say. *Then*, 'tweren' common for servants to be dear to they masters and mistresses, but 'tweren' rare neither.

Our Charlie were mechan'cal same's his father. 'Twere one worthy thing as come out on the War, the bit uv knowledge Thomas learned hissel' on motor engines. An'thing 'lectric or mechan'cal round the Lacey house Thomas ud tend to, and Charlie ud be at his elbow watching he close, passing they tools his dad ud need on.

When Charlie ud finished his schooling – you finished at fourteen then – Thomas were bent on he learning hissel' a trade, 'stead uv wasting his life on the land as he did do hissel'. Mister Jack could see Charlie ud summat, and he 'ranged for he to be a prentice to Garrods, the ag'cultural machine-tool firm in Frome. Be long gone now. But then 'twere the on'y man'factury athin the county, famous for they tractors and traction engines and threshers and harvesters. 'Twere long hours and gruesome hard work for Charlie, athout much for a wage, but we knowed he were lucky. After the War a man – never count a boy – could call hissel' lucky to have his owned job 'tall. We ud never uv got he prenticed uv our own. That were Mister Jack for you. He were thuck with old Mister Garrod and he spoke up for Charlie. Mister Jack allus took care on his owned folk.

So whilst Master Peter were 'way at college a-learning hissel' to be a Navy officer, our Charlie were a prentice for a skilled trade. Thomas were chuffed his boy were doing what he ud allus wanted for hissel', but ud never the chance to.

That ud be 1935. King George's jubilee. What a great pucker that were!

'Twere'n long from then we could see war on the horizon. All the papers, pol'ticians, ev'yone, did promise us 'tweren' so, but we knowed differ'n'. 'Twere same's the headick county folk do get in summer whilst the wind do switch crops this and that way, and the barrow-meter do droop but still it don' rain. Grouty, folk here'bout allus call sich a sky. Ants ull fly and dogs ull keep they noses athin the shadow, afeard on the light'ing they knowed be coming. War were in the weather. Jus' hearing Mister Jack crack his *Times* at the breakfas' table did make us jump. Ev'yone in Europe were gettin' theysel's ready to fight, fas' they could.

But there weren' no big clap uv thunner, on'y that sorryful voice saying over the wireless '. . . and so we'm be at War with the Germans'. I were mizmazed. I jus' coul'n' believe my owned ears. I niver thought to hear sich words agin. 'Tweren' poss'ble.

Compared to Lunn'n or Portsm'th or Brissol we were let off light. We jus' carried on our business as normal. Thomas volunteered hissel' for the Home Guard, being a old soldier, too old to fight – thank God! He were took on be Garrods, soon's 'twere turned over for making chasses for field guns. Not as *he* minded. Not a bit! Not he! Thomas were happy as a sheep in the pink. I ud charge on running the house for Mister Jack.

With fewer servants, 'tweren' easy. German planes ud fly over two, three times a week, on they way to Cardiff or Brissol. Me an' Thomas, same's all Laxfield folk, laid a-bed hearkening to German bombs bursting 'pon they poor devils. Did break your heart.

Master Peter were at sea, a officer on the Royal Navy convoys. His ship, HMS *Centurion*, were sunk in 1941. When the letter from the War Office first come ev'yone were struck dumb. The house were b'shrummed. Doors ud stay shut. Nob'dy wished to eat. Nor speak. Poor Helen Lacey, she rested athin her room, crying her heart out. I did do as I could for her – but what could I do? My eyes were's red as hern. Uddn't I nursed that boy and loved he as my owned?

Mister Oliver were in Lunn'n on War work. Mister Jack did try to carry on as normal. Laceys 'ud allus bin famous soldiers and sailors – for hunnuds uv years. Fighting for England were 'spected uv his folk, how he seed it. But 'twere hard for he too, account on Master Peter were the heir. Holmwood weren' never the same after his death. The house did start to sicken. 'Twere years afore you ud dare say so. Same as a old tree that be shrummed and uv finish' growing. You don' see it a' first. Not for years you don'.

Charlie – he were in the Royal Signal Corps – ud two nights at home soon after news uv Master Peter's death come upon us. The Army ud changed he, an'b'dy could see that athout you were his mother. He were broader in the arm. More knowing, not so much uv a boy. He carried books in his pocket. 'Twere pit'ful to watch Helen Lacey with Charlie, how she did so want to touch he. Often's she could she took his hand athin her owned. Charlie din' mind. They mooped over 'ch other worse'n a courting couple. Both they were broken hearted.

Each time Charlie come home, 'twere plain he were less uv a lad than when we las' seed he. The stripe what grinned 'pon his army sleeve ud took the place uv his lovey smile. The spark ud gone from his eye. Army life ud made he harder'n French stitching. He ud hardy never laugh. Master Peter's death ud shrummed summat athin he. You could see Laxfield and Laxfield folk din' matter to he. On'y his army reg'lation book and his fellows mattered to he. He hated the Army ev'y minute, but he couldn' wait to get back to his unit. It meaned more to he 'n his owned family, you see. 'Twere his family now.

Charlie were killed in France in 1944, next a village called Bosk Dallykim, no bigger'n Laxfield. July 28. Thomas and me did visit there after the War. Dear little place, 'twere. Thomas hired a car in Dieppe and druv me to it. We walked roun'. Seed where our dear boy were buried. Din' speak to a soul, not knowing how to. It chuffed us to see they old village folk walk 'bout they village. Women shopping, talking to 'ch other. Men playing they owned sort uv bowls. We did feel's if Charlie Ufford ud died for summat worthy uv he.

(Pause)

Oh Margery!

I shull be a'right, m'dear.

(Pause)

I shull be right's rain in one minute.

(Pause)

Bisn't a day go by I don' shed a tear for my Charlie. I allus try not to a'front on Thomas. He do feel it terrible keen. Thomas laid off talking uv Charlie a while. For twenny years he din' hard'y speak his name. He do now. We do talk 'bout Charlie when he be minded to.

A' first the sorrow were ramping athin me. 'Twere same's if some'dy ud cut a piece from mysel' and I must carry the missingness along of me, where I did go. I ud cry out at the bittiest thing, when I couln' open a jar and broke it. Over time it did go away. The son we ud once have ud become the son we din'. Charlie were a silence athwart us. A 'visible person, 's if each on they words he might uv spoke were right there atween Thomas and me. The shape on'y. Same's the cupboard where he keeped his clothing and be still in his room. His trousers and shirts be long gone, but the old empty cupboard be still there — and shull allus be.

Do that stand up?

Of course it does!

After years and years uv crying for Charlie we laid off speaking uv he. Thomas din' care to. We din' never quarrel, nothing uv that sort. We did continue as normal. But I did often fear the spark ud blown out 'twixt us.

Missus Lacey weren' no better. She were worst. Mister Oliver, least he ud his work in Lunn'n. Helen Lacey, poor child, jus' mumped athin the house. Couln' 'collect if she ud paid the tradesmen or what you ud spoke to her on five minutes afore. Be then, mind, there were on'y three on us at Holmwood — me, Cook and Samuel Darnell, Mister Jack's man — and a jobbing gardener b'times. Thomas allus mended things soon's they broke — which they did do more'n ever — but he ud chose to stay along of Mister Garrod after the War, where he were made foreman.

Holmwood weren' the same. Missus Lacey were allus poorly and I ud charge on her and the house m'sel'. Old Mister Jack keeped the farm on, but he were showing his years and ud grew budgy. The world ud moved off, you see, and let he catch up best he could. I do 'collect he saying to Mister Oliver as all they changes Mister Attlee ud brung on ud be the ruination uv the county. He did say that. Mister Oliver weren' uv the same mind and he ud stay weekdays in Lunn'n. Weekdays the house were quieter'n a grave and the mice ud the run uv the winscut. You could hear the quiet athin your bones – till Missus Lacey come part uv it hersel'. 1956 she did pass on.

She were a sweet dear girl when she ud firs' come to Holmwood 'pon Mister Oliver's arm. I allus loved Helen Lacey.

Mister Jack were 'lone after she passed on – 'cepting when Mister Oliver chose to come home. Mister Jack ud allus stood head and shoulder over other men, but after Missus Lacey passed on, he did stand distant from they us well. He were the sort uv farmer as ud take his jacket off and load the rick 'longside uv his fellows – *and* see to it none uv they din' bale more'n he. He were's proud on his strength as he were on his stanning in the world. He knowed what were 'spected uv he, his duty to'ard folk under he.

I did love Mister Jack. Same's most Laxfield folk. He were's plump a man's any athin the county for keeping his word. He ud never gainsay hissel'. He were a legend athin the public house. He on'y ud go there one, two time in a year – along uv his fellows after the harvest were barned in. Years afore, afore our young men marched off to France, Mister Jack ud played a innings in a cricket match 'gainst Broughton St Martin what they older men do still talk on. They eighty-two he scored be famous. On a cricket field it don' count who you be, a carter or the Prince uv Wales. All's do count be you hold the catch or put he down. Mister Jack were a famous cricketer us a young 'un, in batting and bowling and catching, and Laxfield men were proud on he. He allus ud a hogshead uv cider sent over for the last home game uv the summer, long after he ud laid off playing hissel'.

I were keeping house for he be then, and I ud worry for he.

He did still walk with a long stride, with his shoulder back. Oh, he were your bluff Englishman a'right! He ud never speak uv Master Peter after he died, no more'n he did uv Missus Helen. He clapped his fillings close to hissel'. I knowed he did think the county were gone to the dogs 'cause he did say so, after Suez he did. (You aks Thomas, he ull tell you what year that ud be.) He did seem to lose faith in what he ud allus believe in, what were 'spected uv he.

'Twere plain to me summat were out uv kilter with Mister Jack soon's I heared folk say things were going poorly with the farm. He ud refuse to plough his pasture for five pun's a acre when Mister Attlee aksed he to, you see, so now he ud too much meadow and fallow on his hand. 'Twere a bad sign when he did rent out his meadows to neighbr'ing farmers for they to plough. He grizzled a'cause Mister Oliver were more fetched be his affairs in Lunn'n than he were be the farm.

When Mister Jack passed on – summer uv 1964, after a stroke – I did think 'twere a blessed release. He weren' a happy man. He ud lived too long a'ready, longer'n were good for he. Ud he seed out the year, he ud to uv watched Mister Wilson win the election on his television. I ud niver uv wished that on the poor devil, even if I did give Labour my vote.

In they las' years afore he passed on he took to setting at the end uv the cut grass along uv my Thomas on an evening, have a pipe with he, a-facing to'ard they old elms atop uv Wufford's Hill. I ud watch they from the house. Poor devils, I thought. They ud be set on the old ironwork seat as were put there years afore for young folk to set on and talk they nonsense athin sight uv the house. I aksed m'sel' what they two could have to talk uv, seeing how they ud come from sich diff'nt worl's. Thomas told me they din' talk uv nothing partic'lar.

'Eve'n, Thomas.'
'Eve'n, Mister Jack.'

'Weather be blooming.'
'Be untimely hot, sir.'

Most the time, Thomas told me, they din' speak 't all. They ud sit quiet and peaceable, neither 'un waiting on t'other to talk. They were happy jus' to do that. I did often watch they with a tear near my eye, hearkening to m'sel' the time me and Thomas and Arthur Marrick and Bert Harrington hid oursel's athin Lacey Wood when this young gen'leman as could bowl and bat and catch, the famous Laxfield cricketer, come jiggeting by on his fine grey horse. Now there they'm be, Thomas and old John Lacey, smoking pipes aside uv 'ch other at the end uv the cut grass. It said summat to me.

'Twere near this time Mister Jack were told he mus' cut down they elms on Wufford's Hill. They were maggoty. 'Twere the last straw for he, you aks me. 'Twere along on that his dear old heart did break.

(Pause)

Be jus' as hard for they as't for us, my Susan – on'y diff'n'. I think they do wish too much from life, much more'n we do. Dis'ppointm'n do touch they worse'n it do us. We do lose our chil'un as tiddlers and in the Wars, but the heart ull allus heal itsel', you do give it the chance to. Most men – all uv the men I ever knowed – do nearly allus set they mind on summat they couln' reach. Soon's it don' come off as they wished, they mump and moan. The mind bisn't like the heart. Be more akin to a motor-car engine. Soon's one bit do go out uv kilter it all do. Bisn't happiness men do seek after. On'y the good regard uv other men ull make a man happy.

The years atween Missus Lacey's death and Mister Jack's, I did do the work uv a half-dozen servants. 'Twere on'y after Mister Oliver come to Holmwood to live and seed with his owned eyes how much I ud charge uv that I ud it easy. First he buyed me a vacuum cleaner, then a Hoover washing machine with a drier. He did pay a char daily to help me. He did fix my hours and put summat into a pension society for me. He did raise my wages too. He were a modern employer and paid for my Nationa'l Assurance stamp.

On'y good thing to come out uv Mister Jack's death were Mister Oliver did move back athin the house. He laid off working in Lunn'n and did work from Holmwood. He were a genl'man, quiet and warm-hearted. He weren' above talking uv his Peter and my Charlie in the same breath. 'Twere a pleasure to he to. We two ud set in the garden athwart a pot uv tea and laugh 'bout what our boys ud got up to. I told he some tales he never knowed uv! When he were moved to we ud talk 'bout Helen. He did miss her, poor devil.

One day I told he uv my fillings for Arthur Marrick. I did cry a piece, and he keeped me company whilst I did. He were there, don' forget. He were a cap'n in the county reg'ment. He ud knowed Arthur Marrick and Thomas Ufford. He ud seed for hissel' what they boys did go through.

Me and Mister Oliver were jus' the same's Thomas and Mister Jack. On'y we ud talk, where's they ud jus' set there to look on they old elms.

Mister Oliver ud come back to live in Holmwood on account uv a promise he ud made Mister Jack he ud do so. He keeped his promise, but his heart weren' here. 'Twere in Lunn'n. Plain as pie 'twere. He ud go up there ev'y weekend uv a fortnight. Athin me heart I allus hoped that he 'ud come back with a lady 'pon his arm but he never did. He did sell off most uv the farm land in 1966. He din' want to bother hissel' with it.

I ud loved Mister Oliver, but I can' deny certain folk in Laxfield did claim he weren' half uv the man Mister Jack were. They weren' been' fair. He were diff'n'. Mister Oliver keeped hissel' to hissel'. His father ud scored his eighty-two runs agin

Broughton St Martin, but he ud niver been athin they trenches in France 'longside uv the men. Mister Oliver weren' easy in company. Folk complaint he din' take no part uv the village. He were gen'rous, no gainsaying it. He did give the vicar a thousand-pun' cheque to'ard the new roof for St Wulfred's. No. 'Tweren' how he discharged his duty. He were athout the common touch.

Laxfield folk din' see as the War ud changed Mister Oliver. The young fellow I ud tilted my hat t'ard and fell at Wipers and his owned son droun'd dead at sea, gave both on us summat in common. He ud changed with the times, and they village folk ud not. He ud no heart to mimp the squire.

One November ev'n summat terrible did happen. Mister Oliver were knock' from his bicycle on the corner uv Thruxton Lane be a lorry going Warminster way. The lorry din' stop, and the poor devil layed there in the road till a car did pass and find he. 'Twere a terrible business. What a thing! To leave a fellow lying half dead 'pon the road in sich a way!

Mister Oliver did die in the Wilton General two days after from loss of blood and fructures. Din' niver gain his conscience. They Wilton doctors did say he must uv ud a chance if the lorry ud stop' for he. There were a pucker in the newspapers over his death. Mister Oliver were a JP, uv a old Wil'shire family. A peaceable man who ud never gainsaid hissel'.

He were put in the Lacey plot 'longside uv Missus Helen.

His friends come down from Lunn'n for his burial. I a'ready knowed most uv they from when they come down to Holmwood on weekends – Diana Graham. Tony Mostyn. Silvia and Henry Harvey-Walker. Max Langham. There were some red eyes 'mong they – if not the congregation. He were missed be his friends. I ud to look after Miz Diana, as were come over so.

Mister Oliver ud allus choosed Lunn'n afore Wil'shire, you see. 'Twere where his heart were. Don' aks me why. I can' say's I ever heared a crossed word atween Mister Jack and Mister

Oliver, but they ud they diff'ences. Be no denying that. Wuther 'twere on'y along of Master Peter's death Missus Helen did mump about so, I can' say. When it do come to affairs uv the heart there be allus more'n do meet the eye, to my knowledge. I don' claim us I knowed half the story. I know us when it did come to probiting Mister Oliver's will Miz Diana ud summat to say.

So there I were in the house all be mesel'. This ud be the winter uv '67. I keeped the old place warm, dusting they old oil paintings, pol'shing the floors, whilst 'twere decided what to do with the prop'ty. 'Twere months afore the will were probited. I did my work out uv habit, a'though there weren' nob'dy living in the house. 'Twere quiet as a barn. I keeped 'specting to hear Mister Jack or Mister Oliver step through the door. I ud seen the whole family pass on, one be one.

After Mister Oliver's accident, 'twere the end uv they Laceys. Be hard to acknowledge, but 'twere so. Not on'y weren' there no more Laceys in Laxfield, but their kind uv folk, old land families, were uv no account. Two wars ud done for they. They were same's they old elms Mister Jack did love so, and if some'dy ever aksed you you ud say were part uv Wil'shire and ud allus be. But they weren'. They be gone for ever, both on they.

The 'heritance uv the Lacey prop'ty were probited to pass to a cousin uv Mister Oliver, Major George Wooton uv Kendal in Cumberland. I knowed he from when he come as a young lad to visit, but he din' have no 'collection uv me, uv course. Servants be 'visible to most folk. Major Wooton a'ready ud a nice house in Cumberland and he din' uv need on another. He did come down and poke his head into cupboards and put stickers on what he ud in mind to keep for hissel' – they old oil paintings uv the Laceys and the best uv the furn'ture, bits and bobs as took his fancy. The rest were put up for auction. Lor! To think uv all they things as the Laceys ud lived with for hunnuds of year, all going unn'er the hammer!

Afore the invent'ry for the auction were made, me and Thomas did go 'round the house and take from drawers and cupboards ev'ything personal: letters, notebooks, lidgers, diaries – and we did burn they 'pon the garden. Din' even look at they oursel's. 'Tweren' our business to.

I did aks Major Wooton if he ud let me buy a silver ring that were Helen Lacey's – this 'un . . .

Margery! It's lovely!

He did jus' wave his hand and say as I should have it. He give Thomas Mister Jack's fav'it silver-topped eb'ny walky-stick, what pleased Thomas, though he don' never take it out uv the house – lest folk do think as he be mimping the gentleman!

Afore the auction, folk as were uv a mind to were invited to step in and walk 'round the house, poke they noses where they wished. And most the village did do so, e'en the vicar. Dealers from Lunn'n come down in vans and buyed up most the dearest pieces, paid hardy an'thing for they too, account uv they ud agreed 'mongst theysel's what to bid on aforehand. Lacey prop'ty still found its way into village houses. I din' mind that. 'Twere the other stuff I did grieve for, bits and bobs as ud stood in a partic'lar corner for hunnuds uv year, ending they days in antiquey shops in Lunn'n and America, cast to the four winds. 'Twere worthy uv a fortune, I dare say, but not owned be no'un partic'lar.

The house did stand empty half a year. Don' aks me why. They were hard times for me – first 'ccasion uv my life I were idle. Thomas were at home and so we did keep in the way uv 'ch other! And we were poor. We ud to scroop our pennies to scrape by.

First I knowed Holmwood did have a new owner were after Thomas seed a light in a window uv Mister Oliver's bedroom. Soon folk were chattering worse'n magpies 'bout who might be the new owner uv the Lacey house. Nobidy knowed an'thing 'bout who he were, but that din' stop they. 'Twere 'nough as he were a man athout a family. They did wish for a young couple, a mother with tiddlers, and here were a young fellow occ'pying a whole house. 'Tweren' right. Afore long, afore an'bidy ud even shook hands with the poor devil, he ud a rep'tation to live down. They did call he the *newcomer*. The first look folk ud uv he on'y proved they worse fears. He din' look how you'd uv 'spect a gen'lman ud look. He weared his hair to his shoulder same's a girl and a beard, checked shirts and blue trousers like a working man! Lor, nobidy ud ever seen an'thing like he round here afore!

(Laughs)

Mister Harris were his name. Well, *you* do know that! When I first did meet he I called he Mister Harris, but he said I weren' to be so formal. I were to call he plain Gregory.

How did you first meet him?

I took mesel' round to call on he. To see for mysel' how he were framed. I were jus' been' nosy.

(Laughs)

We did sit in the garden and talk – uv Thomas and me mostly, and the Laceys and the village. He were keen to know ev'ything. I did warm to he. He were a respec'ful young fellow. Soon after, he aks Thomas and me to come by to have lunch with he. We were took aback, I mus' say. First uv all, he hard'y knowed us. We hard'y knowed he. I weren' raised to be so easy with people I weren' 'quainted uv. Ladysmaids din' sit at table with folk with college ed'cation. More likely we ud wait on they. But he din' see hissel' as a Lacey. He weren' a member uv any partic'lar set. So far's I could see he were jus' a handsome young fellow with respec'ful ways. He did make a big fuss on Thomas, right off.

Well, we called round at the time he did say to. I weren' abashed, but Thomas were pale. He ud refuse point-blank to put his best shirt on, though I did say he should do. But he were right not to. Gregory were in old blue patched-up trousers and one uv they vests with sleeves to here . . .

A T-shirt.

Be that how you do call they?

Yes.

He were very welcoming. Made a fuss on Thomas. My Thomas bisn't a fellow to open his mouth easy, and he can be sour when he do choose to, and I says it as his owned wife. Gregory ud put a table in the conservat'ry, and he brung out the dishes from the kitchen hissel'. He ud baked a chicken-in-the-pot as good as an'thing I could uv put down mesel'. He were the first man I knowed as cooked his owned food. Thomas, I could see, were wrought. He were quiet and did eat his chicken in his second-best shirt. He din' know what to make uv this young fellow in a old man's house, with his hair down to his shoulders same's a girl's, and who not on'y cooked his owned food but brung it to the table hissel'! I don' think he 'pproved on he! He were easy with we, but my Thomas weren' going to let hissel' be hurried. Me, I be jus' the opp'site uv Thomas. Ever somed'y do show hissel' friendly I don' mind meeting he halfway.

After that I ud drop round regular, as were no more'n neigh-bourly. If you want to know the truth, I couln' keep away!

(Laughs)

I ud take he a parsley or mint, account uv he were trying to put back the garden to how 'twere afore Mister Jack died. Else I ud show he how to op'rate the old Hoover washing machine in the scull'ry. He ud say, 'Margery: what ud I do athout you?'

We were soon thuck as two thieves. He ud a wicked spark in his eye. He brung to mind Arthur Marrick afore he did go to France. One day he said: 'Margery. I wager you were a handsome young girl. I believe you were. Did you have a lot uv 'mirèrs?' I told he to go by and tend to his business. I could feel the blood rising into my cheeks! At my old age! He did laugh! He weren' shy uv making a old lady flustrated!

'Margery . . .' he did say, 'I uv need on some'dy to help me run the house. Be too much to do be mysel'. I needs 'nother pair uv hands.' I tell he I should be happy to come by when he ud need uv me. He says, 'It ud make me happy if you ud 'ccept a wage-paying job.'

'Course I did 'ccept – fast us lightning! I were glad to be back in that old house again, us be so powerful dear to me. 'Twere more'n I did dream on, to have a position again. I did allus hate to be idle. Young Gregory said right off 'tweren' my old job he were giving me. I weren' going to be nobidy's maid. I were to be my owned mistress, to come and go as the fancy took me.

Uv course, the money were welcome. I don' deny it. He ud it paid into the post office direct. Thomas and me were living 'pon our pension be then, and on what Mister Oliver ud leaved us in his will.

What about the rest of the village? How did they take him?

Well, they were chattering 'bout he worse'n magpies . . .

106

(Laughs)

But he soon ud they eating from his hand. You knowed he were in the church choir?

Yes.

The vicar couln' believe his luck! Mister Oliver were gen'rous with his money, sich as the thousan' pun' he ud give to'ard the church roof I told you uv, but he were a miser uv his time. He din' niver go to service, and he weren' a man to play cricket or go to the pub and have a drink lick his father. He din' take no part uv village life. He were too shy. Now here were this growed man as did want to sing! The vicar ud allus a half-dozen in the choir – be hook or be crook. 'Tweren' easy. They ud sing the introit at Easter and carols at Christmas.

Gregory did join the choir and he soon ud charge on it. He could play the piano beautiful, and he did have a sweet singing voice. After half a year he ud persuaded some uv the older fellows to come back, men who ud left soon's they voice ud broke. He did uv need on some basses and tenors, you see. After a year his little choir were singing sweet as angels. I on'y heared sich singing at Salisbury afore then. Folk ud go to church on purpose to hear they sing! The singers were's pleased as we.

How did you know?

I knowed acause they wives did say so! You can guess how it pleased they. Eve'y wife be glad when her man do take an int'rest in summat else, aside uv hersel'. I never knowed a man who weren' glad to open his mouth and let forth, you but give he the chance. It come to men's natural as beer-drinking. Where you do meet the one you do near allus find the other handy.

Vicar Matthew soon took a shine on Gregory. Did *adore* he.

You go and aks Missus Matthew, you don' believe me. The pair uv they were allus talking and working or joking o'er a pint in the Mow, a'though Gregory never made no secret he weren' a believer. The vicar din' care two ha'pence. In a queer way 'twere grist unto his mill. I once aksed Gregory how 'twere he got on so easy with the vicar, consid'ring as he were a heathen. All he did say were: 'I allus got on easy with vicars,' 's if he ud knowed hunnuds in his life. And when I aksed James Matthew why he were so thuck with a atheist, he did jus' chuggle. 'Margery,' he did say, 'acause Gregory don' believe Jesus Christ be the owned Son uv God, don' mean he can' be dear to a Church uv Englan' vicar.'

Gregory learned hissel' they old rusty songs from the farm folk, and he ud sing they with James in the Mow. So you could as soon hear a atheist singing in church as a vicar in a public house!

(Laughs)

He allus did have a beautiful hymn-singing voice . . .

(Pause)

Oh Margery . . . !

M'dear!

He's not dead! Please don't talk as if he was!

Susan, m'dear! What a silly old fool I be! He *still* do have his voice! Uv course he do! Lor, I din' mean . . .

(Pause)

You sit tight, m'dear. Let me make you a cup uv tea . . .

Now then. Where were we?

He had a beautiful hymn-singing voice.

Oh yes. And so he do still!

(Laughs)

That be the truth! He were allus singing. I ud be cooking or washing or hanging out the washing, he ud be playing on the piano or one uv they guitars he were mending. He did mend guitars and banjos for a living. Insturments ud arrive all broke up and he ud piece they together so's they did sound good again. 'Tweren' allus classic music he played. He ud play an'thing as took his fancy – old hymns, radio music, songs from shows – you jus' had to cast your eye across they notes he did play from to feel seasick! A tear ud allus prick my eye when I heared he sing they old British Army songs what brung to mind my Arthur, and how my life ud been diff'n' ud he come home from the War.

I told Gregory all 'bout Arthur. He wrung the story out uv me over the years. I weren' sorry he did too. Be true what he did say to me one time. You don' know a person unless you uv knowed how broken-hearted they uv been. I ud never let m'sel' forget Arthur.

But 'twere Thomas Gregory most tickled. And *there* be the miracle!

He ud found out Thomas were having trouble with his old shed, and he come by with his tool bag to help he build a new 'un. 'Twere a lovely job they did do, too. That shed be snug's a railway carriage. Well, you uv seed it for yoursel'. Ev'ry man do want a shed. Don' aks me why. I believe it do comfort they.

Thomas were happy as a lark in May after Gregory ud finished. Both they took pleasure working wood, you see. They ud that in common. They did learn from 'ch other. 'Twere a equal fellowship. No man can be happy athout he do have the fellowship uv other men. Any woman as don' see that be a simpleton.

After'ds they were allus coming and going, doing favours for 'ch other. Thomas did show Gregory how to double-dig his garden.

It be a sweet thing for a woman to watch two men learn they do have summat dear in common . . .

(Laughs)

. . . so long's it bisn't *she*!

They were often in 'ch other's company – *talking*! That were the wonder. Thomas were never what you ud call a chatterbox. Not with me even. But Gregory did pull he out uv hissel'. Don' aks me how he done it. He knowed he were allus welcome to come by our house ever he did feel the need to, for summat to eat or when he wanted company, play a hand uv cards or a game uv dominoes. We all three on us did love jigsaws, and Gregory brung some terrible hard jigsaws with he. A tiger in a jungle storm were one. Did take the three on us a ev'ning to fulfil. Venus – naked as the day she were borned! – stanning on a half-cockleshell with the wind blowing her gold hair. He ud make us do they athout looking at the picture, so neither Thomas nor I never knowed what the picture were – not till after the pretty face and naked belly and bosom uv the girl did come into the picture! Your Gregory were a cheeky boy!

While we played cards or dominoes or filled jigsaws we allus did talk. I warmed to my Thomas, listening to he talk 'bout his time in France. Or the hard life he had on Mister Dilke's farm in the twennies. His War work at Garrods. Things he ud never spoke uv to me. I did begin to see he in a diff'n' light. He allus knowed what he did want uv life. He jus' weren' give the 'pportun'ty. He weren' never hissel' after Charlie were killed, I knowed that.

Then Gregory did do a grand thing. He knowed how much Thomas ud allus wished for a engine to tend, so he buyed a second-hand motor car, a dear little thing 'twere. A Austin, painted grey with maroon upholst'ry. Well, his idea were as he ud drive it hissel' one day. He ud learned hissel' how to drive, but ud never took his licence. Thomas ud have the car till the day Gregory ud his owned licence. Gregory ud pay the assurance and the tax.

It did change Thomas, that little car. 'Twere that dear to he. He druv the village folk where they cared to go – anybidy in the village as aksed he. They ud pass he a couple uv bob for petrol. Thomas were cheerful for the first time since he did read the letter the King sent he 'bout Charlie. He become like a taxi. Did give he summat to occupy hissel' on – summat he ud allus meaned to do. Uv course, he druv young Gregory whereso'er he chose to go. So ev'yone were happy. Nob'dy weren' more happy'n me!

I did join in the talk mesel'. Well, you do know me! I bisn't ever one to sit quiet and make tea! Gregory din' let hissel' forget as I were there, and so Thomas heared what I ud to say. My side uv the story. I 'collected for he the 'ccasion we and Arthur Marrick and Bert Harrington ud hid oursel's up in Lacey Wood and young Master Jack ud jiggeted pas' on his fine grey horse. And the Boxing Day we ud slidged down Wufford's Hill when 'twere froare. He ud forgot that. With Gregory setting at our table, hearkening to us, 'twere easier for both on us. We did warm to 'ch other agin. Do that sound foolish? A married couple uv our years? Foolish or no, it be true. We did look at oursel's from the other side uv the room. When we were 'lone – later, in bed – we ud talk 'bout what we ud spoke uv. Things

111

we ud never spoke uv afore. Thomas and me ended be talking to 'ch other agin. 'Twere a miracle.

(Pause)

M'dear, I shall allus be debted to your dear boy for that. No matter what. Allus.

(Pause)

How did he do it?

Gregory?

Yes.

I aksed m'sel' the same question. All I can tell you, m'dear, is he were open to folk. The vicar. Thomas. M'sel'. The choir singers. An'bidy. He did listen with his heart, you see, not jus' his two ears. He keeped his eyes open. He weren' a fellow to talk 'bout his owned business – not lick m'sel'! He hardy never spoke uv hissel', where he ud come from or his owned folk. But he weren' afeared to put his fillings into words. The commonest thing he did glory in. Cooking toast and cheese, weeding his garden, splitting wood, cleaning a chimney. If you ud seed he restoring they old musical insturments – he ud work so slow and careful it give you a headick to watch. All work meaned summat to Gregory. Nothing he chose to do were tiresome to he.

I ud aksed the vicar how he could be so thuck with Gregory, but I knowed a'ready why.

Why?

He did touch you.

What? Your feelings?

Oh yes! He ud also touch you with hissel. He weren' fussed to do that. Gregory ud take the vicar's arm, or Thomas's, and be easy's fresh cream with they. One even' he did take me in his arm and kiss me g'night, right there in front uv Thomas! What a flustration! Caused the blood to rise to my cheek! I din' mind. Lor, no! Nor more'n did Thomas. I were allus pleased to be kissed, and I wouln' uv complaint if I ud bin kissed more times athin my life than I were.

(Pause)

We were candles in the dark he did set light to, one be one.

(Pause)

He were special in my eyes. If he do love you, Susan, you mus' be special too.

(Pause)

If *he does.*

Sure he do!

(Pause)

Margery. I know you all liked Gregory, but he knew other people, people outside Laxfield. People like me.

Oh, yes! He ud friends his own age, sich as yoursel'. He took hissel' to Bath or Brissol regular. Thomas druv he to Bath on a Frid'y even' and he ud come back Sunn'y or Munn'y under

113

his own steam. I don't know what muschief he ud get up to there. Never aksed he. He brung a friend back b'times . . .

Girls?

(Laughs)

Well, you did say I were to tell you ev'ything! You been' a 'istorian as shouln' be shy uv the fac's!

And I meant it! Of course Gregory had girlfriends.

I knowed he did go to town to have some fun. Listen to music. Have a drink. B'times he took his own insturments to play hissel'. He were a young fellow and he ud need on the comp'ny uv folk his owned age. Be queer if he din'. I did aks mesel' what he got up to but niver he. 'Tweren' my business. I did aks mesel' how ud I uv felt if I were his mother. I weren' troubled 'bout he, a'though I were allus glad to have he back home.

What about the girls?

What 'bout they?

Didn't you worry about them? Or disapprove?

Lor no!

(Laughs)

They were big 'nough to look after theysel's! And they were nice girls. Thomas druv they home, to Melksham or Trowbridge or to the station. But if they did get up to handypandy,

114

they couln' say as they were took be surprise! Anyways, I uv heared you young girls do have pills to stop you having babies.

(Pause)

Well, there you are!
No, m'dear. I din' never worry about they. I were on'y glad to see young girls have they share uv fun athout been' afeard as we allus were. When I were a young girl no'un'd tell you an'thing. You on'y learned how your young man stood athout his clothes on after your wedding night!

(Laughs)

If I ud have they pills my life ud been diff'n', I can tell you!

Perhaps you had better not!

No. Perhaps I ha'n't!

(Laughs)

But he didn' have his friends driving they motor cars through the village, carousing at three o'clock in the morning. Nothing uv that. He weren' that sort. He choosed his friends careful. There were Sydney as plays the banjo so lively. He ud come by. One or two uv they others he did inner'duce me to. They were allus respec'ful to'ard me. Oh yes. Gregory were partic'lar they din' address me 's if I were the char. And then — well, you did come by, m'dear! And I were pleased to see you. I were! I did think you were handsome with your black hair brushed loose and your long dresses with 'brod'ry-work on they. I did tell mysel' you ud do!

Thank you!

Oh, I did watch you with Gregory! I ud never seed a woman who were so easy with her young man afore I seed you! Did take my breath 'way. You were a pretty young girl a'right, but you weren' less than he. You did look he in the eye and speak your mind. I did love you for the free and easy way you had uv he. Same's Gregory did.

Oh Margery!

'Twere allus my wish he ud come back with the same girl on his arm two week in a row. 'Twere my prayer to see some tiddlers running 'bout the old place afore I did go. But you can' eat your cake and have it too, folk say. You young girls shull have your babies in your own time, not when you be made to. After you uv had your fun. Best way round. Don' put it off too long, wull you?

(Pause)

Margery! Don't!

(Sobbing)

Susan, m'dear! I weren' thinking! It mus' be hard for you. There . . .

I'm sorry . . . It's not your fault. I won't have him for . . . such a . . . for years!

What were I thinking on? Uv course you won'! Dear me. How could I say sich a foolish thing?

116

I'm all right. Please go on.

You sure, m'dear? I don' have to.

Yes. I'm all right.

You and me do have summat in common, don' we?

Yes.

I never looked at it in that light afore. Well, you be in a pickle jar, my Susan. No escaping from it. But least your young man bin't going to get hissel' killed. If that be a comfort. He be going to come back whole. God willing.

(Pause)

Let's hope so!

Shall I go on?

Yes. Do. That's best.

(Pause)

Closer he come to me and Thomas – now here be the queer part uv the story – the closer me and Thomas did come to 'ch other. Afore, I ud allus looked on folk from where I were setting. Thomas and me, we ud los' our boy. That were allus there like a bit uv yoursel', a arm or a leg, what uv been cut off. They do say a body can feel a limb long after it be ampt'ated, or you do believe so. Out uv habit. Well, Charlie were sich a filling uv loss athwart us. He were there – on'y he weren' – same's they old elms atop on Wufford's Hill. I do allus feel a ghast run through my body whensoever I do cast my eye to'ard Lacey Wood and see they elms as bisn't there.

Athin my heart I did gain the conviction as Gregory ud los' some'dy dear to he too. He ud never speak uv who 'twere – 'twere be that I knowed. He ud never spoke uv his family, you see. I aksed mesel' if he ud never had 'un. I don' know. He ud niver talked uv an'bidy. That boy, Margery, I did tell mesel', us los' his dear ones. I did feel it athin my heart. Be on'y after listening close to what folk don' say as you do learn they secrets.

I never did speak uv this to Thomas. Thomas be quick as a cat to gauge when summat be out uv kilter with any machine, but he don' unnerstan' folk. Most men be so.

(Pause)

Summat queer were afoot, Susan.

What was that?

In a queer way, us – Thomas and me and Gregory – ud become a family. Athout any uv us saying so out loud.

(Pause)

He din' have no brothers or sisters, see. He were with some sort uv family who ud give he they name. He ud put hissel' back together from the bits and bobs he had learned uv hissel'. Poor devil.

When he come 'pon me and Thomas there were a silence atween us, he ud seed that. He were the missing piece from our jigsaw. You knows how you do turn pieces this and that way? You do pick up 'nother and go on so, till be chance a piece ull come to hand as do jus' fill the space as be missing?

Do give you a queer filling when it happen. Your Gregory were the piece as did jus' fill the space in our life. Me and Thomas felt 'twere so.

Nobidy can stand in for the filling atween a child and his owned mother. It be too close. There be summat too tender – more'n tender . . .

Sexual?

M'be. I couln' never say that word out loud. Bisn't a word I uv ever learned to say. But I did feel queer 'bout your young man. I know a old woman uv my year bisn't supposed to feel tender in sich a way for a young man who bisn't her owned son. But it did take me so. When you shull uv my years, Susan, you shull surprise y'sel' with some uv the queer things as do flit through your head. Mark my word. I couln' never be sure 'twere my fillings for Charlie as Gregory stirred in me – or for Arthur Marrick! Now I ud want to look after he, now I ud want he to look after me!

(Pause)

Do that s'prise you?

Not at all. I think you were lucky – you were all lucky – to have found each other. It makes me sad that you have been so unhappy.

I ud come over hot and cold, jus' lick I did do when I were a young girl and Arthur looked me over. Gregory seed it. He were very gen'man-like with me. He did put his arms 'round me. He were a dear boy!

Is!

119

Yes! *Is!*

But it did cut two ways. He ud need on summat too. 'Tweren' jus' a family he ud need on. He did love living athin a village. It meaned summat to he. 'Twere his wish to belong on a place as were old and ud allus been here. Whilst he were in Laxfield, on'y – what? three year? – he did play his part.

Be thanks to Gregory the church clock do strike 'pon the hour, summat it din' never do after 1947, not afore he and Thomas ud climbered up and looked close on it. He did take the measure on what were needed and sent to Lunn'n, to a old church clock builder in Stepney as were so tickled to hear 'bout our clock, as bisn't so common, they did come up theysel' and fit the new part free uv charge. We did have a night party in the church hall to cel'brate. There were singing and dancing, a hogshead uv cider. Brung all the village together. Gregory's friend Sydney did play on his banjo. Gregory and the vicar sung they rusty songs harmonious. Lor, it did go on most the night!

Gregory did say the clock were jus' a big musical insturment. It did please he to set it right.

Ev'thing do get run-down, you don' tend for it. Be's true uv folk as for St Wulfred's clock. Gregory Harris were what the village ud need on. He were a dose uv Epsoms. He ud a great 'ffection for old things – and he did warm folk. That be what you mus' remember, m'dear. Take y'sel' on a walk 'round the village. Aks an'bidy. You won' find many's as shall have a bad word to say for your young man.

How did people react – to what happened?

We were took aback. And sorryful too. None uv us knowed what to make uv it. We din' want to think bad uv Gregory. No. Mos' folk did feel as 'twere *they* as were in the wrong theysel's. Folk did feel guilty. They ud say so to me. I knowed jus' what they meaned. I did feel the same's they.

They come early one morning. 'Twere in March, so 'twere still dark. I were jus' dressing m'sel'. We heard cars skritch through the village, making sich a pucker you'd uv thought a house were afire! Twenny minutes after, the vicar do knock 'pon the door. He be in a lather. He do aks me to 'ccompn'y he to Holmwood. The police be there. Our Gregory be in some trouble. Gregory ud tel'phoned Mister Matthew whilst the police were smashing his front door with axes. 'Twere solid English oak, that 'un, mind. In the end they did smash a window and climber in and the tel'phone were took off he. The long and the short uv 'twere, Gregory ud need on us. He ud need on some'un to be there.

When we did gain the house – Thomas druv us there in the Austin – there were a druck uv police in the grounds, more'n I ud ever seed at one time in all my borned days! Lor! Dozens uv they! First off, they din' agree to 'llow the vicar and me athin the house, but he did aks to speak to the officer in charge. Mister Matthew ud been a Royal Navy officer hissel', so he knowed how to speak down to men when he cared to. We were led to old Mister Jack's drawing room, which Gregory ud took for his workshop, where he ud mend mus'cal insturments. There were a 'spector and some other policemen in the room. 'Spector Carson were his name. He were polite to the vicar. He din' even look t'ard me. He din' see me, I suppose.

Well, if you'd seed the state uv the room – guitars and banjos all broke to splitherins – you ud uv weeped lick Jesus. All they handsome insturments ruined. The police must uv stamped 'pon they with they boots. You could hear men crashing 'roun' the house, opening and slamming doors, breaking things and shouting to 'ch other. They did act like crim'nals.

Mister Matthew ud control on hisel'. He says he were a friend uv Mister Harris.

121

'A friend uv Mister Harris!' the 'spector do say, rising his eyebrows 's if he ud niver heared an'thing so queer in all his borned days.

'I be surprised t'hear that, Rev'ren',' he do say. 'Your Mister Harris don' allus mix with company so respec'ful as Church uv England vicars!'

Mister Matthew do aks he if Gregory were been' 'rrested.

'Yes,' the 'spector said. 'He be.'

'Can I see he?' Mr Matthew said.

'Prob'bly not,' the 'spector said.

'What charge be he arrested on?' Mr Matthew said.

'Possession and traffic in hashish, Mister Matthew. Cann'bis. Your *friend* bisn't no better'n a common drug dealer.'

You could see he did consider hissel' very mortifying.

The vicar got up on his pulpit.

'That shull be for a court to decide, 'Spector. You shull need to prove your acc'asation with hard evidence.'

'Sleep easy 'pon that score, Rev'ren',' the 'spector said. 'My men be collecting evidence now.'

Mister Matthews did look round hissel' at the broke-up guitars and banjos.

'So I do see,' he said. 'Be this damage necessary? These be val'able insturments.'

The way the 'spector did smile, I were afeard for Gregory.

'Athin one uv they val'able insturments we did find this,' he said.

In his hand were a sort of brick, polished on the outside and of a straw colour where it ud broke off, like a piece uv clay that uv been set athin a mould. He did hold it under Mister Matthew's nose for he to look closer on.

'Fresh Afghan, Mister Matthew,' he said. 'Finest cann'bis in the world. Not easy to come by. You don' get ev'dence much harder'n this.'

Well, 'twere the first time in my life I ever heared uv this cann'bis, but 'tweren' the last, let me tell you!

The vicar, he did look stumped for a reply. I uv watched 'nough cricket matches in m'time to rec'gnize the look as do come 'pon a man's face when he uv missed a ball out uv his crease!

Through the window uv the drawing room I catched sight uv Gregory. He were stanning in the drive, his arms cuffed behind his back. There were dozens uv policemen stanning close by, 's if he were a dangerous crim'nal escaped off the Island. My heart did go out to the boy. I din' unnerstan' what he ud done to fetch so many policemen. I still don'. He ud not killed or robbed nobidy.

The vicar – he ud seed Gregory too – aksed again to speak to he. The 'spector jus' shrugged and led us out uv the house through the front door – what were left uv it.

Gregory did give the vicar a look and the vicar's face were lick a mirror to it. There were a power uv summat in that look.

'Be a friend uv yourn here, Harris!' the 'spector do say. He be very amused, you can see that. I goes straight to the boy and puts my arms round he, and he do kiss my cheek 's if he be Jesus and I be Mary, his mother.

Quiet, so's on'y I ud hear, he do say: 'Don' worry, Ma.'

'Twere what he choosed to call me b'times. Short for Marge.

'What be this 'bout?' the vicar aks Gregory. He be tense. Sicking after the truth.

'I be 'rrested on possessing uv cann'bis,' Gregory do tell he. 'Nothing to worry 'bout. I din' do an'thing wrong.'

He din' seem flapped.

Then he do say summat to the vicar I din' ketch. 'Twere Greek to me. But the vicar did answer in equal measure. (He told me later 'twere Greek to he too!) It took a moment for the 'spector to hear they weren' talking English to 'ch other right under his nose! He were furious. He did push me aside

123

and pull Gregory and Mister Matthew asunder. Three, four police drug Gregory into the van 's if he were a farm animal, and then they druv off. They weren' our local policemen. None uv our men ud dared act so rude to Mister Matthew, nor smash up a house as they did do. They men ud come from Bath.

That were the last I did see uv Gregory till the trial in Lunn'n, where I were aksed to bear witness 'pon his character – as I did do.

Mister Matthew got up a petition as said how much we all a'mired Gregory – and most uv the whole village signed on it. You were there when the old judge did tell they jurymen 'tweren' worthy uv the paper 'twere writ on. What a nerve! He said he were sorry such simple-minded county folk as us ud been 'boozled by a city scoundrel. Gregory ud pulled the wool over our eyes, he did tell they jurymen. He ud took us for chil'un.

Folk in the village don' know what to think.

Gregory do write to Thomas and me ev'y month. His letters do make us laugh and cry so. You ud think he were athin a holiday camp! Thomas don' understan'. He don' know an'thing 'bout this cann'bis, 'cepting some folk do smoke it with tobacco. An' he us allus smoked tobacco, since he were in France.

The Victorians cultivated it as a border plant. It has very pretty leaves.

Be that so? Well, what be all the fuss on? All I can say, if a man do carry hissel' same's Gregory along on he do put this cann'bis athin his pipe and smoke it then I can name one, two fellows as ud be a'vised to follow his example. The Old Bailey judge first off, with all the crick-crank he did talk. He did say smoking cann'bis were agin the law, but many a thing as were agin the law when I were a young girl bisn't so now. Gregory said he ud done nothing he were 'shamed for and I do believe he. The judge did say in court he were part uv a big Lunn'n gang, but they din' prove so. Least, not to my sat'sfaction, they din'. To put a fellow sich us Gregory behind bars for eight year for smoking summat as do grow wild in the garden, it bisn't fair justice.

(Pause)

I do miss that boy, Susan. And, worst, I do fear how much he do miss me.

I think uv Gregory each hour uv the night St Wulfred's clock do strike. His music be's dear to me as the beat uv my owned heart. I know Thomas do lie quiet aside on me, waiting on it. Vicar Matthew do. Missus Matthew did say so athout I aksed. We'm do all lie in the darkness and pray for he.

Mos' Laxfield folk as knowed Gregory do weep athin they heart over that boy.

2

JEANNIE WATTS

14 July 1964

Dearest Rita,

I'm writing this on board SS *Penelope*, the passenger ferry from Naxos to Piraeus, which takes eleven hours. When I say *on*, I mean I'm lying on deck on my sleeping bag in my frock – but not at all sleepy. Matt is somewhere aft, playing backgammon with Doug and Marcia and an Australian called Rod. Finally it's cool! Instead of a single great hot ball of fire in the sky there are a trillion silver fragments, a static shower of ice! Such bliss! Forgiveness after a penance! I never saw such a night in England, not even in Swanage. My skin is still throbbing, giving off as much heat as a two-bar electric fire!

It's moments like this, when I'm cool and quiet and I'm alone, that I remember why I wanted to come here. During the day we seem to spend most of our time chasing after something we want: a bus, a road, a hotel, something to drink, the right phrase in the book. Fortunately – well, *you* should know! – Greeks are very kind and will drop whatever they are doing to help you out, if they can. Outside Athens they stare at us open-eyed, as if we have just stepped off a spaceship, smile, and say *indaxi*. Not a bit like Swanage.

The children in Naxos ran after us, calling us *Inglesi! inglesi!* But laughing, not begging. The girls shyly look up at you from within doorways as you pass. They look at your clothes and your hair, your shoes and your figure. There are some beautiful girls here, but they are all dressed the way our grandmothers in England were dressed during the War – in waisted print frocks down to their calves!

When I left Naxos, Arianna – the girl I wrote to you about – was heartbroken at the thought we would never see each other again. Before we said goodbye we swapped clothes. She was so pleased to have my old cream silk blouse, but it was my full cotton skirt she cooed over. I gave her two of my bras too, as I have practically given up wearing them. I am – as I write – in one of Arianna's cotton frocks which I have taken up but not in, as we are pretty much the same shape. I must say it is much more comfortable to be in a frock. I can lift the top and blow down the front and cool my tits!

Her grandmother is a real sweetie – her mother too. While we were in their village I hardly saw their menfolk, nor mine either for that matter. It's a funny thing, being in a foreign country where you don't speak the language, the way the men stare at you as if you were a cream cake they long to stuff into their mouths but are too frightened to – whereas the women just see you as another woman. They *know*. They understand. I feel we have more in common with each other, even though we don't speak the same language, than either of us have with our own menfolk. Men are strange creatures flapping around out there, to be watched and taken account of like the weather.

The girls and the women want you to come into their homes. They want to show you their sewing machine. They touch your strange hair and undress you and wash you and rub iced rose water into your skin and try on all your clothes. They ply you with sweet things to eat and iced tea. When you have to leave, they hug and kiss you and burst into tears as if you are a daughter or a sister leaving home for ever.

I go back to the hotel where Matt and Doug will be lounging around, playing cards or backgammon. They will grunt some greeting without looking up from their game, perhaps ask where I have been. I can't tell them, if they do. They would never understand. The boys are always outside the places we visit. Idle, amiable, ignorant strangers, they show no interest in the place or the people and take no experiences away with them. I feel sorry for them.

Sleepy now. I feel better for having got that off my chest. I can hear the waves plashing – is that a word? – and the lovely reassuring sound of a ship's engines throbbing in the dark.

Night-night, Rita darling.

Jeannie

18 July 1964

Dear Rita,

We are on shipboard again! This time bound for Heraklion. I left the boys and Marcia sleeping and I have come up to the prow. It's nearly six o'clock in the morning and the sun is just rising above the horizon. The sky is both a deep dark azure and a lovely violent pink. I half close my mind's eye and imagine I am Helen being brought back home after all those chaps died fighting for me.

I couldn't write from Athens. It was madness. Too hot, too sordid. If you could have seen our hotel! My God! I wish I had brought more money with me. I was worn out by the walking and the noise and the traffic.

You will never guess who we ran into there, staying in the

131

same hotel as us. We were drinking in the bar opposite our hotel and this young fellow with a beard, who didn't look a bit English, came up and laid the palm of his hand against my bare arm. I nearly jumped out of my skin! Then he said:

> If I profane with my unworthiest hand
> This holy shrine, the gentle fine is this,
> My lips, two blushing pilgrims, ready stand
> To smooth my rough touch with a tender kiss!

Well, have you guessed? I bet you haven't!

Matt, taking the part of Tybalt, jumped up and shouted across the table:

> This, by his voice, should be a Montague!
> Fetch me my rapier, boy!

It was *Greg Harris*!

Greg and Matt began to fence with invisible rapiers and then we fell about laughing and hugged each other. The Greeks must have thought we were raving mad.

I wish you could see Greg now. He doesn't look quite so odd as he did at school. He's taller and he was always broad so he's quite big, and his beard makes him look a bit like Jesus. He still has that lovely voice. It's exactly two years – almost to the day – any of us last saw him. Over a couple of bottles of Demestica we quizzed him: why had he gone AWOL just two weeks before the exams? He looked a bit sheepish. He said: I could see that soon we were all going to say goodbye to each other. For good, for most of us. You all meant everything to me, and I couldn't bear it that people I loved so much were going to leave me. I decided to leave you before you left me.

That was how he spoke. So open about his feelings. Poor

boy! I wanted to go over and hug him. I didn't, of course. As I never did do.

Later, when we were alone, Matt said he had wanted to ask Greg about the break-in. What break-in, I asked him? (Do *you* remember the break-in?) Apparently some people at school thought that Greg had something to do with it. I was furious. Thank God Matt kept his mouth shut for once. It would have been awful if he had said something. Imagine!

Greg is on his way back to Persia and Afghanistan – for the second time – and we had to leave him to catch our ferry. Just once I thought he looked at me in that way he used to look at me. Do you remember? Wishful thinking, probably.

Greg seems to speak Greek now – enough to make himself understood. (You and he could chat to each other!) You can see him listening to the men talking and echoing back what they say. What I wrote in my last letter – about men being outside the place – is not true of Greg. The Greeks in the bar loved him. They sang their songs and when they asked us to sing ours he sang *The Ash Grove* – beautifully. Sally Tanner did a good job on him.

He came with us as far as Piraeus to see us off. He carried my bag for me and on the quay I hugged him to me. I managed not to cry. He waved to us as the ship left the quay and the sun sank into the Aegean. Then I *did* cry.

Good night, good night! Parting is such sweet sorrow!

Oh dear, Rita. I feel terrible. All that time he was mooning over me at school and I just thought he was too odd and odd-looking. What a foolish girl I was!

The sun is up and already the sky is becoming warm. It's almost morning. I can see land in the distance. Marcia has found me out. My time by myself is over.

Goodbye, dear heart.

Jeannie

22 July 1964

Dear Rita

We are installed in a pretty little fishing village on the south coast of the island. It's called Paleochora. We are the only foreigners here. After Athens the village is mercifully tranquil. The beach stretches for miles and miles without a single person on it! Matt and I have rented a room in the house of an old lady who speaks French. Doug and Marcia have a room in the only hotel in the village. Before she agreed to rent us the room the old lady, like everyone else here, was interested to know if we were German and seemed happy to hear that we were English. They have a very high opinion of the English here. Don't ask me why.

There are two bars. They are rivals. In case we offend one or the other we patronize both: Madame Zariakis for breakfast – delicious cold yogurt, fresh figs and strong coffee! – and we go to Georgi's bar to drink retsina in the evening. I prefer the breakfast bar. In the evening we drink too much and the boys play endless games of backgammon with the old men. Matt and Doug only learnt to play in Naxos, but they seem to have got the hang of it because they win quite regularly. This puzzles the old men who are not used to being beaten by boys. (That sounds rude!) I am hopeless and I always lose.

Yesterday they all took themselves off by bus to a village along the coast, called Omalos. My God, what a relief! They are going to walk down the Samaria Gorge today, spending one night in the Gorge itself – which is apparently very famous and – Doug's joke – gorgeous. They will get a bus back tomorrow. I cried off from the excursion, I'm afraid. For a moment I thought there was going to be a scene. Matt was looking boot-faced but I said my period had come on, and Marcia said in that case I wasn't going and that was an end to it. I *am* due – so it's not an outright lie. Hurray for periods!

I get on with Marcia. She's no great intellect but that's a relief in a way. Her boyfriend, Doug, can be a pain in the neck sometimes when he eggs Matt on. It's funny, being on holiday with people we would never have been seen dead with at school.

I have had a quiet day to myself, walking along the shore in the shade of the fig trees. Bliss! I read some chapters of Lawrence Durrell's *Clea* under one of the trees until I fell asleep.

I was awoken by a dog barking. An old man was looking down at me, grinning with no teeth and chattering in Greek. I don't think he understood that there are people in the world who don't speak Greek! He had a beautiful boy with him, about twelve or thirteen years old. I found myself being regarded by an ancient Greek and a shepherd boy! I could have been in a Jacobean masque: a wood nymph negligently displaying herself. I soon covered myself up. My honour – alas! – was not put to the test. The boy didn't say a word. He just ogled me as if I were a goddess, drinking me up with his eyes. I was probably the first blonde-haired girl he had seen in his entire life, and almost certainly the most beautiful. The old man gave me some warm wine from his leather bottle, chattering all the time in Greek. It was probably ancient Greek.

I had a swim and I enjoyed a quiet meal on my own at the breakfast bar – delicious melon and ham. I shall have an early bed as the others won't be back until tomorrow afternoon. I'm sure they think I'm a bit of a wet blanket. I try not to let them know how much their company gets on my nerves sometimes. It was a mistake to come in a foursome. I should be here with just *you*. That would have been fun! We wouldn't have to get drunk *every* night.

I'm trying to smoke one of those oval Greek cigarettes of Matt's. Urgh!

Rita, I do miss you. Big hugs.

Jeannie

24 July 1964

Darling Rita

Well, here's a turn-up!

I slept like a dog until ten o'clock, delighting in having a
bed entirely to myself! I had my shower – with no one
pacing outside as if we had a train to catch! – and then strolled
down the main street of Paleochora in my own sweet time.
My God, what a luxury! Madame Zariakis, who owns the
breakfast bar, made as if she was scandalized at the lateness of
my rising, but she was only teasing me. I had my usual breakfast
and I was sitting in front of my coffee, smoking an English
cigarette. Who do you think should come strolling down the
street with a bag over his shoulder but Greg Harris! I jumped
up and ran over to him and dragged him back to the bar. He
tried not to show how pleased he was to have found me – *and*
on my own! – but I could see he was. I didn't even try to
hide my surprise and delight. You know me!

I asked him how he had found out where we were.

He said: Matt and Doug mentioned they wanted to walk
down Samaria Gorge. I looked at a map. There were only a
couple of places you could be. By a process of elimination I
guessed you would be by the sea – at Paleochora.

I asked him what happened to his plan to go to Afghanistan.

He said: I can get a boat to Izmir from one of the islands,
which means travelling through southern Turkey. That would
be much more fun than going to Istanbul and Ankara.

I said he had a lot of faith in maps.

He said: They are generally more reliable than people.

He talks about this part of the world as if it were west
London.

I didn't expect the others back until the afternoon, so I
showed him around the village. There isn't much to see. There
is a sweet little harbour, but to get to the beach you have to

walk about a mile on the other side of the peninsula. He was enchanted by my grove of fig trees and he announced he would sleep there tonight. We spent some time selecting which tree he would lie under, pretending he was a wealthy tourist and very choosy. We found a little group that was perfect. Then we walked along the beach, talking. There was no one else there except the two of us – not even the ancient Greek and his boy.

We talked – about me, mostly. I confessed that I had not taken up my place at drama school because I wasn't sure that acting was what I wanted to do. I am wasting my time doing stupid jobs. Greg just nodded. He didn't reproach me. He said: You can't always do what other people want you to do. I told him you were going into your last year at Imperial College. He asked me to say hello. We reminisced about school, the evenings and weekends we spent at Peter and Sally's flat in Holmfirth Road rehearsing *Romeo and Juliet*. Sally, of course, had wanted Greg to try for a music scholarship at the RCM, so we have both failed our teachers.

He announced that he was going to go in for a swim. My first thought was that if I only had a bra I could have joined him. Greg simply took off all his clothes and walked into the water. He has a beautiful brown body.

I must say, Rita, I was in a quandary. I really wanted a swim. He was so unselfconscious and relaxed in front of me. He couldn't give two hoots what I thought or what I did. At the sight of him walking into the sea I thought, this is silly. I took off my dress and followed him in. (I *did* keep my knickers on, though!) His head was bobbing out of the water when I waded in. I knew he was looking at my tits but I didn't care if he was. I'm not ashamed of them!

He swam right out. He's a very strong swimmer, much stronger than me. (He told me later he learnt to swim in the River Thames at Tower Bridge. Urgh!) I felt elated, vulnerable and a bit excited. Is that a dangerous combination, Rita? You were always so much better than me at defining feelings.

On the beach we had no towels to hide in, of course. We sat in the sun to dry. I didn't want to make a fuss about it and so I was as nonchalant as he was. He didn't stare at my tits or get an erection or anything. Eventually I stood up and stepped out of my wet knickers. I did it slowly and deliberately in front of him. I decided I wanted him to see all of me, seeing as I could see all of him. I experienced that tingling in the nipples you get when you show yourself to a boy for the first time. (I've been with Matt for so long I've almost forgotten how exciting it is!) I buttoned myself into my dress and while I did, Greg put his jeans on.

All the time – it was odd – we continued to talk without embarrassment about old times: school, Dawn, Philippa, Dickie, Simon, Nick, Rachel – as if our nakedness was nothing to make a song and dance about.

We found some ripe figs and ate them as we walked back to the village. Greg cut them open for me with his knife. We had some lunch in the breakfast bar and waited for the others to arrive off the little steamer that runs along the coast. You can't imagine the look on their faces – especially on Matt's! – when they saw Greg sitting under the vine with me! We ordered retsina. They were whacked out, poor things, but full of superlatives about the Gorge. They had spent a night halfway down and had a super time, so everyone was in a good mood. I felt a bit light-headed, probably the result of drinking in the afternoon. I was conscious that neither Greg nor I volunteered the information that we had been for a swim together without anything on. It was something between us. I felt a bit uneasy – but not guilty.

I'm writing this during the siesta. Greg and Doug are playing backgammon in the shade of the vine outside my bedroom window. Matt is already fast asleep. He's all in. With the random sound of dice rolling, the tap-tap of backgammon pieces being moved across the board and the beautiful murmur of their voices in my ears, I am going to shut my eyes too.

Oh Rita! What's happening to me?

I shall post this as soon as I wake up.

Kisses my darling.

Jeannie.

I think I'm going to get drunk tonight!

26 July 1964

Dear Rita,

I don't know whose suggestion it was, but it was agreed we should go down to the beach in the evening – yesterday evening, I'm talking about – and have a barbecue. As well as being a welcome change from getting drunk in the evening bar, it would be an adventure. In typically English fashion we divided up the tasks equally between us. I volunteered to go down beforehand and collect wood for the fire. (Anything for a reason to be on my own!) We all seem to get on better when we have a plan and we know what we are doing. Otherwise we lie around reading books and getting on each other's nerves.

I carried out my task conscientiously. On the beach I found a beautifully carpentered wooden crate marked *BRISE MARINE – Sardines portugaises à l'huile*. While I was carrying it I encountered the ancient Greek and the shepherd boy again. They were just the same – one grinning and chattering, the other wide-eyed and dumbstruck. I put my sardine crate down to explain – well, to try to explain – why I was carrying it. Who knows if I succeeded? I thought it unlikely. But when we all went down, a short time before dusk, I found my pile of wood where I had stashed it, only it had been considerably augmented (nice word!). There were some big branches that I certainly had not gathered and – here is the odd bit – the sardine crate had disappeared. I told Greg about this. We concluded that the shepherd boy had coveted the beautiful wooden box and made an exchange – with interest.

And I thought it had been *me* he coveted!

Greg said: What do you mean? This is an offering. If it had been anyone else he would have just taken the box. You should be flattered. Beware of Greeks even when they come bearing gifts.

Neither of us could remember who said that, although I am never sure with Greg. I noticed the previous evenings in the bar, how he never won his turn at backgammon. He said backgammon is a game of chance. I prefer to think he didn't want to win. He wanted to sit outside the bar under the pleached lime trees and talk to me. I know enough about backgammon to know it isn't *just* a game of chance.

The boys had bought some souvlaki, spicy kebabs – what am I telling *you* this for! – and some skinny-looking lamb chops. This was augmented – that word again! – by half a dozen fresh red mullet that Greg had bought from some fisherman. I was pleased he had done this because it was in addition to his own task, which was to make the fire and cook the food. It was a gracious way, I thought, of acknowledging that he uses our places for washing clothes and having showers, all of which will probably be on the bill. Marcia had assembled some fresh fruit and we had plenty of bottles of Demestica. We had all brought our costumes and while Greg got the fire going, we dived into the dusk-blue sea and cooled down.

It was a heavenly evening. You could taste the wild thyme and oregano in the air. I was happy at the way things were turning out but tense, which I put down to the onset of my period. Greg handed me his cigarette while he turned the fish and I must have smoked it and forgotten to hand it back. It was only later I put two and two together. By then it was too late, and things had turned ugly. He cooked the fish on little wooden skewers and handed them round with a quarter of lemon stuck on the ends. Then we had the souvlaki. What a feast!

As the light began to fade Greg rolled a reefer. He offered it round but nobody accepted it. I think we all wanted to but we were too scared. The previous nights we had all laughed at the silliest things, and Greg said it was from the smoke.

It started to go wrong – for me anyway – while I was telling Greg that he had cooked the fish beautifully. (Which was true.) I think I might already have said that once. I can't remember. What did it matter?

It mattered to Matt. He said: The fish is good, Jeannie. I think Greg has got the message.

I don't know whether anyone else understood what he meant, but I did. He meant: Don't labour the point. You're making a fool of yourself. Shut up.

I did shut up, but I felt as if he had put me down in front of everyone. I watched what was happening as if I was watching a film on TV, not as if I was there in person participating in the events.

The conversation moved on. Greg described what happened when the volcano island of Thera – modern-day Santorini – erupted and probably caused the destruction of Knossos with a Krakatoa-sized tidal wave. The submersion of Thera, he said, might have been the origin of the legend of the lost island of Atlantis that Plato talks about. The People from the Sea who invaded Egypt were almost certainly Cretans . . .

Greg had done his homework – which wasn't always the case at school, as I recall. It was quite dark now, and we could only see each other by the light of the fire. I was

141

mesmerized by the sparks flying up from the flames into the night as the wood I had collected earlier cracked and glowed. The brief shards of light not only lodged against the retina of the eyes but inside the mind's eye as if they were, as well as beautiful, full of meaning. Sitting around a fire, cooking meat on this Homeric shore, listening to stories of old warriors while waves plashed in the darkness, I was filled with awe at the tininess of ourselves and our tiny concerns, as if we and the sparks were the same. I felt terribly sad. It sounds trite now, I know, but at the time it was very moving. I thought I understood something. I wanted to tell everybody but I couldn't put it into words. I couldn't even open my mouth!

Apropos of nothing, Matt said: By the way, Greg. Did you know the school office was broken into the weekend you disappeared?

I couldn't believe my ears!

None of us spoke. I could see Greg look across at Matt. Was it? he said.

Matt said: Yes. Just after you left. The office was broken into and some money was taken. Fifteen pounds, I think. I thought you might have known about it.

Greg said nothing. Nobody did. I felt terrible. Instead of telling Matt to shut up or trying to change the subject, I couldn't open my mouth. I was waiting for Greg, like everyone else, to hear what he said. I feel bad now.

The fire crackled softly in the darkness.

Marcia mercifully produced her fruit and we all tucked in. While we were all noisily biting into apricots and peaches, Greg spoke.

It wasn't fifteen pounds, he said. It was fourteen pounds ten shillings and seven pence ha'penny.

Matt, with triumphant grace, was prepared to let the matter drop but Greg wouldn't let him.

Does that satisfy you? he said.

Matt said: How do *you* know how much was in the cash box?

Greg said: Because I took it.

My heart turned to ice. I almost forgot to breathe. Matt laughed – uneasily, I thought. They were playing a deadly serious game, and it wasn't backgammon. It was then I recollected having smoked some of Greg's reefer.

But I didn't steal it, if that's what you are driving at, Greg said.

Matt tried to laugh it off.

I'm not driving at anything, he said. He had made his point, although he seemed to regret it now. I hated him.

Greg said: An accusation of theft normally requires proof of an intention to permanently deprive a person of his property. I didn't deprive the school of the money. I took it because I wanted people to believe that I had stolen it. I was obviously successful in my plan. Later – after the end of term – I sent the same cash back to the school in a registered envelope. Anonymously, of course.

The tension around the fire was exhausting. It was like a scene in Chekhov. Marcia's fruit was forgotten. Everything outside this campfire on the edge of Europe was forgotten. We were alone with ourselves and our feelings for each other.

In the end Matt said what I'm ashamed to say we were all thinking.

Greg, you broke into the school, took some cash – without intending to keep it – and sent it back afterwards?

Greg: Yes.

Matt: Look, it's none of my business . . .

Greg: You're right. It isn't.

Matt: But if you don't mind me saying so . . .

Greg: I don't mind.

Matt: Why would any rational person want to do that?

Greg: Look, I don't know why you want to know. That's your business. I'm not interested in *your* business. I broke into the school office because I wanted to obtain and remove from the school record certain information I suspected it contained about myself – since I was leaving school – and take it with me. I removed selected papers from the file with my name on it. I knew where they kept it. The documents included letters from social services, from my previous schools, my foster parents and my current teachers. I thought I had a right to this information. I took the money from the cash box in order to put people off the scent. I'm not a thief. The information I took I could not permanently deprive the owner of as I considered myself to be the owner.

My God! I wanted to go to him and hug him – but I was made of stone. I couldn't move. He had turned us all to stone.

On one hand it was horrible. I was ashamed of Matt. (Later we had a terrible row about it.) But it was exhilarating too – the build-up of tension and then the release of tension. It was dramatic! Greg had stepped into and out of the noose.

I'm writing this in the breakfast bar early. Madame Zariakis has never seen me up at such an hour. I lay awake all night, turning it over and over in my head, watching it again and again like a film I could not escape from. I wanted to write it down for you, to send the letter, in case I forget the details later.

Now I am exhausted. I don't know what is happening. I feel that Matt is afraid that his position as leader of the pack is threatened. He is jealous of Greg. And he has reason to be. Even in his ugly counter-attack I saw that he had no choice. He was putting up a fight.

Dear Rita. I am completely emotionally drained. I feel

as if I am in a play in which my role is a minor character
who has no important lines to say. It is Juliet's turn to
shut up and listen to what Gregory, servant to Capulet,
has to say!

Never mind Chekhov. This is even worse than Beckett!
I'm going back to bed.

Jeannie

Hotel Paris
Heraklion
Crete

28 July 1964

Dearest Rita,

Just before I sealed my letter to you on the terrace of the
breakfast bar yesterday, Matt appeared. (I sealed it as soon as I
saw him coming!) We had another blazing row about his
conduct the night before. He did not think he had any reason
to be remorseful since he had been proved right. As far as he
was concerned Greg had broken into the school office and
he had taken the petty cash. He refused to see that it was more
complicated than that – or even that there was an issue of
good manners. I was so angry I'm afraid I burst into tears,
alarming Madame Zariakis. I stormed out and went back to
the room and slept angrily until midday.

After a sleep and a cold shower I walked down to the beach
to find Greg. He was in the sea. He waved me to join him
but I didn't. We were too close to the village to go in without
a costume. He was wearing his, I noticed. When he came
out I took him his towel and put it round him. We sat under
a tree and discussed what had been said last night. I was
sombre, he relaxed and cheerful. He didn't hold a grudge
against Matt, but he agreed that it was time he left. He had
disturbed the equilibrium between us, he said. It was his fault.

This was nonsense. I persuaded him to stay — at least one more day. I said: It will look as if you are running away!

He laughed. He said: Of course it will! I *am*! I have always been running away! It's the story of my life!

He showed me a little scar on the back of his thigh where his leg became impaled on the spike of the gate when he had run away from home as a little boy. He was very proud of it. The police had had to bring him back.

He said: But I always felt I was running *to* something better, not from something worse. Even if I was never certain what it was.

I said: Did you ever find it?

He looked into my eyes and smiled and shook his head. My insides turned to jelly because for a moment I thought he was going to kiss me. He didn't.

He talked about Afghanistan, what a wild, dangerous, beautiful place it is. He has a great love for the country. Greg is a real traveller — not a stupid tourist like me, or Matt and Doug and Marcia.

We walked back to the village. I felt very close to him, after what he had told me about himself. When we knew him at school he never let anyone get close to him. Not emotionally. He didn't want to take the risk.

Matt and Doug and Marcia were already having a drink in the evening bar, and we joined them. They acted as if nothing was different and so we did too. Suddenly Matt stuck out his hand to Greg and apologized handsomely for the previous night. Greg took his hand and said there was no need to apologize. I felt proud of both of them. They played several games of backgammon, to cement their rapprochement, and I was stuck with Marcia while they did.

Marcia is a very pretty girl but she is completely stupid. At school you and I chose our girlfriends on the basis of their capacity for keeping information to themselves. She said: Doug thinks Matt was out of order, prying into Greg's past.

I know she meant well, but I wished she had kept her views to herself. It's one thing for me to tick Matt off – in private – but I felt disloyal hearing it from a third person. I just wanted to get away from her.

Greg is right. The equilibrium between us has been disturbed.

We all got pretty drunk of course, and we went home when the bar shut – which is when we were drunk. (Georgi knows to the last glass of retsina when we have had enough.) Matt was in high spirits and he wanted to make love but I reminded him that I was on the rag – which was the truth – and he was soon snoring. When I was certain he was asleep I put my frock back on and my flip-flops and walked out of the hotel, out of the village – quiet as a ghost in order not to wake the dogs – and down the little track to the grove of fig trees, to the group under which Greg had encamped. It was pitch black and I called to him. He struck a match and called back. I slipped out of my frock and went to him.

Greg was lying on his sleeping bag in his sarong. He pulled his sarong over me and we became one.

Do you remember that song by Martha and the Vandellas? 'I didn't know what to say and so I said I love you and he said I love you too and then he kissed me. He kissed me in a way that I've never been kissed before. He kissed me in a way that I want to be kissed for evermore . . .'

Well, it was a bit like that.

I bet nobody ever thought Juliet would bed down with Gregory, servant to Capulet! It wouldn't have been much of a play if she had.

Then something awful happened. There we were, lying in each other's arms under the Greek sky with the Greek sea plashing against the Cretan shore, when we heard someone calling my name in the darkness. It was Matt! For God's sake! He was out there in the darkness searching for me, calling *Jeannie!* in a horrible pathetic whine. He had woken up and found me missing and guessed where I was and who I was with. He passed quite close to us but he couldn't see us without a lamp. Greg was going to come out of me but I held him fast. If Matt Oliver stumbled upon us it would have been his own fault. I felt sorry for him but I was also furious with him. What did he expect me to do, leave the man I was with and come running to him? After that I knew it was over between us. He wandered up the beach, calling.

I wasn't acting rationally. I knew that I was making a mess of things between me and Matt, but I didn't care. I wanted to. I didn't care what happened afterwards.

Afterwards Greg was concerned that we had done it without taking precautions – the dear boy! I reassured him that we didn't need to because I was having my period. Hurray for periods!

He woke me very early the next morning – today, in fact. It was still dark. After we had made love again, we bathed in the sea – we both needed to! – and he packed up his bag and we walked to the village hand in hand. I crept into the room. Matt was asleep in his clothes. I didn't wake him. I threw my things into my bag and left some drachmas for my half of the room and I kissed the dear boy for the last time. Then I closed the door on that part of my life.

I dozed with my head against Greg on the bumpy winding road over the hills to Rethymnon, sleepy and happy, while he studied his Persian grammar.

So, Rita Paprika! The King is dead! Long live the King! Tomorrow we will go to Heraklion and take ship to Santorini – Izmir, Asia and the East! I feel brave and strong and ridiculously happy.

But *poor*! If you can send me some money – twenty or

thirty pounds – please do. Send it care of the British Embassy in Kabul. If you can't, don't worry. I'll live.

Hugs and kisses from your mad happy

Jeannie

ps I'm going to write to Mum and Dad now. I hope they don't have a fit!

11 August 1964

Dearest Rita,

We are in a place called Erzerum, the easternmost town in Turkey. We arrived here yesterday after an overnight bus ride from Kesyri, a bleak, forlorn town miles from anywhere where they make the most beautiful carpets. Greg's theory is that carpets become more luminous the further they are from the sea. The further you are from the sea here, the less European the towns appear. The less Greek. We have been to some splendid places in Turkey but Erzerum, alas, is not one of them, and the bus to Tabriz only leaves twice a week so we are stuck here until Thursday. At least it is cool, as Erzerum is high up in the hills. The town is filthy and uncared-for – but not especially poor. In the streets you see enormous American cars, Cadillacs and Studebakers, alongside donkeys and carts. I don't care for the place much either. Greg has taken himself off on the bus to Mount Ararat, which is somewhere near here. He's going to walk up and down it and come back tomorrow. He suggested I shouldn't go too far from the hotel, as if I had any desire to! After the splendours of Izmir and Sardis and Ephesus, this town is forbidding.

Wherever we are, if there is an archaeological site to explore, a mountain to climb, a lake to swim, Greg will do it. He has great energy and a desire to see what is on the other side of the hill, but he does not make me do these things because he wants to do them. I know that he is more able to move about without a fair-haired, blue-eyed terrifically beautiful girl to look after.

I have never known a person like Greg for wanting to know the reason for things, why they came into being. He has to know the history of every place we pass through. He has a partiality for old men. Seriously! Wherever we end up, one of the first things he does is find out some old boy to talk to. His theory is that old men speak more slowly and more formally and it is easier to pick up the language from them. They often repeat themselves, which helps. They talk about the old days when things were better. Also they tend to be respected members of the community, and it is a good idea to have them on your side. The younger men are ingratiating and just want to know how much you paid for your jeans.

I have to be on my guard in the presence of all men, young or old. It is not the custom here for a woman my age to look at a man directly or even to address him. I try not to catch their eyes, without being submissive. It's harder than you think, because they don't mind staring at you to their heart's content! They don't expect a woman to challenge them and they can get shirty with you if you do. I try to dress and speak and behave according to the custom of the people whose place we are passing through. I do it out of common courtesy, but it goes against my nature. Otherwise you are just a tourist and the people despise you.

The women look at you here with the same interest, but they are even more shy than Greek girls. They behave as if they are grateful just to be alive. It's sickening. In the estimation of the men, I think women come somewhere between Cadillacs and donkeys. The men here are oafs. Even Greg says they are uncouth. In mitigation, he says, the area is in a permanent state of war between its constituent parts. Just south of here you have the Kurds, sandwiched between the Turks and the Iranians and, in the north, the Armenians. This all used to be part of Armenia but there aren't any Armenians here any more. They all hate each other and have long memories and have pogroms at intervals to keep the memories alive. It's bandit country.

I feel quite safe with Greg. We make love every night and are very happy. I enjoy his strength and sense of humour, his knack for picking up languages, his curiosity. He's good at knots too! He adores me, and I am not used to being adored. I suppose Matt loved me in his offhand way, but he certainly never adored me. (He probably hates me now!) I was afraid I might not come up to Greg's expectations but he knows me like the back of his hand. He knows that I would prefer to pootle about and write an overdue letter to you than to climb a mountain for his sake.

There is a funny sort of primitive Woolworths just up the street from the hotel. When I have finished writing this I am going to put on a headscarf and see if I can smuggle myself in and get hold of some soap and toothpaste. At least everything is very cheap here, so my few pounds go a long way. I realize that I am absolutely out of my mind to be here. I am living on love and fresh air and bread and goat's cheese and apricots. I am happy though.

I hope you managed to send some money to Kabul. I wrote to Mum and Dad and asked them to send some as well, so don't worry if you didn't.

I suppose you have spoken to Matt by now. I wonder what his version is. Does he hate me? I think I would if I were in his shoes. Tell him I'm sorry I have hurt him, if you see him. I'm not sorry I left him – but don't tell him that.

Love and hugs

Jeannie

Dear Rita

Well, here we are back in Herat. It's almost like being back home after all the scrambling we have done up and down mountain tracks on ponies, climbing to the back of beyond. I hope you received the two letters I sent from Bamiyan – a secret valley of long-abandoned Buddhist monasteries which we both adored. It seemed unlikely to me at the time that they would ever pass from the hand of the smiling moustachioed official in the ramshackle post office in Bamiyan village, to that of the GPO postman who delivers to your flat in Lancaster Villas in west London. Unfranked stamps here are like currency. Officials have been known to remove them to sell again! It was a relief to get back to Kabul and find your second money order. Thank you, my sweet darling!

We are staying in a majestic crumbling nineteenth-century hotel set back off a modern road lined with evergreen trees, in a walled garden that has a little fountain and mulberries and delicate roses. The rosebuds are small, not much larger than a quail's egg, but the rooms are large and cool with a shower that works when no other guest is using theirs. It is a luxury after some of the dingy lodgings we have had to put up in. Although the place is run-down, shabby even, it has great charm: tiled walls and marble floors and dusty furniture and a shady veranda on which you can drink cool beer in the heat of the afternoon. (There is a fridge which even works sometimes!) It's the only place outside the gardens of the British Embassy compound in Kabul where I have felt so refreshed.

I love the funny old hotel and I love Herat. Kabul, of course, is fun too: full of the bustle of commerce, bicycles, interesting old motor cars, hooting Bedford trucks, men with guns – some in uniform, most not. But Herat is quiet and pretty. The mud-brick buildings are delicately decorated, almost baroque in their detail. The bazaars are out of this world. You can get hold of anything from Persian carpets to a nineteenth-century British regimental sabre (I hate to think how that ended up here!). There are three or four rather elegant minarets that can be seen from almost anywhere in the town. There is also a big brick fort that makes me hot just to look at, built by the Seljuks. Don't ask me who the Seljuks were. Greg can tell you. We were only permitted into the British Embassy compound and to swim in the pool – what utter bliss! – because Greg had impressed a couple of queer Oxford graduate archaeologists who were residents. They weren't interested in me, of course, not even in my swimming costume!

I am impressed how Greg can hold his own with these public-school chaps. They have charming English manners but a person like me can't help being irritated by their enormous self-esteem which their self-deprecating humour cannot conceal. They know all about the social conditions of the Bactrian Greeks in Afghanistan in the third century BC, but practically nothing about those of ordinary people in their own country since 1945. What – I couldn't help suspecting them of thinking – were these two comprehensive school brats doing on their territory? Am I too harsh?

One evening Greg, accompanying himself at the grand piano, sang some Gilbert and Sullivan songs to amuse the ambassador and his wife. After that we were given a pass and could use the pool whenever we liked.

It was too hot when we passed this way in August to appreciate Herat's charm – we were eager to get into the hills – but now it is approaching the monsoon and the temperature is down in the eighties, I am ready for the lush valley. We have had such adventures and met such hospitality, but I need a rest. I'm feeling weak. I need to gather myself together for the journey home. I want to stay still. Greg wants to make one last trip up into the wild. He has heard about an annual gathering of nomad tribes that is due to meet at a place called Chagcheran, somewhere in the desert to the north of here. There will be horse-trading and traditional equestrian sports and tribesmen in their full glory. It's not the sort of place for a woman, he thinks. I'm sure he's right – all those handsome moustachioed warriors on white stallions brandishing decorated firearms! Greg has grown a moustache, and when he puts on his turban and sticks out his chest I have my own fearless warrior!

It's late in the afternoon. I am drinking sweet green tea with cardamoms on the veranda in one of the comfortable chairs. A pair of hoopoes is on the lawn, hopping round the mulberry bush. The crickets have fallen silent, and in their silence a boy is playing a flute somewhere. When we were in the mountains, following the nomad passes under the sun, in the thin air, meeting only supercilious camels and men armed to the teeth and Baskerville-sized hounds (not at all like the Afghans you see in St John's Wood!) we longed to rest our limbs and drink tea in some shady oasis such as this. The sound of the word *oasis* is almost as beautiful as the plashing of falling water itself. I love it here.

Greg has gone to the bazaar to provision himself for his journey. He will take the bus – poor thing! – tomorrow morning. He was in two minds whether to leave me alone for three or four days but I insisted he go. I am perfectly safe here. I have learnt how to be decorous. I am anaemic and I want to rest and read and get my strength up. I'll be able to write to you more regularly, Rita dear, being more settled. The post office in Herat is a solid building with a flag and a soldier on guard.

I'm feeling sleepy so I shall end here.

Love and hugs

Jeannie

ps Greg returned from the market with a present for me. Guess what? A full black veil, with two slits in the front of the eyes to see out through. It's called a chador. Simply a must! Every Herati woman who is anyone wears one.

20 October 1964   Turquoise Hotel

Rita Dearest,

I don't feel very well but I feel better than I did this morning. Well enough to write to you, my darling. I haven't got anything else to do.

I am expecting Gregory to return any moment and I am looking forward to having him back. I have just been moping around the hotel since he left. I must have caught a bug because I feel weak and my head hurts. My tummy is upset too. It comes and goes. I am sipping tea on the veranda, but I can't keep any solid food down. Abdul Rahman, the hotel factotum, brings me broth which I drink for his sake. My life is bounded by the walls of the hotel and the hotel garden, which I share with a pair of hoopoes and my pet quail. Did I tell you I had a quail? We came across some boys torturing the poor bird in a street in Kandahar, on our way here, and I bought it from them. It has nearly recovered from its ordeal and I shall release it as soon as I am well. For now the little caged thing is my only companion. I am very fond of it – perhaps because its situation so resembles my own.

The bounded is loathed by its possessor.

As above, so below.

Yesterday – Tuesday, I think – I left the hotel and walked
to the nearest covered bazaar. I had set off for the post office.
Alas, I didn't make it that far. At a discreet distance from the
hotel – just like a spy! – I had slipped my chador over my head
– *et voilà*! I was invisible! I was able to move along the street
unobserved, to peruse where I chose – even the faces of men
if I felt like it, without their showing the smallest interest in
me. What is so odd about the chador is that this clumsy,
restrictive garment gives a certain freedom to a woman in any
social encounter with men here. A woman may move among
them without revealing any aspect of her sexuality, age, class
or even identity as a person. She could be Jayne Mansfield bare
naked for all they know! Despite my instinctive abhorrence
of the veil, which reduces a woman to something as interesting
as a donkey, I confess I enjoyed my little excursion wearing
one.

The bazaar was – well, bizarre! A maze of turban weavers,
carpet sellers, silver and turquoise merchants, leather and metal
workers. I was so amazed that I overexerted myself and I began
to feel faint. I had to stop two women in the street – a mother
and daughter, as it turned out – and communicate to them
that I was feeling unwell. Fortunately I knew the Persian for
water and the modal verb need: *aa'b ne'ghab*, I said.

They led me, one on each side, into a house not too far
away, which we entered without meeting any men, as the older
buildings are constructed with a curious separate entrance for
female members of the household. You can imagine their faces
– well, I'm sure you can't! – when they removed my veil and
saw my blonde hair and blue eyes! They gasped with surprise!
It was Naxos all over again. Then they laid me down on a
divan and put iced water to my lips and bathed my face. They
were very sweet to me.

They wanted to call a doctor, but I said I wanted to go home because I felt better. They ordered a male relation to fetch a taxi, accompanying me themselves all the way to the hotel. They were such dears and they let me kiss them, both giggling like schoolgirls when I did. I felt like a secret agent in enemy-occupied territory, befriended by sympathetic local citizens. They were on the same side as me.

I'm sorry, Rita. This is all I can manage. I shall try to write something tomorrow. Greg will be back by then and I shall feel better.

22 October 1964

Rita dear! I thought I would be better and Greg would be back. I don't – and he isn't. I feel awful, as a matter of fact, and there is no word from him. I don't know whether to call a doctor or the police. I just want to cry!

Later.

I sent Abdul Rahman to the pharmacy to buy some medicine for bacillary dysentery. The bill was higher than I thought it might be, even taking into account Abdul Rahman's cut. I had enough money at hand to pay him, but there was less in my purse than I thought. I have been racking my brains – racking is the last thing they need just now! – trying to account for what I have spent. When I set out for the post office I had plenty and I didn't open my purse while I was out. I don't understand it. This sudden loss of money worries me. I searched Greg's bag for his money. I found it – fifty pounds in Cook's cheques and twenty in notes – which was a relief.

I have never gone through Greg's belongings before. Even though I had a reason to do so, I was conscious that I was crossing a boundary – not one that was forbidden, but crossing one all the same.

Greg has a waterproof toilet bag in which he keeps his personal documents. Looking through these I found his money – also some old photographs, a handful of letters, a shilling coin and a boxing medal with his name engraved on the back and the date 1957, some official papers, his NHS card. There is a delightful photo of Greg as a little boy at the seaside, grinning in the arms of a pretty young woman in a bathing costume. I wondered if she was his mother.

I heard this morning – from a friendly German couple here – that Labour won the election last week. This is good news, I suppose. It seems very remote to me at the moment. Of course, it is me who is remote.

My headaches are no worse. I feel hot and bothered but not worse otherwise. I have a rash around my tummy. It doesn't itch or anything, though.

23 October

Where is Gregory, Rita?

I feel lonely. Anxious. What do you think has happened to him? I asked Abdul Rahman to fetch the police. He refuses.

I felt so sorry for myself I laid out the stuff from Greg's toilet bag – to comfort myself. I looked at the picture of him again. I held his medal. Among his papers are two old letters in their envelopes. I don't know if I should have read them but I did. They are from – well, you would never believe me if I told you. I hardly believe it myself. I am completely stunned. I'm going to copy them out word for word. What else can I do?

187 Holmfirth Road
London SW7   *27 May 1962*

Darling Crow!

Where have you been? Are you ill? Do you want me to come and look after you? You missed your lesson on Tuesday although you were in school, and you haven't telephoned here. Is something the matter? Are you angry with me because of what I said? If you are, please speak to me! Don't just keep away from me. I can't bear it!

I know you like and respect Peter and the situation is painful for you. What do you think it is like for me? I am tortured day and night! Peter is a decent, straightforward fellow. He trusts me. Whatever happens he must never find out about us. *I owe him that. But I have promised you that I will tell him it's all over between him and me. It won't be easy. I shall tell him as soon as I hear about the Leeds job — one way or the other. What else can I do?*

Please be patient, my darling. As soon as your exams are finished and I have left Holmfirth Road, we will go away together. Peter is working like the devil at the moment. I can't just spring it on him.

Please come to the flat on Saturday afternoon. Peter will be at a matinèe performance of Luther *with some fourth-formers. I want you to.*

Love Sal

ps I hope you have been working on the Schubert song, as we agreed to do. Bring the score with you and we'll go over it together.

Well? Is it credible? Even seeing Sally's words in my own handwriting I can't believe it.

Writing it out, Rita, I felt so sorry for Sally. The poor thing! What she must have been going through! Can you hear the desperation in her voice? While we were all play-acting our stage dramas, Sally and Greg were caught in a real-life tragedy. I wish Greg would come back. I want to know what happened.

Must rest now.

Evening.

Caught sight of myself in the mirror and burst into tears. How dreadful I look!

Sally's second letter is dated June 6th:

> *My sweet boy,*
>
> *Where are you? I am beside myself with worry about you. What are you doing? I'm sure you are not working hard enough. You are hardly ever at school, although you make appearances in the pub in the evening and then you avoid me. When you said you were thinking you might disappear out of our lives for ever, I became scared stiff that you meant it. I feel you are capable of doing that. Please don't torture me like this. I know we are in a difficult position now, but in a few weeks' time we should be free to do what we want.*
>
> *DON'T DO ANYTHING SILLY!*
>
> *Telephone me as soon as you get this — or come and see me. If we don't talk about it we will make a mess of our lives.*
>
> *I have been dropping hints to Peter that all is not well between us. It's very hard because he is miles away and so infuriatingly cheerful. It's going to come like a bolt of lightning when it does, poor dear.*
>
> *Don't leave me in the air like this, my darling.*
>
> *Your own,*
>
> *Sal*

I can't stop crying, Rita. I don't know if I'm crying for Sally or for myself. I feel so wretched. Helpless. Too tired to eat.

My God, what is happening to me?

Sick. Sweating. My body aches all over.

No Greg. Slept and wept.

Woke from a beautiful dream. With Greg in Bamiyan, green and smelling of clover and tall white poplars. The river was roaring. The giant, faceless Buddhas were smiling upon us. Blue dragonflies were skimming the surfaces of the water. Skylarks were piping. The white peaks of the Koh-i-Bab range rimmed the horizon. I was happy to be there but Greg was not happy, not until he had reached the white peaks and looked beyond. He walked away from me. I called after him but he didn't look back.

Woke up in a sweat, alone in a darkened room. I burst into tears when I remembered that in my dream Greg had called me *Sally*!

Am I going mad? Or just delirious?

Asked A. R. to telephone for a doctor and the police. He said: Doctor coming.

Night.

No doctor. No police.

No Greg.

25 October

Hot. All the time.

Spoke to Wolf and Nina. They promised to fetch a policeman.

A. R. is cross with me for doing this. The smelly reptile keeps me like a pet. He said: Time you pay me bill. Quickly! Quickly! I gave him some money. I don't have much left.

My throat is burning. My head hurts all the time. Where is the doctor, Abdul Rahman?

Doctor coming.

Afternoon.

An ugly policeman entered my room. Very stern, as if I had done something wrong. Perhaps I have. But what? To be a woman with blue eyes and fair hair? His God hates me.

I explained – through A. R. – that my husband has gone to Chigchiran for the nomad fair and he has not returned. The policeman did not see anything unusual in this. Didn't write anything down. Stared shamelessly at me – my hair, my clothes, my breasts – as if I were a horse he was considering buying, although he didn't go so far as to open my mouth and inspect my teeth.

Said – A. R. said he said – he would telephone the police station at Chigchiran. I wrote down Greg's name for him. The way he looked at it, I suspected he could not read his own language, let alone mine. It might just as well have been Japanese.

I don't hold out much hope.

I released my quail into the garden. It flew straight into the mulberry bush. Clever thing.

Slept all day. Nina is looking after me. I am so frightened, Rita.

26 October

Woke up in the night – pitch-black, door half open – because somebody was in my room! Called Nina's name and someone hurried out of the door. I could smell the odour of a man – one I know only too well. I screamed and Nina ran in. Spent the rest of the night in her room.

I am so terrified. I thought my door had been locked. Has Abdul Rahman got a key? He is more interested in my money than my body, but the thought that I am not safe terrifies me. Now I bolt the door as well as lock it. I sleep on what is left of my money. Of Greg's money, I mean.

Midday.

I want to get out of here. I have no more money left. A faint cold fear thrills through my veins, that almost freezes up the heat of life. Greg has run away from me. He runs away from everything. It is his revenge on the world. He is climbing the white peaks of Koh-i-Bab. On his quest for Atlantis.

Am I Sally Tanner or Jeannie Watts?

Nina has gone to fetch a doctor. Also the British Consul. Everything will be all right now.

5 o'clock.

Mr Villiers visited me. Lovely man. Ambulance is on its way. I shall give this to Nina to post.

Rita. I love you my darling. Thinkst thou we shall ever meet again?

Jeannie.

Feel awfully sick

C. J. Villiers Esq
Her Britannic Majesty's Consul
The Majestic Hotel
Herat
Afghanistan

Mr Andrew Watts   1 November 1964
17a Cathcart Road
London
SW7

Dear Mr Watts,

It is with great regret that I write to inform you that your daughter Jeannie died in the General Hospital, Herat, on 27

October. She had been admitted to the hospital the previous day suffering from cholera. There is an epidemic in Herat at the moment.

We understand that she was travelling in the company of a young man by the name of Gregory Harris whose return she had been awaiting. It is possible that Mr Harris has also been infected and may be similarly stricken. We will of course inform you of any developments.

Your daughter's property has been forwarded to the British Embassy in Kabul, whence it will be sent to you without delay.

Please accept my deepest condolences for your tragic bereavement.

Yours sincerely,

Charles Villiers

PETER FOSTER

I have thought long and hard about what you said, Angela, when you were last here and spoke your mind so freely. I confess it came as something of a shock to discover the poor light you see me in: a reclusive old sourpuss. I shan't deny I was taken aback. My first inclination was to explain away your uncharitable view of me by telling myself that you can't help seeing me through your mother's eyes. (Even if this is the case, it's no one's fault. I certainly don't blame Alison.) On reflection, however, I decided that I don't want to defend myself. If I am the curmudgeon my own daughter believes me to be, so be it. That's what I am. I don't intend to deny your home truths.

Having said that, it seems unfair – to you as much as to me – that this should be the only picture of your dad you have, because if it is true now, it wasn't always thus. Believe it or not, I was young once, wide-eyed and full of good intentions. I wasn't bad-looking when I could still boast a head of hair. The future was a better place I believed in and worked for. Well, I decided to put dot matrix to paper in order to set the record straight. I want to tell you what kind of young man I was and leave you to revise your picture of me – or not, as you see fit. The period I have written about is the half-decade before I met your mother. It is a snapshot of a part of my life she knew nothing about. I was careful to make sure of that.

I hope your heart does not sink at the sight of such a hefty manuscript! When I started my intention was to write only a few pages, but once I got going I did not want to stop. It gave me pleasure to recall that period of my life. Humour your dad by reading this fragment of his autobiography.

I have to confess too that the task also gave me an opportunity to word-process directly on to my personal computer. I have never done that before, not for a long text. To be able to edit, delete, spell-check, cut-and-paste – things you can't do on a typewriter – was terrific fun. To start sentences with conjunctions *à la* Hemingway! It's the first opportunity I have had to be so authorial!

The most exciting part was to set up the computer to print, press Exit, and watch the numbered pages flip out of the printer, 1, 2, 3, 4, 5 . . .

Peter

In the summer of 1960 I was approaching my twenty-third birthday. For people my age, but not for people very much older, the new decade held out some promise of change – not a lot, but some. With its awful austerity, grey trousers, tiresome round-rim-bespectacled politicians, endless talk of the War, National Service and yet more war, the fifties had never belonged to us and we were happy to consign them to the history book. In some respects we were right. Just around the corner surprises were waiting for us, turnabouts in social behaviour that we could never have predicted. In other ways we got it all wrong – as every generation of twenty-year-olds is no doubt doomed to get it wrong. I was never angry as a young man, but I admired young men who were.

Teenagers had barely been invented, don't forget. We took much longer growing up than you did. I had missed conscription by the skin of my teeth, having been completing my higher education studies when my schoolfriends were being called up. If the Government had not abolished it when they did – December 1960, I think – I would have spent the following year masturbating in some godforsaken place like Aden or, even worse, Aldershot. The one thing that made my contemporaries at university different to young men older than ourselves was that we had never been in uniform, didn't want to be in uniform, and hated listening to the dreadful narratives of men who had been in uniform. They were a generation of ancient mariners and we, only a month or two younger, a generation of reluctant wedding guests. We weren't interested in fighting a rearguard action on behalf of the British Empire against the aspirations for self-determination of her colonies. We had other fish to fry.

After I came down from university – this would be the summer of 1960 – I spent some time in Italy, studying Italian at the University of Perugia for the hell of it. I had no reason for doing this. I wanted to get out of England, that was all. Attending language classes, drinking Chianti and dating pretty American girls was just what the doctor ordered. Those girls 'necked' as no middle-class English girls did at that time. You have to remember that in England attitudes to sex were quite different then. There was no contraceptive pill. Nice girls didn't, which meant that on the whole nice boys didn't either. At Bristol one or two liberated female undergraduates may have gone to bed with their boyfriends, but if they did they ran the risk of acquiring a reputation for being 'fast', the genteel word then for promiscuous. The word 'liberated' had not been coined then, of course – because the social climate in which it would have meant anything did not exist yet. Outside the universities you either got engaged or you went with prostitutes.

Between trips to the beach with American girls, to Venice for the Fenice season and visits to the cinema to see Rossellini films, I had time to consider what to do with my life. I decided I was going to act. I was still young enough to believe that I would have some control over my future, that when I pencilled a ring around a chosen vocation I was engaged in an activity no more rational than putting a mark against a fancied runner at Kempton Park. I had specialized in theatre at university, and I had always been a leading light in the ADS. I had a modicum of talent in that direction, if no other. I think I assumed the chance of stepping on to the boards would eventually present itself.

In the meantime I asked my mother to send out the TES every week, and I scrutinized it for English teaching posts with responsibility for drama. I probably saw myself as a latter-day Auden or Waugh, teaching boys in order to keep the wolf from the door until destiny beckoned. I have sometimes wondered since then whether it wasn't lazy of me not to have tried harder than I did to do what I really wanted to do. Later I discovered that I had a flair for teaching, but I have always been more at home in a theatre than a classroom. The fact is, what else could a chap with a second-class English degree do except teach or join the civil service?

The Tories winning three elections on the trot had put the kibosh on the enthusiasm with which the post-war era had begun, although even by 1951 most of Attlee's cabinet were old, sick and tired. They had run out of ideas. But among younger professionals, planners, architects and educators, there still existed a sense of mission.

Morrison's London County Council had pressed ahead with a radical state education programme. Large purpose-built coed mixed-ability secondary schools were springing up all over London. The idea behind these schools was that all children would be given an equal chance, each according to his or her abilities. It didn't matter if a child failed the eleven-plus or passed it. All children - the able and the less able, rich or poor, the educationally subnormal and the whizz-kids - would be under the same roof, no matter what their background. Such an egalitarian distribution of resources cut right against the grain of English social traditions, of course, because it started from the premise that all children, if not the same, had a right to the same educational opportunities. The Tories pooh-poohed the idea, but they did not go out of their way to frustrate its implementation. It was only later, much later, that they turned nasty.

You didn't need a teaching qualification then to get a job in a classroom. Any kind of honours degree would do. From Italy I blithely applied for half a dozen jobs and got an interview for every one. It amazes me now, when I think about it. That would be impossible today. It amazes me that it was ever possible.

I remember the first time I set foot on to the premises of Fox Hill Comprehensive. It was a gorgeous evening towards the end of the summer holidays. The sun warmed the brand-new brick and the honey-coloured trunks of the old plane trees. The playgrounds and classrooms were eerily deserted. The school was in pristine condition, redolent of fresh wax floor polish. I fell in love with the place immediately.

The campus, cannily sited on the grounds of a grand old London mansion, now demolished, extended leisurely over several acres, contiguous to a park and among plush detached residences, although its catchment area also included swathes of bad housing still waiting to be pulled down after the Blitz. (The word Rachmanism had been newly minted to describe them.) When you stepped through the gate you entered a planned, post-Bauhaus world which gave no clue to the seedy city sprawling hugger-mugger outside. Elevated glass walkways connected specialized teaching blocks: light-filled classrooms, metalwork and carpentry shops, kitchens, gymnasia, typing pools, music-practice rooms.

Everything was brand spanking new, even the grass. The school foyer was a scaled-down version of the foyer of the Royal Festival Hall. This was not remarkable really, since the same LCC architects had designed both. The assembly hall, with a pit and a gallery, could easily seat a thousand, and the stage – I could hardly believe my eyes – had a proscenium arch equipped with flies and lighting gantries. There was nothing of the grimy old second-rate secondary modern here. Here all was light, confidence and hope – above all, hope.

But the architects had also cleverly included into the design mature London plane trees. The yellow-brick modernism of the buildings was softened by green leaves, creating the illusion that the place had been in existence for many years. The original lodge, with its tropical-wood panels and peacock mosaics from Persia, had been incorporated into the design to provide a sanctuary for sixth-formers. The gardens of the lodge, planted with rare trees imported from every corner of the British Empire, was a civilized arboretum wherein young scholars could walk and mentally recite their Milton or the periodic table. In the gardens there were brand-new tennis courts.

It was a pleasant place in which to stroll with hands in pockets. Here was optimism! Here was the romantic radical socialism of our grandfathers triumphing over the gradgrindist impulses of factory owners! Young architectural practice and enlightened educational theory had brought off a complex of buildings whose style was elegantly appropriate to its function. The gobs of the naysayers were stopped by the sheer élan and scale of the enterprise.

I was interviewed by the Head and the Head of English – who, I later learned, had something of a reputation as a poet, a friend of Cyril Connolly. They told me I was just the chap they were looking for: young, enthusiastic and with an interest in the theatre. I got the job and started in September.

It amazes me today when I recall the lack of preparedness with which I launched into my teaching career. To call it blithe would be an understatement. Today I would be appalled if a young fellow straight out of university attempted to do what I did. I would kick him out on his ear. I'm glad nobody kicked me out on my ear. On the contrary, I was given every encouragement. I made a lot of good friends among the staff and the boys and girls. Some of them I am still in contact with today, thirty years later.

I was at Fox Hill for seventeen largely happy years. But it was those first years – between, say, 1960 and 1963 – when we were all finding our feet, that I want to tell you about. It is a measure of how good the idea of the comprehensive school was then that the newly opened model in Fox Hill Walk attracted such a high calibre of senior members of staff. Jack Kemp, head of maths, was a wrangler. The head of modern languages was an ex-RAF pilot who spoke more languages than you could shake a stick at, including Swahili. There was an artist who drank in Soho with Bacon. (I can vouchsafe that because I occasionally kept him company and I was introduced to the great man. I thought he was a shit.) Ratcliff, the international hurdler, did his teacher training there.

Any of these people – unlike lowly me – would have been welcomed with open arms at any of the better academic schools in the country, grammar or public. These people were at Fox Hill and not somewhere more prestigious because they believed in the school, and they slaved like dogs to make it work. What amazed me – still amazes me – and fired my own enthusiasm was that they treated me as an equal. The younger staff members were frightfully talented, and I set my nose to the grindstone in order that my own shortcomings did not become obvious.

I moved into a flat in Holmfirth Road in Fulham, off the North End Road. It was a roomy basement – the euphemism 'garden flat' was not current then. I was soon sharing it with my girlfriend, Sally Tanner, a cellist who taught singing to first years and counterpoint to sixth-formers during the week, and played in an ensemble of old RCM pals at the weekends. Sally Tanner was terrifically pretty and enormous fun to be with. She contributed a lot to my happiness during that period of my life. Although she was not the first woman I had been to bed

174

with, she was the first one who wanted to move in and live with me.

It was a modern, equal relationship, perhaps even a bit ahead of its time. We shared household expenses, did each other's ironing and split rounds in the pub. What we were doing, having regular sex without the commitment of marriage, still wasn't all that common and probably raised eyebrows. The term 'living with someone' was not yet acceptable. It was still an ironically derogatory term, a euphemism for 'living in sin'. You have to remember that. None of our older male colleagues would ever have dreamt of living with a woman who was not married, particularly if he was the man she was not married to. For that reason few of them knew we shared the same address. We forgave them. It was our turn in the driving seat.

Our relationship petered out in 1962. Don't ask me why. Just one of those things.

You have to have lived with a cellist with whom you are in love, who returns your love, to know the joy of it. If you did, you would soon find out that you were not living with one woman but two. As well as a body, the cello possesses a soul – one as greedy for love and gentleness as any woman I have ever loved or been gentle with. Sally played her instrument on days she did not particularly feel like playing it, purely for the cello's sake. If the instrument was not played regularly it went out of tune. It loved to be embraced. You couldn't do anything, go anywhere, without taking it into account. It was like any other living thing in that respect, a pet or a member of the family.

But if you had to make room in your life for a third party, there were marvellous compensations. It was a splendid thing to be working at my desk on a Sunday morning, marking essays, while in the next room the cello part of a French chamber piece was being practised for the afternoon rehearsal. I became as used to having Sally's cello around as I did Sally herself.

When I eventually lost one I lost the other, and I grieved for both of them. Now and then I still hear on Radio Three – when I'm shaving or in my bath or stirring the tea in the pot, something I know you are not supposed to do – rare pieces that she loved. Very occasionally Sally is playing the piece herself – under her married name, of course.

In those days every child in London had the opportunity to learn any instrument in the orchestra and the LCC – God bless it! – paid peripatetic tutors to come in and coach children in pairs once a week. At Fox Hill you had to be good to get into the school band. In addition to the band, we had a choral society and an early music consort which specialized in works by composers such as Palestrina and Orlando Gibbons.

In those days there was a determination among the staff to achieve standards of excellence that even the big public schools could not emulate. We had something to prove. Because the conditions we worked under were so much more difficult than the safe, hermetic world of rural fee-paying boarding schools, we strove to prove our point. Teaching then was a political activity in a way it ceased to be later, when it became just a job. We extracted from our large reservoir of raw talent first-class achievements and performances. It is true that in the realm of sports we rarely carried off the laurels, at least not in any of the traditional team games such as cricket or football or rugby, although we occasionally surprised the opposition in rowing or basketball. But when it came to music or theatre or fine art, we were in a class of our own.

In some respects Sally and I were rivals. At the end of the school day Sally would stay on to rehearse children for a performance of Faurè's *Requiem*, while in another part of the school I would be rehearsing children for a production of *Woyzeck* or *Chicken Soup With Barley*, often the same children. There were numerous clubs – swimming, photography, cinema, chess, poetry, choral. You name it. No one forced the children to attend. They did so because they enjoyed participating in these activities. Any teacher worth his salt will work his pants off for children who show willing. This was particularly true of those from the upper school, who should more properly have been called young adults.

Sally and I and a few other young teachers often felt we had more in common with our sixteen- and seventeen-year-olds than we did with our older colleagues. We would take them to the pub after a rehearsal and buy them drinks, since they usually had no money to buy their own. We shared the same jokes. I can't remember if the phrase 'generation gap' was current then, but, whether or not it was, if such a thing existed we and they were on the same side of it. We were all fed up with the Tories and some of us – not me, you'll be pleased to hear – were CND members. One year a small contingent of us, staff and pupils, joined the march at Hammersmith, marching behind the Royal Court banner and in front of the RCM Branch jazz band.

I suppose we exercised the sort of influence over our sixth-formers that masters have always done in good schools, such as Waugh describes with lugubrious hilarity in his autobiography. The history we taught, the plays we produced, the books we encouraged each other to read, must all have added up to an outlook on life. If they were honest with themselves, those Conservative politicians who naysaid our experiment were probably more fearful of such influences – a cocktail of R. H. Tawney, Orwell, Albert Camus and Roy Orbison – than any of the spurious educational objections they raised. No wonder our boys and girls were lousy at cricket and netball.

I don't want to give the impression that Sally and I always agreed with these young people or that they followed us blindly. As I recollect, we spent a lot of time arguing the toss and we were often the butt of their droll sense of humour. All right, we were teachers and they were our pupils, but out of school we were equals. They could smoke cigarettes, drink beer, vomit in the street, burst into tears, swear or be irreverent – and so could we. We were probably the first people in their lives who gave them the leeway adults are usually more prepared to give to each other than to children. We tended to treat them not as clever children but as rather daft adults. Not so many years before we had been behaving as daft ourselves.

We took them to shows and concerts. Sally was a great supply of free tickets to musical events, funnelled through the Royal College. (We had a lot of sympathizers out there who wanted to see our enterprise succeed.) I must say I always found people like George Devene at the Royal Court most considerate. We saw all the new stuff: Bolt, Wesker, Pinter. Finney in *Luther*, for example. Plenty of Chekhov. Such outings were invariably followed by a row in a pub afterwards on the merits of the event. The English Theatre was dead, and Osborne was its death rattle. Fellini and Jean-Luc Godard and Alain Delon were the people to watch. Chris Barber was ridiculous – but Little Richard wasn't.

I have become friends with a lot of pupils in my time – I still receive Christmas cards from many of the girls, now matrons with children of their own – but I can't say I got closer to any of them than I did to the senior kids I taught during those first two years at Fox Hill, when I threw myself body and soul into my work, when I had energy and still believed something could be made of the British state-school system. Nick Mottram. Rita Papapoupolos. Jean Watts. Matt Oliver. Dawn Reilly. They all showed acting promise, I thought. In the holidays or at weekends, combinations of the Modern Drama Group, as they were pleased to call themselves, would come round to the basement flat in Holmfirth Road to read plays they had seen at the Royal Court. They were the elite.

The hardest thing about being a schoolteacher, in my experience, is knowing that you are putting your best into children

178

who at the end of the final summer term are going to disappear out of your life for ever, often without even bothering to say goodbye. In most cases you hardly ever find out what became of them, who they married, which one went to the dogs, which rose to higher things. I only know that Rita Papapoupolos is a current affairs producer at the BBC because I occasionally hear her name at the end of current affairs radio programmes. I came by the information only recently that Nick Mottram was killed in a canoeing accident in South Australia some years ago, which made me sad. I was always very fond of Nick. With my encouragement Jeannie Watts went on to the London School of Drama but I have not heard of her since, and I have always kept an eye out for her. She was such a talented, pretty girl.

During their final autumn term members of the drama group camped at Holmfirth Road practically every weekend. As their pièce de résistance they intended to mount a production of *Romeo and Juliet* for their Christmas show, held in the presence of His Worship the Mayor, local bigwigs, LCC inspectors and members of the press. We all wanted to show them our mettle.

You can see why schools plump for Shakespeare. His plays offer numerous and diverse minor parts – soldiers, servants, messengers, murderers – for the middle and lower school to get their teeth into. There are colourful costumes, incidental music, plenty of sex and violence; something for everyone. Jeannie Watts and Nick Mottram took the title roles, and the quality of their performance was extraordinarily high. I was pleased as punch. What they brought to their parts was authenticity, being virtually the same age as the two lovers in the play. Their handling of the sexually charged emotions of the half grown-up children was something they hardly needed to learn. Jeannie's rendering of the nightingale speech was electrifying. I persuaded the head to play the Prince of Verona, which he did with just the right dash of headmasterish severity, further accentuating the extreme youth of the lovers.

Sally and I were always happy to take the sixth-formers for out-of-school rehearsals because, I suppose in retrospect, we were drawn to them. As adults with jobs and bank accounts our own youth, not to mention our childhood, was ebbing away with every essay we marked. Their antics and passions gave us a vicarious pleasure, reminding us of our own youth. The kids themselves, when they were not acting or swotting for their A levels, were on an endless quest for the Right Person – to kiss and to be kissed by. Their parties – those we were honoured to receive an invitation to – were simply an opportunity to snog and grope in the dark. This was not true of Jeannie Watts and Matt Oliver, who were almost as established a couple as Sally and I.

After rehearsals we used the public bar of the second-nearest pub to school, the Swan in Dale Street. (I took you there once. Do you remember?) The nearest pub, with hunting prints on the walls, was the preserve of the senior members of staff. Our bar had a dartboard and workmen in overalls were permitted to drink there, as well as under-age schoolchildren. It's hard to believe now that even in the sixties there were public and private bars in every pub, and which one you chose to drink in said something about the sort of person you wanted to drink with. Our bar also had Molly, who served the boys generous light and bitters and warned the girls – not at all *sotto voce* – to Be Prepared and, I suspected, may have been a source of the means for them to be. The regulars tolerated us and called our kids 'stoodents' with mock reverence and, if they felt in the mood, allowed us to beat them at darts.

Sally's old RCM friends – who were not above augmenting the school band for a concert or taking the difficult solo vocal parts in an oratorio – sometimes joined us. The music clique was hardly less boisterous than the drama clique, although they were all part of the same clique: the talented, hard-drinking, handsome sixth-formers whom the lower school lionized. You sometimes got the stray drunk who tried his luck with one of our girls, but Molly was quick to put him straight on that score.

Molly was a warm-hearted working-class woman of a certain age whom we all adored. The sixth-formers trusted and confided in her, since she was neither family nor school. It was she who informed me that Dawn Reilly was pregnant – and then shortly afterwards told me not to worry, it had all been sorted out. She knew that Greg Harris had no proper home to go to before I did. In fact, it was Molly who alerted me.

'Peter. That boy has no mum or dad to look after him.'

It was news to me.

'Well, he has. But they live south of the River – Walworth or Southwark way. But he don't live with them. He moved out. He's on his jack in some bed and breakfast in Hammersmith. How old is he? Seventeen? Can you believe it?'

I made inquiries through the school secretary and found out that Molly was right. Greg had left home and was living on an allowance. His form teacher, Sarah Davis, took an indulgent line over his absences and late arrivals. As there was no one to complain to, what else could she do? She realized that the boy was looking after himself as best he could, doing his own washing and ironing and shopping, getting himself up and going to bed alone each night. He had no one to nag him to get up and off to school, or to tell him off if he didn't. Not surprisingly, Greg spent a lot of time in Molly's public bar, unwilling to forsake the good fellowship to be had there for an empty room in Hammersmith.

The locals in the Swan tolerated our 'stoodents' because they had no side to them, as people used to say when there were still public and private bars. No airs and graces. And they were often a source of humour and drama. On one occasion I was at the bar talking to Celia Hockings, a quiet, amply proportioned girl, a cellist who was a pupil of Sally's. Out of the blue a drunk on the other side of her leaned into our conversation and began

181

to make lewd comments about Celia's anatomy. I ignored him for as long as I could but he did not go away.

'Is he your bloke then?' he said, jerking his thumb towards me. 'Does he give it to you?'

He made an obscene up and down gesture with his middle finger in the direction of her crotch.

Celia flushed. Dawn Reilly or Sonia Hardy would have told him to get lost, but Celia didn't know what to do. I was racking my brains as to how to handle the situation. At that moment Greg Harris – dart in hand – leaned against me.

'Quarrel! I will back thee!' he said.

I looked at him in amazement. But he nodded.

'I will frown as I pass and let him take it as he list.'

While Greg lined up his shot at the board, the drunk pawed Celia's knee and Celia burst into tears. I stood up and said something appropriately pompous. The man put a hand on my chest and gave it a gentle shove.

'Piss off!' he said.

My heart, you can imagine, was going like the clappers. I asked him to remove his hand. The situation was turning ugly.

Greg Harris stepped between us.

'Thou art a villain. Go to!'

The drunk blinked.

'Fuck off. Or I'll take you outside.'

'You will find me apt enough to that sir, and you will give me the occasion.'

I could hardly believe my ears.

'Look, cunt . . .'

'Do you quarrel sir?'

The drunk hesitated.

'But if you do so, I am for you.'

The drunk made to smack Greg around the face. Greg stepped – or rather swayed – back.

The bar had fallen silent.

The drunk threw a more serious punch at Greg's head, but Greg was quick and eluded it like a boxer. It was marvellous to watch. Again the man punched, again Greg removed his head from the path of the fist and shaped a blow of his own which, had he not held back, would have made contact. Greg – he knew how to box, all right – laughed and turned his back on the drunk as if a silly game was over. They had just been amusing themselves. He escorted Celia across the bar to where Rita and Jeannie were sitting. The locals murmured their approval at the outcome, relieved that peace had been restored. The drunk returned to his empty glass but Molly refused to fill it for him. He stomped out of the pub in a huff and as he did, an ironic cheer went up.

We were all proud of Greg, the locals pleased to see that their 'stoodents' had not been humiliated. The boys were cock-a-hoop. Two minutes later, however, the drunk returned to the bar. Before any of us had read the situation he found out Greg, spun him round and head-butted him to the floor. Greg lay in a heap, not moving.

The local men pinned the man down until the police arrived and carted him away. Greg was all right. Coming to with his head on Jeannie Watts's lap, gazing into her tear-stained eyes, almost certainly compensated for the knock he had taken. For a week he wore the bruise on his forehead as a badge of honour – which in a way is what it was.

Greg could be droll when he wanted to be, but he was also a bit stand-offish. He had no intimate friend, neither among the boys nor the girls. For a start, he looked odd. He had one of those adolescent boy's faces that bulge in the wrong places. He was a mess to look at. A loner, which is a hard thing to be in a large comprehensive school – although not out of choice. He just didn't know how to establish relationships. Girls gave him a wide berth. His peers called him Crow, short for Scare-crow. The name suited him. When you see two crows, they're rooks. When you see a rook on its own, it's a crow. Isn't that how it goes? He should never have been at school. Today he would be in a college. The hard thing to know was what – besides the embrace of Jeannie Watts – he wanted.

Sally would have been in a better position to answer the question than me. He was her protègè, if that is not too patronizing a term, because he showed greater musical promise than dramatic. He was not and never would be a thespian. Not in a million years. On the other hand he had a fine tenor voice. He had sung in a church choir and had a repertoire. Such a thing would have been a matter of interest in a suburban fee-paying school; in an inner London comprehensive it was unheard-of. Sally didn't have to teach him the basic elements of breathing, articulation, the importance of tempo. He knew it all already. He could sight-read. Nevertheless, she practically had to go down on her knees and beg him to sing. He didn't want to sing. He wanted to act.

I think a deal was struck in the end. He agreed to sing if she would use her influence with me to make sure he had a role in the production. I didn't mind. I took the view that anyone who wanted to act should be given the opportunity. Even hopefuls as hopeless as Greg Harris. Greg could bring a production to a standstill because he could never remember his lines. When his cue came he froze, paralysed. I don't understand why he wanted to act because he hated being on the stage. He was unable to accept the illusion which actors and audience share when they are in the theatre. I gave him the part of Gregory, servant to Capulet, in the hope that playing a namesake would lessen the ordeal for him.

His reasons for wanting to be in the drama group were social rather than originating from an interest in the theatre. He wanted to be there in a group, to go to the pub, to share the intimacy between stage people which is so delicious. Until Sally told me that he was carrying a torch for Jeannie Watts, I must confess the thought had passed through my mind that he was gay – although I would not have used that word then. Queer was probably the word I would have thought of. He seemed so ill at ease with himself, such a mess. He wouldn't have been the first homosexual to be drawn towards the theatre. In those days it was the only place queers felt safe.

It didn't make any difference because he didn't get a look-in with Jeannie, as far as I know. Any other boy would simply have got the message and transferred his attention to another suitable object, as indeed Romeo does in Act One, forsaking the unresponsive Rosanne for the more easily won over Juliet.

During your twenties you feel like a god. You are both at your most attractive and your most sexually potent – and all your friends are too. You can stay up all night drinking and dancing and go to work the next morning. Money is of no importance, whither it comes or goes. You can tell the boss to jump in a lake if you feel like it. You give no thought to taking out a pension. You are Prince Hal, and the whole of England is your inheritance. It does not occur to you for a moment that one day you will be Falstaff – sad, overweight, bald, ridiculous to your own offspring. You won't die alone and unwanted. Perish the thought!

Throughout October and November and December Holmfirth Road resounded with the voices of teenage boys and girls reciting Shakespeare, working very hard to get it just right. There were periods of intense concentration when lines were spoken and spoken again. Tears were followed by laughter, beans and scrambled eggs, followed by bottles of pale ale. Intermittently the lovely voice of the violoncello could be heard from behind closed doors. The elegiac Romantic repertoire – Saint-Saëns's *Le Cygne*, Fauré's *Après un Rêve*, Rachmaninov's sonata – provided a wistful obbligato to the poetry and the silly schoolboy humour. In my memory the two contradictory

185

moods, high spirits and melancholy, are inseparable. It was only later – I mean, *much* later – that I understood that I was on the verge of losing something. Looking back, it was as if the cello was trying to tell me something I didn't want to hear.

Sally and I were getting on well. We had both got used to living in the same place with another human being of the opposite sex. We would come home and fall into each other's arms in front of the television – or else walk across the road to the local for a pint and come back and make love and, the next day, get up and go to work. It was domestic bliss, pure and simple – with the kids at weekends. We loved it. I liked her friends too. Sally didn't mind that I wasn't a musician. On the contrary, she said she was glad. Musicians have an even lower opinion of other musicians than actors have of other actors.

I was in love with Sally and I had every reason to suppose that she was in love with me. Towards the end of the school year, she announced that she had landed a job on the front desk of a provincial orchestra and she intended to inform the headmaster that she would be leaving at the end of the summer term. I was flabbergasted. The way she put it to me you would have thought that we had only been flat-sharing, and our relationship was no more than a mutually advantageous arrangement for reducing housekeeping expenses. I offered to look for a teaching post in the city where she would be working but she would not consider it. My life, she said, was at Fox Hill. I had too much invested in the school to leave.

There were some tears – from both of us – but there was nothing I could do. We weren't married. It was an open relationship with no strings attached, so I could hardly complain. In the second week of July I helped her to pack her belongings into the back of her dad's old Morris Cambridge – her cello occupying a whole seat just as if it were a real person. I never saw either of them again, although, as I say, I occasionally hear Sally play her cello on the radio.

I still dream about Sally, you know – even now. Once or twice a year. I used to dream about her while I was with your mother. I would wake up in the morning feeling terribly guilty that, moments before, I had been enjoying some mildly erotic dream about another prettier, much younger woman. Alison never knew Sally. There would have been no point telling her and I kept my dreams to myself. I suppose my subconscious was telling me that I was not happy. I was not a young actor living with a beautiful young cellist. I was a middle-aged teacher married to another middle-aged teacher. I missed Sally terribly. I still miss her.

This period of wretchedness was lying buried in the future like a mine for me to tread on and detonate later. At the time I was working so hard – it was only my second year at Fox Hill – that if there had been any tell-tale signs that things weren't right between Sally and me, I'm afraid I missed them. I was too preoccupied with school work to notice. There were meetings to attend, papers to mark, rehearsals to be taken, exams to be prepared for. It was the same for Sally.

It wasn't anybody's fault. When the going is good the person you love becomes part of yourself and if you cease to take yourself into account, you cease to take account of the person you love. But you must always keep some daylight between the negative and positive poles of sexual attraction, if the spark is to jump between them. In *Romeo and Juliet*, it is the separate identities of the two families which generates the heat of their passions. Capulet and Montague are cat and dog to each other. On every occasion they approach too closely – either Mercutio and Tybalt or Romeo and Juliet – the consequences are dire. Tragic in their case, quotidian in ours, but terminal none the less.

Blissfully ignorant that my semi-marital bliss was about to come to an abrupt end, I rehearsed the cast for the Christmas show. After the performance members of the drama group continued to visit us socially, but soon they all had to set their noses to the grindstone for their exams in July. The only one of them who continued as before was Greg Harris. He was still working with Sally on some Schubert songs with piano accompaniment for his grade six. She thought he had a voice and she had put his name down for scholarships at various centres of excellence. If he did well in his A levels he would, she argued, escape the hopelessness of his domestic circumstances. He often came home with us to rehearse and have a meal. Greg was used to messing for himself so he was a good house guest, although non-paying lodger was sometimes a more appropriate way of putting it. He slept in the spare room, where Sally played her cello.

I think the boy couldn't believe his luck in having found two congenial adults who were prepared to give him houseroom. It was what he needed. Because he was living on his jack, as Molly put it, he had nobody to look after him, tell him it was time to get up, have a bath or a haircut, nag him to do his homework. His parlous situation drew the maternal out of Sally, who could not bear the thought that the Scarecrow had to go back to a rented room in Hammersmith.

Throughout the summer term the English A level class – fourteen of them, if they all turn up – prepare for their exam while Rod Laver approaches his first Wimbledon title. We have been together for two years and we are revising the syllabus, languid in the heat. The class convenes in one of the peacock-tiled rooms in the old lodge, well away from the lesser mortals. Through the wide-open window comes the plunk of rackets striking tennis balls in the courts below, unsynchronized with the irregular roar of centre court from the television room next door, which also has its windows open. Donne's poem *A Valediction: forbidding Mourning* has to compete for the attention of sleepy adolescent boys and girls with the men's semi-final.

>'Twere profanation of our joys
>To tell the laity our love.

What, I wonder, do they make of these mysterious lines?

'Profanation is a word from religion, isn't it?' Dawn yawns.

'So's *laity*,' says Sonia.

'He's saying love is like a religion.'

'A religion of two?'

Rita puts her finger on it:

'It's a paradox. This kind of love would have been against religion. When he uses the word joys, he isn't talking about *spiritual* joys, is he?'

'What other kind of joys could he be talking about then?' Sonia asks, wide-eyed.

Jeannie, Rita's bosom pal, takes up the theme.

'He says the foot of the compass is the soul and the other point grows *erect* as it *comes* home. Is this a pun on the male sexual organ during, um . . . ?'

She pauses theatrically.

The inevitable triumphant chorus goes up: '. . . *Seggs-u-al cong-gress!*'

When the laughter dies down Dawn says: '*And makes me end where I begun.* He's talking about the female sexual organ here, surely? Assuming *end* is a pun on ejaculation?'

I probably nod, shocked but no longer flapped by their delicious frankness.

'Look, it's not just a love poem. The whole poem is a pun on love being like death. It's a valediction forbidding mourning. It's about Love *and* Death!'

'But in those days, love was forbidden,' Jeannie Watts says. '"If they do see thee", Juliet tells Romeo, "they will murder thee!" It was a risky business. Detection could mean death. Lovers had to be careful. It had to happen, um . . .'

The cheer goes up: '*Unbeknownst!*'

Unbeknownst, like *seggs-u-al cong-gress*, is one of the trig points all discussion has to pass through, the girls having decided that secret, illicit lovemaking is the sine qua non of all great literature. Each lesson is like an extended game of Mornington Crescent.

'That's because women couldn't sleep with the blokes they liked,' Dawn asserts.

As if woken from a deep sleep, Dickie Chisolm sits bolt upright in his chair.

'You mean,' he exclaims theatrically, '*they can now*!'

We all fall about laughing.

'You never know your luck, Dickie!'

At times such as these I am satisfied I have the best job in the world. Discussing metaphysical poetry with funny, quick-witted, sexually aware sixth-formers is a delight. I am as happy as I have ever been – or will ever be.

All the time I am enjoying seggs-u-al cong-gress with Sally Tanner she is, unbeknownst to me, applying for jobs in other parts of the country.

There was a kerfuffle at the beginning of July, shortly before the exams. The school office was broken into over one weekend and some money taken from the petty cash box – not much, only about fifteen pounds – but the intruder had made a mess of the office in his search for his haul. There was quite a stink about it. People were not so accustomed to crime as they are today, when a stranger can enter a school and spray children with high-calibre automatic gunfire. But then even a small burglary was rare. Even so, I probably would not have recalled the affair had it not taken place the weekend before Greg Harris stopped attending school. He stayed away from the Swan and he stopped coming round to Holmfirth Road. He just disappeared off the face of the earth. I never heard from or of him again.

Sally and I went to his lodgings in W9, a wretched place off

Bloemfontein Road, but his landlady had no more idea of his whereabouts than we did. He had decamped, owing her three weeks' rent and leaving behind most of his belongings, his school books and his clothes, his school tie. It didn't look as if he had had much. The score of Schubert's *Die Doppelgänger* – Sally's copy with his translation pencilled in – was open on a music stand. His homework books were spread on his desk. Greg's landlady knew that he had done a bunk, though, because he had removed his washing things, his shaving tackle and certain articles of clothing, photographs and letters, which were no longer in his room. (She seemed to have a complete inventory of his possessions.) She wasn't concerned about her money because she knew the name and address of the providers of Greg's allowance, a married couple in south London, and they had promised to make good her loss. She gave Sally the address, but nothing came of it. They had no idea where he was either.

The headmaster did not make a connection between the break-in and Gregory's disappearance, at least not publicly. He was a decent chap. It was not because he was worried about how the two events would be reported in the local press – although I'm sure that must have passed through his mind. He knew Gregory's circumstances. He was as worried about the boy as the rest of us. I'm sure he would have willingly hushed up the burglary if that meant Gregory could return to school for his exams.

Sally was distraught. It looked as if he was going to flunk his opportunity of winning a scholarship. All the hard work she had put into the boy had gone down the drain. I know that she didn't look at it like that but I did. It was all so pointless.

The exams came and went. Gregory's papers with his examination-board number on them were placed on a table for him so that his friends and the invigilators – myself and Sally sometimes among them – were conscious of the unoccupied table and chair in the exam room. It was a dramatic expression of the small emptiness in our lives – because none of us expected to see Greg again. We were all miserable. Greg's empty chair reminded us that in a few weeks' time we would be leaving each other for good. There would be no more drinking in the Swan, no more jokes about unbeknownst seggs-u-al cong-gress. The party was over. The Modern Drama Group which had been the vessel of their emotional life would disband. It was hard for Sally – for me it would always be hard, every summer of my professional life – but for Rita Papa and Dickie Chisolm and Dawn Reilly and Jeannie Watts and Matt Oliver, it was going to be the first loss of their lives. Not the greatest, but the first.

It made for a disagreeable exam period. In my experience exams are a curiously emotionally charged avenue at the best of times, more like a rite of passage than a measuring of achievement. The members of the upper sixth were all very fond of each other – and some more than that – but they had overlooked a simple fact: their relationships had been based on their membership of an institution, and when they said goodbye to that institution they would be saying goodbye to each other. Later on – after having observed a number of these enforced separations – I came to look on them as a small death, a second leaving of the womb. Gregory's premature departure focused the minds of the group of friends on the inevitable sooner rather than later. He had cheated them of the illusion – as well as the important ritual of leave-taking. He had disappeared from their lives without saying goodbye, and they didn't want to forgive him for that – although they probably would eventually.

At the conclusion of the exams there were still several weeks of the term left. A lot of tennis was played. Sixth-formers began to slope off one by one. The drama group gave their last performance at the farewell party to which selected staff were invited, including the head: a send-up of *Romeo and Juliet* in which the cast performed dressed as tarts and queers and pimps

– in bras, fishnet stockings and suspenders, enormous codpieces. It was a hilarious shambles, saucy and very funny, in some ways better than the original production. I had nothing to do with it. Lines were forgotten and improvised on the spot. Jeannie Watts, the only person to remember her part, brought the house down in her outrageously sexy outfit. Sally put her hand in front of my eyes when she came on stage. I have always remembered her doing that. It was one of her last intimate gestures to me.

We all hugged and kissed each other and afterwards some of us repaired to the Swan – one or two of the girls omitting to change out of their costumes. We were soon happily tipsy. Molly – who was as sad as any of us – let the double entendre fly. Nobody mentioned the Scarecrow that night. He could go to hell, if he wasn't there already.

I was much more philosophical about his departure than Sally. I thought Greg Harris would always be able to look after himself, but Sally was hurt and upset. She took it personally. It only occurs to me now – as I am typing out this memoir – that her disappointment at her protégé's failure to fulfil his promise might have been a factor in her decision to pack it all in, leave me and Holmfirth Road and start afresh somewhere else. I know she would have needed to apply and be auditioned for her new job up North well before this happened.

Still, it might have been the last straw. She had had enough. After the experience she never taught in a school again, as far as I know. The emotional intensity and stomach-churning despair the work engenders was too much for her. I don't blame her. She did well to get out when she did. I'm sure she had a pleasanter time playing Saint-Saëns and Rachmaninov for a living.

The school year came to an end and, with it, my relationship with Sally. I was too exhausted and fed up to go on holiday and I just sat in the garden and read thrillers. I missed her terribly. I think I must have been in some kind of shock. My belief in myself, I realize now, had been completely shattered. I had not realized how much I had become used to her energy and vivacity and the sound of her music-making. After Sally had gone, the fizz went out of me for a while. I mean quite a while. It wasn't for another five or six years that I met and married your mother. During that period there was nearly always a girlfriend somewhere in the picture – invariably a teacher, I'm afraid – but never one I wanted to live with, never a musician.

Whether by accident or design I became less involved with my pupils. I stopped inviting them into my home. There is a difference between a couple inviting boys and girls to visit them and a single bloke doing it. It wasn't the same. I began to take a back seat in the school drama society. To tell you the truth, I don't think anyone noticed. It's a thankless task. There is nothing more ephemeral in the world than a school production of a Shakespeare play.

Slowly – over a period of ten or fifteen years – I watched the school go downhill. The head and the older heads of subjects retired, and they were replaced by staff who were simply not of the same calibre. Later still the Government declared war on state-school teachers and there were strikes which – I am sure you would have disapproved – I participated in wholeheartedly. We were fighting for our professional lives. It's all ancient history now.

The Government won their battle and teachers were broken and the children came off worse. The Education minister could not get rid of mixed-ability egalitarian schools, but he could make life hell for people who worked in them and no more were built. Brand-new schools began to look scruffy and old ones were allowed to fall to bits. When I entered the profession, the provision of books and textbooks was the responsibility of the Education Authority. After years of rate-capping we don't have books any more. The Authority has had to cut waste and books are seen to be waste. We have tatty photocopies from which we encourage the children to mug up the facts, facts, facts which the Education minister in his wisdom has decreed they should know. There is no discussion of ideas or opinions. Not surprisingly, the children are as bored as their teachers and hate school almost as much.

My present school is falling to pieces. The head has a Master's in Business Administration. He thinks he's running a business. The staff, who have to answer to line managers and be appraised and meet performance indicators, are demoralized and lazy. And who can blame them? I am myself. We teach the same curriculum as every school in the country and if we don't score high enough in the league table of results, parents will enrol their children in other schools and then our capitation will fall and our grant will be cut. The school will become even poorer and teachers will be made redundant. There are no clubs or societies following the strikes in the eighties, during which teachers were vilified in the *Sun* and *The Times*. There is no sport to speak of any more, no music and no music teachers and – since I am no longer prepared to undertake the chore – no drama.

Teaching, you see, is no longer about educating the child for life, it's about training him for a job.

Perhaps you are right. I *am* a disillusioned curmudgeon waiting for his pension. But I wanted you to know that I did have enthusiasms once, and I loved my work. I fought for an idea that I believed in. It was a good idea. It still is. If we failed it was because the Government didn't believe in it and the Government was stronger than we were. Market-place mechanisms have taken the place of passion and altruism. We have all become meaner and more selfish. Collective cooperative behaviour is seen as an anachronism, if not downright subversive. In the sixties we were able to rub along with the old Tories, all of whom had been in the trenches with men – Macmillan,

Butler, Mcleod – but once the aristo property-owning class allowed their party to be hijacked by shopkeepers and property speculators, it was only a matter of time before the whiff of fascism entered through the back door. I and my colleagues were openly talked of as the Enemy Within.

I have a black and white photograph stuck on my fridge which I look at a lot, even though it terrifies the life out of me. I look at it in disbelief. I would not believe it if I had not cut it out of the *Observer* myself. The photo is a snap of the wedding of an affable-looking young man – about my own age in 1962 – with half a dozen of his mates, all in morning suits, standing outside some college in Cambridge. The young man getting married is a future Education minister. In the photo are two future Chancellors of the Exchequer, two Home Secretaries and a Minister for the Environment. This little gang of middle-class public-school boys eventually conspired to abolish the Inner London Education Authority, in essence the old LCC, with a campaign of lies and disinformation and in the teeth of the opposition of Londoners. They handed over Fox Hill to the local Tory council. Finally, after thirty years, the naysayers – small businessmen, Masons, Chamber of Commerce grad-grinds – were in a position to make sure the school failed.

Shopkeepers have no interest in learning, culture or intellec-tual pursuits, never have done. Never will. They contribute nothing to the cultural life of any society. All they care about is selling things.

You must not think I am having a go at you, Angela dear, because – silly girl! – you voted for Margaret Thatcher. I don't blame you for doing that. You were your mother's daughter more than you were ever mine, I regret to say. I have never tried to alter your political persuasion. If Alison and I had stayed together, you might have grown up to be a completely different person. At least you would have heard my side of the story.

I'm sorry I abandoned you to her influences, although under the circumstances I can't see what else I could have done. You are old enough to make up your own mind, and one reason I have written this memoir is because I wanted to put it in the balance, to show you that I was once industrious, optimistic, cheerful even. I loved my work. I loved my pupils. I loved a woman too, and it is my tragedy that she was not your mother. I could never have told you this while Alison was alive. I hope reading my account will help you to understand – if not forgive – your father.

When Gareth and Rob are old enough I expect you will want them to try for a scholarship to a direct-grant school. I wouldn't blame you if you did, or even paid for them to go to a private school. If that's what you want, I will do what I can. I shall be taking early retirement this September and I have thirty years' superannuation due to me. I should be able to help out with the fees. You would be out of your mind to send your boys to their local comprehensive. If it's anything like the one I teach in it will be a dustbin, full of smart-arsed young bastards, lazy, unprepossessing little shits. And the pupils aren't much better.

Write soon.

3

ARTHUR MORRIS

Time to take the weight off the old plates of meat, eh, lad? Get some shut-eye. Yes. That's what you want to do. Make yourself comfy. Stretch out, that's right. Cop some of this. That'll put some lead in your pencil. I'n't a bad old gaff, eh? I told you. You won't find a better gaff than this to kip down in.

I've kipped in some worser places. In the Army you dossed where you fucking could. In trains, trenches, under tanks. You wasn't supposed to sleep under your tank – it was against standing orders – but we all did it. You was hungry and tired, shitting yourself in case your own fucking artillery shelled your position in the night. More than anything you wanted a kip and the safest place from mortars is under a tank. A mortar i'n't going to dent a fucking tank, not even one of ours. A 88, mind, well you'd know about it. What am I talking about? You wouldn't know a fucking thing. Brew you up in two shakes. Your 88 was a class weapon, could shoot the shit out of a Sherman. Lucky for us Jerry was nearly always short of ammo and he didn't waste it on night firing. So we never paid no attention to standing fucking orders no more than the officers did.

After we were pulled out of Africa Jerry had us under the cosh all the way up Italy. It was no fucking picnic, stand on me. German weapons were miles better than what ours were. We just had more of them, plus we had the bloody Yanks' hands to hold. Those dozy fuckers couldn't piss in a hole if they were standing in it. So in some ways it was worse than Africa. Either it was cold enough to freeze your bollocks off or else it fair pissed down – but at least you could get hold of a tart. I had a bint once or twice in Egypt but it weren't easy. If a soldier wanted a bit of cunt he had to go looking for it there, in the bazaar, and more'n one Tommy never come back from a brothel-creeping expedition. A lot of Gyppos hated our guts worse'n what the Germans did. And if you did come back you more'n likely brought summat you hadn't took with you. Italy was different. You was fighting through villages, house by house, see, and those Eyetie girls would drop their drawers and give you a bunk-up for a tin of spam or a bar of mouldy Army chocolate they were so starved, or their kids were. All the young Eyetie men were away in the Eyetie Army, see.

I came across a girl one time – she was only about fifteen or sixteen, hard to say – crouching alone in a house that was all smashed up. Our company had just shelled her village to bits and the Germans had fucked off ten minutes before. She was sat in the corner of what was left of her yard, staring at nothing with her mouth open. I could see she was in shock. She didn't try and stop me when I got her titty out, so I just lifted her dress up and stuck it in her, gave her one while I had the fucking chance. Wallop! Didn't make no difference to her, did it? Never said a bleeding word. I left her where I found her, with her mouth open.

Yeah. I've kipped down in some places, lad, you wouldn't want to shit in. Of all of them, ships was worst by a long chalk. You want to try getting some bo-peep in the hold of a fucking rolling ship with men wanking and pissing and shitting themselves and being sick all over you. If that weren't bad enough, you had fucking U-boats out there looking for you. We lost two ships in the crossing from Egypt. Poor bastards didn't stand a fucking chance. There were cock-ups in Africa – I mean whole fucking divisions wiped out because the la-di-dah generals didn't know what they were fucking doing, least not till Monty took over. Jesus! When you think of the clobbering those poor New fucking Zealanders took at Minqâr Qaim! Italy weren't much better, worse even because Monty had fucked off by then. But a night in the hold of a fucking troopship takes the fucking biscuit. Stand on me.

How old are you, son? Twenty? Twenty-two? Is that all? Well, I weren't much older than you are. There was a lot of lads like you, I mean skinny little runts. No disrespect to you, lad. Poor cunts should never of been put in a fucking uniform. I'm not saying I never wanted to piss my pants when Jerry was sending it over – I weren't no fucking hero – but those poor cunts started running away and calling for their mummies. You had to knock them to the fucking ground before the battle police shot them.

By then I knew how to hit a man. There's different ways, of course. Oh, yes. You can knock him about a bit, cut him up around his face, or you can hit him in the solar and take the wind out of him so he feels fucking awful and wants to crawl into a hole – or you can put one on him under his jaw – wallop! – so he goes down like a wet kitbag, happy as Larry. When I joined the Army I could handle myself all right but I was just a pub scrapper, you know what I mean? I could throw a punch at a bloke after I'd a drink or two in me. Or butt the cunt.

It was the Army taught me how to box. There's nothing in the world more boring than a fucking Army camp and boxing gave a bloke summat to do. I won cups. Straight up. At Benghazi I fought for the regiment and I'd of won all my bouts if we hadn't had to strike camp and fuck off sharpish. Rommel had took over the Afrika Korps and soon had us under the cosh. In Italy, when we had a tournament with the Yanks in the next Sector, I did all right until I came up against this fucking nigger who beat me on points. He was a fucking gorilla. He was fighting at his wrong weight, but there was no one else big enough to match him with. That was one of my best bouts, funnily enough. The Yanks lost loads of money on that fight because they bet with our boys the nigger would stop me before the bell did. But I took him the distance. I gave them a good fight and they paid up smiling. In fact they gave me a fucking grand time afterwards. Got me shitfaced on American whisky. Saved the honour of the regiment, the sarn't major said. He never expected me to walk away from three rounds with the nigger no more than they did. Even the nigger shook my hand afterwards like a real gent. I asked him to join us for a drink, but he wouldn't. Yanks don't drink with niggers.

A good big 'un will always beat a good little 'un. Remember that, lad, and you won't go far wrong.

Boxing's an art, you know that? The noble art, they call it. You attack and you defend, and you get points when your attack gets through your opponent's defence. It's the feet you want to watch. Your footwork gets you out of trouble – and into it if you're not careful. If he can't hit you he can't hurt you. It's fighting but it's honourable. You're not allowed to hit a bloke below the belt. Only a cunt would do that.

I haven't been in a ring for donkey's years. After I left the Army it was harder to train and keep the weight down. When I got into Civvy Street I kept it up for a few years, but there was fuck all money in it, so why fucking bother?

Those were the days, lad. The Army made men out of lads like you. Here. Pass it over. Let's have some of that. Don't be vague, ask for Haig . . .

That's more like it. Where was I?

Demob and Civvy Street. Well, it was a fucking free-for-all for a while. Hundreds of men chasing after a few jobs. I fucked around London, in and out of work, never short of a quid or two in my dummy. Did a bit of navvying on the sites. I bounced for a club in Poland Street for a while. Freddie Mills, Brian London, Terry Downes. I knew all the boxers. They all used a club called The Stork. London in the fifties was fucking paradise, stand on me. Plenty of drink, women with tits and men who wore proper suits with a tie and a hat, not like the scruffy bastards who have money today. In them days people had a bit of flash. If you could of seen the Edmondo Ros Club in Bayswater Road of a Saturday night, you'd know what I was talking about. Gents in black ties, beautiful tarts in pretty dresses, the most expensive tarts in London – and I shagged my share of them on the house. I was bouncing for Mr Ros then. A real gent, he was. Had more front than Selfridges.

One time this naval officer type tried to come the gold lace with me. He'd had a few and he talked like pound notes. I said, 'Leave off. The fucking War's over, mate.' He got snotty and started to 'my man' me. Well, I dropped him. I weren't his fucking man and the cunt woke up with a broke nose and claret all over his clobber. The Old Bill done us for A and B. When the case come up in Marylebone Magistrates, Mr Ros stood up in the box and said how it weren't me started it. My brief gave the beak the old moody, how I was a Desert Rat what'd fought Rommel at El Alamein. The old git just wagged his finger at us and bound us over to keep the peace. I slipped the noose on that one!

London was fast, then, and dirty, much more'n what it is now. Look what happened to Freddie Mills – shot in his car outside his own fucking club! You've heard of Freddie Mills, I suppose? No? Jesus Christ! Well, he was a professional boxer. British middleweight champion. One of the fucking best.

Lovely bloke. Gave us a couple of his suits. We were the same size, see.

It wasn't long after that, while I was still bound over, I got swagged off to Pentonville after I sorted out this spade who tried to cut me. It was about then you started to see spades all over London, fucking pimps every fucking one of them. They all carried fucking weapons and dealed in reefer. I got a lagging for that one, but the black cunt I sorted out lost his teeth and got a nice stripe across his boat race with his own fucking blade. He never got his gnashers round a tart's titty again, stand on me.

Matter of fact it was then, while I was in Pentonville doing my bird, I first had what you do. We never had that in the Army – no fucking fear! – but nick was different. All the big 'uns looked after the little 'uns in nick, and the little 'uns looked after the big 'uns. Simple as that. And there was always queers, blokes who'd gobble your dick for a quarter of snout, take it up the arse for a full ounce.

April 1955 I come out. Didn't have two fucking pennies to rub against each other, and the National fucking Assistance wouldn't give me fuck all. I had to odds it best I could. Slept rough. Spent a few nights in the Sally Army hostel in Shoreditch before I got a break. The weather weren't too bad, thank Christ. I was knocking around south London – Lambeth, Bermondsey, Wapping – sleeping in bombed-out houses or the Sally Army. It all looks different round there now. You wouldn't hardly recognize what it was then. Whole streets have gone, even the ones Hitler hadn't got round to bombing. But in the fifties it was a right bleeding mess.

I was going to this church hall at night for a bowl of summat hot and a slice of bread. I gave them the old moody, how I was an old soldier fallen on hard times. They never tumbled I was straight out of nick. I kept stum on that score. They soon had me doing odd jobs about the church and before I knew it, they were talking about us helping out in this boys' club the church paid for. Well I did that for a spell, kept my nose clean, and blow me if they didn't give us a fucking job! Straight up.

The Two Feathers Boys' Club was on this Peabody estate what'd survived the Blitz. Fucking miracle it did, an' all. I was to be a sort of caretaker. All I had to do was look after the place, open up, lock up, put the rubbish out and keep the boys in order. It was a dead cushy little number. I didn't pay no rent and the money weren't bad: seven nicker a week. A fiver was good money then. The club was run by this young couple who were summat in the Church and lived on the estate. They were in charge. There was loads of things for the boys to do in the club – table tennis, gym, football and cricket – but it was boxing they wanted. Couldn't get enough of it. Well, I soon got them sorted out. I had local boxers down to talk to them and sign autographs and one of them had some old equipment from his gym sent over.

It was a cushy billet. I stuck it a couple of years – the longest time I ever spent in one place. Best of all, I had most of the day off. It was just evenings I had to be there, to open up, get the equipment out, put the equipment away, lock up. To tell you the truth it kept me out of the pub. Either I was keeping everything shipshape and Bristol fashion, or I was teaching boys how to box. It suited me down to the ground. For one thing it was quiet work, not like the kind of jobs I had before I done my bird. I had to do set things at set times of the day like in the Army, only there was no cunt shouting at you if you was late or you felt like a lie-in. I was on my jack. Cooked my own grub and shifted for myself. It was all right.

The part of London where the estate was there was no late-night clubs or fast set, hardly any tarts or blaggers, just ordinary south Londoners trying to put their lives back in order after the War. The War had been over ten years but things were still bad there. I just got on with it. I had a drink in the local pubs. Made a few friends. I soon got to know everybody on the estate. I think they liked having an Army bloke in charge of the boys, someone their sons could look up to. Well, I know they did because they told me they did.

A few of the families had television sets and they'd invite us in to watch it if there was summat on. Lad your age can't imagine there was a time when hardly anyone had a television, but it's the truth. Before you were born we only had the radio, bit of variety, the pub.

I still think about them days I spent at the club. I kept out of trouble while I was there and I had neighbours who thought I was doing a good job. I'd be sitting in my little garden in the back of the club, reading the paper, and some nipper would poke his head round the corner and say his dad had bought a new cooker or summat, what he wanted was us to help him hump up the stairs. Well, I'd go up and take one end. I didn't mind. I'll always help a bloke out so long's he don't act like a cunt. A lot of the men on the estate had been in the War, in the Army or the Navy, so we knew how to rub along with each other. Come Christmas I got loads of presents and I was always asked in for a drink and a knees-up.

Tuesday and Thursday nights I taught the boys how to box. An official from the ABA helped me affiliate and sent me on a referee course. You had to be a member of the ABA – which I was – but the club had to affiliate for fights to take place. There were plenty of retired boxers in Bermondsey, old pros who were only too happy to come out of an evening and help coach the lads. One or two of them had boxed at a much higher level than I ever did. Old boys. Real characters. We soon built up a gym and our lads began to put in for competitions. We done terrible at first, but after a year or so they began to win bouts. Mark had to go out and buy a cabinet with a glass front to put the cups we won in.

Mark was the bloke in charge. He was the one I told you about who was summat in the Church and had give us the job in the first place. He was in the Church but he weren't a fucking creeping Jesus like the old sky pilots you got in nick. He was always dead straight with me. One of the reasons I stuck the job so long was because Mark didn't act like a fucking officer or NCO. He was my boss, but he never pulled rank. In the Army officers were either la-di-dahs or else NCOs who'd gone on courses.

Mark weren't working-class – but he weren't a la-di-dah neither. When he asked you to do summat, he didn't talk down to you as if he was one notch up the fucking ladder from you. He'd ask you if you thought such-and-such was a good idea or not, as if he was interested in your opinion. He was the first bloke I ever met who gave a toss about my opinion. Mark didn't treat us like a cunt. And when I wanted *him* to do summat for *me*, like get hold of some bleeding form he had to get hold of and sign it for us, he just went off and did it, like I was his boss. He never pulled any of those old Army strokes. The thing I hated most about the Army was the fucking NCOs. The officers were either wankers or cunts but the NCOs were *all* cunts. Mark weren't a wanker and he weren't a cunt neither.

He was a Christian, a proper one. He knew I wasn't and he'd never try and convert me to be one. He went to church on Sunday morning and believed in God, I went to the pub Saturday night and believed the Gunners would win the cup. Field Marshal Montgomery was the only bloke I ever believed in – and that was under fire, which don't count. And Monty could be a right cunt when he wanted to be.

I suppose they were thirty, thirty-two or summat, Mark and Dawn – about the same age as me. They had a kid, a boy of twelve or so, a nice lad who spent a lot of time in the club. I don't know if he was their kid or what, I can't remember. I often wondered because he didn't look a bit like either of them. If it was anyone else but her, you'd of thought he was got on the wrong side of the blanket. She'd of had to of been about

209

eighteen when she had him, which was possible but not all that likely in her case. They probably never told me and I was just guessing. I can't even remember the boy's name now. It's on the tip of my tongue. Hold on. I'll get it in a minute. I called all the boys by their surnames, like you did then. He was Harris to me. I couldn't show any favouritism just because his dad ran the club. I liked young Harris. He helped us around the place. Ran errands to the shop. He was a willing lad. More important, he couldn't half box.

The boy was coming on. He was a good height for his age. Had a good pair of shoulders on him and he moved well in the ring. What's more, he had a punch. He went in there and he hit hard, which is what counts. The lad was going to shape up into a good-sized welterweight if he kept at it and was handled right. I had to be careful because he weren't scared of nobody. He'd of fought boys what were too big for him if I'd of let him. You can match boys that i'n't the same age, you can match boys that i'n't the same height, but you're not supposed to match boys that i'n't the same weight. But boys his own size, thirteen, fourteen-year-olds even, none of them could beat him. I spent a lot of time with young Harris. I came to the sport too late to do anything – and there was always some bits of technique I never got right. But a young 'un, if he shows promise, you can make into a good boxer.

In the summer when the weather was hot I'd take a group of the boys swimming. We'd walk up Jamaica Road to Tower Bridge and cross the River. In them days people used to swim in the Thames off of the little sandy beach just in front of the Tower. Nobody does that no more because of the fucking state of the River, but then families'd take their kids to swim there. That's what we used to do when it was hot. It was free and we had a laugh. Their mums'd let half a dozen of them go if they was with me. I was in charge and I never let them down. I was strict, see. That's why. I let the boys lark around but I

210

didn't stand for no nonsense. They knew where they stood with me, and if one of them stepped over the line he got a thick ear – and that was that. They got it into their heads I'd been a sergeant in the War. The grown-ups knew I weren't nothing of the sort, but we let the boys think I was if they wanted to.

And so they called us 'Sergeant'. Yes, Sergeant. No, Sergeant – but I made sure it weren't three fucking bags full, Sergeant. I tried to be with them boys how I'd of been with men if I had of been a real sergeant. I didn't want them to think I was a cunt like we all thought our sergeant was. They were working-class south London lads, hard as nails and twice as sharp. I met some of them in the old Tank Corps, lads not much older than my boys. You always knew where you stood with them.

After a swim we'd get fell in and march back up Jamaica Road singing 'It's a Long Way to Tipperary', hot and dirty and red from where the sun had got us, our shirts round our waists, handing the old Tizer bottle round. We traipsed home like Fred Karno's Army, late for tea but happy as fucking larks.

It was like being in the Army, only without the Stukas and the fucking 88s up your arse, or the horrible sounds your mates made when they was hit. You stuck together, see, and you didn't let each other down. You'd die first. That's what I taught them. If a group of you was up to a bit of no good and one of you was captured by the bogies, you took your medicine and kept stum. If the Old Bill put the feelers out you got took by an attack of the old dockers' asthma. You never grassed on your mates, see. If I caught a boy up to no good, he knew if he told me who was with him the punishment he got would be half what it would be if he didn't tell me. My boys always took worse punishment than they had to before they grassed on their mates. If you want to make a unit of men out of a group of boys, what you don't ever do is make them feel small in front of their mates. They won't forgive you if you act like a cunt. Never.

That was what their mums and dads wanted, an Army bloke their boys could look up to. Boys need to be kept busy and they have to know where they stand, not unless you want them swagged by the Old Bill for breaking into places and nicking things. All my boys were boxers but they still got up to mischief. I knew they did. I just told them to make sure they didn't get captured, but if they did, they shouldn't act like cunts. I know Mark sometimes talked to them about Jesus, how they must tell the truth and turn the other cheek, but that never meant fuck all to them. What little they knew about right and wrong, which weren't saying much, they got from Arthur.

I hope you're listening to me, lad. You might learn something. That's right. Have a drink. Put some fucking lead in your pencil.

This bloke Mark had some other job in the day. He ran the Two Feathers Club in his spare time, in the evenings. In the day Dawn, his wife, was in charge. She was a funny, mousy little thing, never wore no make-up and always dressed herself plain as an old maid. She had sort of washed-out blonde hair what she put up in a bun. She looked completely the opposite to her boy, who was big-boned and dark-haired, lively. She was a Christian, of course, same as her old man, and she was always straight with me. Sometimes, if she'd cooked a meat pie or a duff pud, she'd send her boy round with a helping for me. A few of the women did that. They must of felt sorry for poor old Arthur Morris – 'Arfa Mo'' their boys called me, cheeky buggers! A single bloke with no woman to cook for him. Well, there was a char come in twice a week to the club and she did for me, cleaned my gaff and washed my stuff. She was an old bird who'd been on the game in her day. Said I could poke her for a couple of quid and I did too a couple of times, but it weren't all that much fun. I did it for her sake.

Most of my meals I ate in the Venus Café on Dockley Road, or else I walked to the pie and mash on Bevington Street. I liked to sit with my paper and pass the time of day with the blokes from the building sites. They were nearly all ex-Army or Navy, or else in the merchant navy. Hard nuts. There was a lot of buildings coming down and new ones going up in them days. A bloke could always get a job on a site. I never fancied it myself. I stuck it for a bit before I done my bird, but I chucked it in. The foremen carried on too much like fucking NCOs for my liking.

I'd been at the club coming on two years. I was well settled in. I could see I'd got myself a nice little billet, all found. I bought myself a second-hand BSA from a bloke on the estate, which meant I could buzz over to Haringey for dogs' night when I felt like it and get back any time I wanted. Things was looking up for me. I ud calmed down a bit since the War. Didn't get into fights or blagged by the Old Bill. I just opened up the club, did the job, had a few drinks and fucked a tart when I felt like one. Then, blow me, just when I was settled in, summat happened. Not sudden, like. It took months and it weren't nothing to do with me. Straight up. That's the fucking truth.

I'd be in the club getting the equipment out and Dawn'd be in her office writing letters. Dawn did all the paperwork from a little office in the club, see. She had to raise money by writing letters to charities and famous people. She organized the football fixtures and got the shirts washed and mended. I don't think she got paid for doing it. I don't know. She might of. I'm telling you this so that you'll see the lie of the land. Dawn Harris weren't the kind of woman normal blokes would of looked at twice. I i'n't saying she was bad-looking. She just didn't tart herself up the way most women do.

One afternoon I went in there to ask her something, and I could see that she was shaking like a fucking leaf. I didn't say nothing about it. Women go up and down like fucking yo-yos all the time. In my experience it's best to leave them to it. They don't want some bloke poking his nose in.

One day – she was sitting at her desk and I was standing in

front of her – blow me if I couldn't see down the front of her blouse! She'd forgot to do some buttons up and I could see her white brassiere. Well, I thought to myself, this is a bit of a laugh. Then it happened again. I could see the top of her brassiere clear as that. Aye, aye, I thought, this is a bit queer. I kept my eyes peeled after that and, soon after, I went into her little office and her frock was sort of open in the front. I could see her tits because she didn't have a brassiere on. All the time the poor woman was shaking like a fucking leaf.

Well, I got the horn straight off – I could see she had a nice pair of top 'uns – but I weren't going to do anything about it. No fucking fear. I weren't that much of a stupid cunt. Still, the feeling in the room was electrical. I weren't going to do anything about it no more than she was. I left her and went off to my room and tossed myself off to cure the horn.

What happened next I couldn't of stopped if I'd of wanted to. I'm telling you the truth, lad. Next time I saw her it was the same. She had her blouse buttons sort of undone accidentally on purpose, and I could see the nipples of her titties when she leaned over her desk in front of us. All the time she was trying to act normal. She never looked at us or said a word, but I could see her chest going up and down. I'm telling you she was in a right two and eight. You just wanted to put her out of her fucking misery. I got the horn straight off and I felt like getting it out and showing her. I didn't, though. I didn't know what she wanted us to do. I didn't know if she even knew herself.

Well, suddenly neither of us could stand it no longer. She sort of stood there dithering in front of us, looking down at some piece of paper in her hand, the front of her blouse undone and one of her titties poking out of her blouse, right there under my nose, going up and down as her little heart beat like a fucking drum. I undid the rest of her blouse – she didn't do anything to try and stop us – and took it off of her shoulders. She just stood there, looking at the floor, without anything on

214

her top, with her little nipples gone all stiff. I moved behind her and put my hand over them and stroked them and she sort of fell against me. I lifted her up and carried her into my room.

The bed weren't made or nothing but I put her down, lay her face down and pulled her dress up. The little mouse had even left her knickers off! Well, I stuck it in her from behind and gave her one, which must of been what she wanted because I didn't need no Vaseline. It slipped in easy as that. All the time, though, she never looked at me. She kept moaning *No!* and *Don't!* She didn't want me to kiss her face or speak to her. I gave her a good fucking and afterwards I left her alone. I left the club and when I came back she had scarpered.

That was how it was every time. I could tell when she wanted it because she had the button of her blouse undone and she was shaking. And every time it was left to me to take her, and she'd try and act like I was doing it against her will. She'd try and pull her dress down, but it was just a game. She even put my hand on her fanny hill where she wanted me to rub her and she went fucking wild when I did, and she came louder than any woman I ever fucked. She wanted it worse, too. It was always the same. She left it up to me to make the move and she never touched my cock. She always wanted me to do it from behind so that I could rub her fanny hill at the same time I was giving it to her. And we never spoke about it. The game she was playing was that she weren't doing it, I was doing it – against her wishes. Which was a fucking laugh!

After the first time I found a box of johnnies in my room. After that I had to pretend to take her and put a fucking johnny on my cock at the same time! I could never of done it if she didn't want me to. She liked it as much as I did. More.

And that was the trouble. Sometimes I felt like it just seeing her, and I would just take her and do it right there, without even putting a johnny on. She'd pretend to resist and say stop, but she ended up moaning when she came just the same. We

215

were doing it a couple of times a week. I got used to her little titties and that bit of her legs between the tops of her stockings and her wet little cunt. If she weren't around I had to toss myself off to cure the horn, just to stop thinking about her.

I thought I had it made. A cushy little job coaching working-class boys in the noble art. Nice gaff with no rent. A char to do for me regular. A BSA handy for running over to Haringey to put a half-sheet or two on the dogs. On top of that, I was getting my bit of pud twice a week like a married man – free, too. It weren't like paying a tart. You can have a laugh and a slap and a tickle with a tart but underneath it all you both know it's your wad she has her eye on. Even a tart with class can't hide that. Dawn was different. She wanted it. It weren't me she wanted, I didn't kid my fucking self on that score, because she didn't want me to kiss her or even look at her. I was an uneducated bloke who liked a drink and went down the Arsenal to watch the Gunners. But Dawn was a well-brought-up lady who spoke nice and went to church.

I don't know for certain, but I don't reckon she'd ever had a good bloke inside her before. If she did it was only Mark she ever done it with. I reckon either he wouldn't do it with her or he couldn't. That was what I thought. Maybe he had summat medical wrong with him that stopped him getting the horn. I knew a bloke in the Army who couldn't get it up. Terry Hargreaves from Watford. Poor cunt copped it in Italy. But he weren't a fucking queer. Maybe Mark was a queer, I don't know. If he was he didn't act like any of the queers I ever knew. There weren't nothing pansy about him. I reckon him being a Christian had summat to do with it. Perhaps he turned to Jesus because he couldn't shag his old lady – or the other way around, more like. I honestly can't tell you. Just a feeling I got. Whatever the reason was, I'm sure he weren't putting it in her, and I was happy to do the job for him.

All right, so it weren't a nice thing for a bloke to do, to shag a bloke's old lady who has given him a break, but she wanted someone to do it and it so happened it was me. I can't see how you could of blamed me. I was a good-looking feller then. I had all my teeth and a full head of hair and you could see what kind of body I had on a summer's day when I wore a vest.

You don't believe me? I don't blame you, lad. I'm not half the man I was then. Best time of my life it was. I was in clover. Didn't want for fucking nothing. Once in a while some of the lads from the Regiment would get together up West. We'd have a slap-up meal and get shitfaced and go to a strip club and have a fucking good night out. When I told them what the deal was, how I was getting it regular from my boss's old lady, they didn't believe me. Thought I was telling a tall one. The truth is they didn't *want* to believe me. They was nearly all cash and carried themselves by then, with an old lady of their own, a couple of nippers and steady jobs, council houses with little gardens, TV sets on the old h.p. They'd all quieted down since the days when we got some Eyetie girl tied up in the back of a covered Bedford truck and fucked her stupid, one after the other, queuing up outside like we did when we was getting a jab from the MO.

This went on through the summer of 1957. It was a scorcher too, and the boys kicked their heels around the estate all through the school holidays. I felt sorry for the poor sods. If you don't keep boys busy they get up to no good. They nick things. Not things they want. Stupid fucking things like the park keeper's spike for picking up paper which they had no use for. But it isn't easy to nick something like that. It's a laugh — and that's all they want. On Saturday mornings they'd go to the flicks at the Essoldo on the High Street, the girls too, and the club was always open in the evening. I might take some of them swimming, either in the River or the new open-air pool in Southwark Park. But there weren't a lot for them to do except mess about in the park, catapulting the cars as they went past, or go down to the docks and hang about watching the River flow.

Some evenings we took a bat and ball and some stumps to the recreation ground and played a game of cricket. I was never much of a cricketer but they wanted to play. The Australians were in England that summer and all the boys wanted to be Dennis Compton – or else Jim Laker, but it was Compton they worshipped. He never seemed to give a fucking toss how many runs he got, if it were a hundred or he was out first ball, which weren't often. Of course, playing for the Gunners in the Cup Final as well as batting for England, well, he was like a god to them.

I saw a lot of young Greg Harris – that was the boy's name. Gregory. I knew it'd come back to me. There was an ABA tournament at the end of August that him and a couple of other boys had entered in for. They were training. It's all very well having a couple of good punches and being quick with your head. The hardest thing for a young lad is just holding up his arms with a pair of size six gloves at the end of them for three rounds. I tried to tell them they had to put more weight on their upper body. They should eat lots of meat. They had to do the right exercises. All the boys who qualified for the tournament were given some instruction in exercising by a trained boxing coach who knew more than I did, paid for by the ABA.

Greg Harris was the cock fighter of the bunch. He already saw every fight as a whole, with a beginning, a middle and an end – not just a scrap where you threw everything into knocking your opponent out in the first round.

Greg would come round the club and I'd open up the gym for him, and he would skip or use the weights for an hour or so every day. I think Dawn found it a bit hard having him around the house all day, and she was glad to have him out from under her feet. He never gave me no trouble. It weren't easy for him neither, in some ways. All the other boys came from working-class families, they all knew each other's nan and had uncles and aunts all over Bermondsey. Greg was different.

His mum and dad had come from outside. Mark worked in an insurance office in the City and Dawn was a trained secretary. Her typing sounded like a fucking Kraut 42 machine-gun. I almost pissed my pants the first time I heard her open up.

What I'm getting at is they weren't like other families on the estate. Because Dawn and Mark were in the local church, Greg had to spend a lot of time singing in the choir. I wanted him to bang that on the head, but he said he didn't mind. When the ABA instructor heard he was a choirboy he said it was the best thing a boxer could do if he wanted to get his breathing right. So I kept my mouth shut after that. I even taught him a few Army songs – 'Christmas Day in the Cook-house', 'Roses of Picardy', 'Wash Me in the Water That You Washed Your Dirty Daughter in'. I don't know if he really enjoyed the hymn-singing, but he stuck at it because his dad wanted him to and I think that was why he didn't bang it on the head.

I never heard his dad have a go at him. He never had to. The other dads were always having a go at their boys, shouting, laying into them with the belt, when they weren't larking about with them. Mark never raised his voice or larked about. He weren't like that. They were both very polite to each other. Listening to them talk together was dead queer. I mean, they were more like a pair of off-duty regular officers than a father and son. 'Please don't stay too long, Gregory,' his dad would say. 'You know you have to be at practice in twenty minutes.' 'All right, Mark,' his boy says to him.

Greg always called his mum and dad by their first names. I tell you, lad, it was dead queer. I wouldn't of let my son do that, if I'd ever had one. It i'n't right.

When he was with the other boys he was just like them. Spoke like them. Larked about and probably nicked stupid things like them, for all I know. When he was alone with his mum and dad, though – if he didn't know I was there – he talked different. He didn't sound like a boy from the estate. He spoke to me the same way all the boys did. I was the Sergeant.

He lived in two worlds. The boys liked him. His mum and dad liked him. I liked him. His teachers liked him. He didn't go to the grammar. He went to Wolsey Road Secondary Modern along with the other boys. He had failed his eleven–plus exam like they all had, but he told me that when he found out what would happen if he passed it, how he'd have to go to the grammar in Southwark Park, he fucked it up on purpose, so as he could stay with his mates. That was one reason I liked him: he stuck with his mates. Passing the exam would of been like saying he was a notch up the fucking ladder to them. He didn't want to do that.

But he weren't a great talker. He'd pass the time of day, talk boxing or cricket or the rubbish boys talk, but when it came to himself I never got much change out of him. I tried to find out what went on between his mum and his dad but he kept stum. He wouldn't talk about them. I found it hard to believe that Greg was really Dawn's boy. I didn't push it, though. A boy might feel funny about something like that, if his mum weren't his real mum. He might not want the other boys to know. That was fair enough. In fact it was right. Boys that age have a strong sense of honour. He didn't want to talk about his family to an outsider, same as he wouldn't of done about his mates. I respected him for that. It was what I taught him, keep stum and you won't go far wrong.

Are you asleep, lad? Well wake up, you cunt. I'm telling you summat. Have a drink. You can have some bo–peep when I say you can. I i'n't finished.

Where was I? The inter–clubs tournament. Yes. It was in the last week of August, and young Greg worked hard over the summer preparing for it. For the week before it came up, his dad had arranged for him to spend a week at the seaside some-where in the West Country with some vicar and his wife,

220

friends of Mark's. Greg was looking forward to that because he liked the people he was going to be staying with. He was dead lucky. None of the other boys had a holiday, not unless they had an aunt or a gran who lived somewhere they could go to stay with. I thought it would do him good to get out of London, rest up a bit, have some fun on the beach. You can overtrain for a fight, you know.

With the boy out of the way I was having it off with his mum nearly every fucking day of the week, almost at the same time in the afternoon, regular as clockwork, like it was a part of my job. We still had to go through the same old palaver, though. She never came to me when she wanted it. She still sort of shuffled around her office in the club, pretending to work, with her tits half showing. I'd get the horn and do it just how she wanted me to, as if it had nothing to do with her and I was the sex-starved monster, not her. I stuck it in from behind and rubbed her special place until she went crazy and then I came myself. Afterwards I left the club and let her make her own way out. I didn't kid myself she liked me. I knew I was being used. She was using my cock as a wanking-off post. Not that I was complaining. I was living the life of fucking Riley.

The boy came back cheerful and sunburnt. He'd had a smashing time at the seaside – I can't remember which one. Paignton or Torquay, one of those two. He done a lot of swimming, he said, because the couple he was staying with were both swimmers. It was just the sort of all-round exercise he needed. It was good to have him back. I could see he was in great shape. He was in peak condition when we came into tournament week.

The tournament was spread over two days. The first day boys were matched against other boys the same weight, which meant Greg was fighting boys a whole year older. He won his first bouts easy and came through to the second day and got to the final of his section. By then the weight difference between the boys was more than what it was at the start of the tournament. Greg had to fight a good 'un, good in his technique and strong. Greg put up a terrific fight, landing some sweet right-arm punches to the head I wouldn't of been ashamed of myself. But the other boy was bigger and stronger and he got through Greg's defences more than Greg did his, and that's what it's about.

I was sorry he didn't win the cup, but Greg weren't bothered. He got a silver medal and, more important in boxing, he got himself noticed. There were a lot of old pros in the crowd for the finals and I know – because they told me after – they thought young Greg Harris was a boy to watch. It wouldn't of surprised me if he weren't sent an invitation to join a top-notch club where he would get much better instruction than what I could ever give him.

Soon after the tournament, school started. It'd been a good summer. We'd had some laughs. The boys had done well at the tournament, England had beat the Aussies, and the boys hadn't got into too much mischief. But we was all glad they was off the street and back in school. One or two of the dads stopped me and said so, and some even bunged me summat – smokes or a bottle of summat, to show their 'preciation. I'd done a good job, they said. They thanked me. I can't say as I've done many things in my life what people came up to me afterwards and thanked me for.

I was happy as Larry, I can tell you. When I think of the geezers I'd been in with before I got weighed off for a lagging, the strip clubs in Soho, the whores and the gangs, I reckoned I was dead lucky. I'd been a whisker away from falling in with some dangerous people. Real villains. When I say villains, I'm talking about geezers who carried shooters. I'm talking about the south London heavy mob who blagged banks. I'm not talking about fucking little pimps who ran tarts. Now here I was, doing a proper job of work that brought home the bacon and weren't fucking navvying on a site. I weren't throwing drunks out of a club. I weren't banged up in choky for trying to top some poor cunt. The boys' dads – ex-Army, Royal or merchant navy, mostly – came up to me in the street and said, *You done a good job with our boys, Arthur. Thanks.* Things like that. Well, I was dead chuffed.

After the War there was too many blokes come back to Civvy Street knowing more than was good for them about how to top a bloke. I was dead lucky – but it was a points decision.

School started. The football season again. The weather turned shitty. After the hot summer we'd had it pissed down. I took a week's holiday myself, most of it I spent reading the *Daily Mirror* in the pie and mash on Jamaica Road, or changing the carburettor on my BSA in the club garage while the rain banged on the roof. The club closed for a week. I went to the dogs at Haringey once and lost more than I should of. If I'd been on the ball I'd of seen the writing on the wall then: my run of luck had broke.

I've often thought over what happened next. I honestly don't think I could of done nothing different. Nothing that could of stopped it. It was too late. In the War it was often like that. Some dozy cunts miles away from the front would cook up some fucking whizzo plan. The artillery would go into action at the same time and when they'd smashed up Jerry's tanks, our tanks would break cover in front of the infantry. Only it never happened according to plan. Our artillery would be off target by miles and our tanks would be hit shitless by the camouflaged 88s, and our own fucking ATs wouldn't arrive on time and the men would have to try and take the position against fucking armour with fucking bayonets. If you weren't there you couldn't believe the fucking clobbering we took. The officers on the ground could see the cock-up coming, but they couldn't do fuck all about it. Once it started, they couldn't call it off.

They knew they was fucked. They had to tell their men to fix bayonets and advance – and advance them fucking selves – when the dozy cunts miles away from the line told them to. They and their men did an' all, knowing the show was going to be a fucking cock-up. Well, it was like that.

Young Harris come into the gym one afternoon – I hadn't seen him around for a while – to do some training. I was pleased to see he was kitted out in his shorts and vest and gloves but he didn't say nothing. Come right up to me and when he was standing in front of me he didn't take his eyes off me – it was a trick I taught him – and he hooked a right-arm punch into my solar. It was a well-aimed punch and I bloody near went down. The little bleeder had taped a strip of lead or something on to his knuckles, inside his glove, and he hurt me. While I was doubled over, coughing, he caught me again, this time on my left temple. He had me off balance and he come in quick for a third punch which clipped my right cheekbone. He got in three good punches before I came to and when he come at me again, I gave him a couple of short jabs around the head, not all that hard. I was shouting at him. He was crying now but it weren't my punches made him blub. That didn't stop him, though, and he came in again, ducking and diving like he could do. I went to belt him on his upper forearm, I mean really hard to make it dead, but he read what I was doing, stepped back and came in like a snake and landed one on my lip, cut it and there was my own fucking claret all over the shop. Well, I'd had enough. I banged his arms down and cracked him a good 'un just below the jaw and his legs went and he went down like a wet kitbag.

It was all over. I lay him out and got his tongue free, and called 999 from the office. I must of hit him hard because he was still woozy when the ambulance came. They carried him out of the club on a stretcher, through a crowd of nosy women that had come to see what the excitement was about. They

224

took him to St Thomas's Hospital and kept him till his mum came to collect him. There weren't nothing wrong with him, but with a knockout to a youngster they don't take no chances.

The coppers came round in the evening and asked me some questions. Why had I knocked the boy out? What had he done? I told them he hadn't done nothing. He had come at me and there weren't nothing I could of done to stop him. My lip was up so they could see he had put one on me. They were all right. They didn't charge me or nothing. The boy hadn't told them nothing. He didn't deny to them he had attacked me but didn't tell them why. I didn't know why neither, but I could of made a fucking good guess. I don't know how he found out about me and his mum but he had all right, I knew that. While he was away we might of got slack. I don't know. I wondered if he'd clocked us at it. He could of, I suppose. He never said nothing, though, if he did.

A couple of days later I came home and found my BSA smashed up. It had been hammered, I mean smashed with a hammer. There weren't a bit of it that weren't smashed. He knew how much I loved that bike. That got me really narked. I'd of killed him if I could of laid hands on the little sod.

After a week Mark came by and had a chat. He was dead sorry about what happened, he said. He couldn't understand it. From what he said I knew the boy had kept stum. He hadn't told his dad. Anyway, Mark was very sorry but he was going to have to ask me to work out my notice. He said it weren't his decision. There'd been a committee meeting and it had been voted unanimous, excepting for him, I had to go. Dawn was on the committee. I knew she must of wanted me out bad. I never saw her again hardly, not to talk to.

On the estate most people blamed the boy. They came up to me and said so. They said he was a juvenile delinquent and what he needed was a fucking good thrashing. They were all dead narked I was getting the old heave-ho. What happened had got in the local newspaper, a youth club boxing instructor had knocked a kid out cold, and a couple of days later I got a visit from some geezer at the ABA. He told me I couldn't work with boys in a ring no more, not until they had made an enquiry. They said my membership of the Association was suspended. I was put on a disciplinary. The tide had turned, I could see that.

I worked out my two weeks' notice but the club was closed all that time, so there weren't nothing for me to do except go down the pub and have a few beers. Some tart I knew in the Roxborough Arms found me a rented room in Walworth. I had a few bob put by in the post office, but that weren't going to last long if I didn't get another job soon. Mark helped me move my stuff in the club van. He was decent about it even then, and I was glad he never found out. He kept saying how sorry he was it had happened and I had to go. He still couldn't understand what had got into Greg. I had a pretty good idea. Dawn must of an' all. He knew. We all knew, excepting for Mark. Mark felt sorry for me and I felt sorry for him. But the boy never grassed on me. It were something between him and me. Mark never found out I'd been having it off regular with his wife because his boy never told him. Unless his wife did, and I can't see her doing that. I have to thank Greg for that.

To Greg, *I* was the one who had acted like a cunt. I had let the side down. The Sergeant who drilled into the boys that you never pissed on your mates had done a dirty on him. I'd hit him below the belt and he hated my guts because of that. I can't say I blamed him neither. From his point of view I was a right cunt.

Not that you fucking care! Oi! I'm talking to you, you toe-rag! Wake up, you miserable little tosser. Get that fucking gob of yours open! It's all a shithead like you's fucking good for!

That's right. That's more like it. That's a good boy.

LIZ BRODIE

Friday   31 March 1950

After the doubts I had entertained on the journey – and then
the mix-up of my baggage at Crewe – I had become quite
dispirited. A doltish brake porter refused to unload my trunk
because it was not on his list, even though it was quite clearly
labelled. The guard was about to blow his whistle for the train
to leave! I put my foot down, and eventually the trunk was
transferred on to the Plymouth train. I couldn't help
wondering whether the two circumstances – the confusion
on the platform and my own inner uncertainty – were not
allied. Was I meant to miss my connection? Whenever I step
out of my routine I have the sensation that what happens to
me is not so much a consequence of my actions or conduct,
than a description of my state of mind. External events are
metaphors for my inner life. The more probable explanation,
I suspect, is that I read too many nineteenth-century
novels.

   I had to change again at Exeter St David's. The branch line

followed the serpentine estuary as far as Exmouth, where the sea jumped into view and my spirits revived. The loveliness of the countryside confirmed me in my decision to come here and I knew that my earlier doubts were unfounded. Dawlish, Teignmouth, then – as if to tease me – the train puffed inland, arriving at Torquay after skirting the Teign estuary via Newton Abbot.

I was met at the station by a tiny, grey-haired woman in a grey uniform, Sister Cleary, and a black limousine driven by George, who is the factotum here. We drove a short distance up from Torquay, past the golf course, to a large ugly greystone building on the cliff road with a superb view across Babbacombe Bay. I was thrilled to bits. The blue of the sea with the afternoon sun shining on it filled my heart with joy. I immediately wanted to get my bathing suit out and run down to the beach and jump in, but I forced myself to remember my reason for coming here and I meekly followed Sister Cleary into the house.

Cliff House is large and rambling, an L-shape on its side, the refectory comprising the length of the L and the playroom the foot. French windows open on to the garden which is a grass play area. Sleeping quarters, the dormitories, are at the front of the building, and the staff rooms are at the rear on the second floor.

I could write much more, but I must not get carried away. I must try to sleep. My room, although small, is adequate. I gather the size of the sleeping quarters of staff members is in proportion to their length of service. That seems as fair a way of apportioning them as any other.

Sister Cleary is a mouse. Grey, gentle and of a timid disposition.

Sister Hiller, the senior officer, greeted me when I arrived and showed me to my room. She has requested a formal induction meeting with me tomorrow.

George is not, as I had first thought, a deaf mute – merely chronically taciturn.

I take up my duties on Monday.

Walk worthy in the vocation wherewith ye are called!

Saturday   1 April 1950

Today the children buzzed around me, sniffing and touching me, clambering over me like small animals. They are such dears. Their ages range from four to twelve. In their homes for motherless children, the Church Army permits siblings to remain together in the same establishment. Upon the boys' reaching thirteen, however, they are separated. The boys are moved to all-boy homes. This does seem a bit harsh to me.

My interview with Sister Hiller went off all right and then she introduced me to the rest of the staff. She is a very upright, neat woman of about fifty – not tall but with a spry, Montgomeryish air. Her features are not those of someone who is accustomed to smiling often, and so when she suddenly does smile, it's so much of a shock you want her to stop. She asked me why I had chosen to work with children. I was stumped for a reply. I wasn't prepared for another interview for the post. She might just as well have asked me why I wear spectacles. I ended up saying that I had trained in nursery care at the Church Army centre in Chester and I had liked the people I had worked with. She nodded at my reply but I got the feeling my answer fell short of satisfying her. Perhaps it did, but we had only just met. These things take time. She assigned 'Doyle' to show me round. To Doyle she referred to me as 'Brodie'. Indeed, all the younger staff are addressed by their surnames.

Mary Doyle is a Northern Irish lass with a delightful brogue.

231

The children adore her. There are forty of these resident at the moment, and every one of them wanted to touch me and hold my hand. Later, Mary gave me a piece of advice.

'You have to learn to parcel yourself out in equal parts, otherwise there will be fights. It's a horrible thing to say, but they are like hungry animals. They don't know how to share a person's affections with someone else. Each child wants you all to himself. There isn't enough of you to go round. You have to be fair.'

Sunday   2 April 1950

Before breakfast I took in my uniform which was rather too ample around the hips for my figure. It is a grey cotton tunic-dress with a broad maroon belt. I have grey wool ankle socks and a grey cardigan on which I wear a silver brooch, a sword in the shape of a crucifix – or is it a crucifix in the shape of a sword? I felt very proud when I put it on. I have also been issued with an ugly grey broad-brimmed hat.

The children assembled in a huge crocodile down the length of the garden path and I accompanied the troop on the short walk to church. The sermon was on the proposition that a little bit of yeast leavens the whole loaf, which I like to think was appropriate. I fancy I saw myself as the little bit of yeast in question. Was that terribly vainglorious of me?

After tea, I walked out of the grounds along the golf-course road. What a gorgeous expanse of blue water as far as the eye can see! The sweep of Babbacombe Bay is breathtaking. I stood for half an hour on the cliff path at the edge of the golf course, watching the silent, distant white horses, and gave thanks to God for having placed me in a spot so charmingly airy. I prayed that He would give me strength to do my work well.

My first day!

I was up at seven and I have hardly sat down once! It's not like being at work, with set hours and time off. We are one big family and you are expected to work around the clock like a woman in any family. There are quiet moments – a lot of the children attend the local primary school so they are out most of the day – and the littler ones lie on their beds in the afternoon. Still, with so many children to get up and wash and dress, cook for and give breakfast to . . . The list never ends until the children are asleep, and by then you are too exhausted even to listen to the wireless. We spend our time shepherding the children from one stage in the routine to another. The silly things prefer to run around and play and dawdle when that may not be what the routine requires them to do.

I have had to learn so many names quickly – James, Sarah, Anne, Nicholas, Paul, Colin, Amy . . . I am glad that I have been assigned to the smaller children who are very affectionate and not so obstreperous. There are twelve of these in the Blue Room, which is more of a dormitory than a room. Twelve high iron cots on the polished parquet floor. Twelve children who will go to bed without the kiss of a mother or a story read to them by a father. All they have is Sister Slater and Sister Brodie. Poor mites!

Sister Slater is tall and slim with a profile reminiscent of Charles de Gaulle. I am to work with her and Sister Rackham, who is short and round. She is the cook, and I am to help her out sometimes. She told me I was to call her Alice.

There are set ways of doing things here. That goes for the staff as much as for the children. I was helping Sister Slater settle the children this evening, tucking them into their cots, calming them down in the semi-darkness. As I did I kissed each child goodnight. It seemed to me the natural thing to do. Later, Sister S. suggested that this was perhaps not such a good idea. I asked her why on earth not. I found the reasoning of her reply difficult to follow, but I think she wanted to say that if I allowed myself to get too close to the children, they would be able to use that against me later. They would be able to manipulate me, which might create discipline problems. I was a bit nonplussed. I wanted to ask her who was going to kiss the children if we didn't. Were they to grow up without kisses and cuddles? But I didn't.

In every outward respect the children are like any other children, boisterous and eager for affection to the point of plain naughtiness. As you get to know them, however, there are tell-tale signs that they are not ordinary. This one is incontinent, that one prone to tantrums, another is violent, another withdrawn and listless. Several are epileptic. But every one of them wants me to be their special friend.

Thursday   20 April 1950

A warm, blousy day. Large white cumuluses – do I mean cumuli? – billowed across the sky. What a fine spring we are having this year.

In the afternoon I accompanied Alice on her weekly visit to the shops to order provisions. It was such a warm day that we walked down, and so I saw a bit of Torquay. It was fun. Alice calls me 'pet' and puts her arm around me and says she's going to have to fatten me up. We are already friends.

Annie Get Your Gun with Doris Day is showing at the Roxy.
I shouldn't mind seeing that.

Letter from Aunt Vera.

Friday   21 April 1950

My day off. Walked to Torquay and bought an inch to the
mile Ordnance Survey map and joined the library, but didn't
get anything out. I went down to the harbour and watched
the fishermen tending their boats and nets. I have always enjoyed
watching men handle their gear and tackle. I think it is their
repose I envy.

I finished *Cranford* and wrote a letter to Aunt Vera, who is
grumpy on account of her hip.

Sunday   23 April 1950

Here at Cliff House the sabbath is celebrated – perhaps not
quite the best word – with much solemnity and seriousness.
From the moment the children wake up until they go to sleep
they are urged to remember that Sunday is the Lord's Day.
No running is permitted in the house. Voices may not be
raised. All boisterous behaviour is frowned upon. They are
ushered from one place of worship to another. Viz:

8.30–8.35	Chapel
10.30–12.00	Church
2.30–4.00	Sunday School
6.00–6.30	Chapel
Bedtime	Prayers

I can't help feeling that this is an arduous regime for such tots — to say nothing of the staff. We have to polish shoes and spruce up our charges in ironed clothes for the church service, which we must remove as soon as we return for lunch. The children's notion of Our Lord must surely be of a very strict headmaster in whose presence they must Keep Still and Be Very Quiet. I noticed in church when a boy of eight, Simon, was whispering to his neighbour, Sister Hiller administered a sharp rap on his temple with the clenched knuckle of her forefinger. I was shocked. As I watched the silent tears roll down Simon's face, I wanted to take him in my arms.

My own belief is that the path to Our Lord need not be made so forbidding for such little souls. They do not need to fear God but to love Him. I refuse to believe that their misdemeanours are, as they are frequently reminded, recorded in heaven, which they will be punished for at some unspecified date in the future. The Kingdom of Christ is not a harsh penance!

I sometimes wonder whether the emphasis on chastisement and the virtues of cleanliness, obedience and punctuality which the Victorian Church promulgated is compatible with Jesus' teaching. There is an unhealthy closeness between C of E virtues and those of the Conservative Party.

But the sermon was beautiful! The young vicar officiating at St Jude's has a very engaging manner. He smiles a great deal and is quite mischievous with his congregation. He took as his text the verses in Matthew when Jesus talks on the Mount of Olives: *Consider the lilies of the field, how they grow; they toil not, neither do they spin.* These are such beautiful, dangerous words, and how I love them! It is always the outward form of religion that Jesus castigates, not the quiet, inner yearning for Him. *When thou prayest, enter into thy closet, and when thou has shut thy door, pray to thy Father which is in secret.* He was very amusing on his text. At one point I nearly laughed out loud!

I was thrilled to have my own feelings about these words confirmed by a vicar of Christ.

I was introduced to the Reverend Richard Raleigh after the service. He asked me if by chance I sang. When I told him I had done my grade five in the choir at Chester he was delighted, and invited me there and then to join the church choir. I said I would be very happy to, and he promised to speak to Sister Hiller and get her permission. His open-hearted and compassionate manner is a contrast to the strict sabbath regime at Cliff House.

Monday   24 April 1950

Letter from Major Willmot-Smythe officially confirming my appointment and wishing me luck in my chosen vocation. When I met him at the HQ in London he looked like a real old soldier in his uniform.

Tuesday   2 May 1950

I was seated on the bench in the garden with my mid-morning cup of tea, keeping an eye on the little ones. I was going to say I was on duty, but this doesn't mean anything here as staff are on duty all day. One of the younger boys, Gregory, brought me a pair of snails he had found. The snails were clasped together in what I can only call an embrace. We watched them on the bench for several minutes. A tiny white filament was lodged in the slime of one of them, on its route to the other. Gregory wanted to know what it was and what they were doing. From what I was able to remember of my biology lessons, snails are hermaphroditic gastropods. Their stomach is in their foot. One of the snails in its male cycle was in the act of passing a small package of sperm to the other snail, in its female cycle. Since the boy was showing a healthy curiosity in the world around him, I did my best to describe the process to him, leaving out the hermaphrodite bit, which seemed to complicate the explanation unnecessarily.

After a moment the two snails disentwined themselves and we raced them along the bench.

I was happy to have the opportunity of using my biology. It was always one of my favourite subjects. I'm sure I could still draw a cross-section of the frog and the spirogyra and the human reproductive system as well as I did in the matriculation exam – the vas deferens, the oviduct, the glans penis – although my understanding of the process itself is likely to remain academic for the foreseeable future. Still, I *am* a female of the species. I am not ashamed of my body. Whatever takes place in my physiology is natural and – because it is God's work – beautiful.

I can't pretend I am not conscious when men are looking at me in that way – and there was that awful young man in Chester who got me hot under the collar! Until I have met the man I shall give myself to and – if it is to be God's will – we have consecrated ourselves to each other in holy matrimony, how male and female humans reproduce will remain a model answer to a matric examination question for Liz Brodie, along with that of the snail and the frog and spirogyra.

Wednesday   3 May 1950

After tea this evening we had great fun with fire drill. There is a fire chute attached to the rear of the building, access to which is through a hatch in Sister Slater's bedroom, two rooms along from my own. The children thought it was terrific fun, sliding down on mats cut out of old carpet into the arms of Mary Doyle, and running around to the back door of the house and up the stairs and along the corridor to Sister Slater's room for another go. It was as good as a fairground. I loved hearing the children's voices squealing and hooting around the building.

Mary, calling up from the bottom of the chute, persuaded me to have a go myself. I must confess I was longing to try, so I didn't need much encouragement. I crawled into the chute and whizzed down, bowling Mary over. The two of us ended up in a ball on the floor, legs a-tangle, laughing fit to cry. The children thought our turn was very funny and tried to get us to repeat it. We declined. Apart from anything else, my glasses had flown off when I hit the coconut matting and one of us had rolled on top of them and crushed them.

Sister Hiller, drawn to the commotion, appeared round the corner of the house. Mary and I felt a bit sheepish. She didn't say anything to us, but even without my glasses I could see how she was looking at us. We felt as if we were two of the children and we had a job holding down the giggles. Being naughty is such delicious fun!

The bore is I have to use my spare glasses now, which are years old and are not right for my eyes any more, and one arm is held in place with a paper clip. When I mentioned this to Sister Slater she suggested I make an appointment with the optician in Torquay. At least I won't have to pay for them on the National Health.

Mary and I could not look at each other all evening in case we got a fit of the giggles again. I do love Mary so. She is a sweet, simple girl without a malicious bone in her body. She hasn't been to grammar school, and is happy to polish floors and wash clothes singing 'Lead Us Heavenly Father, Lead Us' while she does. She has the simplicity of faith that Jesus urged upon all of us. *Except ye be converted, and become as little children, ye shall not enter into the kingdom of heaven.*

239

Do we prize learning too highly? I know at school when my teachers wanted me to apply for a place at university I gave the option serious consideration. I decided not to apply because I was too impatient to serve God. I just wanted to get out into the world and do something useful. I have to admit now that I harbour a secret regret that I did not apply. I have a longing for books and essays, poetry and fine talk. Playing the fool with Mary is good for me. She brings me back down to earth and confirms me in my belief that God loves a joyful giver.

Thursday   4 May 1950

After school Gregory brought me two blue halves of a robin's egg. He took me to the spot at the end of the garden where he had found them and we peered together up into the tangled branches of the may tree, which is really a kind of thorn, but we couldn't see the nest. We could hear the robin singing his heart out, though. Gregory wanted to know why birds sang to each other. I said they did that to tell other robins to keep out of their patch. Also, when the male sang to the female, he was telling her 'I'm best! Choose *me*!'

He said: 'What do the baby robins do when they grow up?'

'They learn to fly and then they leave the nest and start a family of their own.'

'Don't they stay with their mum and dad?'

'Never. The mother bird pushes them out of the nest.'

'My mum and dad are dead.'

He passed on this piece of information without any emotion.

'Are they? So are mine. We're the same.'

'Was yours killed in the War?'

'Sort of.'

In the secluded corner of the garden under the may tree, I

reached for the boy and drew him to me. He laid his head
against my breast and I hugged him. He held on to me, very still.

'I love you, Brodie,' he said into my tunic.

'I love you too, Gregory,' I said.

Friday   12 May 1950

I woke up feeling moody. Sad and a bit lonely – not exactly
sad, more 'beset by doubts', and not lonely either, more
alone. My normal cheerfulness seemed to have deserted me.
At least it was my day off, so I lay in bed watching the
sunlight dapple the ceiling, listening to the children stirring
along the corridor and the squeak of the composition soles
of my colleagues toing and froing past my door. Outside my
window a thrush in the pear tree was singing his heart out.

My original plan had been to walk into Torquay, do some
shopping and explore. I had made a list of items I needed to
buy. (I have a horror of running out of Tampax, since I am
not certain I could turn to any of the women here, not even
Mary, if I suddenly needed one. I don't know whether or not
they would disapprove.) Instead I dug out my new OS map
and plotted a completely different day. I filled a knapsack with
stuff I might need and persuaded Alice to make me some
sandwiches, and she let me take a bottle of lemonade. While
the children were at breakfast I stole out of the house and left
by the back gate – which I had to ask George to open for me.

I walked west along the cliff, past the golf course for about
a mile, until I came to the narrow opening in the trees I was
looking for. Cars don't often use this road; it is so steep and
winding. Along this part of the coast the reddish seaward
cliffs are thickly wooded and as you descend, the trees make
a canopy overhead. The light is almost completely shut out.
Without warning you are in a cool, damp, moss-smelling wood

in which there are bluebells, dog violets and primroses. Deep inside the wood I left the path – although there was no one else abroad – and quickly took off my uniform and slipped into an old cotton skirt and jumper I had brought. I exchanged my flat-heeled shoes for a stouter pair. I felt like a naughty schoolgirl doing this, which soon shook off the doldrums.

At the foot of the cliff I emerged into the sunlight with a whoop of joy, kicked off my shoes and ran across the white, ashy shingle.

The beach was deserted, even though the weather was so fine. There wasn't a cloud in the sky. If you half closed your eyes so that the deciduous English trees looked like tropical palms, the red rock cliff-side could have been Crusoe's island, Tobago or the Bahamas. The red rock met the white sand; the sand met the sea and the sea met the sky. I was an upright among horizontals! The world was clear-cut and I alone was different, confused and beset by doubts. But no longer sad nor lonely, because I knew that Jesus was watching me.

I tucked my skirt into my knickers as I used to do at school and explored the rocks and the pools at the crescent of the cove at Little Tor Point, prodding the kelp and stirring up the water with a stick in search of interesting marine life. Considering the sandstone marl of the area I thought I might find some fossils, but I didn't. After an hour of this my eyes became accustomed to the chiaroscuro of sea-wet pebbles, waving water, algae and creatures of the seashore: hermit crabs like rocks, rocks like whelk shells, barnacled mussels, pretty sea anemones and mermaids' purses, delicate starfish. Here were my school biology lessons come to life.

I was so happy just prodding about. This was my world – oystered and ambiguous. I was reminded of the ever-changing ambiguities of light and marbled textures celebrated in the poems of Gerard Manley Hopkins: *All things counter, original, spare, strange;/Whatever is fickle, freckled (who knows how?)* The rich diversity of life on the margin between land and sea – what G. M. H. called *the bole, the burling roundness of earth* – was just as true of the inner life as well. There is no shame in seeking out the complex and the subtle in preference to the Unalterable. *Christ plays in ten thousand places.* The soul is alloyed, not pure. My Jesus is a lover of the human.

> *Glory be to God for dappled things –*
> *For skies of couple-colour as a brinded cow . . .*

Then I cartwheeled across the sand and sang snatches from *Ancient and Modern*. When I became hot, I changed into my swimsuit and swimming cap and ran into the sea.

Lord, it was cold! But what utter bliss! I swam far out into the bay and, looking back towards the sweep of Babbacombe, I fancied I could see Cliff House perched upon the horizon. Without my spectacles I couldn't be certain.

After my swim I sat in my towel on a rock and warmed myself up in the sun, watching shags skim the surface of the Bay while I wolfed my sandwiches and drank my lemonade. I dressed and – walking, leaping and praising God – I retraced my steps up the narrow path into the wood. But this was not Dante's wood. There was no leopard or unicorn to confront me. I changed back into my grey tunic dress and returned to the main road. I entered the house by the front door, my heart filled with love and faith, happy and tired – and hungry. Alice could not believe her eyes when she saw the quantity of fish pie I put away this evening!

Sunday   14 May 1950

St Jude's is a very old local parish church. It was here long before the Victorian suburbs of Torquay engulfed the village of Babbacombe. It has Saxon walls and a beautiful twelfth-century font. The church was hit by a bomb during the War and the tower is in a heartbreaking state, although work is in hand to make good the damage. It seems incredible to me that such a short time ago, men climbed into huge planes and flew across the sea in order to drop bombs on people they didn't know, one of which landed on this ancient village church. You can understand why Jesus wept. If the parishioners who were first baptized in the font nearly a thousand years ago had witnessed the attack, they would have believed they were witnessing Armageddon. For their descendants it is just a piece of recent history they would prefer to forget.

Richard, who had changed into an old rugby shirt and cotton trousers, showed me round the old building in the afternoon while the little ones were in the hall with the Sunday School teacher, sticking coloured picture stamps of scenes from the New Testament into their books. He is still eager for me to join the choir, of which he has great expectations. He showed me the piece he wants to start rehearsing for Ascension: *A Hymn to the Virgin*, a four-part harmony for solo voices and choir by Benjamin Britten. It is certainly a bold piece of programming. He stuck the music on to the old Brentwood and played it through for me. It was very beautiful and I didn't need much prompting to have a go at it, and I muddled through the soprano line. I did it much better the second time though. He took the tenor line himself. I think he was impressed by my sight-reading. I'm not just a pretty face!

It's not up to me whether I join the choir, of course. That will depend on whether Sister Hiller is prepared to release me. Richard is confident on that point. He seems to think he has her eating out of his hand.

Perhaps he has. I don't know. He has that English public-school charm which I usually find insufferable in most men, but in Richard it is mitigated by a gentleness and a wicked sense of humour.

If he keeps a diary – which I'm certain he doesn't, as it is a sure sign of immaturity – he is probably jotting down some equally patronizing observations about myself.

Tuesday   16 May 1950

This morning at breakfast a rather difficult situation arose. I was serving out porridge from the hatch. Alice was in the kitchen, dolloping it into bowls as fast as I could dish them out. I was so preoccupied with the task I was probably the last person to notice anything was amiss. I was in mid-stride when Sister Hiller suddenly addressed the children in her shrill, no-nonsense voice. I froze. I only noticed then that none of the children was eating. They were making the groaning sounds of a person dying from poison. A sort of unofficial down tools was taking place.

'There is nothing wrong with the porridge!' Sister Hiller insisted. She moved from table to table like an officer urging on reluctant troops.

'Eat it up. Come on!'

One or two of the smaller children lifted their spoons to their mouths – but they were unable to swallow. I poked a finger into a bowl and tasted it myself. Urgh! It *was* revolting. Alice must have used milk that was off. I thought the children were quite right to refuse to eat the slop. Sister H., equally, was not going to give way. I couldn't believe what I was seeing: a refusal on the part of the children to obey the senior officer. An act of mutiny. I watched with bated breath to see how the situation was going to be resolved.

The children weren't going to give way.

'There is nothing the matter with it!' Sister H. asserted.

Eventually she tasted it herself.

'It's perfectly good,' she said.

Whatever she thought privately, I could see she was not going to back down. She was white with fury. Taking hold of the nearest boy, she gripped his hand and lifted a spoonful of porridge into his mouth. The boy resisted, clamping shut his jaws, and the porridge spilled on to the table, at which she slapped his face, quite hard, and then pushed the spoon into his mouth. The boy chewed while tears ran down his cheeks into his mouth. I was horrified. The conflict seemed so pointless. If it had a point, it was to uphold the principle of obedience to the authority of the senior officer. The matter of the porridge, whether or not it was fit to eat, was of no consequence.

She moved on to the next boy, my friend Gregory. She attempted to force his spoon into his mouth but he wasn't having any of it. He mumbled something which I could not hear. Sister H. yanked him out of his chair by his hair and stood him on it. Then she slapped his bare calf several times. She ordered him into the corner where he stood crying quietly, as fingermarks reddened on his left leg.

I had had enough. I walked the length of the refectory with the intention of leaving. I refused to bear witness to such violence. I had not reached halfway down the length of the hall before the senior officer called after me.

'We have not finished breakfast, Sister Brodie.'

I stopped dead and turned to face her. I was very angry, but I am glad to say I had the presence of mind to remain professional. It was not easy.

'The children are going to be late for school,' I said.

She glanced down at her watch, clapped her hands and dismissed the children.

Looking back, I realize I had given her the opportunity of ending the situation without backing down. Nevertheless I was disgusted with myself for not speaking out more decisively at the injustice.

Later in the morning – I was making the beds in the Blue Room – Sister Hiller, from the door, asked me to come and see her in her room as soon as I had finished the beds.

She wasn't angry any more – although I have to admit I was. Fortunately she did not ask me for my views on the disagreeable events at breakfast. She gave me a talk, the gist of which was that these children were either the offspring of parents who had been killed in the War, or they were the unwanted issue of criminals, thieves and prostitutes, and when they left Cliff House they would need to understand the difference between right and wrong, to obey the law and respect authority – otherwise they would end up like the men and women whose fornication had brought them into the world in the first place.

I could have argued with her analysis as well as her reasoning. All I said was: 'The porridge was disgusting. The milk was off.'

Sister Hiller gave one of her ghastly smiles.

'Rubbish! And even if it was, they'll eat a lot worse than that before they die!'

Wednesday   17 May 1950

I got Alice to wangle me on to her rota and spent the day in the kitchen, scouring porridge plates, polishing the cutlery and then peeling potatoes. It is real skivvying but I don't mind. I enjoy it. In the kitchen Alice is in charge. There is something reassuring about her and the place where she has authority. Although the kitchen is, at least geographically, at the centre of the house, it has the feel of being apart from it. Alice has her copy of the *Daily Mirror* on the table and she turns the wireless on when there is a job to do. This gives you a sense that there is a world outside Cliff House. A submarine has sunk in the Thames. Arsenal beat Liverpool in the Cup Final. George Orwell has died. The Government is getting us into another war.

It is, of course, Alice's personality which establishes the friendly atmosphere. The kitchen is her domain, and her bulk is a reassuring bulwark against the predominant thinness of the senior staff members. She has delivered and reads her *Daily Mirror* notwithstanding the scantily clad young woman in the cartoon that paper is notorious for. There is no question but that she will do what she wants to do. The kitchen is out of bounds to the children, so there is no danger of their coming into contact with reality. I'm beginning to sound cynical.

Alice is different. She is a good-natured Geordie hinny without any air of piety about her – and she loves the children. Of course, I am mindful of the obvious fact that she alone among us has had children of her own. Is it this which gives Alice her down-to-earth air and authority over the other members of staff, women for whom men are a dangerous mystery, if not an anathema? Her own life has been tragic. Her family were destroyed in the War: first her children in the Blitz, and then her husband in the merchant navy. We are her family now.

Alice looks after me. She talks freely about the family she has lost – and she lets me talk about mine. When I told her what happened to my dear father and mother she held me gently in her big arms while I had a little weep. She doesn't mind if I take ten minutes off to sit down and read her newspaper over a cup of tea. The only other member of staff who works with us is Mary Doyle – presumably because the younger women are thought more suitable for skivvying – so the three of us make a happy team. We have such a laugh, sometimes we have to close the door.

Whenever I am in the kitchen, chopping vegetables at the

table while Alice is at the cooker, stirring the pot, the overwhelming feeling I have is of safety. I don't have to think about what I am doing. Chopping vegetables, stirring the pot, never changed anything and require no great skill. It is a chore that has always been done – by women, mostly – between wars, death, affliction, conversation, work. I take heart that there is nothing in it to be understood. My doubts are calmed.

Thursday   25 May 1950

Gregory seems to have struck up a relationship with George – something of an achievement, considering nobody else can get a word out of him. I suspect that theirs is not the kind of friendship in which words play a large part. Perhaps a six-year-old boy and a sixty-year-old man have things in common. I am very pleased when I see them both pottering around in George's greenhouse. It is good for a boy to have a man to talk to and do things with. This afternoon he took my hand and dragged me over to show me what they had made together: a *snailarium*! Using one of George's glass seedling boxes – they had half filled the box with earth and plants and a number of snails. It made a perfect viewing chamber.

They also have a cardboard box with a muslin cover in which they keep little red chrysalises. I was pleased to see this interest in natural history, and the friendship between a small boy and an old man. George was unwilling to catch my eye, but I could tell that he was pleased too.

Friday   26 May 1950

I took the train from Torquay to Brixham to have my eyes

tested for my new spectacles. Any of the opticians in Torquay would have been adequate for the job but we have a five-year-old, Godfrey, who needs to be seen by a qualified optometrist, as he has recently undergone an operation at the Royal Infirmary at Exeter to correct his strabismus, which I think is another word for boss eyes. I didn't mind. I enjoyed the ride. I had put on a dress so as not to advertise to the world that we were different from anybody else.

The train followed the sweep of Torbay, taking in Paignton and Goodrington Sands, which is all very pretty. Brixham is delightful, a working fishing town with trawlers rubbing shoulders with the yachts and dinghies. (I know! Trawlers don't have shoulders!) I can't wait to return and explore the area more thoroughly.

Godfrey is a funny little chap, very fearful to be outside the environs of the home. With the pink patch over his National Health specs, he is anxious at the traffic and bustle of Brixham. He never let go of my hand. Nevertheless the optometrist's assistant kept him amused while I had my own examination.

The young man was very pleased with himself and made a great fuss of me. I have always enjoyed having my eyes tested, being the sole object of another person's close scrutiny. It's even better than having your hair cut. In the darkened room the youth placed the red and green lens in my hand, alternating from my left and right eye, all the time prattling about the Devon coast. Only when he mentioned that his father owned a skiff that was moored down in the marina, and invited me to see the magnificent view of the coast from the sea, did the penny drop. I don't often find myself alone in a darkened room with a member of the opposite sex! As I was in the hands of a professional I hadn't thought anything of it. I realized that from where he was standing, he had a magnificent view down the front of my dress! I disengaged my hand from his and extricated myself from the situation. What a novel place for a girl to have a pass made at her!

Godfrey and I had fish and chips in a little restaurant overlooking the marina. And very good they were too. No disrespect to Alice, whom I love dearly, but the food at the home is pretty unimaginatively prepared. It is as if the austerity of the War years has become a permanent fact of life. The habit of making a little go a long way that was urged upon the nation by Lord Woolton refuses to die. We have all become used to a dull diet.

I found a bookshop and treated myself to the handsome new Penguin edition of *Daniel Deronda*.

Petrol rationing ended today.

Sunday   28 May 1950

The crocodile of scrubbed necks and polished shoes and combed and brushed heads wound its way down the pavement to St Jude's at twenty-five minutes past ten – on the dot. Most of the children's Sunday clothing is new, having been purchased by local charities, the Rotarians or the Women's Institute, with the result that our children are always much better turned out than the local children. Wouldn't it present a truer picture of their situation, I ask myself, if our boys and girls were dressed in old hand-me-downs? Wouldn't that more accurately reflect their true situation in life? Our children seem to be acting a part, making a false statement about themselves: We are just the same as other children. Don't worry about us. We are clean, and cleanliness is next to godliness.

It was a beautiful service. The choir sang Howells's lovely *Ascension Cantata* and I longed to be up there to sing it with them. I know the work well because we studied it at Chester.

While Richard was trying to interest the congregation in

251

his interpretation of Jesus' words in Matthew: *Beware of false prophets, which come to you in sheep's clothing, but inwardly they are ravening wolves*, Gregory, who was sitting next to me, turned his hand to and fro in the multicoloured sunlight that was being refracted through the windows, fascinated by its beauty. Richard was very amusing, I thought, asking us to consider what Jesus might have meant by a 'false prophet'. He urged us to ask ourselves what the modern equivalent of Baal and Mammon might be. He suggested that respectability, what others think of us, might be a wolf in sheep's clothing. Fashion another. And advertising. He went so far as to hint that many religious rituals were humbug, reminding us how often Jesus had said that the outward form is only the raiment of virtue; it may fool the Pharisees, but it does not fool God.

Moreover when ye fast, be not, as the hypocrites, of a sad countenance: for they disfigure their faces, that they may appear unto men to fast.

This theme seems to be a hobby horse of his, for he often returns to it. He would have us believe that words are like clothes; they cloak the naked intention. Although I recognize the obvious Neoplatonism in this way of thinking, I am nevertheless intrigued. Since words are public property, and the meanings we give to them are private, we should rather distrust them than put our faith in them. If we were more alert to ambiguity, there might not be so many misunderstandings.

Richard seemed genuinely disappointed that I would not be bringing the children to Sunday School in the afternoon.

Tuesday   30 May 1950

I had a bizarre conversation with Sister Slater in the kitchen this morning. We were sitting across the table from each other, shelling peas from a paper sack into the mixing bowl between us. Alice had made us both a cup of tea.

Sister Slater is the oldest member of staff, not counting George, so she has the ear of Sister Hiller. Because of that, I can't help wondering whether she doesn't function as an unofficial NCO.

The popping of pea pods punctuated our conversation.

Apparently, Mr Headley, the headmaster of the primary school, has telephoned Sister Hiller with some disturbing information. It had been reported to him by a teacher that one of our boys, a six-year-old in Year Two, had expounded authoritatively to his class on the subject of how animals mate.

'Do you mean the sexual reproductive system?' I asked her.

Sister Slater gave a startled nod. I think even being present in a room when the word 'sexual' is uttered is difficult for her.

'Are we talking about animals in general,' I asked as innocently as I could, 'or mammals in particular?'

Pop!

'The headmaster was shocked. He couldn't think where the boy had got such information from.'

I deliberately pretended to be obtuse.

'How disgraceful!'

Pop!

'I hope she told him it should have come from *him*. Elementary animal biology is a necessary part of every boy's education. And of every girl's too, for that matter.'

I hoped that would take the wind out of her sails.

'No, Brodie! Quite the reverse! She *agreed* with him.'

'Really?' I said. 'How odd. I'm sure boys who don't know how babies are born do more damage to girls than those who do.'

She looked at me aghast. I had a job keeping a straight face.

'He's a bit young to know about *that*, don't you think? According to Mr Headley he used the word *sperm*!'

Alice and I exchanged glances but we quickly looked away from each other. Thank heavens Mary wasn't there! I didn't know whether to explode with laughter or fury. I bit my lip – with what I supposed Sister Slater took to be a sign of Great Concern.

'Which boy was it?' I asked her.

As soon as I spoke I realized that it was a mistake. She surely already had a good idea that I knew who we were talking about. I was convinced she was delivering a coded message to me from the senior officer, who would have told her. And who, by a not very difficult process of deduction, had guessed that it could only have been me.

'Gregory!'

I just looked at her.

'I really can't understand where he has picked up such filthy talk! It seems most unlikely that it could be one of the other boys attending the school.'

I took a deep breath.

'There is nothing filthy about sperm, Margaret. None of us would be here if there was. The Good Lord gave the boy a penis. I suppose He knew what He was doing when He did that.'

Her jaw dropped.

The insubordinate popping of pea pods had ceased.

I had used her Christian name for the first time. I don't know which shocked her more, that or my Augustinian theology. The way she looked at me, you would have thought I had just denied the transubstantiation of Our Lord. Alice leaned between us and picked up the bowl of shelled peas.

'That's plenty, my dears,' she said. Then: 'Brodie, pet, the groceries need to be checked into the larder.'

She shooed me out of the kitchen. And that was the end of our conversation, one in which much had been implied and much inferred, although not necessarily the same things.

I felt uncomfortable with myself afterwards. Neither of us had been honest with the other. Sister Slater had acted as a mouthpiece for another person. She had also not been entirely honest, giving me to understand that she did not know where the boy had obtained this forbidden knowledge. I had colluded in the dishonesty by not confessing outright that I had been the one who had introduced the 'filthy word' into the boy's innocent head.

It is very disagreeable to find yourself accused of conduct which you do not consider in the least bit reprehensible. Am I to confess to an act for which I do not feel the slightest guilt?

Paul spoke a lot of nonsense about the evils of sex, but Jesus never did.

Sunday   4 June 1950

On the way home from church Sandra soiled her knickers. She was walking ahead of me when Amanda drew my attention to the piece of faeces that was sliding down Sandra's leg. The poor child. I cleaned her up as best I could, but she was very distressed.

I was going to ask Richard during Sunday School what response he had got from Sister Hiller about my request to join the church choir. Before I could speak, he let me know in no uncertain terms what he thought about her decision to reject my request on the grounds that rehearsals would interfere with my duties. He was nonplussed, because it was not at all the response he had anticipated. He paced and fumed. I thought it was very amusing, because I was not in the least surprised. It is not unknown for a woman to sing alongside boys but it is, after all, more generally frowned upon. (On the grounds, I believe, that our presence pollutes their purity!) I had already convinced myself that, since I wanted to sing so much, it would be congruous with my position here that I should not be allowed to. I was sorry but not surprised. Jesus alone knows my heartbreak. My sacrifice is my gift, and He loves a cheerful giver.

I told Richard not to carry on so. I almost got cross with him. What on earth did he expect? The fact is, Richard is progressive even to consider me for his choir. She has not said so, but I suspect that the senior officer disapproves. You could say we had an argument. As soon as he realized how upset I was, however, he quickly engineered a change in our mood. He drew me to the piano and produced the music for the Britten piece. On this occasion, while I was singing, he gave me precise directions on breathing and articulation, and he knew what he was talking about. He was very strict when it came to tempo, as all good musicians are. We worked hard for half an hour, and I noticed sweat on his forehead when we decided to call it a day. He did look pleased!

As he rose, he accidentally placed his hand on top of mine. We were both aware that we were in physical contact with each other, but neither of us was prepared to acknowledge the fact. And then it was too late. It was a funny, tingling, dangerous moment.

For both of us, I think.

Monday   5 June 1950

Barely three months in post, and I am already one of the fixtures. I have got to know all of the children and I love them all, particularly the littler ones. I understand now why it is necessary to be quite firm with them. Persuading forty-two children to line up, wash and clean their teeth, all within the space of fifteen minutes, requires a degree of regimentation. Unfortunately there is not always a reciprocal disposition on the children's part to feel hungry or sleepy or to wake up at the same time as each other. But I refuse to shout at them or to invoke the threat of punishment, not to say damnation. My view is, if you can persuade your charges to cooperate with you, you have won half the battle. I take some quiet satisfaction from the fact that I have not had problems of discipline. Touch wood.

I am afraid I do have favourites, although I hope I do not practise favouritism. Among the girls, Mandy and Wendy are both sweet and helpful, doting on their own little families of dolls and bears. It is a bitter irony – mercifully one that will remain hidden from them – that both girls were dumped on the Church Army by mothers who did not share their maternal instincts. Among the boys, Robert and Simon and Andrew are dears. Gregory, of course, has taken a shine to me and sits near me at every opportunity. He will do anything I ask of him – and he can be one of the rougher boys when he wants to be. He loves an intelligent conversation and can ask subtle questions. He is a dear, warm-hearted boy.

Wednesday   7 June 1950

An overcast, blustery day. Out in the bay sails were running in front of a stiff breeze as the yachts huffed and yawed – or whatever it is they do. Mary says the summer season will soon be upon us. Soon there will be many more visitors. The model village will open, as indeed the cliff railway already has. I am conscious of the fact that the world outside the home goes about its business, as unknowing of us as the weather – men play golf, women walk with their children along the cliff road to shop in Torquay – while we remain inside a closed world criss-crossed with routine, guilt and fear. Freedom is on the other side of the garden wall that has broken bottle-glass

257

cemented into it, to keep the children in as much as intruders out. For the motherless children who live here, Cliff House is a place they may not leave, with rules they must obey. In some ways it conforms to a definition of a place of detention. It is hard for love and mercy to flourish where there is coercion.

For these boys and girls I am afraid there will always be a wall with broken glass bottles cemented on to it, albeit an invisible one, all through their lives.

Thursday   15 June 1950

Oh dear! A chain of events this afternoon showed up both the weakness of my way of controlling the children and, at the same time, the harshness of the regime that is administered by the rest of the staff.

As a treat, I had got down the dressing-up chest for the younger children. This always raises the temperature as the little ones step in and out of role, but it is such fun. We made a pirate ship of the big table in the nursery and there was a lot of bloodthirsty braggadocio. Perhaps I let it get out of hand. During the excitement Gregory forced Viola, whom I know he is fond of, to walk the plank. (Boys, I have noticed, are often most physically robust with the girls they like best.) The girl fell awkwardly and set up a piercing howl. I was in charge, so it was my job to deal with the situation. Normally I would have got the culprit together with the victim, extracted an apology and a hug from one and a gracious acceptance from the other. But first I wanted to make sure that Viola was not hurt. While I was inspecting her, Sister Hiller entered the nursery and took control.

She ordered Gregory and Viola and myself into the chapel, which is just along the corridor from the nursery. There, she extracted from me an account of the circumstances of the mishap. I was put in the position of having to betray Gregory in his presence, since there was no denying he had been a bit too boisterous. Fortunately Viola was not seriously hurt.

Sister Hiller asked Gregory if my account was correct. He nodded. Without further ado she seated herself on one of the prayer-chairs and pulled down Gregory's trousers, put him over her knee, slipped off one of his own plimsolls and beat him with it on his bare behind six times. Gregory burst into floods of tears and that set Viola off again. I left the chapel and went to my own room and burst into tears myself, certain that this humiliation of the boy had been intended as an object lesson to me in the preferred disciplinary practices of the home. That this punishment should have been administered in a place for devotion and the contemplation of Jesus' example made me see red. The senior officer was paying lip-service to Our Lord's injunction to forgiveness and compassion.

Blessed are the merciful: for they shall obtain mercy.

Blessed are the peacemakers: for they shall be called the children of God.

Friday   16 June 1950

Letter from Aunt Vera, who is still having trouble with her hip.

As it was my day off, I put on my raincoat and set out along the coastal path. I forgot to take my map. I had no provisions with me and no clear idea of where I was going. This, alas, seems to be true of my entire life at the moment. I felt a bit sorry for myself. The sky was grey and the sea was grey. Everything was grey, including me in my uniform. I let the wind blow my hair into a tangle and thought hard about things. After an hour or so of playing Merle Oberon to the gallery, I couldn't help laughing at myself.

I returned home, feeling much better.

Saturday   17 June 1950

After breakfast Sister Hiller produced a tray of wrapped chocolates. They had been donated for the children by a local confectionery company. The chocs were all different shapes and sizes: cars, animals, tools, etc., individually wrapped in shiny paper. All the children, after they had finished their breakfast, were told to line up and choose a chocolate. It was my job to hold the tray for them. I was amused to watch their reactions to this treat. Not surprisingly, they were all very excited.

Most of the chocolates were more or less the same size. There was one large gold medallion, however, three or four times larger than any of the other sweets. This presented an ethical conundrum to a small child – not by design, I hope. It is a measure of the sense of 'good form' which the home instils into the children that none of them chose the medallion, although they would not have been normal not to have wanted to. I assumed their reticence was out of fear of looking greedy in the eyes of Sister Hiller and their peers. When it came to Gregory's turn he couldn't make up his mind, and Sister H. had to hurry him along. He reached out and picked up the gold medallion. Good for you, I thought.

Later in the morning I came across Gregory skulking around the toilets, which are at the rear of the house. Usually he is pleased to see me, so when he showed no sign of being so I knew something was up. I asked him if he had enjoyed his chocolate and he burst into tears.

It took me a little while to coax out of him the whole story.

The other children, when they had Gregory alone, had tormented him for having taken the largest chocolate, kicking him and calling him horrible names. Gregory had run away. In shame he had flushed his chocolate down the toilet.

It's sad that the outwardly noble gesture the children had made in refusing the larger chocolate did not spring from any genuinely generous impulse on their part, but rather from a fear of censure. Their dishonesty had merely laid the seed for envy and anger later.

If our duty is to nurture in the children in our care a proper Christian conscience, to be generous and have consideration for others, can we be said to have succeeded if all we have done is to have instilled guilt and fear in place of love? Do even the most laudable ends ever justify such ignoble means?

Monday   26 June 1950

Half-term. The children are home all week! My God, what a prospect.

Tuesday   27 June 1950

Following a disagreement between two of the children, one of them – Gregory, who else? – ended up sleeping on the landing floor all night. The original quarrel was the sort of thing that happens at bedtime when the children are fractious. I thought Sister S. handled it very badly. Who knows what the boys were arguing about? These things are nearly always six of one, half a dozen of the other. Sister Slater chose to believe that one of the boys was more at fault than the other. She gave Gregory a sharp scolding. I thought she was being less than even-handed. Gregory was furious at the injustice, and he retaliated by hitting her where it hurt: 'I don't love Jesus! I love Satan!' he shouted at her. I did want to laugh! I was impressed by the boy's defiance. Sister S., unfortunately, did not see the funny side. She lost control of herself and dragged Gregory by his ear before Sister Hiller. His punishment – for blasphemy, I suppose – was to spend the night on the parquet landing floor with just a single blanket.

I dare say he will survive the ordeal. My concern is that things are going wrong for Gregory. Either his behaviour is deteriorating and he is acting in a delinquent manner, or else he is being too harshly punished – picked on, I would go so far as to say. Personally I never have any trouble with Gregory. Nor does George. He spends a lot of his free time in George's greenhouse, improving his snailarium and attending to his collection of chrysalises. I am worried that the senior staff do not see any good in the boy, only his defiance. I feel powerless.

Thursday   29 June 1950

The children woke up in a state of high expectation. They had been promised all week that as a treat, if it was fine today, we would be going to the beach – and today *was* fine! What excitement there was! From the moment they woke up it was like trying to get a cork back into a bottle of champagne! I was excited myself. Alice had prepared packed lunches and orange squash for forty-five! These – along with buckets and spades and other necessary articles – George would ferry down to the beach while the rest of us followed on foot. At an agreed time he would return and ferry the littler ones back up the cliff road, making several trips if necessary, while the rest of us came back on shanks's pony. Sister H., who remained behind, reminded me twice not to forget to take my swimming costume. As if I would! It had not crossed my mind until that moment that my Life Savers' Association gold medal had been the qualification that had secured for me the post I hold!

Babbacombe beach was crowded with holidaymakers. The arrival of our troop – in double file, singing in unison:

> Onward, Christian soldiers,
>   Marching as to war,
> With the cross of Jesus,
>   Going on before.

– caused something of a stir. The silver and maroon flag of the Church Army was carried aloft and then planted in the sand, staking out our claim to a separate identity.

I already had my costume on under my dress in order to be able to make a quick change. This was fortunate because children were soon running headlong into the water, even though hardly any of them can swim a stroke! I spent my time fishing them out and tossing them, spluttering, on to the beach, where Mary showed them how to make sandcastles. It was glorious fun!

While I was in the water playing with the children, a man's head, shoulders and torso burst out of the sea in front of me. It took me a moment to recognize who they belonged to. I had never seen a minister of the Church without a shirt on before. I must say, it was a bit of a shock. Richard had got wind of our little outing and had decided to join us off his own bat. His presence was very welcome because he larked about in the water with the children, throwing the swimmers into the waves as if they were sacks of potatoes, which, of course, they loved. He was wonderful with them, and it brought home to me what these children, the boys particularly, are missing more than anything: a strong and loving father. He is very fit. It is obvious how he comes to be in possession of those old rugby shirts he likes to wear when he's not officiating.

It's a curious thing about swimwear, when you come to think about it, how the context of the swimming pool or the beach sanctions a dramatic reduction in the outer garments men and women may be allowed to wear. What would be grossly inappropriate in another context is, under these circumstances, perfectly acceptable. My own costume is a faded blue Jantzen which I have had for years now. But I would be lying if I said I was unaware that it possessed a décolletage. You could hardly call me flat-chested!

Richard, who was in very high spirits, tried his best not to ogle, but I couldn't help observing that his attention was drawn towards the neckline of my costume, and once or twice in our horseplay I – and he – pretended not to notice when my breasts accidentally brushed against his bare skin. It was a terrifically exciting sensation when this happened, making my flesh tingle in all the extremities of my body. I have never felt anything like it. On several occasions I suppose I might have taken greater pains to prevent that area of my anatomy from coming into contact with his, if I had wanted to.

I don't just *think* he likes me. I know he does. I have been aware, ever since I was seventeen, that I am attractive to men because I have had to deal with the occasional advance, or even quite crude pass. This is the first time in my life, however, that I have felt at all inclined to reciprocate a man's interest in me. I am pleased that Richard is intrigued by my breasts. I know, though, that it is not just those bits of me he would like to see more of. He likes *me*, who I *am*. I have always believed that God in His own sweet time would steer me towards a good and devout man. I continue to pray that this will be so.

We all traipsed back across the sand as the teatime hour approached, more of a ragamuffin army than when we had arrived, hot and tired and happy. What a splendid day it had been! George ferried some of the littler ones back to the house in the car while the rest of us climbed the steep cliff road. Richard took Amy on his shoulders and Gregory walked between us, holding my hand and cleverly interesting Richard in his collection of shells and marine objects.

Richard – who had changed into a blue and white striped rugby shirt, faded blue shorts and old white plimsolls – looked perfectly at ease with himself, affable and unaffected and unpompous.

We said goodbye to each other at the gate. I wanted him to touch me again, even though I knew that would have been impossible. I think he knew what I wanted.

I have caught the sun. I have a white costume mark. Pink arms and legs and neck. I stood before the mirror in the bathroom and wondered what Richard would think, if he could only see me now!

Friday   30 June 1950

Much of the day spent in a happy daze after yesterday's fun. There are a lot of pink faces among us, including my own. Sister Hiller has not said anything on the subject, but I sense a rebuke to the staff responsible in her order that the children must not go out into the sun today, which in effect means they may not use the garden. We have had to try and persuade them to stay inside and lie down, when all they want to do is go out and run around and play. They don't understand, poor things. I can't say I do either.

I was laying the tables for tea with Mary when Sister H. marched Gregory through the french windows from the garden. She had found him in George's greenhouse, which was strictly out of bounds. She was furious with him in her subdued way, hissing angrily at him. Gregory made no attempt

265

to defend his action, although I knew why he had been there: he had gone to water his snailarium. In such hot weather it is vital to keep the earth moist. I had been the one to drill into him the need to do that, since gastropods are, strictly speaking, displaced aquatic creatures which need a very moist environment. I couldn't see what I could do to mediate between them without making a bad situation worse. The little chap was sent to bed without any tea. I felt very sorry for him.

After tea I went up to speak to him. I found the boy sobbing into his bedclothes in the darkened dormitory, into which splinters of sunlight penetrated through the cracks between the shutters. I stroked his head and tried to comfort him. He was still anxious in case the snails suffered in the heat. I only reassured him by promising to go and inspect them later myself and give them some more water.

I found Sister H. and explained the boy's preoccupation with the snails. I told her I thought that his concern for their well-being mitigated his offence. Anyway, it was my fault. He had only been following my instructions. I then ventured the opinion that he should not be too harshly dealt with. Unfortunately the senior officer did not see his transgression in this light. She informed me that she had ordered George to remove the snailarium and to dispose of it. For a moment I was speechless.

'You can't do that!' I said. 'The boy will be heartbroken!'

'Brodie. Please don't instruct me as to what I can and can't do. Gregory has deliberately disobeyed orders. He must be punished.'

I stamped out. I think I might have shut the door behind me rather more firmly than I had intended.

What can I do? I feel powerless.

Where to start? I am so distraught I can hardly think. It's late at night and I am writing this in bed because I can't sleep. I don't *want* to sleep.

The day started badly and ended disastrously.

I had a stand-up row with Sister Hiller on the subject of the destruction of Gregory's snailarium. I told her I thought it was a small-minded and vindictive act. I wanted to make her angry but unfortunately she remained icily in control of her emotions, whereas I was the one to lose my temper. I said that destroying the boy's snailarium was an unChristian act and unworthy of her. Her response to that flabbergasted me.

'Your opinion on the theological implications of my decision is interesting. I shall note it down. As you know, I must send a report to Major Willmot-Smythe on your progress here. I am sure he will be interested to hear your views.'

I expressed satisfaction on that score and told her – quite untruthfully – that I intended to write to the major myself. Then I retreated to the kitchen to lick my wounds and quite alarmed Alice by bursting into tears. She took me in her arms as if I were one of her own children. She gave me a cup of tea and some forks to polish. I was at the kitchen table polishing forks when Mary ran in and announced that Gregory could not be found and the fear was that he had absconded.

The fear proved to be justified. He had run away. The police were called and a couple of officers in a car arrived, asked some questions of Sisters Hiller and Slater and then drove off. It is now eleven o'clock and the boy still has not returned. It is dark and I am worried sick about what can have happened to him. He is only six!

I telephoned Richard to let him know what had happened

to Gregory. His housekeeper said he was at a school governors' meeting.

How on earth can I sleep while his bed in the dormitory is empty?

Dear Lord – look after that poor, sweet boy!

Sunday   2 July 1950

Sister Hiller called the staff together before breakfast and informed us that Gregory was still 'at large' – that was the form of words she chose, as if he were an escaped criminal. The police, she said, were confident he would turn up soon. He was an emotionally disturbed child and his delinquent behaviour made him a danger to himself. I voiced the opinion that he was an emotionally *distressed* child, and that as far as I was aware she was not qualified to determine whether or not he was disturbed. She ordered me to leave the room, which I was glad to do.

The routines of the house continued as normal. Because it was Sunday, the children were scrubbed and dressed in their best and then packed off to church. The service went ahead, as it has done for nine hundred years, notwithstanding the individual sufferings of the congregation. We sang the hymns and repeated the prayers. Richard, in his white cassock and with his wise aperçus upon Our Lord's utterances, was in the eye of the storm, a centre of peace within the maelstrom. The children were as good as gold. Nobody has told them anything, of course, but they know what is afoot. They can sense how tense and worried we are.

I had no opportunity to talk to Richard until the afternoon. While the children were in the church hall with the Sunday School teacher I waited for him in the sacristy, and when he entered the room I ran to him, straight into his arms. I did it without thinking.

I tried to tell him everything but I was too upset and I burst into tears. He already knew Gregory had absconded. He had not been told of his reason for doing so: because his snailarium had been confiscated.

My dear Richard held me in his arms. My head rested against his shoulder. His hand stroked the nape of my neck. Suddenly, without premeditation, we were not two but one and gradually I became calm. I don't think I had realized until then how fraught I was. We sat down and I told him everything that had happened, what had passed between Sister H. and myself. After first obtaining my consent, he made a telephone call to Sister H. to request another member of staff be sent to relieve me. In his view I was too upset to be in charge of children. I was very reassured by his courteous, professional manner.

As we were leaving the sacristy he said: 'Lizzie, dear . . .'

Before he could continue I went up to him and he did what I wanted him to do. He kissed me.

I am so happy!

'We seem to have lost Gregory and found each other,' he said. 'All we have to do is find him and everything will be all right.'

'I doubt it very much,' I said. 'After my conversation with Sister Hiller I shall almost certainly be disciplined.'

'Lizzie. You're an officer in the Church Army – not the Brigade of Guards! They aren't going to cashier you!'

'But darling—'

I had said *the word*, and he kissed me again.

He assured me everything was going to be all right and I felt happy because now I knew it would be. I am not alone. I have Richard!

I was relieved by Mary. I waited until the end of Sunday School and then accompanied the children back with her.

At about six o'clock a police car drove up the gravel drive and Gregory emerged from the back. He looked so small between the two officers, holding a hand of each of them.

Sister H. met them halfway and they released Gregory into her custody. That was what it looked like because she did not hold him or come down to his level. He stood at her side until she and the policemen finished talking. I watched the silent tableau from the nursery window, filled with anger at the woman and admiration for the boy.

The County Hospital had contacted the police after a member of the public had brought in a small boy with a wound in the back of his thigh and a doctor had put in a couple of stitches. Gregory had escaped Cliff House by climbing over the wall where the slope of the garden made this possible. He had slipped and a fragment of glass had gashed his leg. He had spent the night in a bus shelter.

I wanted to go to him but Sister Hiller made sure I couldn't. He has not returned to the dormitory but sleeps on a cot in Sister Slater's room.

I want to cry and laugh! Shout with fury and dance for joy!

Richard darling – I do love you!

Tuesday   4 July 1950

George has handed in his notice. I understand he has got a job as driver-gardener at one of the residential hotels in Torquay. He will take up his new employment on Monday, having been released from the obligation of working out his notice. This is all very sudden. George was never one to discuss his feelings. One can only guess at his motive for leaving.

I found him in his greenhouse, pricking out some seedlings into clay pots. I wanted to say goodbye to him but he would not look up from his work. He is not voluble at the best of times and he clammed up when I mentioned Gregory's name. He didn't want to talk about what had happened. As I made to leave, though, he shuffled over.

'I'd like the boy to have this, miss,' he said.

He handed me a shilling.

'I promised he a farthing for ev'y snail he ud catch. He catched us forty-eight. I owes'm a bob.'

I have put George's bob in an envelope in case I spend it by accident.

Friday   7 July 1950

It was my day off and I fairly swanked out of the house after lunch. Without bothering to go through the charade of leaving in my uniform and taking a change of clothes, I left for the beach in sandals and my summer frock to meet Richard on the sands. I had my swimming costume on under it too. I was tingling with anticipation. I didn't know what was going to happen, but I couldn't wait for it, whatever it was.

Richard, as arranged, was waiting for me at the end of Petit Tor head. We kissed and walked along the coastal path until we came to the secluded little Watcombe Cove, which is only accessible on foot. We descended hand in hand to the beach. There were hardly any other people around and no parishioners, Richard was certain. He had brought a rubber football with him and we played with that until we were hot, and then we swam. He is almost as good a swimmer as I am. We swam into the bay until we were well out of our depth!

Afterwards we lay side by side on our towels and ate our sandwiches and talked. We talked about everything! Dorothea and Mr Casaubon, Charles Darwin and the Church of England, the Labour Government's chances of surviving on its tiny majority. Each other, of course. He wanted to know all about me, what had happened to Mum and Dad. He was very sweet and sympathetic. I realize how starved I have been of adult conversation!

In the afternoon, after a final cooling-down dip, we changed to leave – not just the beach but each other. Reality was edging in as inexorably as the shadows lengthening in front of the rocks. We grew quiet and less jolly as the sun moved towards the horizon. Soon we would have to say goodbye, and we were not ready to do that. While he dressed, I wriggled out of my swimming costume inside an ample Church Army bath towel. Richard gallantly occupied himself with a knot in one of his plimsoll laces. Once I had achieved the difficult manoeuvre I said his name. He turned towards me. Wrapped in my towel, I pulled him against me so that my breasts were against his body and we hugged and kissed. Whatever happens to me in my life I know I will never be kissed like that again – not even by Richard. By certain physiological changes that were occurring in specific areas of my body, I realized that I was becoming sexually aroused. The same was certainly true of Richard. His hand caressed the small of my back. It was quite unnecessary to speak.

We walked back up the track, every few hundred yards pausing to kiss and to touch each other. We were so happy and full of giggles. Each time we embraced, our explorations of each other were in small, but increasingly less small degrees, more adventurous. We are both so inexperienced and clumsy we had to stop to laugh.

To delay our imminent separation we had a drink in a pub. In the event we had two drinks! I couldn't believe my unlooked-for good fortune. One moment I had been peeling potatoes in my uniform, the next I was in a pretty frock, drinking beer in a public house with a young man who I wanted to kiss me. I felt I had been rewarded for something I had not deserved.

It was nearer eight than seven when I entered Cliff House. I tried not to swan in but I was brim-full of joy, with the confidence of a woman who has just been kissed by her lover. I couldn't have hidden that, even if I had wanted to.

I am sure it was only because of Richard's forbearance that we had not gone any further in our delight in each other. I am happy that we did not, because it is a further confirmation to me of Richard's worth. He is a man above other men, no less subject to the desires of men, but blessed with a deeper understanding and with a greater compassion and capacity for love.

Saturday   8 July 1950

Gregory has become withdrawn. He continues to sleep in Sister Slater's bedroom and he attends school with the other children. It is understood that he is in disgrace and he walks alone, as if the other children are afraid that some of his 'badness' will rub off on to them if they approach him. I have tried on several occasions to engage him in conversation, but he has lost his enthusiasm for the subjects that interested him previously, as if they were partly the cause of his troubles. His anger is not directed at Sister Hiller or the home but at himself – and, I fear, towards me. Sister Hiller's policy of punishment and blame are having the effect she desires. Gregory blames himself and accepts that his punishment is the result of his own 'badness'. It is damaging his personality and sense of his own worth.

All this done in the name of Jesus!

Tuesday   11 July 1950

The staff were informed this morning that Gregory is to be moved to the boys' home in Gosport. Normally boys are moved when they reach their thirteenth birthday, as it is Church

Army policy that pubescent boys should not be in the company of girls, even their own sisters if they have any. Gregory is very young to be in a boys-only home. I know he will be very unhappy. I ventured the view that such a move would not be in his interests and his behaviour, even if he had contravened some of the rules, had not put any of the girls in danger. Sending him away was an expression of spite rather than a just and reasonable punishment. This time, instead of ordering me from the room, Sister Hiller asked the other staff if they shared my opinion. Nobody said a word, of course.

I happen to know that Richard has interceded with Sister H. on Gregory's behalf, but I could not publicly point this out without compromising Richard.

I went straight to my room and wrote a letter to Major Willmot-Smythe at Church Army House in London, stating my objections to the decision that had been taken, adding details to the background of the case which I was certain Sister H. had omitted. I posted the letter on the way to school to collect the children at three-thirty.

Thursday   13 July 1950

I received a letter from Major Willmot-Smythe this morning, so our letters will have crossed. His was dated 11 July.

Dear Sister Brodie,

I am writing to you in response to a number of serious complaints that have been made concerning your conduct by your superior officer at Cliff House. Sister Hiller has written to me at length. She has expressed herself concerned about your suitability for this demanding post. Her complaints against you are as follows: that you are insubordinate and disrespectful;

that you have made grossly false allegations about her in front of other members of staff; that you have encouraged small boys to use foul language; that you have developed an unhealthy relationship with one boy in particular; that you are slipshod in your work.

With great regret I am terminating your post at this establishment. You will be required to attend a disciplinary hearing at Church Army House on Monday 23 July. Please go to Room 108. Sister Hiller will also be present.

I should emphasize to you that you will be given every opportunity to put your point of view.

However, you should understand that when you leave Cliff House to attend the hearing you must remove your personal possessions since it is unlikely that you will return to this post, whatever the outcome of the hearing.

I am very sorry that this posting has not worked out for you.

Yours sincerely,

Mark Willmot-Smythe
Staff Organizer.

As the only telephone in the building is in Sister Hiller's office, I went straight to the Rectory to see Richard. Alone in his office we kissed and I showed him the letter. He was appalled and very angry. It went against his sense of fair play and he wanted to do something to help. He said he would write to Willmot-Smythe and support my case.

I explained to my sweet darling that if he did this, the important relationship he had built up with Cliff House would almost certainly break down. If he sided with me those close links would be terminated. The children would suffer. I told him I did not want him to write anything. I wanted to present my own case and I would judge the organization on how it meted out justice to me. He had been right when he reminded me I was not in the Brigade of Guards. There would be other ways I could serve God besides wearing the uniform of a sister in the Church Army.

Then – quite out of the blue – he said, 'Lizzie, darling. I'm sorry it has to be under such unfortunate circumstances, but as you are leaving Devon and I may not see you for some time I want you to know, in case you are in any doubt, that I would be very happy and honoured if you would agree to be my wife.'

I could hardly speak, I was so happy. I fell into his arms and wept – not just for joy but with release from the pent-up emotion of recent events.

Richard then rummaged in his drawer for something and then fished out a Bluebell matchbox, from which he produced a gold ring with a single green stone.

'These turn up now and then in the church. I think women work them loose with the emotional tension of marriage and funeral ceremonies. Will you accept this as a pledge of our engagement? Or would you think I was being stingy? I'm afraid I haven't had time to go out and buy a real one.'

I let him slide the ring on to the second finger of my left hand.

'May the Lord give us his blessing and bring us together very soon as man and wife.'

I said Amen to that.

I feel so very happy. I am upset at losing my job, and I am terribly worried about Gregory, but when I think about Richard I burst into smiles and I want to sing!

I left today for London and the Church Army hostel in
Edgware Road, a day early in order that Richard could see
me off, tomorrow being Sunday.

I couldn't help crying when I said goodbye to Alice and
Mary and all the dear little ones whom I have dressed and
washed and put to bed and comforted. They were bewildered
and most of them cried when they saw my tears. I will turn
out to be one more adult who has passed into and out of their
lives. I tried to put out of my mind feelings of guilt and
failure. I so wanted to be happy here.

I had sought permission to say goodbye to Gregory, but
Sister Slater informed me that he did not want to see me.
That may have been true. I gave the envelope with George's
shilling in it to Richard to pass on to him, since I did not trust
Sister S. to do so. I find it hard to believe that such spite and
hatred could find a place in the heart of a woman who has
chosen as her vocation our Lord's work with children.

Gregory is due to leave on Wednesday for a Church Army
boys' home, Thorpeness House in Gosport.

The taxi-driver − since George has taken up alternative
employment − helped Richard with my trunk. I don't know
what the staff thought about Richard's presence at my
departure. It could be put down to a proper exercise of his
ministry. It is his job to comfort and help those in time of
trouble. Frankly I don't care what they thought. Mary admired
my ring but I gave her no hint of its provenance. Alice, on
the other hand, took me in those huge arms of hers and
whispered into my ear: 'Congratulations, pet. You got yourself
a good 'un there.'

At the station I broke down completely. Richard was
wonderful. There he was in his dog collar, holding his fiancée
in his arms. He kissed my tear-stained face for anyone in

Torquay station to see who wanted to look. He held my hand and murmured his encouragement and faith that we would soon be together again. He made me promise to write. Eventually the train drew into the station and I was on the train and he was on the platform. We kissed through the open window. Then the train moved slowly away and he became very small until I could not see him at all, and I was alone in my carriage.

My journey repeated in reverse the route I had taken four months earlier – full of such hope! – from Torquay to Exmouth via Paignton, changing for the Plymouth to London train, although on this occasion I did not need to change at Crewe. I said goodbye to that lovely coastline.

Will I ever see it again?

VIOLET HOSKIN

Jack was a decent, old-fashioned bloke, one in a million. I don't blame him for how he took it when he found out what I did. I don't blame him and I can't complain. I deserved it. I'm just sorry I hurt him. I couldn't be more sorry. He took it how you'd have expected he would. When he wrote me that letter saying he wasn't coming home and he wanted a divorce and he didn't want to see me again, I knew there was no use trying to put things right. He was finished with me. He had put his trust in me and I'd let him down. All the married men worried themselves sick what their missus was getting up to while they were away – nearly always with good reason. Not my Jack. Jack slept easy because I wasn't flighty like the women the other men talked about, he said.

So when he found out how the very thing his mates were afraid of had happened to him, it was more than he could stand. He was broken-hearted. The horrible names he called me in his letter – I was a filthy whore and he never wanted to see me again – was because he was hurt, not because he hated me. I knew how he felt. He couldn't understand what had happened no more than I could myself.

Jack Hoskin loved me. I'd always been happy with him. I never even looked at another man while I was with him. If you'd have seen him you'd understand why. Jack stood six foot two in his socks and had that quietness and strength mixed together a woman likes. I used to laugh, watching other women stealing looks at him, flirting and trying to catch his eye, how he'd give them the old wink and make them blush, but that was all. He never led them on. It was me he wanted.

So long as he had me he was happy because he was that kind of man, a lovely bloke with a smashing smile and no roving eye. One in a million. He worked hard and looked after me, never raised voice nor fist to me once – and didn't we have some good times together! I'll say we did! Jack was a good husband in all departments. He always did the job to my satisfaction – and I've had a few men since then, some good 'uns too. Even Charlie, even that shiftless bugger who I loved in the end almost as much as I loved Jack, even he didn't measure up to Jack. Charlie had blue eyes and a smashing smile of his own, but he was never the man Jack was.

I used to wonder how those two would've got on if they'd had to share a billet. They were both big men – popular with the boys as well as the girls – but they were different. You'd never have caught Jack blowing a wad on the horses or the dogs and then laughing it off in the pub afterwards. Jack was more careful of his money. Charlie didn't value money nor property, neither his own nor anybody else's. For him it was easy come, easy go. You could never have got Charlie to stick a regular daytime job if you put a ball and chain round his leg. Still, that don't mean him and Jack wouldn't have got on with each other. I like to think they would have. Then all this might never have happened.

Even if I had my time over again, I couldn't put my hand on my heart and say I would have done it different. Seeing as

I'm not going to have it over again there's no use thinking about it. It's not as if there was one big mistake I made. There wasn't. I made a lot of little mistakes. None of them, on their own, was a hanging offence, but when you add them all together what you get is the mess I made of my life.

That's why I don't blame Charlie. It wasn't his fault. He may have been a bit of a rogue and he may have been involved in some dodgy business – well, I know for a fact he was – but it was just bloody bad luck the way he was picked up, a chance in a million – but I can't honestly say I wish I'd never met the bugger, or if I had that I wouldn't have gone with him. I did and that's that. But if you want to nail down the moment when I left the straight and narrow, it was when I let Charlie take me back to his flat after the pub shut instead of dropping me off at the end of Coldharbour Lane like he did usually. It didn't seem such a terrible crime at the time. Charlie showed me a good time and looked after me when that was what I wanted.

What's the use in blaming the past? If Hitler had been killed in the First War like he would have been if there was any justice in the world, everyone would all have lived happy ever after, wouldn't they?

I don't think!

On Jack's last forty-eight in Torrance Street we had a really good time, starting out at Vera and Maurice's and ending up at the Eagle on Dalton Road. Jack was with his mate Maurice Pearson who was in the same unit as him and had a forty-eight too. The morning after, me and Vera saw them off on the tram to the station. We all had hangovers and we were sad to say goodbye to our men, but at least we'd given them a good night out. From the Eagle Jack and me had gone home and got down to business. I know some women saw it as their duty to make sure their man went back shag-happy – because if she didn't, she could lay a bet some other tart would. But I never saw it as my duty. Jack and me'd been married three and a half years by then. We understood each other. He was a randy bugger, but that never bothered me. I always wanted it as much as he did. He never gave me no trouble. When it was my rag time he stayed away from me and never forced himself on top of me. He never had to.

Funny, now I come to think of it, I never got pregnant with Jack, when you count all the times we did it without using anything and how much we both wanted kids. If there'd been a nipper or two for me to look after things might have turned out different. I couldn't have gone out so much. And then, no sooner than I didn't want one, I joined the club. I don't understand how it happened. Perhaps funny isn't the best word for it. Bloody unlucky, more like!

Life's more about luck than most people give it credit for. Charlie understood that. He was a great gambler. There was nothing he loved more than a day at the track – especially if it was Brighton. He loved spending money, drinking with the friends he'd gone with or the ones he met there, losing some notes, winning some. He taught me to love it too. Charlie would always prefer to lose close on an outside bet than win a percentage on a short-odds dead cert. He was like that. He didn't care if he won or lost so long as he had a good time. He used to say it don't matter what you do, what you think will happen, it makes no difference. Most of what happens to you has more to do with luck, things you can't plan for one way or the other, so why not make the best of it while you can?

After Jack rejoined his regiment that time, I honestly thought it'd only be another four or five or six months before he was given another forty-eight hours and then we'd do it all again. While he was away he wrote every week if he could. Then he was sent somewhere – I didn't know where – and I didn't hear from him for weeks. When his letters started to arrive again there was nothing in them to say where he was. Men weren't supposed to write anything that could tell the Germans where they were or what they were doing. An officer had the job of reading the men's letters, crossing out whatever he thought gave the game away. All I knew was it was hot, too hot – but it wasn't Africa or India. So he didn't have another forty-eight, or any leave at all, at least not with me. He was overseas, that's all I knew. Vera Pearson said she thought he and Maurice were in Palestine. I had to look on a map to see where it was.

Jack wrote to me every week. His letters turned up in twos or threes and when no letter came at all it was awful. All I needed was to see the envelope with Jack's handwriting on it. What was in the letter was nearly always the same: the terrible food, the terrible weather, the terrible things he and his mates had to do and who won the football match. It wasn't to read his words I wanted so much as to get them, to see in his handwriting *My dearest Vi* . . . I kept all his letters in a box. I didn't often read them but I got them out and looked at them now and then.

What I'm saying is, that morning when I saw him off on the 36a tram to Victoria station, neither of us knew it would be for ever. It never entered my head I'd never see my husband again. I didn't see him again – at least not during the War I didn't, not until after it was all over, years later, in the Prince Albert in Notting Hill Gate. I was with Ray then. Ray nudged me and said there was a bloke on the other side of the bar looking at me, and I turned round and my heart stopped when I saw it was Jack. Our eyes met and he turned away and walked out of the door and didn't come back when I called him. We didn't know that then.

Jack's letters kept arriving after I had started going with Charlie, and I still looked forward to them and worried if they were late. None of the other women in my family knew about Charlie, of course. I was careful to make sure of that. I thought I was just having a fling, a bit of fun which I could stop any time I wanted to. It wouldn't have surprised me if Jack wasn't

285

getting it when he could and I wouldn't have blamed him if he was, so long as he didn't catch anything. I couldn't see what harm there was in a bit of fun, if no one knew about it. Charlie always took me across the River, up the West End where the pubs had something to drink, you could dance and go to the pictures and no one knew Violet Hoskin from a hole in the ground.

That was one of the reasons it happened. It was easy enough to get a bus across the River before dark. Getting back, though, was murder. There was no buses or trams after the blackout and there was nearly always an air raid on.

I can see now I had nothing better to do. Nothing ever happened in Camberwell. If you didn't have children, either you went to work in the Decca electric components factory in Coldharbour Lane or worked in a shop – or you joined up. The women with families had their work cut out trying to make ends meet. There was nothing in the shops, and even if you had the money and the coupons you'd still be lucky to get any fresh meat or vegetables or what you wanted. I used to give my coupons to the married women when I could.

Of course, after I started going with Charlie I didn't need them. He had coupons for anything you wanted – and money to buy it. More than likely it was the stuff itself he had. Drink, clothing, meat, cigarettes. If he didn't have what you wanted, he knew where to get hold of it. There was more than one woman in Torrance Street, including Vera Pearson, who gave her old man meat and onions I had put her way and never took a penny for.

Charlie had the use of a car, too – a Baby Austin. A tall, fit young fellow like him you'd expect to be in uniform and he would have been if he hadn't thrown it out the window of a train going to London on his first leave. He was in a training camp somewhere in Yorkshire with a London infantry regiment and he decided it wasn't for him. He wasn't a coward. He just found it hard to keep his rag when the NCOs shouted in his face and made him beeswax the floor with a nail brush, that sort of thing. The sergeant major could stop your leave because he didn't like your face. It had nothing to do with soldiering, in Charlie's opinion. After he deserted he drifted around London, into one thing and another, on the lookout. More than once he said to me he'd have given himself up if it weren't for the amount of choky he'd have to do if he did.

Worth more than the car were the coupons for petrol. Charlie knew a bloke in the AFT garage who didn't mind swapping them and a bottle of gin for petrol. In the boot of his car he had cans of petrol, apples, leeks, clothing, tobacco, razor blades, whisky. He would swap the leeks for the apples and the razor blades for the sugar and the sugar for whisky, the whisky for petrol. He always ended up with more whisky than he started out with. It made me giddy.

I didn't know any of this when I first went with him. I was too simple. I see now he turned my head because he had more pound notes in his wad than I had seen in my whole life – but at the time I thought it was because I liked him. I was just a girl. I wanted a good time. To go to the pictures and dance. Have a bit of fun. That was all. It didn't seem such a crime to want to dance to Al Bowly at the Alhambra – or Snake Hips Johnson at the Café Royal – any more than it was to see Vivien Leigh at the Odeon Marble Arch. I didn't set out to leave Jack, or turn my own mum against me.

My mum never forgave me for what I did to Jack. At first me and Charlie would go back to his flat in Paddington in the afternoon. Later I'd spend the night and, after my mum found out, I moved in permanent. The flat wasn't his, of course. He was looking after it for a mate of his. Nothing of Charlie's ever belonged to him. He was always just looking after it for some other feller – and that went for old Gubbins too, I suppose. Stuff just passed through his hands. Sometimes even his money wasn't his. He was just delivering it for some party who had a sudden desperate need for a box of nylons or a side of beef. He took the risk and ended up with a percentage. I know because he'd pass meat and stuff on to me and I got rid of what we couldn't use ourselves round Torrance Street.

I found out later that Vera Pearson saw me get out of Charlie's car and give him a kiss in Brixton High Street one afternoon – and that was that. Jack probably heard by the next mailboat. A month after, I got a letter from Jack telling me to fuck off out of his life. I cried for days. I honestly never meant it to turn out like that. I never wanted to hurt Jack because I still loved him.

It wasn't easy for me after that because my mum thought the world of Jack. She and my dad had gone to school with Jack's mum and they were all old friends, so it wasn't just my family I let down, it was half of Camberwell. I knew Mum would murder me if she thought I was having it off with another bloke, so when she found out I was I had to move in with Charlie at the place in Sussex Gardens he was looking after. And that was the end of my life in south London. I'd have gone down on my knees and pleaded with Jack if I thought it would have done any good, but I knew he didn't want me no more. I wasn't his. I wanted Jack but he didn't want me, and I couldn't go back to Torrance Street. I couldn't face my mum or Jack's mum or our friends. Vera cut me dead when I ran into her.

After that me and Charlie did everything together – just like Jack and me used to do. Without meaning to, I'd swapped one man for another. First time I'd done that, and it left me feeling light-headed for days.

Probably one reason was because I was drinking more than I was used to. Before, I used to drink a light ale or two – or a sherry sometimes. Charlie started me on Scotch and cocktails and I took up smoking. I also dressed better than most girls could afford. It does a lot for a girl's confidence to know that what she has on under her frock is dearer than anything any other girl in the room is wearing under hers.

I slept with a lot of men during the War – well, nineteen to be exact, not counting Charlie. Is that a lot, over two years? Maybe not by today's standards, but it was a lot then. Eleven Americans, five English. Two Scotchmen and a New Zealander. I liked them all as much as they liked me, and Charlie didn't mind who I slept with. He said he just wanted me to have a good time. We went to pubs or parties together and now and then I left with some other bloke. We'd all be pretty drunk. Often it just happened early in the morning. You'd be at a party and you and some soldier would slip out into a bedroom, and you'd do it without even taking your clothes off and return to the party, and no one was the wiser.

I thought!

Of course they knew! I can see that now. But then I thought I was just having a bit of fun on the side. It wasn't until years later that the penny dropped and it dawned on me that Charlie must have known all along. He'd be over in the corner talking business with some chap, but he almost certainly took something on the side from the feller I went with. Not money necessarily. All of those boys were in a position to put something Charlie's way. Bacon. Scotch. Motorcycle parts. Charlie wasn't all that interested in money. He swapped goods for goods.

It was years later – if you can believe a girl could be that simple! – before I even suspected I came into that category myself and I was part of the merchandise Charlie was dealing in. That just shows how simple I was. I didn't think of myself as a tart because I knew all those boys' names. It was just a bit of fun I enjoyed as much as they did. There was one or two boys I got to know who'd ring me up when they were on leave, and we'd meet and go out on the town. I never went with anyone I didn't know and I never did anything dirty. One RAF chap liked to put me over his knee, pull my drawers down and spank me, but not so it hurt. It was all in good fun. I didn't mind that, and he was such a dear. After I didn't see him for a while I asked his mates what'd happened to him. They said he'd gone MPD. His plane hadn't returned from Germany and he was Missing, Presumed Dead, poor boy.

Even when they slipped some pound notes into my pocket – which the Americans always did – I just took them as a friendly thank-you present. I didn't look on it as payment for services rendered. The time one of the Americans Charlie had introduced me to telephoned me at home and said a friend of his would like to meet me I wasn't sure, and when he said his friend would pay handsomely for the privilege, I got on my high horse and asked him what sort of girl he took me for. He laughed and told me to keep my hair on. I met his friend in his hotel and I let him do it with me without taking a penny off of him – just to show him I didn't mind a bit of fun but I was no whore. Believe me, I was the simplest girl in London!

Charlie was nearly always out during the day and I spent a lot of time alone at his flat, sleeping through the morning and most of the afternoon. I was done in after a night in one of the cocktail lounges in Mayfair or the Paddington gambling clubs the Americans all went to. I didn't gamble myself but nearly everyone I knew did. And how! I'd never seen so much money pass hands in my life. We might go to the dog races at White City on a Saturday night. Or we'd go dancing in a whole gang or see a new film. Wherever we ended up we always had a drink or two. I never got back home until three or four in the morning and then I probably had to hoof it. At night you could hardly see anything because of the blackout. Even cars couldn't shine their lamps. But who wanted to see anything? London was bombed to bits.

It wasn't just the buildings, the burnt-out houses and flooded streets. The faces of people were so downcast. Hardly anyone wanted to be nice to you. Londoners were snappy. You got on a bus and the bus conductress would be sulky. Shopkeepers talked to you in a way they never would have dared before the War. The boot was on the other foot, you see. They had something that was in short supply, and in a lot of shops they didn't mind letting you know it. If they didn't like your face they wouldn't let you have what you asked for. Shopkeepers had favourites they kept the best stuff for. Of course, I didn't have many problems getting what I wanted. I could always put the grin back on their face, no trouble. I knew their game. But if you weren't young or pretty any more, like my mum, or you dressed bad like Vera and the other women in Torrance Street, it was hard work just getting what you were entitled to. Butchers were worst.

By the light of day it made you feel ill to walk around London. I stayed in bed until blackout and the guns started firing at the German planes. They were my alarm clock. First the siren, then the roar of the planes and then the AA guns firing. As soon as everyone else was in bed or in a shelter, I nipped round the corner to the Victoria and Albert and met up with Charlie and the gang, and we all had a good laugh about it and drank and sang songs.

There were pubs and clubs that had spirits where you could stay late. The police couldn't do anything about it. Those places were full of uniforms. The MPs would have had to arrest the boys who were doing all the fighting. You couldn't send the poor blighters out to some godforsaken part of the world to fight and then tell them they can't have some fun on their leave. The authorities didn't like what was going on, but they had to lump it.

The bombs never bothered me as I didn't have a house or a family or a job. I had no property to lose, no loved ones living with me, no pet even. I just had me. A bomb could have fallen on top of me but I didn't expect one would. Everything was a gamble then, the races at Brighton, roulette or blackjack at the Upstairs Club, or even who you landed up with in bed.

The chance of a bomb landing on you and not some other poor blighter was something you had to live with. If you had something to lose you were more likely to worry but if, like me, you had nothing, you didn't care. You were excited.

The most exciting days of my life I spent in the Blitz, though I don't say they were the happiest. I was a pretty girl with a good figure. Men liked me and so I was always in a crowd. When the bombs were falling the best place to be was a long way from your family, with people you could have a laugh with, but who you might never see again. Whether you were dead or just dead drunk, what difference did it make? No one would miss you.

Everyone was in a crowd in those days. There was Charlie's crowd and then there was the Upstairs crowd. They weren't always the same people because they weren't always the same kind of people. All Charlie's mates ran some kind of business: most of them were from south of the River so I got on with them. At the Club it was a different story. Most of the men there were junior officers, British and American. The girls all had nice teeth. In those days you could tell the class a person came from as soon as they opened their mouths. I've always been lucky with my teeth, but most working girls then never had good teeth. At the Upstairs they knew I was a working-class girl and I never tried to hide it. They pulled my leg and laughed at the things I came out with but they didn't hold it against me. I was popular.

In the War people from different classes mixed more than they did before. If they wanted to be on friendly terms with you they didn't care how you spoke. It's hard to explain now, but then it was a new thing. For a girl like me who grew up in a street of two-up two-downs in Camberwell, it was a new world. Once I'd seen it, how the girls dressed and spoke and how the men behaved to them, I could never go back. I was careful not to give myself fancy airs because people don't like that. Still, I learnt a trick or two – what to drink with what, how to wear nice clothes without looking like a tart. I could never have changed the way I spoke in a million years, so I didn't even try.

Some nights Charlie'd take me to one of the grand hotels, the Mayfair or the Dorchester or the Park Lane, to meet some friend of his, usually an American Army officer or NCO. (Ordinary GIs weren't allowed to drink in the same posh places as the officers.) I'd sit next to them at the bar with a drink while they talked business and when they finished, we might have another drink and then go out and have some fun. Americans had more stuff than they could ever use themselves, and you could get hold of anything you wanted from them in the way of food or clothes or make-up or, especially, spirits and cigarettes. I always carried a tin box of fifty 555 Express in my handbag and, while Charlie and his friend talked business, I smoked and looked at the people in the bar. It was better than going to the cinema.

You'd never believe the swank those places had if you hadn't seen it for yourself. I met some very charming Americans, very considerate young men. I liked Americans. Even the ordinary GI was much better mannered than your average Tommy. They were big and healthy and had smiles that made a girl's insides go funny. They really knew how to make you laugh. A few of them I let take me out dancing at the old Alhambra, before it was bombed, and I didn't mind giving them what they wanted afterwards.

Charlie didn't mind either. Nothing put him out. He breezed in and out of those swanky places and drove his Baby Austin to the races at weekends if he felt like it. He could get hold of anything he wanted.

It was weeks before it dawned on me I was pregnant. I'd missed my period but that had happened before. I came over a bit queer, and so I went to the doctor and he told me I was going to have a baby. He seemed to think it was something I should be pleased about. Charlie told me there was nothing to worry about. He could fix it for me if I wanted him to. We were living in Paddington after all, which was notorious for that kind of job then. I couldn't have been better placed. Praed Street was the abortion capital of the world. He started to make inquiries. I think he saw it as a challenge. I'd probably get an abortion for two pounds of old beef and a couple of bottles of Gordon's gin.

I wanted to see my mum. Which was stupid of me, as it wasn't as if it was Jack's child I was carrying. You do funny things when you're pregnant. I got a tram to Brixton and walked up the hill to Camberwell. I walked as far as the corner of Dalton Road and Torrance Street which, thank God, was still there. It was quiet. The sun was shining through the dust that used to hang in the air all over London then. Torrance Street looked normal, just as it did before the War. It was like going back in time. I hoped my mum would step out of her door but she didn't and I didn't have the nerve to go and knock. She would never let me cross her front step. I wanted to see her so much, but she didn't want to see me ever again.

I missed my mum – and Tilly, my sister, and my little brother Ron. I wanted to see how they were all taking it, what the damage was. They all thought I was a bad 'un, I knew that, but even if I was, that didn't mean I didn't have feelings like anybody else.

Just seeing the old Eagle and the shops I used to go into as a girl brought tears to my eyes. These were the places I'd grew up in and where Jack and me had courted. An invisible piece of glass was between me and those places now. Something had happened. I couldn't change it and I could never go back.

I walked back down Mill Hill Road towards Brixton. I didn't want to look at people in case I met someone who knew me. Luckily for me there was no one about. The only person coming up the hill towards me was a boy scuffing along in the gutter. I recognized him at once. It was Ron on his way home from Ditchling Rise Primary School, where I'd gone myself. What a scruff he looked! He was miles away. He'd probably have walked right past me if I hadn't called out to him.

'Ron!'

He squinted up at me for a moment. Ron hadn't seen me for nearly a year now, and it took him a moment to recognize me. My heart stopped while I waited to see what he would do. When he saw it was me he ran into my arms.

'Vi! Where you been? Have you come back? Are you going to live with us again?'

He hugged me so hard I burst into tears. I could hardly speak. I told him I couldn't come back quite yet. I had an important job in town and it was hush-hush. Some nonsense.

Ron had grown since I last saw him. He was ten now, and would be going on to the secondary school in September. I'd brought presents for all my family and I put them into Ron's hands and told him to give them to Mum and Dad. I missed my dad too, but I knew he would never go against Mum. It was Mum wore the trousers in our house. I gave him a US Air Force paperback book of aircraft identifications. His jaw dropped.

'I must go, Ron,' I told him, crouching down in front of him. 'Will you promise to think about me sometimes? Even if you don't see me for a long time? I'm always thinking of you and Tilly Mint and Mum and Dad.'

Ron promised he would. I hugged him again and remembered I had something else for him: an American chocolate bar and a pack of chewing gum. That made his day. He waved to me from the top of the hill until we couldn't see each other.

I sat in the tram with tears in my eyes all the way to Victoria. It'd been stupid of me to go back. None of my family, except Ron, wanted to know me. Later on Dad was killed in an accident at his work and then, after the War, Tilly went to college in Croydon, too much under my mum's thumb to make contact with me. She got married and bought a nice house in Purley and voted for the Conservatives. The last thing she wanted was to be reminded that she had a tart for a sister. I was the black sheep of the family. But Ron always had a soft spot for me. He's always kept in touch. He didn't hate me. He was too young to know what happened and when he found out he didn't care two hoots. I was always his big sis, Vi. And I still am. He still has that US Air Force identification book.

Crossing the River and seeing the state of the houses in Lambeth was a shock. Bombs had fell all over Paddington and the West End and whole streets of shops had gone, but along the River it was worse. You couldn't imagine it if you didn't see it for yourself, and there were no pictures in the newspapers. People were frightened to talk because if you were heard moaning about the situation you could be had up in front of a magistrate and put in prison. The newspapers had plenty of stories about cases where that'd happened. When I saw the damage and all the mess, my heart broke for the people who had lived there. Those houses had belonged to families like mine, ordinary working-class Londoners who liked a pint or two and a sing-song and stuck together.

All that had gone. The faces I saw looked awful, as if someone had boxed their ears two minutes before. If you ask me, one reason they were so shell-shocked wasn't just the planes dropping bombs on them every night, it was because the Government told them they weren't allowed to moan. Having a good moan about things comes natural to Londoners. It's what keeps them cheerful. It didn't do them good bottling it all up. London Can Take It! the newspapers said – but it wasn't true. London couldn't – at least not in Lambeth and Stepney and Wapping.

I walked across the park to Lancaster Gate. It was sunny and warm and it cheered me up to see all the soldiers and sailors walking with their arms round their girls or lying on top of them in the bushes. Good luck to them, I thought. People was desperate for every little bit of fun they could get. Of course, the real fun only started after it got dark. The grass was littered with used rubbers to prove it. I was propositioned myself half a dozen times just walking that short distance, but in a laughing way, and I was careful not to give any encouragement.

I was glad to be back in Paddington, I'm not ashamed to say so. There was something reassuring about the sight of the buses and private cars, the young people walking around in groups, a bit of bustle. The shops had things in the windows and there was always beer in the pubs. There were even taxis. It was like a different city. Practically everyone was in uniform, which meant they didn't live there. They were here today but they might not be tomorrow, so what did they care?

And then there were the boys in beige cotton twill, sauntering and loafing around in a way that only they knew how. Americans – most Londoners called them Yanks, but I didn't – moved in a way no British person did; more relaxed, GIs as well as officers, as if they were made of India rubber. And when they spoke to you it was always 'yes ma'am, no ma'am'. They looked bigger than our boys and they had smarter, better-made uniforms and, no use hiding it, more money in their pockets. You can't blame London girls for being impressed, even if the men weren't. But whether you liked them or you didn't, American soldiers gave London – the West End, anyway – a jaunty feel. These boys weren't going to lose a war – ever!

Visiting Torrance Street had made me miserable. I knew it wasn't something I was going to do again. I didn't belong there any more. My home was in Paddington and Bayswater and Mayfair, places where people were still cheerful and faces lit up when you went into a pub.

Charlie was out when I let myself in, as I knew he would be. I was quick to get my clothes off and fall into a hot bath with a cup of tea. I was dead beat and fed up. A good soak always cheered me up. I wanted to wash all that south London grime off of my skin and step into some brand-new underwear. I felt like pampering myself. There were plenty of boxes of nylons to choose from, as well as pretty brassieres, the kind American women wore, to go with them. Once I'd got myself dolled up and had put some perfume on and brushed my hair, I began to feel my old self again. Unless a bomb fell on the block where Charlie's flat was – which could happen anywhere – there was nothing for me to worry about.

Charlie was already propping up the bar of the V & A when I walked through the door. The gang was all there – Gordon, Tommy and Brenda Grey, Jock McCullum, Alex Castle. I've always liked walking into a pub that's full of people you know, watching their faces light up when they see you and offer to buy you a drink. I could forget the War, Jack, my family, even that I was pregnant. The men knew I was Charlie's girl and so they didn't try anything. I was like a mascot.

'I got it from this rating who was stationed on the ship that did the job . . .'

Jock McCullum was telling them one of his stories. It was a story doing the rounds of London pubs then. It wasn't the first time I had heard it.

'. . . They took a load of old iron from the dock at Portsmouth – Pompey, he called it. They steamed out a mile or so from port and then winched the lot over the side and let it go into the sea. The rating asked one of the officers what it was and why were they dumping it overboard. The officer told him it was supposed to be hush-hush, but it was the railings from Kensington Gardens and the other London royal parks. It turns out that they found out the iron in the railings was useless after they had taken them all down, good for nothing, but they couldn't very well put them back because it would make them look pretty stupid, so they dumped the lot in the sea. Can you believe it?'

Everyone agreed it was a typical cock-up. There were lots of stories like that going round. Balls-ups, cock-ups, fuck-ups. You'd never have thought we were supposed to be fighting a war, the way people in charge carried on. I didn't read the newspapers much because they just made me cry, thinking about Jack and Maurice and their mates. Even I could see we weren't winning. Tobruk. The *Prince of Wales*. Singapore. They were just names to me, but I knew they weren't names of battles our lot had won.

Everyone – I don't mean everyone in the gang, I mean everyone in the country – was waiting for something and nobody knew what it was, or if they did, they didn't hold out much hope it would ever happen. You had to wait in shops to find out what they had for sale, for buses and trams that never came, for letters that never arrived, and were in the wrong order when they did. You waited for the air-raid siren to go off, then for the sound of the German planes going overhead, and then you waited for the bombs. You sat in silence, waiting for the all-clear. More than anything you waited for the bloody War to end.

I'm not sure if this was true in Charlie's case. Whatever you were waiting for he could probably get hold of it. He was in no hurry for the War to end. He had a thriving business, getting hold of what people wanted.

When the first planes were overhead a quiet came over the whole bar while we all listened, trying to guess how close they were. A couple of redcaps came in to get off the street and went up to the bar. Margaret, who knew her business, gave them a shot of something each and shook her head when one of them put his hand in his pocket. I couldn't hear what they said. We'd all missed the moment when we could've gone to a shelter, not that any of us would leave a pub to go into a shelter. Charlie would always rather sit out an air raid with a drink in his hand than go underground with all those terrified people and their children and pets. The battery in Kensington Gardens was firing at the planes, which sounded as if they were right over our heads.

You could hear the exploding bombs getting nearer. I was frightened. It wasn't going to be the East End that copped it tonight. I must have become a bit hysterical because Charlie told me to shut up. Nobody spoke and then we heard it coming. One of the MPs shouted something but the noise was too loud to hear what it was. We all hit the deck. Everyone, including me, was lying on the floor with their hands over their heads. The noise was terrific. I thought my ears were going to explode. I had my head buried in Charlie's chest.

There was a bloody great crash very close by and I thought the floor was going to hit the ceiling. The doors blew open and the little windows shattered – the big ones had already been replaced by board. The lights went out. You could hear the explosions following one after the other as the stick fell from west to east. The planes just kept coming and although no explosion was so close, the sound of bombs falling all around went on for a long time. I couldn't move. I didn't want to look up.

The inside of the pub was wrecked. All the mirrors and glass were smashed and dust and debris from the street had been blown in through the open doors and window frames. Even before the all-clear people were pulling each other off the ground and looking at each other, dazed. An AFS man poked his head through the opening where the door had been. He shone a torch into the darkness and shouted something. It took about twenty minutes to make sure but – it was an amazing piece of luck – nobody was hurt except for some scratches from the broken glass. The pub hadn't been hit, but two doors down was a building that had.

We groped our way out of the bar and looked around at the destruction. Practically a whole side of the square had been wiped out. Two of the big trees had been lifted out of the ground and thrown across the road. The pub had been between two bombs in the stick. My God, we had been lucky! Already the ARP and the police were attacking the buildings to pull out people trapped underneath. Margaret – bless her! – was handing round a bottle of brandy which had survived the blast. Everyone took it and drank from the bottle, even the policemen.

Then a queer thing happened, one of those flukes that changes the whole of your life. We were all standing outside the Victoria – what was left of it – our heads spinning. We were in a daze. Firemen were already shifting what was left of the block of mansion flats that had disappeared into a pile of rubble. All we knew was that we were alive and other people were dead – for no reason we could see. The two redcaps were inspecting their car which'd been smashed to smithereens. One of them came over to where we were standing and asked if any of us had a car. Everyone shrugged or shook their head, including Charlie who had one, but I couldn't see him lending it to a military policeman. They began chatting to us in a friendly way. One of them went off to look for a telephone. While he was away the one left suddenly turned to Charlie and looked at him.

'Don't I know you, mate?' he said.

Charlie handled it really well, as he always did. He always had papers on him that wouldn't tie him to his past life. I'd seen him do it.

'Charlie, isn't it?' the MP said. 'Charlie Mercer. Catterick. 1940. Remember me?'

Charlie brassed it out. He put on a posh voice, which he could do well enough when he wanted to.

'I'm sorry, officer. My name's Clarence Percival.'

Without being asked, he handed over his identity card which had his picture on it over the name he'd given.

The MP looked at it and then handed it back to Charlie.

'My mistake, Mr Percival. For a moment you reminded me of a soldier in a company I had in training.'

'That's all right,' Charlie said.

While he was sliding his ID card back into his wallet, the MP slipped a handcuff on to his wrist and snapped the lock shut. Just like that. You can see why they call them bracelets.

'Don't make a fuss, Mercer. You're up to your fucking neck in it as it is.'

His mate came back and in a few moments they had us all lined up to examine our cards. Up until now I'd been watching in a dream I couldn't wake up from. I was standing in a line waiting while a policeman looked at my papers. I didn't think to make up a story or even wonder if I was in any danger. I hadn't deserted from the Army. When it came to my turn, the MP glanced at my card and handed it back to me.

'Where do you live, Mrs Hoskin?' he said.

Instead of saying 147 Torrance Street, like a simpleton I gave the address in Sussex Gardens. He walked over and spoke to his mate and then he came back and said those frightening words.

'Would you step this way please, miss?'

I was so simple I gave them the same address as Charlie had. Can you believe it?

Charlie and me were taken to the police station in Seymour Street in a police car, and I spent the night in a cell.

And that was it, the end of my life with Charlie. I never saw him again, and it was the beginning of everything going wrong for me. Whenever I look back, the only thing I feel rotten about is that stroke of bad luck, Charlie running into that bloody redcap during a raid, something he could never have planned for in a million years. I sometimes wished the bomb had fallen on the Victoria and Albert and killed the bloody lot of us that night, instead of all those other poor people.

I spent more than one night in that police cell. At first I didn't worry as I hadn't done anything wrong. After a couple of days and they still hadn't let me go, it began to dawn on me that I was in it almost as deep as Charlie was. They refused me bail and they weren't very friendly about it either. When I told them I was pregnant they laughed and said they weren't surprised, but they didn't believe me. I'm sure I didn't look it. They asked me questions, all of which I answered. I told them the truth because I don't know how to lie. I just wanted to get out of there.

There weren't any policewomen at Seymour Street so they had to move me to the station in Notting Hill, at the top of Ladbroke Grove, where they had some. Before they did, though, something happened to me. I often thought things were going to get worse and worse, but even though it was always bad later, this, what happened to me in Seymour Street nick, was the worst thing that ever happened to me.

Charlie was moved back to Catterick soon after he was arrested, though I didn't know that then. They never told me anything. It was a long time before I found out he was a prisoner of the Army and I was being charged with a civil crime. Charlie had committed his share of civil crimes, I can promise you that, but desertion was a military offence and once the Army got their hands on him, they never bothered to charge him for what he'd done in Civvy Street. He had his court martial and did his time in the glasshouse. I'm sure it wasn't a picnic for him, but at least they treated him decent and never laid hands on him. The moment he was in Army custody he was in uniform and all the Army rigmarole applied to him again. After his sentence he'd be put back in the ranks and have to start over again where he left off. The number of his dice had fallen on to the mouth of the big fat snake that swallows you and takes you down the whole length of the board, just when you were about to reach Finish, and shits you out on number 2.

I know that's how Charlie would have looked at it, just an unlucky fall of the dice. Soon as he was let out he'd have another throw and then anything could happen. If I knew my Charlie, he'd desert at the first opportunity they gave him, if they did give him one, which wasn't likely. By then the Army knew Charlie Mercer as well as I did.

On my second night in nick I was asleep on the bed, still in my clothes because they hadn't given me anything to sleep in, when I was woke up by something interfering with my skirt. It was dark and it took me a second to realize someone was in the cell with me. Someone was touching me under my skirt, but not roughly, more as if he was trying not to wake me. I lay there – I was on my front – not believing what was happening to me. I was terrified. I tried to turn over but as soon as I did the man suddenly jumped on top of me, holding me down. I cried out and then I saw stars. The man had smashed his fist against the side of my head and I went limp as a rag. I couldn't move a muscle while the man's other hand continued to pull down my knickers. He yanked them down to my knees. When he had done this he pushed my legs apart and then, leaning on top of me with all his weight so that I could hardly breathe, shoved his cock into me. I couldn't cry out because he had his other hand over my mouth. I thought he was going to suffocate me. I tried to bite his hand and he hit me on the side of the head again. I couldn't do anything because I was on my front and he was on top of me. The bastard was grunting like a pig.

I don't remember how long it went on. It didn't matter. My mind seemed to leave my body as if my body was something that didn't belong to me. It wasn't mine any more, but the property of this pig on top of me. Then it was all over. All of a sudden I was alone in the cell. The bastard had gone – all the time he never spoke a single word – and I was lying face down in the dark with my legs apart. Slowly my mind returned to my body. I just cried and cried. I wanted my mum.

The next day they moved me to Notting Hill police station. I hadn't washed properly, not for two days. I didn't look at any of the coppers when they brought me out of the cell and signed me out and put me in the wagon. The way they talked to me, any one of them could've been the pig. Whichever one of the bastards it was he knew I still had his come inside me, and I didn't want him to look at me in the eye and see me looking at him, him knowing that.

I never told a soul about what happened to me that night in Seymour Street nick. I tried to forget about it. What would have been the use in telling anyone? In the eyes of the law and the police I was a whore. That was what they called me. Over the next few months that word was thrown at me wherever I went. If some copper had raped me, then good luck to him. It was no worse than a whore deserved.

It wasn't as bad in the Notting Hill station. The policewomen were all dykes, hard as nails and strict, but at least they were women. I was allowed to shower once a day and they let me keep the suitcase of clothes that Brenda Grey had brought in for me. From the questions the police put to me I began to get an idea what I was going to be done for. They'd raided the flat in Sussex Gardens and came away with clothing and petrol coupons, cigarettes, liquor and a pile of US PX stuff. I was going to be charged with being in possession of uncustomed goods 'knowing them to be stolen'.

Worse than that, they were treating me as a common prostitute. They'd got hold of Charlie's address book and contacted the names in it. Some of the men had made statements saying how they'd slept with me for money. I didn't know what Charlie had told them about me, but if he could have dropped me in it to save himself he would have. What's more, they knew all about Jack, that I was married to a serviceman who was overseas fighting for his country, which made it a hundred times worse. It was probably Charlie who helped the police with their inquiries in that direction. Things weren't looking good for me.

My case came up in Marylebone Magistrates' Court. The police warder in charge of the cells was a warm-hearted old sergeant who made me a cup of tea. He did his best to reassure me that I didn't have anything to worry about. His was the first friendly voice I'd heard in a week.

'What you been done for, my dear? Soliciting? Your first time, is it? Don't worry. They'll give you a twenty-quid fine and probation and you'll be out of here by this afternoon. Mark my words.'

I didn't argue with him. I'd given up trying to put my side of the story.

I came up from the cells and found myself looking at a baldheaded man with horn-rimmed glasses who reminded me a bit of Stafford Cripps. After the charges were read out and my plea entered he sat reading the documents through his glasses, every so often glancing up at me over the top of them. I'd put on the plain suit that Brenda had packed for me and a clean blouse. It still looked expensive and, probably in the magistrate's view, not within the reach of an ordinary London girl with no visible means of support. The police went through the case against me and then the magistrate spoke to me in the dock.

'Violet Hoskin. Your husband is a member of the armed forces. Is that correct?'

'Yes, Your Honour.'

'But you are living with another man.'

'Yes, Your Honour.'

'And you are a prostitute.'

'No, Your Honour.'

He glanced down at the piece of paper in front of him, surprised. You'd have thought I'd said I was Snow White.

'I have the witness statement of the man you have been living with, Mrs Hoskin. Mr Charles Mercer states that you worked for him as a prostitute. What do you have to say?'

I said nothing. The fight went out of me when I heard that. The magistrate read out bits of Charlie's statement. The gist of it was he'd confessed to a charge of living on immoral earnings.

306

According to Charlie's version, all the stuff at the flat was mine, what I received from my clients while I was on the game. Pimping was a normal peacetime criminal business, but black marketeering was a new crime the War had created and was treated harsher. Charlie had dropped me in it to make it easy for himself. It really shocked me. That's how simple I was.

The magistrate said what I'd done was the sort of thing that could lose the British Empire the War, damage the moral fibre of the troops and injure civilian morale by creating shortages. I had undermined the ration system. He found me guilty on both charges. He was about to pass sentence on me when the clerk interrupted him and they whispered to each other.

'I see. I understand you are pregnant, Mrs Hoskin. Is that correct?'

'Yes, Your Honour.'

'What date did you last see Mr Hoskin?'

I told him. It was over a year before.

'Do you know who is the father of your child?'

'It's Charlie's.'

'He denies that.'

'He would, wouldn't he?'

He looked at me over the top of his spectacles.

'But it isn't your husband's, is it?'

At that point it all became too much for me and I burst into tears. I could see I was on trial for leaving my husband.

'Hmm! Well, if your child was your husband's I think we could take that into consideration. I don't think a custodial sentence would be appropriate for a woman carrying the child of a member of the armed services. Since this is not the case, I see no reason why I should not pass sentence. Violet Hoskin, I sentence you to twelve months' detention in an appropriate institution. It is necessary to make an example of women who behave as you have. I hope it will serve as a warning to other women who might be considering acting as you have done.

The court will deal firmly with such antisocial behaviour.'

Behind me some people at the back of the court started to clap and shout, 'Hear, hear!'

I was taken back down to the cells. The old sergeant gave me pea soup and bread for lunch and afterwards a van took me to Holloway.

At first I cried a lot. I was miserable. On top of prison, the pains of pregnancy were an extra punishment for what I'd done. Even though the old lags accepted me and treated me as one of themselves, I didn't feel like one of them. I know it wasn't right leaving Jack and going with Charlie, but it wasn't against the law. And I'd never have moved in with him if Jack hadn't written to me saying he wasn't coming home. I'd slept with some soldiers, I don't deny it, but that wasn't a crime either. I was being punished to make an example to the wives of other servicemen. It wasn't fair.

Junie, the old lag who shared my cell, stroked my hair and rubbed my back and laughed at me for being such a simple girl. It was Junie who kept my spirits up and passed stuff to me from the kitchen. She got me through those first awful days – and the nights, when the bombs fell all around the prison and you had to sit tight in your cell until it was all over. Junie was a coloured girl from Liverpool with a Scouser way of expressing herself, and she was very protective of me. She was doing her time for sticking a knife into a Polish soldier who tried to cheat her after they'd agreed a price. She was always a bit cheeky with the screws and they sometimes smiled at her cheek – and sometimes they didn't. If they weren't as bloody with her as they were with some of the women, it wasn't because of her sense of humour. There was something strong behind those jokes. They respected her.

Junie and me told each other our stories. When she heard mine, how simple I'd been, she wept with laughter.

Most of the women at Holloway were in for ordinary offences, from murder and GBH to petty crimes, some so petty it made you wonder what the courts were doing. (I knew a girl of seventeen who was doing a stretch for stealing a bottle of milk from a doorstep!) These were the old lags. I came into that category. The rest were Nazi sympathizers like Sir Oswald and Lady Mosley and members of the British Fascist Party. We came across the Fascists now and then because they didn't always segregate us as they were supposed to. The difference between them and us was not that they supported Hitler and Mussolini and we were thieves and murderers and prostitutes, but that they spoke better than us, had better teeth and had been to good schools. We were nearly all working-class girls, as a general rule.

Both lots of women thought themselves a cut above the other, though. Certainly the old lags were better at managing the system. They had ways of getting hold of extra blankets and cigarettes and light duties. On the other hand, some of the Nazi sympathizers were well connected. They had posh visitors and were given privileges. It was rumoured the Mosleys were served wine with their meals. Strictly speaking, they were remand prisoners. They hadn't been charged with a crime as there was no law against believing Hitler was a good bloke.

After a couple of months my belly began to stick out. I started feeling awful and I was hungry all the time. The food in prison was exactly what a person was allowed on her coupons, no more and no less, but it was bought and cooked without any of the craftiness a woman outside would have used. I was sick a lot, probably because of the disgusting slop they expected you to eat. If it hadn't been for the other women, the things they got hold of for me from the kitchen – pieces of chocolate or jam or even fruit – I'd have starved.

The first time it really dawned on me I was going to have a baby was when the old magistrate asked me if my child was

Jack's. Until that moment the fact hadn't sunk in. Charlie had told me not to worry, he was going to fix everything and I'm sure he would have if that bomb hadn't fallen on Lancaster Gardens and we were both nicked. After that I was scuppered. Day by day the bump inside me got bigger and then began to kick and make sure I knew he was there. I never was in any doubt the baby was going to be a boy.

The other women always talked of him as 'he'. How is he today? Is he being a good boy? I expect he's hungry. For them he was a person already, with his own personality. I wasn't one person, I was two people. They were always interested in his well-being – at first, more than I was myself. I hadn't wanted a child and if I had, I wouldn't have wanted one that wasn't Jack's. I'd told the magistrate he was Charlie's, but I couldn't be a hundred per cent sure it was. It could easy have been someone else's. For a long time I talked of 'it'.

Then one day what I was carrying stopped being 'it' and became a 'he'. I had a child inside me! Later – years later, when I wasn't so simple – I realized it was the other women who'd made him real for me. They knew what they were doing. They wanted him to be strong and healthy and beautiful, and it was important I ate well and they gave me food if they thought I wasn't eating enough.

At the time I took it for granted. They were being good to me because they were good women – I'm talking about women who had been sent down for thieving and causing grievous bodily harm, murder even. They were old lags who knew how to play the system. Later, I wondered if in some funny way I wasn't having my baby, I was having theirs. I was having a baby for all those old lags. My child was the baby they'd either had or wanted to have. He was important to them. I could have been pregnant in nicer surroundings where the air was fresher, with better food, but I couldn't have carried a baby where I was looked after better.

I didn't want to let the old lags down. Once I realized that as far as they were concerned I was one of them, I couldn't. In prison there are all sorts of favours prisoners do for each other. You do this for me and I'll do that for you. Swap your ciggies for my sugar ration. It went on all the time. You didn't get anything without giving something up. As most of the wardresses were bent there was always 'specials', stuff you weren't supposed to have. Some of the old lags were dykes and there was business you could do in that department, if you were desperate enough. I didn't have to do any of that. No one ever asked me for a favour. The other women ran around after me and got cross if I even stirred off my backside. All they expected from me was to have a healthy baby. My nickname was Princess.

'How's His Lordship then, Princess?'

'The bugger's fine.'

'I've got something special for him.'

The old lag would palm me a raw carrot or cold bacon butty.

There were women I never saw, women who worked in parts of the prison I never visited – in the laundry, the kitchen or the garden – who sent things to me through other women. Junie would pass me a bag of boiled sweets.

'Phyllis sends you summat, sweetheart.'

'Who's Phyllis?'

'She's an old jailbird – who do you think, the Archbishop of Canterbury's daughter? Works in the uniform shop. Done her old man in in thirty-six.'

That's all I ever knew about Phyllis. Or Doris. Or Alice.

But it was Junie, the old lag I shared my cell with, who was most devoted to me. Bombs were falling all over London nearly every night, don't forget. Before, I'd never worried about them. When I was on the outside I was having too much fun and if I didn't go down to the shelter it was because I didn't choose to. I was the kind of girl who didn't. Prison was another kettle of fish. You were in a cell with one small, high window and the door was locked. You couldn't go anywhere, even if you wanted to. And that made it worse. Because you were in the same place night after night, the odds in favour of a bomb landing on you seemed greater.

Every night there was an air raid on Junie took me in her arms and rocked me and sang songs to me from her childhood and told me stories, things that had happened to her or her family. While bombs fell on Holloway and Islington the building shook and reflections of searchlights, the ack-ack and houses on fire lit up and criss-crossed the cell. I lay in the dark in Junie's arms, watching the ceiling, thinking sometimes about Jack, sometimes about Mum or even – so help me! – about Charlie Mercer, while His Lordship kicked around inside me. The air raids always woke him up and started him thrashing like a drowning man. He must've felt like I did in there – trapped. Junie stroked him and rubbed me where it hurt.

In prison there's a set rigmarole for women who are pregnant. There is for everything. You're only supposed to do light duties, and so they put me in charge of the library. They called it a library but it was just a room with a lot of bashed-up books in it. At least it wasn't a cell and there were some soft armchairs. Hardly any of the old lags read books and so I often spent the afternoon reading them myself. I hadn't been a great reader before, except for magazines. In prison it was something I did because I had nothing else to do. The only women who used the library were the Fascists, and I got to know some of them. I must say, they were a funny old lot. They talked as if their stay in prison was just temporary, some terrible mistake. (I knew how they felt!)

I became quite friendly with one of them, Silvia, who came from Parson's Green. She hated being in with the Fascists because she claimed she wasn't one. She hated Hitler, but she'd had an affair with an Italian before the War, a man who was now an officer or some high-up official in Italy. Apparently her affair with him made her a danger to the British Empire. Silvia suggested books I might like to read and we talked about them afterwards. She said she knew some writers. She told me their names but I'd never heard of them. The writers I liked best were Dornford Yates and Daphne du Maurier. I read *Rebecca* twice.

I still read books sometimes. The habit stuck. The thing I've always liked about books is that when you're in the middle of one you can forget where you are, that you are in prison and miserable. You're somewhere else – in another country even. You find yourself crying about something that happened to people you don't even know, who are completely different to you. And while you're reading, the end is already there in your hand waiting to happen. It made me wonder if my own life wasn't like that, already written down somewhere. I hoped it was, because then it wouldn't make a blind bit of difference what I did.

The rest of the rigmarole for pregnant inmates had to do with the medical side. Once a week I was sent down to the infirmary to see the doctor, who was a lady doctor not much older than me. I looked forward to my visits to the infirmary. I liked feeling Dr Wakefield's cool hands examining me as if she really cared about me. The way she talked to you, you wouldn't have thought you were in prison but in some swanky hospital. She talked to all her patients that way, the old lags, the Fascists, the prison staff. We were just women to her.

Dr Wakefield – Hazel, she said I was to call her when the screws weren't in earshot – prescribed me fresh milk, and there was a bit of a ding-dong about whether I was entitled to more than my ration. She gave me a toothbrush and a cake of Gibb's toothpaste. She would sit me down and make me a cup of tea, open a packet of biscuits and have a nice chat. She told me all about herself. Her young man – a nice-looking chap – was a

313

medical officer serving with the Eighth Army. I didn't try to hide what happened between Jack and me. I told her everything and she listened. If she thought I'd done something terrible she didn't say so. We could go through a whole packet of arrowroot biscuits between us.

'Your Tony's a lucky chap,' I told her.

'He probably wouldn't agree with you, Violet. I don't think he likes Africa. He has that kind of skin that turns pink in the sun.'

'I mean, you're not going to run off with some American flying officer, are you?'

'I haven't time to. Besides, Tony and I aren't married. There's every chance our relationship won't last the War.'

I was shocked to hear her say that. It was the first time I'd ever heard a woman talk like that. After the War – perhaps *because* of the War – it was more common to hear people talk about their 'relationship'. But then it was new to me.

'You mean you wouldn't mind if he fell for some pretty nurse?'

'Of course I'd mind! But I want Tony to be happy. Obviously, if he fell for a pretty nurse she'd be the best person to make him happy, not me. People can't always help who they fall in love with.'

'You wouldn't blame him then?'

'I might. I hope not. We blame people we love when we are angry with them. When people I love are angry with me, I want them to forgive me.'

That was how she spoke, from the heart. Nobody'd ever spoke to me like that before. I loved Hazel Wakefield.

I like to think I wasn't so simple when I came out of prison as I was when I went in. If I wasn't, perhaps it was because the time I did in Holloway was the only time in my life I didn't have men around. Junie, Silvia, Hazel Wakefield, the old lags, the Fascists, even the screws – they were the people I met in prison. Women. I missed men – most of us did – but it wasn't the only thing we talked about. I felt safe in there, not from the bloody bombs but from the world. I didn't have to worry about what I did because there was nothing I could do and nobody to let down. In Holloway nobody blamed me for anything, and the old lags looked after me as if I was somebody very special. To hear Junie talk you'd have thought I was a beautiful princess locked up in a castle who one day a knight in shining armour was going to come and rescue.

The sweltering summer we had that year was followed by a bitter winter. First you boiled, then you froze. The German bombers stopped coming over every night but came whenever the fancy took them – which was worse in a way because every night left you guessing. Were they going to come tonight or weren't they? Spring came, but you hardly noticed it as there were no trees or flowers to look at.

In April I was called in front of the Board of Visitors. I was just a month off from having my baby, so I was as big as a pig. When I saw the usual stony-faced crew of old women wearing hats and fox furs, holding crocodile handbags, my heart sank. There was also a bald old chap, a solicitor, who looked like Dr Crippen and did most of the talking. He asked me some questions – how was I feeling, what did I think I would do at the end of my sentence – as if he really cared. Even if he looked like a murderer he was kind-hearted and spoke like a gentleman. I showed him the lawyer's letter that said Jack had put some money into his hands for him to pay the rent on a flat for six months after I came out. Good old Jack! I sometimes daydreamed that me and Jack would get back together again, but it didn't seem likely. Still, it meant I had a place to go when I got out.

They sent me outside and then, after about twenty minutes, they called me back into the room.

'Violet,' the old solicitor said. 'We have taken into consideration the good reports of you from the prison staff and the doctor and, of course, there's your condition. We've decided that you should be released in a few weeks, so that you can have your baby in a proper hospital.'

I was so happy I cried! I didn't care that my knight hadn't come in shining armour but looked like Dr Crippen. I would be out by the end of April!

I promised the old lags and the screws I would send them a picture of the baby. Some of the girls pulled my leg and said I was getting special treatment because I was royalty. A few weeks before, Sir Oswald and Lady Mosley had been let out. There was a bit of a hoo-ha about that. People were cross that he was allowed to live with his wife in connecting cells, and then they were cross when they let them out. The old lags were glad to see the back of them. After they heard that the Mosleys were served wine with their dinner there was some sarcastic comments made to the screws, who were all snobs.

One afternoon – it was a Sunday, the 10th of April it must have been – I was taken queer. I began to sweat and I felt tired and wanted to lie down but I couldn't. I started to have pains and so Junie called Rachel, the wardress on duty, because she thought my labour was starting. It was, even though the baby wasn't due for another three weeks. I was walking up and down the cell, stopping every ten minutes to hold on to Junie while the pains came on. Rachel came in and went out and then told us they were trying to get hold of Dr Wakefield, but it was a Sunday and they couldn't find her. They decided I should go down to the infirmary and the nurse came up to get me. I wanted Junie to come with me but Head Wardress Cooke said it wasn't allowed. I went down to the infirmary supported on each side by the nurse and Rachel.

About eight o'clock the head wardress came to see me. She said they had telephoned the Royal Free for an ambulance and one was on its way. By nine o'clock the ambulance still hadn't come and so she telephoned a local GP – 'just in case'. As usual they told you one thing but you never knew what was really happening.

The local doctor was a doddery old chap of about seventy, and he looked well put out when my waters broke and poured out on to the floor in front of him. I wasn't especially worried about what was going to happen to me, I just didn't want my baby to be born in a prison. The doctor wanted me to lie down on the infirmary bed, but that was only more painful. I wanted to walk up and down but he insisted, and the nurse and the wardress held me down. The doctor gave me an injection and soon after I was sick, all over the nurse's hand. It began to dawn on me that there wasn't going to be an ambulance – that's if one was ever called for – and I started to cry.

If the air-raid siren went off I didn't hear it. The first I heard was the roar of the planes and the AA battery in Parliament Hill Fields. I knew an ambulance wouldn't be leaving hospital for the prison now. The infirmary had larger windows than the cell and the sky outside was lit up with searchlights and ack-ack. It was a big raid, and you could hear the bombs going off one after the other all round the prison. That set His Lordship moving and kicking as he did every air raid. I wasn't scared, or if I was it wasn't of the bombs.

The nurse was wiping my forehead with a damp flannel when a big one landed close to the prison – it sounded like a landmine. I don't know if the prison itself was hit or if a bomb had fallen in the grounds, but the whole building shook and the windows of the infirmary blew inwards on top of us. Plaster showered on us from the ceiling. There was pandemonium. The wardresses were running about like headless chickens, screaming to each other, and the doctor seemed to have fainted. The nurse, bless her, never left my side and held my hand. Her face, I noticed, was covered with blood. On the infirmary walls I could see reflections of the fires burning outside. I wondered if I was going to die before my child was born. Many's the time since then I've wished I had.

The sound of the planes passed, and soon after the all-clear the bells of the fire brigade were ringing all over north London. My baby was born at one-thirty – a boy, of course. He was put in my arms and I cried my heart out with a kind of broken-hearted joy. I could hear through the shattered window the fires still blazing and the men shouting to each other, but I didn't care. My little boy had fine black hair and beautiful dark eyes. I wasn't so lit up on what the doctor had injected me with I couldn't see that with those features he definitely wasn't Charlie's, whose eyes were bluer than Max Miller's jokes.

I slept with my baby on me until the next afternoon. Every time I woke up to feed him and I saw this little chap on my breast I burst into tears again. In the morning the nurse took the boy away to wash him and I was soon fast asleep again. Later, Head Wardress Cooke allowed the old lags to come down in twos to see the baby and each one of them brought some small thing she'd made or stolen for him. A little vest. Some socks. A rattle. I couldn't help crying because these were women who had nothing, and here they were coming to me with beautiful gifts. I felt like Mary in the manger and I had just given birth to baby Jesus. Junie had made the dearest little bonnet from a scrap of parachute silk, and she'd embroidered *His Lordship* on it in blue cotton. All the women wanted to hold the baby – something they all knew how to do better than I did.

On our third day in the infirmary, Head Wardress Parker told me to get ready as I was going to be released soon. Rachel had my things packed in a suitcase. I asked her where we were going.

'The Royal Free in Hampstead. They want to give you an examination and have a look at the baby.'

I could hardly believe it! The day had come! I wanted to say goodbye to my friends, but Head Wardress Parker wouldn't let me. Prison staff aren't cruel on purpose. They have regulations to follow and if they don't follow them they get in trouble. I can't say it's a job I'd ever volunteer for.

While I was in the shower the nurse took my baby off to bathe him and dress him in the clothes the old lags had made. I put on my suit. I must say, it felt odd to be putting on my own clothes again. I said goodbye to the nurse and the wardresses. Then I got into the ambulance while Head Wardress Parker sent Rachel to fetch my baby.

It was nothing to do with the prison staff. I know that now. It was the local Watch Committee made the decision, and the county court made it all legal. They took my baby away from me while I was in the shower and shut the ambulance door on me without giving him back. For a long time I refused to believe they would do such a thing. I cried and cried and cried. Later, when I was told official, the reason the court gave was that my profession as a prostitute made me unfit to bring up a child and so he had been taken away for his own good. They said he would be found a good home.

Three days in his mother's arms, that was all the poor little bleeder got.

I went to a solicitor to try and get him back but it was no good. I didn't have the money to pay him and nobody knew where he was. I never saw my boy again.

After I stopped crying I couldn't have cared less what happened to me. I went on the game to prove they were right. I *was* a common prostitute and I wasn't fit to bring up a child. I don't think I could've gone on living if I thought there was a chance they might have been wrong.